CYCLES OF THE LIGHTS

The Seed of Life

Ava Reiss

Space Tigers

Publishing LLC

For more information, visit space-tigers.com

Copyright © 2020 by Ava Reiss
All illustrations (including covers) by Ava Reiss

ISBN: 978-1-949195-18-7 (paperback)
Library of Congress Control Number: 2020931186
First Edition

For my husband

... and my social media friends—anyone who's ever helped share a post, or beta read a volume. You're the best!

Titles in the
Cycles of the Lights Series
(in chronology)

Fall of Ima Recap

(includes spoilers for *Fall of Ima*)

The sole heir to the kindgom Priletoria, Meliora is faced with difficult decisions after her father's passing. Her mother, Queen Vesper leaves their planet, Ima, in search of a cure for death. As a woman who had lost much, Vesper refused to lose her husband.

Vesper enters the school of sorcery on planet Jema and loses communication with Ima. With much needed to be done on behalf of Priletoria, Meliora assumes the crown as ruling monarch—an action that cannot be undone. She rules with her childhood friend and sweetheart, Jedrek, a prince from the neighboring kingdom of Carpecillero.

While on Jema, Vesper suffers humiliation and suppression. She bears it all in hopes of finding a sacred object that might reverse the effects of death: The Seed of Life.

In an accident, Vesper falls victim to a battle of powers between Master sorcerers. To her—and others'—infinite surprise, she arises as the sole survivor.

Vesper makes a quick getaway back to Ima; in hopes of putting her nightmare behind her, she seeks solace in the little bit of control she retains: She is still the ruling monarch of Priletoria.

Vesper returns to find her daughter has been crowned, usurping her title as Queen. With her better nature lost to the battling souls of dead Masters trapped in her body, she unleashes her rage.

The result: A planet that came to her heel.

Controlling Ima wasn't enough. Vesper now sets her sights on Jema, the planet that houses the school of sorcery. The school that held her down in misery.

As *The Seed of Life* opens, Vesper has spent two decades preparing for conquest. Taking Jema is the only thing on her mind.

Little did Vesper know, Ima and Jema are not the only planets in the universe that houses sentient life. Unbeknownst to all Imans and Jemans, there is a planet at the outer edge of their system: Teroma...

Vesper's Curse Recap

(includes spoilers for *Vesper's Curse*,

and *Fall of Ima*)

In trading for Jedrek not to die at her mother's hands, Meliora swears a vow to the universe: She'd gladly give her life in place of his a second time.

Intrigued by the idea, Vesper casts a curse that ensures the scenario plays out.

After their deaths on Ima, Meliora and Jedrek incarnate on Earth as Agatha and Ivan in the late 60's. With no recollection of their previous lives, they meet one another by chance when she is a child, and he a young veteran. He rescues her from human trafficking. Ivan leaves her at a hospital and slips away.

Years later, Agatha finds herself working as a secretary for Ivan's partner at their law firm. They hardly speak to one another until one night when a purse snatcher strikes Agatha. In the area, Ivan comes to her assistance.

As Ivan's past catches up, he and Agatha are found in harm's way.

The power of Vesper's Curse is too strong. Agatha saves Ivan's life by catching a bullet meant for him.

Yet, as she lay dying, deep down Agatha knows they'd see each other again...

Cycles of the Lights

The Seed of Life

Ava Reiss

Prologue

Multiverses existed in no real order, hovering nondescript in gauzy clouds. Rarely did they intersect, and if they did, entities of one could not cross into another. In some, time cycled in one direction. In others, it occurred disjointedly in bubbles of events.

The sources of dynamic existence, En and Il, were exceptions. They had ejected their cores into the ether of their creations. There, their tiny sparks drifted asleep. A natural attraction between the two drew them close, stirring En and Il to awaken.

Gradually, they formed eyes. Peering around, they searched for the thing that pulled them at their cores.

In the moment En and Il's gazes met, a truth so profound shook the foundations of actuality. The force casted them apart.

Asleep once more, they drifted for eons at the outer reaches of existence.

The rest of creation settled and patterns emerged again. Time continued to cycle. Worlds blinked in and out of existence. En and Il wandered among endless birthing and decaying universes. At the center of their idling essences, each sensed the other's voice, calling.

It pulled them closer and closer, until finally, they tumbled into the same universe.

Yet, their path to each other was complicated. Firm structures governed this universe. Constructs were held together by consciousness. It fueled separation of the corporeal and ethereal. Time folded in an intricate fashion. Only in pockets of the corporeal did it pass in linear form.

En and Il found themselves subjected to the universe's laws. In ways it protected them. Should their gazes meet again, they'd no longer be cast apart.

But their paths to one other could not be direct. Each time they came in contact with a soul, a line of karma formed, amalgamating their destinies to others.

They wove in and out of incarnations. Fate threads wrapped tighter and tighter. Though they held no waking awareness of it, their voices called to the other's soul. They began sharing contiguous incarnations, culminating towards a rubicon.

~*~

A hierarchy of souls existed in this universe, best explained in a pyramid. The bottom contained seedling souls. They were simple beings, incarnating as mortals with no memory before birth. Life lessons acted as nourishment for spiritual growth.

En and Il found themselves as seedling souls, not comprehending the existence of the pyramid.

If a seedling soul were to reach its epitome, it'd transform into a celestial soul. They were the second tier of the pyramid. Significantly less in number, celestial souls remained connected to the ethereal realm. Even if they chose to enter the corporeal.

The connection gave abilities to affect the physical world. However, if they used the abilities, it taxed their suits of flesh, shortening their time in corporeal form.

Celestial souls could also choose to enter a life without previous memory. Sometimes, recollections can be blocked by another celestial soul. Especially one more powerful.

To seedling souls who came across them, celestial souls have been referred to as gods, angels, and demons. The drastic variance in perceptions was due to an unforgiving nature of celestial souls. Unfalteringly, they cycled between angelic and demonic states.

Angelic souls were benevolent. Demonic souls were self-serving. None could permanently remain in one state, and neither could they hold characteristics of the opposite. This led to dramatic fate clashes, generating karmic debt.

Like seedling souls, celestial souls were to learn lessons and resolve karmic debt.

Karma flowed like water, attracted to the path of least resistance or strongest pull of debt. It held the greatest sway on reincarnation. Sometimes, extreme strength of will can alter the direction of karma. This can be caused by a change of heart, or powerful consciousness.

Once a celestial soul cycled through adequate existences between angelic and demonic to satisfy their debts, they become a deity soul. Deity souls sat at the peak of the pyramid. They existed beyond known realms and were untouched by space and time.

To those below, the existence of a deity soul couldn't be proven. Upper-tiered celestial souls theorized their presence by the echo of inexplicable changes in the realms.

The believed goal of a deity soul was to find ultimate harmony with universal energies. Once achieved, it's conjectured the particles of their being would dissipate. They'd then fuse with other forms of consciousness and reconvene as fresh seedling souls. Thus repeating the cycle.

Ima

Jema

Oli6

Oli5

Oli4

Ia System
(not to scale)

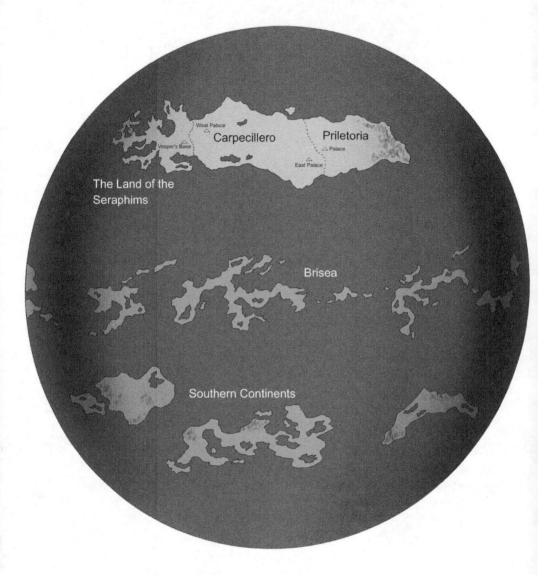

IMA

Diameter: 4,003 miles

Axis: 23° tilt

Surface Water: 80%

Distance from Sun: 0.9 au

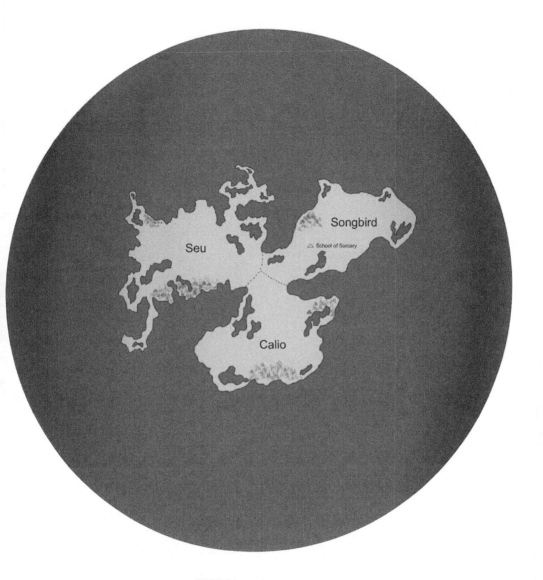

JEMA

Diameter: 519 miles

Axis: 23° tilt

Surface Water: 94%

Distance from Sun: 1.2 au

Chapter One

Kameclara stepped to the edge of a half-mile drop. An enormous cavern spread before her. Wall to wall of habbadite clay waited, capable of changing into myriads of dangers in an instant. She felt clacking beneath her mission boots. The clay kept solid… for the moment.

Her expression remained serene. She was never one to display much emotion. Yet beneath her skin, blood drummed, anticipating a rush of excitement. She flicked her wavy, black hair over her shoulder. This was her final evaluation to become a green-lit operative of the Intergalactic Military—one of the planet's elite. Since she was a child, Kameclara had looked forward to this day. Why?

Because operatives traversed stars.

Truthfully, it was no further than the Molta Belt—the asteroid ring outside their planet, Teroma's, orbit. The "Intergalactic" part of their military name was more hopes of reaching further in the future. Yet it was beyond where many on their planet ever hoped to go.

Kameclara celebrated her twenty-third birthday days ago. This final test was the perfect present. She adored a good challenge.

Her hand went to the weapon at her hip. She wouldn't need it. It remained a rite of passage for each team to finish their graduation run by the grace of their skill. She had completed five ans of intense training. Not to mention the two ans of vetting before that.

That's seven birthdays.

Once they aced this final test—and there was little doubt they would—the nation of Orareca's present operatives would retire with commendations, or become officers.

Kameclara already knew she'd never retire. Not if she could help it.

She lifted her arms, appreciating the material hugging her skin. Highly elastic, it allowed for a full-range of movement. Yet remained resilient enough for space travel. Lengthening her spine into a stretch, Kameclara's eyes caught a smooth rectangle in the ceiling—the only object not made of habbadite clay. Somewhere behind the one-way window, Teroman officers watched.

She knew there were more than usual to judge the graduation run. They were probably in the midst of cooking up a surprise or two, preparing to send electric signals to the habbadite clay. On command, the substance would take on various properties. The material was confiscated from enemies over a millennium ago. With Teroman engineering, it became a valuable training tool.

Beside Kameclara, her squad-mate let out a whistle. "What'll it be this time?" the white-haired young woman stared across the expanse. She kept her locks short and pulled to the side.

"Don't tell me you're nervous, Sy?" Kameclara teased. She knew none of them were.

Kameclara had two partners she lived and trained with, Syralise and Leera. They were on their nation's Alpha Team. Each team comprised of twelve squads of three. Those squads were ranked by ability. Kameclara and her partners made up Alpha-Je—the leading squad.

Syralise gave an easy laugh, "Nah. I think we've seen it all over the ans."

Leera shrugged, "Remember, real test's when we're alone in the field."

A shrill siren echoed across the expanse, a warning the exam was about to begin. Bumps formed on Kameclara's skin. Her composure kept steady. A characteristic she inherited from her father.

"Here we go!" someone cried.

The edge of the cliff lurched upwards and she braced with thirty-five teammates. She noticed the habbadite floor shifting. Large boulders peeled from now fluid surfaces. They lifted lazily into the air and hovered.

Pressure on her feet eased. Kameclara nodded to herself. Gravity was neutralized for this exam. It wouldn't be a first. She'd run thousands of similar scenarios. Scoffing, she thought the training cavern strangely felt like a second home.

"Yeah!" Syralise cried enthusiastically. She bounced energetically on her toes. The rapidly rising cliff didn't affect her footing.

Kameclara glanced to Leera to get a read. The lanky woman crouched low as she slapped on her helmet. Bits of auburn hair poked around her neck. By her posture, Kameclara knew the eyes behind the protective glass were keenly studying the unfolding landscape. It was Leera's turn to lead. The three rotated command every mission. Syralise led the last, and Kameclara would lead the next.

"Operatives prepare," an officer's voice came from inside her helmet. Kameclara had it balanced around her crown. She pushed it down. The sphere glided seamlessly over her glossy hair, keeping thick waves in check. Compression lining calibrated, hugging comfortably to her skull. Her coms were synced with her squad-mates.

"First squad to strike the buzzer wins," an officer announced, the voice piping directly into her ear.

No sooner were the words spoken, thirty-six operatives leapt from the cliff, keen on being first to complete the mission. The ledge they stood on a moment before smashed into the ceiling.

Air rushed past Kameclara as she landed on a floating boulder. She noted wind generators firing at random intervals from the walls. Objects chancing near them swirled mercilessly, pushed at frenzied speeds. There was enough force to cause permanent damage. Even their jumpsuits suits couldn't save them. Kameclara made a mental note to steer clear.

She kept her squad-mates in periphery while hopping around, avoiding careening blocks. Kameclara scanned the cavern, searching for anything that could be a buzzer. Nano-particles in the fabric of her gear compressed when needed, decreasing joint impact. Should the material be torn, the rest would constrict a small degree, mitigating blood loss.

"I need assistance," Syralise's voice came through.

Kameclara landed solidly, grabbing onto a nook. It was safer to adhere to large boulders. They offered some protection to debris compared to her free-floating. She craned her neck above. Syralise had landed too, but her boulder proved amorphous. Her legs were sunk into soft habbadite.

"On your left," Leera's voice came through as she dashed passed Kameclara. Syralise reached out an arm. Leera pushed from a rock and grabbed hold of Syralise, yanking her from the mire. They separated mid-air and landed on fresh boulders. Both proved solid.

Leera's helmet swooped in an arc, scoping a wide range. Kameclara knew her partner liked to take in as much information as possible before announcing a plan of attack.

As she stood by, Kameclara noticed other squads also discovering the erratic nature of their environment. Some had trouble getting unstuck.

She couldn't help but grin. Habbadite caverns had always been her favorite. Anything could happen. In previous weeks they'd finished exams in stealth, weapons, and labyrinths. All with strategy incorporated. She found those routine and a bit tiresome.

Kameclara recalled an evening a few weeks ago. She had gone to a lounge with her partners to enjoy music. Some people their age attempted to chat them up. "What do you do for fun?"

Kameclara smirked playfully, dodging a piece of habbadite. *If only we could show them this…*

Leera had curtly explained they were not out to make friends. "We're unwinding before our next Intergalactic Military exam."

The others took a step back, giggling nervously. Kameclara wished her partner hadn't given up their vocation, especially so coldly. Some citizens were afraid of them. Keeping a healthy image was important.

"Stay scattered," came Leera's first command, as she switched to another boulder.

It snapped Kameclara to the present. "Heading?"

"Most squads are checking boulders individually for the buzzer," Leera observed.

Kameclara's hand became stuck to a boulder she tried to push away. Grabbing hold of a smaller rock, she shoved it into the mire and wriggled loose.

"There," Leera pointed to the furthest wall. "There's a permanent wind stream firing from the base of the wall. All others are intermittent. Worth inspecting."

"Roger," Syralise chirped as she somersaulted from her perch. The three propelled from hovering habbadite as they navigated the gravity-free field.

Kameclara spotted two members of Alpha-I squad heading in the same direction. "Interference on left," she radioed her squad.

"Sy," Leera commanded, "Inspect boulders in the wall blocked by the wind stream. Kame, assist me in interception."

"Got it, Boss!'" Syralise responded. As the most agile of the three, she wove her way through flying objects. She was careful to make contact with one appendage at a time. Should she be ensnared, her other limbs could grab onto neighboring chunks to pull herself loose.

Kameclara and Leera greeted members of Alpha-I with straight-on tackles. They were ranked just behind Alpha-Je.

Kameclara's target leaped and she missed. Following with a quick pivot, she pushed off the boulder and grabbed his foot. Catching sight of the emblem on his belt, Kameclara recognized Brock. She grinned. His right knee was still weak from a previous exam.

Brock pulled Kameclara into a wind stream. The rush of air slammed them both into an amorphous block. Kameclara's arms and shoulders were caught. Only Brock's hand was mired. Before he could clear himself, Kameclara quickly wrapped her legs around his right knee. She jerked mercilessly and he lost balance. His right side fell into the sticky boulder. Placing a hand on his back, Kameclara pulled herself loose.

"That's for the last run," she shouted playfully, kicking away. He'd stolen her ladder.

Kameclara noticed Leera in a grapple with Embledon. As she dashed to help, a shadow caught her eye. It was Verniv, the third member of Alpha-I.

A burst of air came from the wall. Kameclara pushed into its path, far enough to not be injured. It launched her into Verniv. The Alpha-I member detected her a split second before, and rolled out of reach.

Kameclara grabbed an outcropping to reposition herself. She caught a fist from Verniv as she recovered her balance. The two sparred amidst dancing boulders, neither able to best the other. Physically, all members of Alpha Team were equally matched.

Syralise's voice came through Kameclara's helmet. "Found a button," she breathed. "It was hidden behind a rock I smashed." She grunted in annoyance. "I've tried to strike it but the wind stream's too strong. It pushes away anything in its path."

"Kame, to the button," Leera commanded.

Kameclara abandoned the fight with Verniv and followed orders.

Syralise's discovery drew the attention of other operatives and all raced towards the same destination. One reached Syralise and they engaged in combat.

Leera was known for speed. Kameclara observed her squad-mate grab a fist-sized rock as she dashed from one habbadite structure to the next. Soon, Leera was near Syralise. With a quick whip of the arm, the rock struck the opponent's helmet. It distracted him long enough for Syralise to land a well-placed kick. The opponent fell into a boulder.

Good! It's amorphous!

He was stuck.

"Sy, you're on defense. Keep all away from the button." Leera somersaulted to avoid a habbadite collision. She continued, "Kame, strike the button on the count of three."

Alpha-Je positioned themselves.

"One," Leera landed her feet into the mired block that had trapped Syralise's opponent.

He whipped his head to her in alarm, wondering why anyone would choose to be caught.

"Two," Leera twisted her torso, pulling the boulder with her. The large structure bowled towards the wall, mere yards beneath the button.

"Three!"

Kameclara launched from her perch as Leera's boulder cut off the wind stream. Her palm struck the button, but it wasn't enough force. She grabbed hold of a groove in the wall and threw her shoulder into the nub.

Kameclara felt a click.

A buzz filled the cavern as Leera's boulder rushed upwards. Kameclara flipped backwards, missing it by a hair.

Before Alpha-Je could cheer, gravity laid claim to the cavern. Habbadite boulders dropped suddenly. All members of Alpha Team scrambled to avoid being crushed. Kameclara propelled herself against one large rock to avoid another. Pushing off falling objects, she made her way to the top.

When she did land, shock absorbent boots protected her ankles and knees. Nearby, her squad-mates peered about in anticipation, unharmed. Officers hadn't announced the end of the exam. Anything could still happen.

The habbadite clay crumbled into tiny pieces, enormous boulders melting. Kameclara jogged towards her squad-mates. Her eyes narrowed as the clay reshaped itself. "Are those arms and legs?"

No answer came. Hesitant postures alerted her to their uncertainty.

Kameclara crouched near Syralise and Leera as her eyes rose with the formation of the clay. They turned into creatures she knew all too well. Each stood four to five times taller than the average Teroman. These were Ressogurey forms. One of three alien races threatening Teroma. Their size, matched with intelligence, made them an exceptionally difficult opponent.

Without warning, a half-formed Ressogurey struck. An Alpha Team member was slammed into the ground. She cried in pain as her squad-mates rushed to her side.

A crackle came over the coms as Leera switched her channel to include the entire team. "Take-down formation Cephei!"

When no officers were present during a mission, command was determined by squad rank. Alpha-Je ranked first, and Leera was presently in charge. When not in competition with one another, the squads of Alpha Team trained in countless configurations. Cephei was one devised against Ressogurreys.

As the creatures thundered towards them, Alpha Team commenced their counter-attack. The weakness of the Ressogureys was their soft abdomen. The habbadite rendered these enemies with plated armor covering their undersides.

Kameclara raced towards a looming beast with Syralise by her side. Leera reached it first and pinned a leg as wide as her body. With a well-placed kick onto the other leg, the creature crashed to the ground.

Syralise evaded a swinging arm and launched herself into the air. Kameclara aimed attacks at the creature's head to keep it distracted.

Syralise landed on its back and reached down, grabbing hold of its plated armor.

Kameclara ducked from a blow and slipped beneath the creature. She struck a crucial joint in its armor as she exited between its legs. Syralise yanked off the protective plate. Kameclara and Leera simultaneously landed devastating blows, felling their opponent. Around them, other squads of Alpha Team did the same.

Ressogureys were the reason they were grouped in threes. In direct combat, they could efficiently neutralize them.

Alpha Team continued until all beasts returned to inanimate lumps of material.

The cavern fell silent. Kameclara huffed, bending over her knees. From the corner of her eye, she noticed a rock twitch. It skittered until it met with a larger lump of habbadite.

"They're reforming," she observed. The hairs on her neck raised in excitement. She loved it when situations changed in an instant.

"The button's reset," Brock reported to Leera. Kameclara swung her eyes to the far wall and ascertained the large button had indeed popped out. In the back of her mind, she wondered what retaliation Brock had planned for their next skirmish.

"My guess is the Ressogurey structures will likely come at us repeatedly until we hit the buzzer a second time," Syralise reported.

"We've an opening," Leera observed as the first Ressogurey simulation reared its head. Its arms had yet to form. "Pyramid formation. Beneath original target. Now!" she commanded.

Immediately, members of Alpha Team raced to gather beneath the button. The wind stream had shut off, so none could ride it upwards.

Alpha-Je had been furthest from the button. By the time they reached the pyramid, they were near the top. Leera stood on Kameclara and Syralise's shoulders. Even then, she couldn't reach.

"We don't have time to restructure. We need to vault," Leera ordered, eying a charging horde. The operatives were vulnerable, stacked against the wall.

Kameclara laced her hands with Syralise. Leera placed a foot into the crook and they launched her into the air. The slender operative lifted her arm high as newly formed Ressogureys reached the pyramid. Kameclara could only imagine her teammates at the base bracing for assault. She tensed too, should she fall.

Leera struck the button with all her might.

Another buzz ripped through the space. Ressogureys crumbled into loose habbadite pebbles, cascading around the feet of operatives sighing in unison.

They caught Leera as she came down.

"Disband," the redhead ordered.

Alpha Team lowered themselves to solid ground. All operatives still on high alert.

"Exam complete," came over their coms.

Kameclara exhaled sharply, filled with relief and disappointment. She was just getting warmed up.

Habbadite pebbles at their feet skittered to form a staircase. Clay on a wall peeled aside, revealing double doors. The operatives stood in formation, awaiting permission to exit. Kameclara noticed lasers weapons on the ground, previously embedded in the habbadite. They had defeated the Ressogureys before the forms could utilize them.

"Proceed to briefing hall," an officer commanded.

The operatives trooped up the steps, giving one another supportive pats. They wanted to congratulate each other, but hadn't heard affirmation if they'd passed.

They entered a large space and took their places before a Captain. Not long after, a Major appeared. The name, "Uteni" emblazoned on her chest. She marched to Leera. "Very clever. You've beaten the record. Congratulations on holding the shortest time in completing the final evaluation."

Leera saluted, "With respect, Sir, the victory belongs to all of Alpha Team."

A proud look shined on Major Uteni's face. "Absolutely. In training we pit you against each other because competition bears improvement. But the real test is how quickly you recognize the need to work together."

"Sir!"

Major Uteni's eyes shone with pride. "It's the one thing you can never forget when you're in the field: In unity we triumph."

Leera nodded sharply. "I'll remember, Sir."

Major Uteni faced the team, a wide grin across her face. "You're all green-lit for missions!"

Kameclara saluted with the rest of her team. No more chaperoning from experienced operatives. Next time they were in the field, they were on their own.

Her eyes gazed at the slate-gray ceiling, knowing a star-studded heaven spread beyond. She hoped to see it in person soon.

Chapter Two

The Land of the Seraphims- 2210 Iman Year

A hand fluttered to Vesper's chest as she surveyed her domain. She stood in the high tower of what was formerly the Land of the Seraphims' palace. Now, it was her command base.

Without realizing, she rubbed a tender spot in her breastbone. An ache had resided there since before she came to power.

Before she lost something.

... Or someone?

The thought caused forlorn to rise. Vesper gasped as sentiments crowded in from the edges of her mind. "No! I've too much to do!" she struggled to cast them aside. The melancholy refused to obey, pushing through with memories in tow. A flash of curled hair. A dash of wistra flowers' scent. They threatened to disempower her, and Vesper bit down hard. "This *planet* is mine," she snarled. She had taken Ima, and everything was in order for her next phase. She wasn't prepared to let foolish emotions cripple.

A breeze whipped her earth-colored hair from its pins as if aiding Vesper's emotions in rebellion. It stirred ribbons around her robes and snapped banners displaying her crest, a green serpent on a field of red.

A hand snatched a fistful of air. "Even you belong to me." She twirled the wind into a ball. It beat about, at the mercy of the sorceress.

Vesper seldom recalled days before magic. Days with her husband. "… And Meliora," she whispered, giving an inch to her daughter's name.

The wind around her subsided as if it'd received what it'd wanted—her to acknowledge the young woman.

Staring into the ball of air, Vesper fathomed smiling eyes. The green the same shade as her own. But with a joy and love she could not feel. It sent a shiver down her spine, and she released her hold. Watching the ball dissipate, it took her melancholy along.

Vesper gazed to the sky, swallowing the last of rebellious sorrow. An incomplete task irked. There was a faint outline of a planet.

Jema.

She imagined it jeering at her. "Once I conquer Jema, I'll have control over both planets." Her eyes narrowed, "And the kingdom Songbird is there."

She clenched the edge of a decorative bannister. It seemed a lifetime ago when she had gone there to test into the school of sorcery. All Vesper wanted then was to find a way to bring her husband back from death.

That desire was now as lost as his grave in the rubble of the Priletoria palace. The very mention of Songbird, home to the school of sorcery, brought bitterness. That was where she had suffered indignity. Such a place could not be allowed to exist.

Vesper grinned crookedly, swimming in dark, violent emotions. Those she was familiar with. They fueled her spells.

In the last twenty years she'd toiled to comprehend the magic in her veins. Without a Master's guidance, it'd brought struggles and dead ends. She wouldn't receive a Master sorcerer's help. Not on Ima, because there were none. On Jema, she had left behind destruction. None would aid her.

Vesper had consumed a number of Master sorcerers in Songbird and inherited their power. It nearly drove her mad. With the abilities came the Masters' souls, locked inside her own. Though they had no conscious bearing, their vicious demise made them restless.

She'd searched through their memories. The voices preached countless approaches to sorcery. It led to confusion. Through strenuous experimentation, she had managed to acquire some finesse.

"I've often found myself going back to Cleodell," Vesper grimaced at the thought of her first instructor. He'd taught her to use negative emotions to cast.

Vesper straightened. She shouldn't waste time divulging contemptible recollections. She jerked to face south, where new structures were built. She had climbed the tower to review them. They protected her dragons—interplanetary ships, recently fitted with weapons of war. In two years, she WILL launch for Jema.

The sorceress frowned. There was one kingdom on Jema she knew could prove a challenge.

Seu was known for military prowess.

Yet for millennia, they'd been unwaveringly clandestine.

Vesper shuddered to recall the black shooting stars she once saw take flight from behind Seu's walls. Their roar terrified her. She again searched memories consumed from Master sorcerers, as she'd often done. Even they knew next to nothing about Seu.

Except Master Reynoro…

He had been the eldest Master. In his memories was an incomplete reference tying Seu to the Seed of Life. She had gnawed around this partial memory for decades, but couldn't wring more information.

It made her uneasy. Vesper feared Seu might house a weapon that could neutralize magic. Then, she'd be nothing but a mortal, and the invasion of Jema a fool's errand.

Gray clouds formed over the ocean. Weak thunder reached Vesper's ears with a strong scent of rain. She paid no mind, deep in contemplation on Seu.

Vesper wasn't willing to take blind risks. She had concluded her best option was to conquer Songbird and Calio first, the only other kingdoms on the small planet of Jema. She could safely command from Songbird where her powers were amplified by the school of sorcery. She would then scour Songbird and Calio's records, searching for Seu's weakness.

... And its connection to the Seed of Life. With so much secrecy shrouding both, it can be assumed they're somehow connected.

Vesper had spies on Jema. They were Priletorian officers sent to search for her decades ago. Vesper had been imprisoned then, as the result of a foul plot. At the time, she was Queen of Priletoria. Those soldiers, without complete knowledge of her takeover on Ima, pledged continued loyalty to Vesper. Using coded transmissions, she'd kept in contact.

They updated her on Jeman situations. Most of the small planet continued their operations without much concern for Ima. Seu closed off borders and limited immigration.

The greatest change was the disbanding of the school of sorcery. Four of seven remaining Masters stayed in Songbird. The other three kept their whereabouts quiet, but were rumored to have moved to

Calio. The consensus on Jema was that the Master sorcerers' era had ended.

"As for the soldiers of Songbird and Calio?" Vesper scoffed; eyes locked south. A circular structure encrusted with glyphs stood wide. It was her own school of sorcery. She'd been training loyal mages. With the Master sorcerers of Songbird scattered, the pitiful armies of Jema were no match for her magic wielding soldiers.

Nothing on the two worlds could stop her.

Chapter Three

Kameclara's steps were lax, shoulders shifting naturally. On the inside, she throbbed with anticipation, marching at the front of Alpha Team. They filed into a briefing room, prepared to have their first official meeting as green-lit operatives.

Syralise chatted heatedly with others, speculating on state secrets they'd soon learn. Leera brought up the rear with intent focus, a signature of her Pinghe training.

Across the nation of Orareca, other freshly green-lit teams were receiving similar briefings.

Captain Hilme entered and the team settled in their seats. After a swift introduction, he dimmed the lights. Their sun appeared on a viewing screen, comprised in a rainbow of colors. It was a spectrograph image. Kameclara gazed warmly at the star's unique halo, extending roughly two astronomical units from its surface.

Her eyes narrowed. There were two anomalies in the halo. She twitched to raise her hand, but hesitated. It was unlike the Intergalactic Military to show an image with errors.

Is there a reason the spots are there?

"What do you see?" Captain Hilme asked as if reading her mind.

Syralise lifted her hand, "It seems we need better photographing equipment. There are two specks in the sun's corona." From the hesitation in her voice, Kameclara gathered Syralise shared her doubts. But her partner wasn't one to keep quiet.

Captain Hilme pursed his lips, expression souring. It was then Kameclara realized the specks were the focus of the briefing.

He spoke, "The Intergalactic Military's scanning and observation equipment are state-of-the-art and routinely maintained. There are no errors."

In response to everyone's eagerness, the Captain pointed to the dark dots on the image. "You're gazing at the Ia Solar System's best kept secret." Giving his audience a grave expression, he announced, "Our system has nine planets, not seven as you were taught in primary school."

Kameclara glanced to Leera with tempered alarm. The minute muscles on her partner's face tightened. Beside her, a sharp noise came from Syralise's throat.

The captain added, "The sun's corona naturally shrouds the inner two planets and distorts communication." His eyes narrowed as he growled, "Before I continue, I want to stress clearly. This next piece of information must absolutely NEVER be revealed to civilians of Teroma." There was a long pause as he allowed the gravity of his words to sink. "You must NEVER let slip these inner planets exist. Let alone house life."

Kameclara felt her throat tighten. "Life?" she sputtered under her breath. She wondered if Captain Hilme meant microscopic organisms. She got the inkling he didn't.

Syralise lifted her hand, slower this time. The captain nodded for her to speak. "Are they also an alien threat?" she asked, referring to their familiar enemy.

"No. Other questions?"

Leera voiced, "What about the six Oli gas planets between Teroma and the sun? Are they the same as we learned in primary school?"

"Yes. They're uninhabited."

Kameclara mulled over the information. Then, calmly raised her hand. The captain pointed to her. She made an assumption on the type of life. "What people are on the two planets in the corona?"

"Jema and Ima? They're Teromans, like us."

Kameclara turned down a street, sighing contentedly as she took in the view. Silver arches stretched across the sky. They were the rings of Teroma. Her eyes shifted, focusing to stars beyond. She thought to the many hours of her childhood spent in her father's study. He had dozens of instruments, some rudimentary, many advanced. All were for observing the stars. It was in those early ans Kameclara developed a love for the heavens. She always knew she belonged somewhere out there.

A long breath escaped, clouding in the air. Kameclara flexed her shoulders, a bit sore from training. Joining the Intergalactic Military started as a chance to fly to the stars. But as she continued, Kameclara discovered unparalleled comradery and a sense of accomplishment. Now, she held two passions. "Serve the planet, explore the beyond," she grinned.

And indeed, there's so much to discover...

Still processing the existence of Jema and Ima, she whispered to the sky, "What other secrets do you hold?"

The wind shifted and flurries of snow gave chilled kisses. "What a lovely summer," she sighed, sporting a single-layer coat. During winters, three or more layers were needed. Kameclara couldn't imagine what Teroma's climate would be like without their atmosphere. The planet would be at absolute zero all the time.

Still, their bodies were unique. At least, compared to their enemies. Teromans were naturally tolerant to extreme temperatures.

Kameclara strolled past an entryway to an underground city. Warm air brushed her skin. She slowed to soak in heat, using it to imagine life on Ima or Jema.

It must be hot... They probably have flowing water on the surface, and not just underground like Teroma.

Chatter reached her ears as a group emerged from the tunnel. She picked up her pace. She didn't feel like interacting.

A few yards later, her ears perked. The people were catching up. Kameclara moved aside to allow them to pass.

Then she heard rushed steps. Not panicked, rather clumsy as if someone tried moving quietly, but failed. She slowed her steps, exhaling with displeasure. She had an idea what was coming.

A young man darted past. The strap of her shoulder bag snapped. Instinctively she rolled her wrist, wrapping the strap before he could get away. He didn't loosen his grip as he kept running. She tightened her core and jerked. As he fell back, she commanded her shoulder forward. Her fist followed into his nose. A crunch reverberated as he fell to the ground without a twitch.

Without batting an eye, she pivoted to face three others. One pointed a five-shooter at her. Kameclara took her time and knotted her strap before sliding the bag back over her shoulder. She eyed the muzzle and man's posture. Ans of practice told her if he squeezed, the bullet would careen left. At her distance she could easily evade.

"Lady, we need to borrow some money," he spoke impudently. His friends snickered.

"Come and get it," she challenged.

Kameclara wondered if she should reveal she was an operative. On a planet ruled by martial law, harassing a member of the Intergalactic Military was met with heavy punishment.

"Do it," his friend goaded.

But… these kids don't look too bright.

The young man hesitated for a moment as the muzzle lowered. The other friend called him a coward. The gun lifted towards Kameclara's head once more. Her trained eye gaged it to still be off, with less than five percent chance of hitting her—assuming the barrel held no deviation. She was in no real danger.

The young man inched with false bravado. Kameclara waited until he came within reach. His face showed he believed he was still at a safe distance.

Her feet slid forward. Kameclara's right hand snaked as her left assisted. Before he could blink, the weapon was in her hand and disassembled.

The three gaped for a second before turning to flee into the tunnel. They left their unconscious friend in the snow.

Kameclara tossed the gun into a dumpster and kept the ammunition. Though ballistic weapons were allowed for special-circumstance civilian ownership, ammunition was illegal. Only in times of global emergencies would bullets be distributed.

She knelt beside the unconscious man and pulled back his eyelids. "Don't worry. You'll be awake in a few minutes." She dragged him into

played pranks from time to time. This must be one.

"It's not mere legend," Procias' face grew long. "Not only did she devise a way to heat our planet's core, she also taught us useful skills. Some might sound absurd unless you witness it, like how to estimate future events and use what was known as sorcery… But it's all true."

"Alright. But why?" A skeptical grin lingered on her lips.

"The Goddess visits for reasons only she knows," Procias shook his head. "We, however, are obligated to protect her, or it means the obliteration of our race." He added in a low voice, "She's tied her safety to the existence of every single Teroman. It's literally written in our DNA. The nevino sequence."

"The ghost sequence? The one that flickers?" Kameclara's eyes glimmered with fascination.

"Yes."

Her face changed as Procias' words turned in her mind. "Let's say I believe," she spoke levelly. "What does this have to do with your work?"

Procias patted his daughter's hand. "You know of Jema, right? The planet that means 'first mother?' There's also Ima, which means 'second mother.' They're named similarly to Teroma, 'earth mother.' Because of your clearance, you should've been informed they hold intelligent life."

"Affirmative."

Procias sipped his drink. "A large part of my duties is to communicate with Jema. There's a facility there called Seu. We, the Teromans, established it seven thousand ans ago. Its sole purpose is to be a safe haven for the Goddess, should Teroma ever come under attack while she's incarnated."

"Does she appear at a specific place and time?" Kameclara asked, still hunting for an impish spark in Procias' eyes. She found none. Only steadfastness.

"A select few have the skill to calculate the time range and approximate location of her return. Fortunately, our enemies cannot. And just as blessed, for the last millennium or so, Ia hasn't returned." Procias stared into his glass. Speaking on such heavy topics fatigued him.

"Our enemies. Your mention of them implies they're linked to this Goddess." Kameclara struggled to wrap her mind around her father's words. It went against her logical nature. It had to be one of his jokes.

But… they were never this elaborate, and never involved his work, which he takes gravely.

Doubt shaded her thoughts.

Procias nodded, "Legend has it, Ia can bring immortality to a race. It's believed that's why they're after her. This 'child's tale' as you call it, is the true reason we're under constant threat of attack. And why the Intergalactic Military exists."

The back of Kameclara's neck tingled. If immortality existed, the quest for it would make any civilization bloodthirsty. Yet as she stared down at her body, though impervious to algid weather, she knew she wasn't the least bit immortal.

"It leads me to why I'm here. We know civilization evolved naturally on Jema and spread to Ima. We've left them alone," he brushed it aside as a mere convenient mention, "all the while keeping Seu's true purpose secret. Millennia passed and nothing's affected the sanctity of our base." His eyes hardened, "Until now. There's a threat on Ima. We believe it'll soon spread to Jema." Procias took a large swig of his drink.

"Father?" Kameclara's voice grew uncertain as he polished off his beverage. "What is this? Seriously. Aren't you kidding?"

Hoarse from the liquor, he announced, "It's believed the Goddess is returning to Teroma. She might already be here." Fear flashed in his eyes. "That's why it's of the utmost importance Seu's secure." Face distorting, he confessed, "I fought with my conscience. I didn't want to because you're my daughter…"

Kameclara sensed something else bothered him. Something personal. She watched Procias cover his eyes with a trembling hand. His next words dribbled sadly. "In the end, I did what was best for Teroma and Seu." Procias locked a mortified gaze with Kameclara. "I gave a *strong* recommendation to send Teroma's Intergalactic Military to Jema. To subdue the situation. Because it was the only option with even a chance at success."

"Are you saying...?" A rush flooded Kameclara, making her skin tingle. This was out of the ordinary. The Intergalactic Military faced enemies from outside their solar system.

Not inside.

"Yes," he wheezed.

She'd never seen her father this upset. The gray streaks in his black hair appeared more pronounced. Kameclara steadied his hand.

"You'll need to go," Procias barely formed the words. "When you're there, you'll face myriads of dangers I can't begin to detail."

"Like what?" Kameclara no longer believed her father to be joking. Yet the information processed slowly. She braced against a sensation of awe, enveloping her like an unexpected snowstorm.

He gulped. "There's a powerful sorceress on Ima. She single-handedly took control of the planet. Use utmost caution dealing with Vesper." His hand squeezed hers, the name moaning from his lips with angst.

"Ima... first from the sun," Kameclara didn't know how to begin addressing a sorceress.

"Yes. And as far as we know, our enemies in neighboring star systems aren't aware of Jema and Ima." He gulped. "We must keep it that way."

Kameclara ran numbers in her head. "It's about an eight-ans journey from Teroma to the inner planets, isn't it?"

"That's why it's hard for me," Procias stuttered. "When you leave for this mission, I'll likely never see you again." He blinked back tears, adding in careful cadence, "It pains me to say this, but I believe this path's always been your destiny."

Procias had read the stars. He'd caught glimpses of his daughter's future. But he couldn't share them with her, lest it affect the decisions she needed to arrive to on her own.

Kameclara's eyes softened. She embraced him, "You, mom, Acile and Rito will always be with me."

He patted her head, knowing it would be one of the last times he'd see her. "I wish I could answer more questions, but I've already committed treason in saying as much as I have. You can't volunteer a word of this."

She pulled away. "Understood."

"I've stayed too long," he glanced at his timepiece. "The situation on Jema's tense. An urgent message can arrive from Seu any minute." Procias planted a firm kiss on her cheek. "Be safe, sweetie."

"I love you too, dad."

A damp mood settled over the room when Procias left. Kame-clara returned to the kitchen. Pulling out a glass for herself, she poured the same stiff drink.

Chapter Four

Retractable skis on Kameclara's boots squeaked across the snow. Beside her, Syralise's laugh echoed through frozen air, the only sign of warmth for miles.

"Hey, thanks for coming to my party last week," Syralise peered from her hood. Stray pieces of short hair, the same color as the snow, poked out. Her golden eyes twinkled. When Syralise smiled, the corners of her lips creased more than average. It made her come off mischievous. Kameclara felt it suited her.

Syralise's family had thrown a celebration for her becoming green-lit.

Kameclara puffed, "Of course! I wouldn't have missed your dad's world-famous cooking!"

In the back of her mind, Kameclara thought to her visit from Procias. It was drastically different from Syralise's joyous occasion. She wanted to confer the information with her partner, a woman she'd grown to trust with her life. Yet, Kameclara honored the promise to her father and kept quiet. A pale sense of betrayal slithered at the edge of her mind.

The two traveled in silence, enjoying their last few hours of freedom. They were to report for duty the next morning. Soft powder beneath their feet indicated an unusually cold summer. Normally the snow was wet. "The planet core must be cooling," Kameclara observed.

"It happens every few millennia. It kicks back up again on its own, doesn't it?"

Kameclara shrugged. An enormous nevite crystal in the core generated heat for the entire planet. Deep rivers wend between layers of crust, acting as a conduit for warmth.

"Where did Brock say this new river is?" Kameclara asked. The team liked to dive, exploring underground terrain.

"We're almost there. His brother's a developer and found it last week." Syralise had an impeccable sense of direction.

Kameclara peered to her friend and cocked an eyebrow. "Last week? So it should be a restricted area. What if we're caught? How'd it look if newly active operatives were arrested?" She wasn't really worried. Few braved barren snowfields.

Syralise opened her arms and spun, "That's half the fun!"

It was Kameclara's turn to laugh, "It *would* put our skills to the test."

Each nation of Teroma held a specialization in the Intergalactic Military. Some produced fighter pilots. Others scouted, engineered weapons, or focused on a defensive tactic. Orareca's was stealth—one of the few offensive specialties. In the event of invasion, they were to board enemy ships and disable from within.

"Leera said she'd meet us there. She's leaving from her Pinghe reservation."

"Where we're still not welcome," Kameclara added soberly.

The Pinghe were an ancient order of martial warriors who kept out of the public sphere. They harbored centuries of disgruntlement towards the Intergalactic Military. Leera had been disowned when she left.

"They think we're 'too violent.'" Syralise's voice grew small. "Leera's only allowed back for limited visits because her mother's a Grandmaster."

"My father told me their practice has been around since the dawn of civilization. They were the original protectors of Teroma. Long before the Intergalactic Military."

"I didn't know that," Syralise said in awe. "Nothing against Leera, but I don't get it. I mean… their belief system is based on martial arts. Why're they so against us?"

"I know what you mean. But they're so secretive, there's no way to ask."

The two climbed a snowy ridge. On the other side, they spotted Alpha Team. Verniv waved and Kameclara called out in greeting. She and Syralise braced their knees and rushed down the slope. She loved the sting as wind reddened her cheeks.

A history lecture came to mind. Kameclara spoke above rushing air, "I think the Pinghe pulled away because they didn't like how the Intergalactic Military handled sleeper agents."

Syralise waited until they were at the bottom of the slope. "I don't like how we handle them either. But…" she sighed, "… orders are orders."

"They're here 'cause of that one time… four millennia ago was it? The only time the enemy made contact with Teroma's surface," Kameclara recalled.

After a grueling battle, Teroma had stood victorious. Many alien soldiers were left behind as the commanding enemy fled. Prisoners of war were forced to live in penal colonies, but their offspring were released to assimilate into Teroman society.

"Yeah… And shortly after, domestic attacks grew prevalent," Syralise chipped in. "The nations discovered secret societies formed from the enemies' descendants."

"Sleeper agents," Kameclara declared in a low voice.

"What about 'em?" Brock asked as they approached.

"We're talking about the falling out between the Intergalactic Military and the Pinghe," Syralise filled him in.

Brock nodded. "I get it. I think it's b'cause of the raids. Usually conducted by North Deron operatives." Their specialty was identifying sleeper cells.

"The Pinghe don't like how brutal we are," Syralise puffed.

"But sleeper agents are a real threat," Verniv pressed. "Remember the attempted bombing two ans ago? Stuff like that happens all the time."

"When I was first vetted as a possible candidate to become an operative, I couldn't even come close to the training field until they did an extensive background check," Syralise spoke. "It went back sixty generations!"

"I recall you started a month late," Kameclara commented.

"That's how long it took!" Syralise flashed a grin to Kameclara, "Your dad's worked for them for decades and Leera's mom is a Pinghe Grandmaster. Bet they held the door open, shooing you two in!"

"Well, your mom's a star athlete in the Ring Games. That's pretty awesome too!" she complimented. Kameclara loved watching the Ring Games with her brothers. The planet's top athlete's competed in various sports hosted in orbit.

"Yeah, I'm still waiting to get her autograph!" Brock laughed. "And speaking of the Pinghe, where's your third?

"Coming from her reservation, two nations away," Syralise answered. It was common for operatives to be transferred to where they were best suited.

"Oh, respect!" admiration crossed Brock's face, a common reaction to the Pinghe. The Intergalactic Military didn't harbor the same resentment.

Every few decades, a Pinghe Master or two emerged of their own volition. They faced exile to train the Intergalactic Military. It was their personal belief Pinghe skills added to the defense of the planet. Leera's father had been one of them.

"Speak and you shall receive..." Verniv peered past Kameclara.

They turned to see Leera ski down a hill, hair whipping freely beneath a hat. Kameclara lifted a hand to wave. As Leera drew close, her hand lowered. Anger tightened the redhead's angular features.

"Hey," Leera greeted the group abruptly, dark eyes flashing.

Kameclara stepped near, "What is it?"

Leera's teeth clenched, but her eyes softened. "Tell you later. Everything's green." It meant there was no threat.

Syralise casted a concerned glance Kameclara's way. Though habitually serious, Leera seldom appeared as upset as she did now. Kameclara wondered if her partner had an argument with her mother.

Leera stepped past them. "Yo, Brock! Where's this dive site? I needa blow off steam."

"Just waiting for you, Pinghe!" Brock pushed off, skis gliding effortlessly. "Let's go!"

The rest of the team followed with yips of exhilaration.

Brock led them down a steep ravine, shielded from tundra winds. They cut through a construction zone, disobeying trespassing warnings. There wouldn't be any workers. Progress halted when new underground rivers were discovered. They needed to be mapped first.

When they reached a climb, the operatives tapped the side of their boots. The skis retracted, allowing them to scale an ice shelf.

"Stick to the left of the outcropping," Brock instructed. "There's a prison on the right. We don't want to be seen."

A vengeful gale bore down and Kameclara doubted any guard would be on prudent watch. As she climbed, curiosity got the best of her. She'd never seen a prison before. They were built aboveground, to discourage escape.

She inched right.

"What you're doing isn't very stealthy," Syralise hissed.

"I just wanna look," Kameclara whispered back.

She found a shallow ledge to the right of the ice shelf and perched solidly. Peering beyond the bend, she spotted a large box on a sleigh coming to a halt. "Prison transport," she barely made out the plain letters on its side.

A guard hopped out, hat pulled low and wrapped in layers. Kameclara imagined his teeth chattering. He yanked open a door, the wind nearly taking it off. He shouted something but there was no movement. The guard reached in and jerked on a chain. A man spilled out, wearing bright yellow. Shoulders hunched, he fought the wind pressing fabric to his skin.

"What'd you do, buddy?" Kameclara whispered in mild amusement.

A gust howled across the plain. The man in yellow turned his face away. He struggled to walk as his legs sunk into snow up to his thighs.

Kameclara felt a tickle at the base of her skull. An unseen thread tugged in her ribcage, connecting to something distant yet close. Before she could comprehend the sensation, the man's head jerked up. He peered the mile or so between them and Kameclara felt his eyes lock onto her.

The thread pulled taut.

Her breath froze. *He can't see me, I'm in shadows,* she thought logically.

A chill went through her body as a sweet melody rose in her soul. It urged her to answer the tug.

The man didn't move. Standing tall, the cold no longer troubled him.

"I see you," Kameclara mouthed, feeling an old connection.

Her rational mind chalked it up to amusement at the uniqueness of the moment.

The guard struck the man. He shuddered, again drooping from the temperature. He hurried through the gates, disappearing behind thick gray walls.

"Let's go!" Leera sniped.

Kameclara mentally shook herself and joined her friends.

Chapter Five

Orareca 14.236 ans

Stanten felt his stomach tighten as they went down a slope. He peered from a slit in the metal transport box. A glimpse of a yellow glow and green vegetation told him they were in the north underground sector. His city, Pudyo was one of many in Orareca. The far north primarily supported agriculture. Beyond it was his destination.

Prisons were far from cities. Escapees succumbed to hypothermia before nearing civilization.

Due to the distance from its sun, Teroma remained frozen on the surface. A core of solid nevite emanated heat and smaller chucks of the material were embedded in the crust. Stanten lived underground like most citizens. Buildings above were for commercial use, rich snobs, and military. Installing nevite to heat homes was a luxury.

He'd heard soldiers went without because they were trained to tolerate extreme temperatures.

The middle class lived deep in the crust where it was warmer. Steam-powered cable cars safely commuted them to work on the surface, passing people like Stanten. His home sat in the shallow tunnels where it was perpetually cold.

A loud rap came at the back of the metal box. It took him a moment to realize they'd stopped moving. Obediently, Stanten lifted his shackled hands above his head. A hook reached in from the slit and pulled his chains tight, preventing him from attacking should he get the idea.

The door opened and freezing air poured in. Stanten tightened his jaw, refusing to let anyone hear his teeth chatter. His issued garb did nothing for warmth.

Once the convict's yoke was attached to his neck by a mechanical device, the guard commanded him to exit. The cold made Stanten hesitate. A yank came at the chain attached to the yoke, and he tumbled into the snow.

Stanten held his arms stiffly at his side, refusing to cross them and appear weak. Sharp wind sucked away his breath and he squeezed watering eyes. He prayed his legs wouldn't give out as the cold sapped the last of their strength.

Unexpectedly, a flame stirred in his chest. It locked him in place as a sensation took over his body. Stanten's eyes shot open, searching the distance. Someone had called to him. "Impossible," he muttered. The wind howled savagely, carrying away any sound.

He stared intently. The feeling someone watched flooded him stronger than anything he'd felt before. "Hello?" he muttered. His eyes searched frantically, finding nothing but snow and dark.

A thud between his shoulders forced him to continue. As he stumbled, Stanten quickly forgot the sensation. By the time they made it to the shelter of the prison, he'd surrendered to wrapping his arms around his torso. The building wasn't much warmer, but at least protected against wind. Stanten hid envy mixed with disdain for the officers' thick coats and heavy boots. He slowed his steps, hoping to keep warm air lingering around him longer.

A yank on his neck deferred efforts.

The begrimed hall lacked windows. Silenced filled the space, broken only by marching feet. Three officers escorted him. Standard procedure for someone convicted of manslaughter.

As his feet dragged, Stanten's thoughts went to his mother and how disappointed she'd be. Her life had been hard, working odd jobs because her birth certificate didn't verify her father. Life for people with obscure lineages proved difficult on Teroma. No one wanted to hire for fear they were sleeper agents.

His mother was a rare beauty, with a head of dark green hair and eyes as bright as ancient ice. It brought her trouble with men. Stanten was the result of a trouble. He didn't know his father, and neither did she. As a child, he'd spent hours studying his plain brown eyes and flat cheekbones. Whenever he ran into men with similar faces, Stanten wondered if they were related. If they were his father.

A shove from an officer caused him to trip on the chains around his ankles. His nerves grated. Stanten warned himself to keep his temper in check. It was what landed him in this mess.

He looked down at his large hands, the bones of which had been broken countless times. Growing up on the streets of Pudyo, he'd learned to survive at an early age.

By his teens, Stanten grew adept at ending fights. Once word spread not to mess with the "grumpy guy," things grew somewhat quiet.

He'd left primary school before finishing. Not that he was learning anything there anyway. Stanten found employment collecting waste, and for a while, dared say he felt content.

He and his mother had lived in the same dump of a place since he was born. They'd always found it difficult to make ends meet. Paying rent was a struggle. Living on his own was only a dream.

Stanten looked around at the prison and shook his head. He was getting a private cell. *I didn't want my own place this way.*

Their old landlord had always given them an extra week here and there. Things went sour when he passed away. His less-than-honorable son took over the building. He always asked for rent at the door. Stanten could handle the unsavory personality but what bothered him was the way the younger man looked at his mother.

"Ma, he shouldn't be at the door all the time," he said one day.

She told him to keep it to himself.

The new landlord raised rent every few months. Things became increasingly difficult. At first his mother hid the raises from Stanten. She paid the difference by spending adult time with the new landlord.

One day, Stanten ran into him alone. The man let slip about his mother and Stanten flew into a rage. He left the landlord barely breathing. By the end of the day, he and his mother were on the streets, hiding from authorities.

"Son," she said as they huddled behind a building, "Just because something's wrong doesn't mean you gotta fix it. I know that temper of yours. When it goes off, you can't think. Promise you'll keep it in check."

"But he was using you!" he shot angrily.

"And I let him," came a tired response. "I'm not saying it's right, but I chose to let it happen."

As he gazed at her sagging face, Stanten understood she did it to keep a roof over his head. Worse, they were the kind of people who didn't have a better choice. She couldn't report the landlord. No one would believe her—and even if they did—they didn't matter.

"I'm sorry," he jerked away, ashamed for his actions and of who he was.

"It's alright. We'll find a way to make things work," she smiled. "I just want to see you find little pieces of happiness in your day."

She ruffled his hair but misery clung to him, the way foul odors clung to their parts of the tunnels. He'd seen past her expression. She knew all too well happiness wasn't meant for people like them.

Stanten's trek with the officers ended at a documenting station. They took his fingerprints and collected a cheek swab. Next, they pushed him into a small room and told him to undress. No sooner did he disrobe, foul-smelling liquid shot from the walls. It stung, but Stanten invited the lukewarm suds.

Afterwards, a moderately thicker garment was issued. The officers screened his body for contraband before placing him in quarantine.

The room wasn't much bigger than the kitchen in the new apartment he'd found with his mother. Stanten shuddered to remember the place. It was in a worse part of town. He had insisted his mother take the single bedroom while he sleep in the open area. Quite a few times, they had returned home to discover their apartment was broken into. There was never much to steal and they joked, "To poor for even burglars."

Around that time, Stanten had considered seeking out sleeper agents and asking to join. Having an undocumented lineage meant the world saw him as one of them anyway.

However, there were no guaranteed benefits. Sure, he might score a few cash jobs here and there, but it was dangerous.

And Mother would be disappointed.

Despite the way the planet treated her, she loved Teroma. He quickly did away with the thought.

On Stanten's nineteenth birthday, he had returned home early from work. As he approached their front door, he saw it ajar. Peeking warily, he discovered a letti cake on the table with "Happy Birthday" written across the top. A rare smile crept to his lips. He called out as he closed the door, sliding deadbolts in place.

Scuffling in the kitchen drew his attention. He went to see if his mother needed help. In a few steps, he was peering in and stopped abruptly. A bloody knife confronted him on the floor. Gasping reached his ears. Stanten turned to see his mother scrunched in a corner, coated in crimson.

He could never unsee the look in her eyes. They glossed with relief, recognizing her life would soon end.

"Don't go!" he cried, recognizing the selfishness of his request.

A bang behind him made Stanten jump. A man was escaping through the window, his mother's purse in hand.

Stanten's vision filled with white spots. He grabbed the man's ankle and the intruder careened across the floor. As Stanten descended on him, the bloodied knife swung. He ducked, swatting it out of the man's hand. His other fist caught the intruder by the throat, slamming him into the ground. Meager kitchenware clattered around them.

A pair of scissors appeared and the intruder slashed wildly, striking Stanten in the arm and leg. He wrangled it away and pinned him. Anger overtook and Stanten's fists met the man's head in frenzy. He didn't stop until officers wrestled him away.

His mother and the intruder were taken to the hospital. Later, both were reported to have passed. While in custody, Stanten was denied temporary release to attend his mother's recommitment to the earth.

For the first time since he could remember, Stanten bawled.

He became indicted for the death of the intruder. After a four-ans trial, he was found guilty, earning a life sentence without parole. A typical sentence for the poorly documented.

A green light buzzed in the quarantine room, driving away his recollections. A voice informed Stanten he had passed scans for infectious diseases. He blinked away wetness as the door opened.

The yoke was replaced around his neck. Shuffling obediently, Stanten entered a long hall with metal doors lining both sides. Aggressive voices called, but he tuned them out.

"Sorry Ma," he mumbled under his breath. "I messed up. I know you never wanted me here."

They stopped at an open door. The yoke was removed and he dragged his feet inside. The door clanged shut and he was alone. Those convicted of severe crimes often were. Stanten didn't usually mind loneliness. It gave him space to sort out thoughts. But this time, he was confronted by a lack of closure he could never shake. It sat heavier than the yoke, leeching exhaustion into his bones.

"I didn't even get to say goodbye," he choked. "Can't think of anything worse."

The only solace he found was making the resolve to keep his rage in check.

He sat tall and drew in breaths. His mother often told him to breathe a certain way to get a rein on his anger. The advice was all he had left of her.

Breath by breath, he used it to distract from pain.

Chapter Six

Orareca 14.236 ans

"How bad was it?" Syralise implored Leera while holding a handstand. They lingered in one of many training halls at their base. Alpha-Je was squeezing in a warm up before reporting for duty.

Leera shared with them that she had indeed argued with her mother the day before. "She told me never to set foot on a Pinghe reservation again. That I should think she was dead to me." The redhead sniffed in annoyance. "Ever since I quit my path to becoming a Pinghe Master, she's been this way. I never guessed her hate for the IM was this deep." Leera used the abbreviation for Intergalactic Military, an unspoken right earned by those green-lit for duty.

Kameclara thought to her father's warning. Operatives were likely to be deployed to Jema soon. "Maybe you should call her and smooth things over." She hated the thought of her friend leaving on bad terms with her last living relative. Leera's father had died in a training accident with the Intergalactic Military. It could've heightened her mother's prejudice.

"I tried," Leera stepped to a bar. With a hop, her left arm grabbed hold. Aggressively, she did a chin up. "She won't take any of my calls," she announced, pausing at the top.

"I dunno, maybe since you've been green-lit, your mom wants you to commit to the IM and forget all else," Syralise tried to be helpful.

"Whatever," Leera did another chin up.

Kameclara detected that her friend didn't want to talk about it anymore. "So how about last night?" she spoke cheerily. "That cavern we found was amazing!" They had dived fifty miles of underwater river before chancing on a dry pocket. There they stopped to rest, marveling at the stalactites embedded with nevite shards. They glittered like the sky.

"Yeah! It was so breathtaking I'm glad I brought an extra oxygen canister," Syralise snorted.

Kameclara groaned at the joke. Thumb-sized compressed oxygen cans latched to their regulators. Truth was, none used their spare can. As part of training, operatives were made to run drills in oxygen deficient environments. Should they ever find themselves in a vacuum, the training gave them an edge to salvage their situation.

"What'd you think our first assignment'll be?" Leera changed the topic. "Think we'll be stationed around Molta?" she referenced the asteroid belt circling beyond Teroma's orbit.

Syralise laughed spiritedly, "I see you wanna get far away from your mom!"

One Teroman ans—which the women recently learned was equal to one Jeman year—matched one-sixtieth of Teroma's orbit around the sun. It served as their main measurement of time. Teams stationed around the Molta Belt could remain there over twenty ans at a time.

"You know it," Leera switched arms and continued her exercise.

Kameclara stretched nearby, keeping her lips tight. She'd promised her father not to volunteer information from their conversation. If she were to mention the possibility of going to Jema, difficult questions would arise.

"Think Chi Team would be stationed nearby?" Syralise wondered aloud.

"So... you and Nolram are steady?" Kameclara asked about the closest thing to a boyfriend any of them had.

"Not really. I just like having him around," she winked.

Operatives were forbidden to be involved with anyone in their own team or a team above or below in rank. On rare occasions when the Intergalactic Military deployed large missions, similarly ranked teams worked in tandem. For Alpha Team, there was only Beta Team. It helped Syralise narrow down her romantic options.

"Why do you see someone from the IM?" Leera huffed.

"It's easier this way," Syralise explained. "We've an understanding work comes first."

Kameclara couldn't argue with the logic. Personally, she saw dating as a waste of time. If she had needs, it was easier to meet a random person and never call again. That way, she didn't have to deal with pointless banter or mismatched emotions. Work didn't leave a lot of free time and she liked to spend it in the company of known associates. Men would always come and go. An operative's oath was for life.

Leera's wristband beeped. "Time to report in," she grabbed a towel as Syralise lowered from her handstand.

The three changed into uniform before filing into a briefing room. As they found their seats, the rest of Alpha Team spilled in. Excited murmurs filled the air. They were to receive their first mission.

Kameclara propped her elbows onto the table and sighed in contentment. She would finally have the opportunity to leave orbit.

Thoughts darted to her father. A small part of Kameclara still questioned if his words were part of an elaborate prank. Yet recalling his expressions, it seemed doubtful.

Jema and Ima are much further than Molta stations. A mission there is virtually unheard of...

She knew sometimes seasoned operatives were tapped for discrete task forces. It wasn't beyond the realm of possibility that higher ranked officers would execute classified missions to unreported locations. Jema or Ima could believably be one of those.

But would they send an entire team?

A door slid open and Wyzenkor Gatta entered. Operatives rose. Wyzenkors ranked above Captains, but below Majors and Generals. The Wyzenkor saluted and Alpha Team followed suit.

Behind him, a decorated General appeared, one Kameclara didn't recognize. Her uniform was from another nation, West Jebbun. The Intergalactic Military held authority over the planet. It was natural for officers to coordinate in foreign nations.

The portly woman took time cleaning her glasses. "I'm General Phinnas, here to brief your mission." The words filled Kameclara with anticipation. She noted the General appeared uncomfortable. Her eyes focused low, as if carefully selecting her words. "Alpha Team, along with Beta, Chi and Delta of Orareca will join other nations of the Intergalactic Military on a large-scale endeavor." As she spoke, the General marched around the room. She paused every few steps to inspect operatives.

Once the General felt satisfied, she approached a model generator. Tapping the side, a miniaturized terrestrial planet appeared. "Your destination is the planet Ima, where you'll subdue a threat before continuing to Jema."

Kameclara glimpsed stunned expressions across the room.

Another tap and a much smaller planet populated beside the rendered Ima. General Phinnas pointed, "On Jema, you'll work with the Seu base to maintain civil obedience."

Kameclara's head swam. Her father's recommendation was approved much sooner than she'd thought possible. The General's casual mention of Jema and Ima were equally disorienting.

It's as if they'd always been an extension of Teroma.

General Phinnas' lips pressed into a frown, "I'm reminding you all, it's illegal to mention Jema and Ima outside the Intergalactic Military." Her eyes roasted the operatives to drive home the point. "You're to inform civilian contacts you're departing on a long-distance mission." The corners of her lips deepened. "It can last up to fifty ans."

Kameclara noticed twitches from her teammates. General Phinnas adjusted her glasses, revealing no emotion. "You'll be given details in following weeks as preparations are made. In eight days, report to Base Shech-I," she referred to Base Twelve. "Until then, you're dismissed to address personal affairs."

"Yes, sir!" Alpha Team responded in unison.

The General nodded, turned on her heels and departed.

"Dismissed," Wyzenkor Gatta announced before following her out.

As soon as the door shut, the room buzzed. "Jema?" Brock asked in disbelief. His partner, Verniv shook her head, equally dismayed.

"I have a family. How am I supposed to leave them behind?" Embledon frowned.

Kameclara exchanged looks with Leera and Syralise. A rare grin spread across the redhead's face and Syralise raked fingers through her hair. Her eyes rolled with eagerness. "This is a rare opportunity!"

"Why're so many teams being sent to Jema? Are there going to be enough to protect Teroma should anything happen?"

Procias swallowed hard. "You ask too many questions. Perhaps I trained you too well with all those games growing up."

Kameclara implored his eyes, but found they'd grown steely. "That answer makes me uncomfortable."

Her father stood tall, "Don't you worry," he tried, and failed to put on a soothing expression. "We've come to an agreement with Ping-he tribes across Teroma. They've vowed to step up in your absence."

Kameclara gawked. "Dad! That's monumental! Why isn't it in the news!"

It suddenly made sense why Leera's mother pushed her away. She must've known about the upcoming mission and wanted to make her daughter's departure less difficult.

Procias shushed his daughter. He peered to make sure the door was still shut. "If we made the public aware, they'd know something is different. There could be widespread panic."

Kameclara's concern didn't alleviate, but she understood the logic. She gulped, "I'll keep silent."

Procias cupped her chin, face melting. "I love how you're caring. From the day your mother told me she was pregnant, I knew you were special. I've no doubt you'll be amazing on Jema."

Kameclara sensed there was more Procias held back, but trusted his judgment to do so. "I'll make Teroma proud."

He gulped, "I'll say the only thing a parent can. Be safe, sweetie."

Chapter Seven

Base Shech-I sat outside Cronmus, one of Orareca's largest metropolises. Kameclara and her partners rode the train and arrived two hours before reporting time. It offered a rare chance to socialize. The separate teams didn't see each other often. Their bases spread equidistant across the nation to ensure any populated location could be accessed within the hour.

"It's been a minute," Syralise hailed a man from Delta Team. They'd enrolled in military school together, from the same town. As she strolled to speak with him, Syralise passed Nolram, her sweetheart on Chi Team. She gave him a wink and they touched hands as she passed.

Firek of Beta Team approached Kameclara and Leera. "What'd you think's the threat on Ima? A military that grew too strong?" They'd all been speculating.

Kameclara said nothing. How could she explain a sorceress when she held doubts herself?

"I'm more curious how much Jema knows about Seu," Leera said. "We're told citizens of the planet aren't aware of Teroma."

Kameclara tightened her lips, flicking her hair as a distraction. She thought to her father's words on the Goddess. She pondered if the entity could incarnate directly on Jema. If so, they could be sent to protect her.

If there truly is a Goddess.

Two hours passed quickly. Soon, it was time to report in.

The teams marched through large armored doors of a hall. They took their formations and awaited instruction. It wasn't long before a General entered.

"Attention!" her voice rang out.

The operatives stomped and saluted in unison. With a glint in her eye, she introduced herself as General Briggands. Behind her, marched a row of Captains, flanked by two Majors. They formed a line before the armored doors, as if barring operatives from escape.

Kameclara stared at them in admiration. Staggered every twelve to fifteen ans, Teroman nations sourced new operatives. Only a select handful advanced in rank. She recognized a Captain with dark, curly hair. She was formerly an Alpha-I member. Kameclara had shadowed her in the field.

"I want to address personal issues first," General Briggands' voice cut straight to business. She didn't appear pleased with the topic. "Due to the anticipated length of this mission, we'll be clearing a limited number of civilians for travel." She straightened her uniform. "This means some members of your immediate family may accompany this mission."

The training hall remained silent. Kameclara guessed everyone shared her astonishment. *Never* in the history of Teroma have civilians been cleared to accompany a military operation.

General Briggands added, "However, they must understand the risks of such a journey. They'll be exposed to circumstances that can result in premature death. Most importantly," her eyes hardened, "they'll not be privy to our destination. You may not speak of Ima until we've arrived. And Jema shall *never* be mentioned." She stressed the last sentence.

Kameclara wondered at the wisdom of the decision. Having civilians alongside created vulnerabilities. If a military strike were to go wrong, having family around would distract operatives from peak performance.

General Briggands straightened her sleeve. "Our departing fleet will consist of forty-two warships. You'll live and train there. Eight civilian ships will be nestled among us. On your days off, you may be shuttled to see family." Kameclara caught a twitch under the General's eye. It seemed as if she were uncomfortable with civilians tagging along too.

Firek raised his hand. The hairs on the back of Kameclara's neck rose as an annoyed expression appeared on the General's face. Operatives didn't ask questions. They took orders.

General Briggands' eyes flashed before giving a nod. She was being generous.

"Sir, why're civilians cleared for this mission?"

"Consider it a courtesy for your service on this particularly long assignment. No more questions."

Firek lowered his hand, appearing dissatisfied. Kameclara shared his feeling.

General Briggands' expression changed to steeliness as she moved on to brief about the enemy. Clearly a territory she felt more comfortable with. "The targets on Ima are not as experienced in warfare compared to us. However, they do have unique methods of defense

limited fields. Kameclara speculated on reasons for cross training. It could be to make use of time during an eight ans journey. It'd add versatility to the operatives.

She gulped. Another reason was a high expectation of casualties. Operatives would need to know other specialties should they be called upon in a pinch.

General Briggands' words cut through her thoughts, "At the start of each day, you're required to attend an hour of Jeman dialect training. It shouldn't be too challenging, since their language spawned from a Teroman root."

Languages weren't Kameclara's strong suit. It wasn't Syralise's either. Intergalactic Military operatives trained in alien tongues. Leera did excel, however. Ancient Pinghe techniques were transcribed with similar linguistic patterns. It supported the belief that the Teromans were descendants of their enemies.

"Each team will be assigned training officers. They'll be your point person for the duration of the mission." General Briggands waved and the dark-haired woman Kameclara recognized stepped forward. "Captain Nanti will command Alpha Team."

"Yes, sir!" Alpha Team saluted. Their Captain fell in line beside them.

Kameclara stole a glance to her new Captain. A dusting of freckles covered her cheeks. Kameclara could usually get a read on a person, but Nanti's eyes showed little. Even on their few shared missions, she'd been impassive.

What type of leader is she?

~*~

Hayes received a notification from his supervisor, Ashmarah. She had confirmed his recommendation. Captain Nanti would be assigned to Alpha Team of Orareca.

He opened his closet and continued packing. He was to report in with his Alpha Team in a few hours. Normally he'd fuss over the comfort and style of his casual wear, but that day, he felt numb. He threw things indiscriminately into his bag.

When finished, Hayes tiptoed to his sleeping daughter's room. There, he packed her things as well. She was excited about joining her father on an Intergalactic Military operation. She loved it even more when he told her it was a big secret. He'd smiled at her jubilance, but inside Hayes drowned with terror.

Not much bothered a seasoned operative like him. Yet, his hand trembled as he zipped her backpack.

Chapter Eight

Stanten's back hit the ground. His body felt strange, as if it didn't belong to him. Straining his neck, he peered at his hands. They were covered in blood. Clumsily, he placed his palms over the searing in his midsection. His breaths came too fast and his heart beat off-rhythm.

"Hey, buddy!" he heard his friend, Tibor's voice. "Stay with me!"

Stanten's body slumped sideways. Through blurred vision, he realized Tibor was rolling him under a table. Shouts and confusion came from all around and he closed his eyes. To shut everything out.

More gunshots went off as a cloak of darkness settled in. Stanten greeted it complacently. *Wherever I'm going, it's gotta be better than this world.*

As the sounds faded further and further, Stanten grew calm. He felt himself drawing deep into his body.

At a place so small, he felt he could hide from it all, he found a pinprick of light. There, a tiny voice—his voice begged him to hold on. That he came here for something.

He knew then, his time with the living wasn't over.

~*~

Daegan ran the largest underground crime syndicate in Pudyo. The police were foolish to think prison could keep him. Problems had started when some new guy in town gunned for his territory. The wise-ass concocted a story about Daegan running a sleeper cell. It wasn't the first time someone tried to take Daegan down that way.

Somehow, this guy produced believable evidence. The police decided to call in the local militia. An inconvenience, but at least it wasn't the operatives of the Intergalactic Military. Those dicks would've taken out his entire crew. No questions asked.

Now, Daegan fumed in his cell. He still had people on the outside. It took a few weeks, but he finally he got them a message with an escape plan. It wasn't elegant, but he only cared for the result.

He had men on the inside too. They were going to instigate a riot. The guards friendly with Daegan's people agreed to leave a few weapons lying about. In the madness, Daegan would slip out the food delivery gate. They might have to take out a few guards, but it'd be even trade for men he'd lost. A sled was arranged to wait out back. He meant to be long gone before the local militia could be called.

On the day selected, his boys started a melee. Taking opportunity of its cover, Daegan and two of his people headed towards the kitchen. He didn't know it then, but one of his boys had beef with a guy named Geraldo. The boy was escorting Daegan during the riot. He broke away, having seen his enemy.

"Just lemme get at Geraldo!" he cried.

"Damnit, we gotta go!" Daegan hollered as his other crony struggled to keep the fray from blocking their path.

In the confusion, Geraldo had a friend, and he got in Daegan's face. Annoyed, Daegan took a plank from a broken table and swung it hard. It broke against the back of Geraldo's friend. The kid lost it, grabbing a piece of splintered stone, stabbing wildly.

Daegan scrambled to get his gun. As he let a bullet loose, the kid stabbed him in the eye. He squealed revenge as his men carried him away.

~*~

Stanten heard dripping. He dragged his eyes open to see himself in the clinic. A gray lumped moved nearby. Stanten's eyes took a moment to focus. It was Tibor with his arm in a sling. He stared down in a worried expression. In Tibor's hand was a glass jar. He shook it and a bullet clinked.

"You're one crazy bastard," he said in disbelief.

"Just tryin' to help Geraldo," Stanten croaked. It hurt to speak.

"You 'member what happened?" Tibor raised an eyebrow.

"Yeah. Fight broke out. Happens."

Tibor shook his head and leaned in close. "You stuck Daegan's eye. You know who he is?"

Stanten knew him by name only. Not someone to be trifled with.

He squeezed his eyes, trying his best to recall the fight. At some point he'd lost control and stabbed furiously. The object in his fist had caught something. A sick feeling squirmed in Stanten's gut. His mouth went dry, "Did I kill 'im?"

"Nah. Daegan's alive. He was bouta get away too, but had to come back for a doctor. He was bleedin' so much, he would not've made it." Tibor showed concern. "He lost his eye 'cause of you."

Stanten felt the will to live evaporate. "Guy like him's gonna have me killed."

"Shh, keep your voice down," Tibor hushed, "No one knows it was you and we wanna keep it that way!"

"He's gonna figure it out eventually."

"That's why we gotta getchu outta here."

Stanten didn't think it was possible. His spirits sunk lower. "There's no escape from prison. I don't got people like Daegan."

"I don't mean escape," Tibor pulled a chair next to the bed and plopped down. "I'm talkin' 'bout space." Stanten waited quietly. "Geraldo told me 'bout it. He was gonna get outta here anyway 'cause o' trouble with Daegan's people."

"I'm listenin'."

"Well, the Intergalactic Military regularly staffs prisoners at their off-planet bases to do dumb chores. They only take ones wit' good behavior."

"Coupla ans witha small chance of running into a Daegan lackey sounds good," Stanten wheezed.

Tibor gave a lopsided smile. "Daegan's men are problematic. With their records, I doubt any'll qualify." He shook his head, "Anyway, I'm talkin' 'bout a new assignment that came up. More than twenty ans or somethin'. Geraldo's got a pretty clean record. He's got pull with the head warden and's puttin' in a good word for ya."

Stanten thought for a moment. "I'll hafta get on a spaceship, won't I?"

"Yep."

His hands grew cold. "Tibor."

"What?"

"I'm afraid o' heights."

His friend laughed, "Itsa good time to get over it!"

~*~

Inmates approved to work for the Intergalactic Military operation were chained together. The cuffs chafed Stanten's wrists, but he didn't care. He was getting away from Daegan and his people.

Out of habit, he checked over his shoulder. A man caught his eye and glared back.

Are any of them secretly working for Daegan?

Probably not. Normally if an inmate belonged to a crew like Daegan's, they were loud about it.

A warden bellowed and the inmates marched outside. Cold, dry air made Stanten's legs buckle as they piled into a large van. The inside remained unheated; metal stuck to skin.

No one said a word as they jostled along. Stanten wondered if his expression appeared as worn as the others. Every soul in the van was running from something. They'd been trying to evade trouble their whole life.

Wonder if there'd ever be a day when I run towards somethin'.

He fell asleep and didn't wake until guards clanked open the door. He overheard they were in Cronmus. Rolling his creaky neck, Stanten climbed down. They marched under an awning, where he noticed a gap in a canvas. He craned over the shoulder of the man before him, wanting to catch a glimpse of what lie beyond.

The man noticed and purposely blocked his view. Stanten clenched his jaw, but swallowed aggravation. It wouldn't be good to start a fight now.

They were led underground and waited in a medical facility, still chained together. Nurses administered vaccinations, and after a few hours of observation, they were released.

The warden ordered them aboard a large structure. Judging by the military markings on the walls, Stanten devised they were aboard a warship. One by one they were unchained and assigned private quarters.

His room was about twice the size of his prison cell. He had a bed with a real mattress, and a padded chair.

Luxuries.

He shared a bathroom with five other men in the same hall. It was loads better than sharing with two dozen, like in the prison. That night, he slept the best he had in ans.

The next day, they were taught to maintain the ship. There was a screen embedded in each inmate's wall. Every morning, around the time their hall was unlocked, a list of chores populated. If Stanten finished tasks early and to satisfaction, he earned commissary points. They were redeemable at a pantry on their level.

Many areas of the ship were prohibited to Stanten. They were reserved for operatives and officers. He hadn't seen any of them yet. They weren't due to board for another week.

"Don't mess with 'em," a warden cautioned. "I'm a big guy. And one of 'em could take five of me." He added with a sneer, "Also, know if you feel like causin' trouble, we're allowed to jettison you at will."

The wardens were well-built and exuded discipline. Far more domineering than the ones at the prison. Stanten couldn't imagine any of the inmates winning a one-on-one against them. He heard a rumor they were washouts from the Intergalactic Military's recruiting program. Someone said it must mean the ships were headed someplace remote, where everyone fended for themselves.

"Where do you think we're goin'?" He asked Geraldo one day.

He didn't know more than Stanten. "The only thing I'm guessin' is our destination is far. There's a shit ton of food in storage."

"Any place Daegan's people can't get to me, I'm good."

"I hear ya."

Stanten didn't mind his new life. At first the wardens were hard, testing the inmates. The labor was intensive too. A few who couldn't cut it were kicked off the ship and replaced with fresh faces.

Stanten kept his head down, mouth shut, and did the work. Once the wardens realized he didn't want trouble, they eased up. Back in Pudyo's prison, some wardens harassed inmates no matter what. Stanten decided early on he liked the ship better.

~*~

When it came time for takeoff, inmates were locked in their halls. The screen in Stanten's room broadcasted the operatives boarding. The crowd seemed enormous, as if the entire nation had gathered to see them off. Rows of media lined the path leading to the gangway.

Orareca's Chi and Delta Teams appeared and waved before heading to the ship. With them were two teams from East Jebbun. The announcer declared Orareca's Alpha and Beta Teams were boarding in South Deron with their teams.

Stanten listened carefully, but the broadcasters never mentioned their destination. "Guess they gotta keep it secret," he muttered to himself. He briefly wondered if he'd be in danger.

Nah, there hasn't been any global alarms. Ammunition hasn't been distributed.

Not long after the hull sealed with a hiss, rumbling quaked his bones. Stanten hugged his bed and gripped the edges. He'd never flown before and didn't know what to expect. The noise grew louder and he sucked in a breath. His fingers went numb from clasping the frame.

Moments later, pressure bore down as quaking intensified. It lasted for what felt like infinity. When he dared peek at the clock, only ten minutes had passed.

The sound gradually lessened, as did the pressure. His room ceased shaking and Stanten ventured a foot over the side of the bed. Carefully, he stood. The metal still hummed, but didn't threaten his stability.

If this was flying, it wasn't so bad.

Chapter Nine

The vehicle hit a bump and Leera's knee knocked into Kameclara. Her partner shoved back with a smirk. Across from them, Syralise didn't notice. Her eyes trained out the window on Warship-12. "Forty decks. It looks as big as a small moon!" she cried.

The vehicle swooped in a semicircle through a cordoned lot. Alpha Team climbed out with Captain Nanti at the head. She led them towards the warship.

As Kameclara fell in step, she observed barricades in a wide radius. Excited crowds gathered behind them with cameras. Out of habit, she swept her eyes, seeking signs of threat; despite knowing every person had been pre-screened.

A roaring crowd waved and cheered as Alpha and Beta Team marched in formation. The public knew the teams were headed to subdue a situation, but weren't given details. This didn't deter them from fawning over the planet's heroes.

Kameclara thought sentimentally of her family. They were watching from home. Her mother had expressed it was too painful to witness her daughter leaving in person.

Alpha and Beta Team crossed the threshold and made their way through a long hangar. Soft, violet lights illuminated the ground, directing the path. They were flanked on either side by state-of-the-art fighter jets. Some recently designed for the mission.

Upon exiting, they passed through a short hall, emerging in a common lounge. Alpha and Beta Teams of South Deron greeted them. There, the Captains gave room assignments.

"This is mip," Kameclara found their assigned hall, numbered four. They turned the corner as a squad from South Deron's Beta Team came from the other direction. Teams of other nations seldom had the opportunity to socialize. Though joint operations were common, they relied solely on officers' commands. Kameclara anticipated the cross training would open doors in collaboration. They exchanged a few pleasant words before retreating to their rooms.

"We have a window!" Syralise squealed as the door to their unit slid open. It was little more than a sliver following the curve of the hull. Opposite from it, three beds bunked against the wall.

"I call top!" Leera grabbed the edge and hopped up. There was little headspace and the tall operative lounged on her side. She scanned her palmprint on a screen embedded in her headboard. It glowed red, Leera's assigned color. Her schedule and entertainment preferences loaded.

"I call middle!" Kameclara threw her things on the second bunk. Her palm loaded a blue screen.

Syralise's would be purple.

Their uniforms were corresponding colors. Orareca's teams differentiated each member of a squad by red, blue, or purple. A shoulder patch emblazoned their team and squad insignia.

"I wanna camp on the floor next to the window," Syralise joked. She stood reluctantly, eyes lingering outside. She tossed her bag on the bottom bunk and explored the bathroom. "Not bad! Two showers!"

"Guess hygiene's a priority," Kameclara laughed.

"I should take one now," Syralise scratched her stomach lazily. "We report in one hour after launch. Then we'll be on duty for eighteen hours."

"They say 'on duty,' but it's all still training," Leera tapped her toe on the ceiling in aggravation. "Can't believe it. We're freshly green-lit and go straight into more training. Stupid."

"Orders are orders," Syralise shrugged. She started to strip off her uniform.

"Do that in the bathroom!" Leera threw a pillow, with a snort. "Nobody wants to see that!"

"Whatever, I love my curvy body!" Syralise shimmied to the bathroom, still undressing. The door slid shut as muffled singing arose.

The energy of the room settled as Kameclara and Leera unpacked. She came across the box her father had given her. Kameclara peeked at the syringes before shoving them deep into her assigned stowage space. There were plenty of other things for her to deal with at the moment.

"I'm takin' a nap," Leera announced, pulling a blanket over her head. "Wake me when drills start."

"Will do," Kameclara responded.

She stretched out on her bunk too, but sleep was the furthest thing on her mind. As Syralise softly gurgled a tune in the bathroom, Kameclara thought to her conversation with Procias. It reminded her of the mission's exigent state. The legend of the Goddess had the power to galvanize the Intergalactic Military on a one-way mission.

"Therefore, it's believable our species truly depends on its success," she whispered into her pillow.

"Prepare for launch," an automated voice spoke coolly through the room's coms.

Syralise bounced out of the bathroom in a towel. Hopping onto her bunk, she dressed in seconds. Kameclara watched her rush to the narrow window. She wished she shared Syralise's optimism, but her father's words weighed her down.

The sound of triple-shielded doors clamped in the distance. A long hiss indicated vacuum-seals activating. Across Orareca, people tuned in for the televised send off. Kameclara pictured her parents and brothers seated in their living room. In her heart, she said a final goodbye.

As blast off occurred, Syralise squealed. Adrenaline surged through Kameclara. This was it. Her destiny waited among the stars.

~*~

Forty-two warships hovered in Teroman orbit as they checked communications. During that window, eight civilian ships launched to join. Once everything cleared, the fleet used the gravity of Teroma to slingshot towards the sun. Nevite powered thrusters would adjust course as needed. Based on calculations, they had enough momentum to reach the third gaseous planet on its orbit, Oli3. From there, they'd use its gravity to aid maneuvering. Another slingshot would be done around Oli5, two planets from Jema.

"May Ia's wings fly with you," a communications leader on Teroma sent in a final transmission.

The fleet was to travel in silence. An especially violent solar storm was on its way. Long distance communications would be severed for the next decade. It was Teroma's plan to leverage this storm. The destination of the fleet was to remain hidden from all but the most secret organizations.

~*~

"We inherited a project from our predecessors," Damas of South Deron explained through controlled breathing. "It involves a new way to tap nevite for energy." The four teams aboard Warship-12 headed into the eighth mile of their warm-up run. They took the opportunity to get to know one another, conversing as they paced through the decks.

The operatives of South Deron had been active for two ans. Their concentration was Tactical Engineering, which meant generating innovative weaponry. When faced with an enemy, South Deron operatives were also responsible for reverse engineering. The expediency needed of the task required them to be endlessly creative, and to study new methods at all times.

"The hardest part of our job is anticipating weapons the alien threat could devise," Damas explained as Kameclara pulled beside him. "And to make sure we have surprises up our sleeves too."

"This new energy use," Syralise brought him back to his original topic, "you said it could telepathically manipulate objects?"

Damas nodded, wiping sweat off his brow. "There's a way to tap into our genetics, the nevino sequence to be exact." He grabbed a water bottle at his hip and sprayed into his mouth. "With it, we're able to manipulate objects in our vicinity."

"I'll believe it when I see it," Leera sniffed.

"Fine. I call you as first sparring partner during open training," Damas challenged. "Bring padding," he added with a snicker.

"How?" Kameclara's spine gripped. What Damas was saying sounded like sorcery. She needed to know the science behind it. She couldn't be sure if she wished her father were right, or sought evidence to prove him wrong.

"We created gloves that sends a continuous, low electrical pulse through our cells. It doesn't hinder bodily functions, but blood tests show the nevino sequence vibrating at a higher frequency." He let out a short laugh. "It burns energy like crazy too, and you're starving after an hour. But we think it activates a natural link that living beings have to all matter."

"So, you don't know *exactly* how it works?" Kameclara concluded.

Ullon from South Deron spoke up, "It was discovered accidently in a weapons test. It took our previous operatives fifteen ans to duplicate the results and package it."

"So, you can chuck a rock without touching it?" Syralise asked brusquely.

"Well, yes," Ullon chuckled. "And things like generating a protective force field."

"We have a limited radius to work with," Damas added quickly. "Our bodies can't handle more than ten to twelve feet. Pushing for more leads to blackouts."

"Not great on the battlefield," Ullon shook his head. "But definitely worth further exploration."

"Leera," Damas added with seriousness, "Batra has the best range, 'bout fifteen feet. If you wanna get a real taste, challenge her."

Kameclara glanced over her shoulder at Batra. Her eyes caught Captain Nanti nearby. The officer averted her gaze. The Captain had been watching her.

"Watch it!" Leera cried as Kameclara stepped on her heel.

"Sorry," she faced front, flicking her braid over her shoulder. "I call second spar with Damas. I wanna check out these 'magic' gloves."

In the back of her mind, she wondered if she had imagined the

Captain observing her.

Why would I garner special interest?

The teams pushed on for two more miles. Kameclara stole a few more glances at Captain Nanti. The officer appeared actively disinterested in Kameclara.

After the run, the Captains marched all four teams to Deck Seven. In a training hall, operatives were ordered to set two rows of tables. One they lined with empty water canisters. The other held a few pens.

"Beta-phen," South Deron's Captain Rycien commanded his squad, "retrieve Project S-48."

"Yes, sir!"

Three men moved to seamless lockers in a wall. Scanning their handprint, doors swung open. They carried large cases to the center of the room. Their Captain unlocked each with his thumbprint. "These are experimental weapons," he explained. "We plan to have them fully developed before arriving to Ima." He turned to Orareca's Captains, "Outside of North Deron and us, you'll be the first to test these."

Kameclara observed with curiosity as South Deroners lifted trays of fingerless gloves, carefully stored. Ullon fitted a pair to his hands. Upon contact, a faint glow ran along the seams. He snapped his fingers, and a canister fell. Grunts of alarm went through the room.

"I can agitate the air on command," he explained.

Orareca operatives were distributed gloves. A few tried to manipulate objects, but at most, pens shuddered. Kameclara noticed the gloves sent a cool trickle through her palms.

"Don't be discouraged. It takes an exorbitant amount of practice," Captain Rycien announced. Pulling a pair of gloves on himself, he circled his arms. The air around him distorted ever so slightly. "Pick a weapon," he commanded a member of Orareca's Beta Team.

Len lumbered to the gun rack at the far end of the room. He selected a sonic rifle.

"Shoot me," Captain Rycien commanded.

"Sir, you're not wearing protective gear and this can't be set to stun."

Captain Nanti took the rifle from Len. In the blink of an eye, she pulled the trigger. The weapon sent a shriek through the air and the distortion around Captain Rycien rippled. He remained unharmed, though his face reddened from strain.

Captain Rycien exhaled, arms dropping. "It takes a lot out of you, but with practice, you can create resistance strong enough to withstand all sorts of assaults."

Kameclara examined Captain Nanti. She had seemed confident the technology would work.

Perhaps some officers already experienced Project S-48.

She wondered how an Orareca Captain would've been exposed to the gloves.

Kameclara felt a nudge against her arm. It was Ullon. "That pen is begging you to move it," he gestured to the table. She realized all the operatives had given the gloves an attempt except for her. Stretching hands, Kameclara imagined pushing the air.

Moments passed. The pen didn't twitched. Pursing her lips, she rooted her feet in a deeper stance. Stiffening her fingers, Kameclara pictured the pen sliding.

Still nothing.

"How'd I know if I'm doing this right?" she asked Ullon.

He moved away from assisting Syralise. "What're you feeling

when you're trying to affect your target?" he asked.

"That I want it to move," Kameclara cocked an eyebrow.

Damas overheard, "You might think this sounds ridiculous, but how do you *feel* about needing the pen to move?"

"How am I supposed to feel about moving a pen? It's such an inconsequential thing in this moment."

Damas tapped his chin with a contemplative expression. He then blurted awkwardly, "Your mom's fat."

"I don't believe you've ever met my mom." Kameclara couldn't quite figure what he was trying to do.

"Did I make you angry?" Damas asked, hands moving to hips. Ullon covered his mouth, embarrassed for his friend.

Syralise laughed, "Cool-headed Kameclara? Good Luck." She stretched her fingers. "Lemme guess, the gloves work by emotion?"

"Yeah. But not unfiltered emotion. It needs to be focused," Damas explained.

"Hmm, who's the most focused person I know…" Syralise peered around the space. She stopped, spotting her partner. "Hey Lee!" she called. "What does your mom remind you of?"

"Stupid rules," Leera grumbled.

"She's…" Syralise took a breath, wincing, "fat?"

Leera flashed a warning glare. Besides her connection with her mother, insulting a Pinghe Grandmaster was distasteful for any Teroman.

"Here!" Kameclara whipped a canister at Leera, catching on to what Syralise attempted.

Leera swiped the air, gloves glowing bright. The bottle changed direction, jerking across the room. Brock ducked, narrowly missing a black eye.

"Excellent!" a few operatives complimented.

Damas patted Leera on the back, "You're a natural."

"You know I didn't mean it!" Syralise quickly added. "I think your mom's awesome!"

"It's alright, I know you didn't," Leera marveled at her gloves. She wiggled her fingers, "I think you helped me figure these out."

Ullon turned away from the excitement and faced Kameclara. "See what you can do," he encouraged.

She closed her eyes and brought her family to mind. Kameclara pictured the happy moments. Then imagined never sharing them again. Disappointment weighed on her chest. Opening her eyes, Kameclara focused on the pen, trying to disappoint at it.

It didn't even tremble.

Perhaps knowing her family was safe on Teroma mitigated negative feelings.

What if I think about happy times?

Filling her heart with fond memories, Kameclara stared daggers at her target.

It quivered ever so slightly.

"Th… this really can work!" She felt a rush of endorphins. Channeling the excitement through her hands, the pen shifted an entire millimeter. "If we master these gloves, it'll give us an edge!"

Ullon sassed her, "Told you! And hate to break it to ya, but it looks like YOU still have a long way to go!"

Syralise's laughter drew attention. Kameclara gawked to see her partner sliding a pen across the table.

Syralise's always been excitable. I'm happy it's enhancing her ability.

Kameclara's emotions had always been steady. It gave her an edge in being an operative. She had never been last place when it came to the Intergalactic Military. She frowned at her hands.

I've gotta figure this out.

Chapter Ten

"The main target to be contained is named Vesper," Wyzenkor Kace announced during their first briefing aboard Warship-12. Kameclara felt odd this information was released only after communication to Teroma had been severed. It must mean it was abnormally sensitive.

Of course, she'd already heard the name from her father.

"In ans 14.213, she seized control of Ima. Because of her interest in Jema, the IM classified her a threat to Seu." Wyzenkor Kace strutted about the room, jaws tight, biting back superfluous words. Kameclara sensed there was much more unsaid.

They were shown photos taken from high orbit. A dark-haired woman marched across a plain, surrounded by legions. Kameclara studied the troops carefully. The soldiers carried arcane weapons. There were no other munitions.

She raised her hand. "How did one woman achieve so much power while garnering a loyal following? What's her leverage?" From the corner of her eye, Kameclara noticed teammates perk. They wondered the same.

Wyzenkor Kace steeled himself, posing in a wide stance. "Vesper eliminated opposition and seized control of resources." The answer remained vague, like most of the mission.

Kameclara chewed the inside of her cheek, attempting to find satisfaction with the response.

There was a click. The next image of Vesper showed her head tilted, peering at the heavens. Kameclara stared into her eyes, glossed by indifference. A tickle came at a sensitive part of Kameclara's neck. She scratched as a shudder traveled down her spine. In the color terrifyingly similar to her own, Kameclara detected simmering in Vesper's eyes. She cocked her head. It seemed like self-loathing.

She raised her hand again. Wyzenkor Kace braced, but nodded. "No one stood against her?" she asked.

"It's believed Vesper devised technology that gave her power to control others." Wyzenkor Kace saw Kameclara's hand start to lift again and added, "The nature of this technology cannot be confirmed." His face remained impassive, ignoring baffled glances around the room.

A hex, Kameclara heard a whisper in the back of her mind.

She shook herself and focused on the briefing.

Wyzenkor Kace finished his slides. He didn't take any more questions before dismissing the operatives. All noted the peculiarity of it.

Orareca's Alpha and Beta Teams changed into uniform and met with South Deron teams. "Drills and tactics for the next ten hours," Syralise sighed.

Usually, training cleared Kameclara's mind. Not this time. As she sweat, she pondered the briefing, but found nothing to be clearer.

~*~

"What're you thinking?" Leera asked as they headed to the showers during their first break. She had noticed Kameclara's distracted expression.

She grabbed a towel, tossing it over her shoulder. "I'm stuck on Wyzenkor Kace's words. If our enemy has the ability to conquer a planet—and we have no reliable intel how she did it—how effective can we be?"

"Was thinking the same," Syralise moaned. "In past instances of alien interference, we've gathered hoards of info long before contact was made. Molta scans tell us so much about weapons, class of ships, and directionalities." Her lips pulled into a line. "With Ima, all we have are a few photos. You'd think with Seu being a Teroman base, they'd have tons of intel…"

Leera brushed hair off her neck, "According to the briefing, Ima's chosen to live the simple life. It'd be easy for anyone with advanced technology to make an impact."

Syralise added, "Maybe Vesper made technological advancements. The planet probably didn't like it, and in the disagreement, war broke out."

"Hmm," Kameclara followed Syralise's logic, but something didn't feel accurate. She couldn't place her finger on it. Perhaps it was the look in Vesper's eyes. Kameclara sensed the events were personal.

The three entered the locker rooms as Leera added, "Ya know, Teroma was simple once too. Pinghe culture was prevalent a few eras ago. And you how we like to keep things minimalistic."

"Wasn't Jema settled during a flourishing age of the Pinghe?" Kameclara asked, calculating dates in her mind. Pinghe history was Teroma's history, and likely Jema's as well. The information was worth exploring.

"Yes!" Leera's eyes sparkled.

"But we've advanced because of our enemies. We have the IM

now," Syralise added. "Ima didn't have extra-planetary foes. If Vesper commanded a weapon the planet wasn't ready to contend with, it easily explains the outcome."

Leera bobbed her head in agreement. "Wished we knew what it was."

Kameclara thoughtfully grabbed shower items. "I bet," she spoke carefully, "Higher command knows all about Vesper. We're not being told for security reasons."

"I certainly hope that's the case," Syralise griped. "I don't like how blind we are going into this."

"It might have something to do with them being Teroman," Leera chimed.

"Yeah… and that. I'm not sure how I feel about assaulting our own people," Syralise appeared irritated.

"You can't hold reservations like that," Leera advised. "It paralyzes you when time for action comes."

"What do you mean?" Syralise snapped. "Don't the Pinghe believe violence should be the final resort?"

Leera scoffed, but not from disdain. Kameclara turned to the redhead, recognizing homesickness. She'd been feeling it too. "That perspective seems like a privilege an operative can't afford. Not if Teroma's to remain safe," Kameclara spoke tenderly, trying to reason between the two.

"I know what Sy's saying!" Leera cried in exasperation. "True, Pinghe teachings are about peace first, but also protection of the planet at all costs. How can we do both!" Her eyes beseeched her partners. "And now? The enemies on Ima are our descendants!"

Kameclara wrapped her arms around her partners. "Don't forget, we're distant descendants of our enemies from a neighboring star system too."

The words struck a chord with her squad. Syralise and Leera's eyes cleared. Rawness of the moment melted away.

Leera sucked in a breath, changing the topic, "I never told you two, but I finished my certifications to become a Pinghe Master. All that's left was to train sixty disciples."

"Wow, Lee," Syralise appeared genuinely impressed. "You're kinda... young for that." The youngest known Pinghe Masters were in their late thirties. "Or did you lie, and you're not twenty-three ans like us?" she joked.

"Nah," Leera sniffed, "I started earlier than normal. Trained a lot with my dad."

Syralise gave her friend a squeeze, earlier prickliness forgotten. "Bet you're a natural too."

Leera grinned sadly, "That's what he said. Though I thought he was just being nice." She hugged back. "I miss him every day. He's the main reason I joined the IM. He supported it adamantly."

"I'm sorry he passed away during an IM accident," Kameclara felt deep sympathy.

"Theoretically, could you gain permission from the IM and train operatives as disciples?" Syralise asked encouragingly.

"No," she shook her head. "First and foremost, a disciple needs to give up all things for twelve ans and focus on training. Operatives can't afford that." Leera straightened. "And a Grandmaster must recognize a Master. There are sacred scriptures to pass on." She threw her hands up in defeat. "I don't know a single Grandmaster who'd be happy to recognize an IM operative! My mother especially!"

A buzzer sounded, indicating training was to recommence in ten minutes. The friends dispersed.

As she showered, Kameclara recalled a news report she had heard as a child. A Pinghe Master, Hegmin died during an Intergalactic Military training exercise. She didn't know it then, but it was Leera's father. A young operative testing flight equipment had run into a malfunction. Master Hegmin managed to board and ejected the young man.

Unfortunately, Master Hegmin couldn't pull the craft back under control before crashing into the rings of Teroma. Fine particles further compromised the ship's life support. Oxygen depleted in seconds, long before assistance reached him. In his rush to save the young man, Master Hegmin hadn't donned proper gear. He didn't survive the incident.

The name of the young operative was kept private. Anonymously he'd written a public apology. Grandmaster Jamarinne, Leera's mother had accepted it. Though she'd been an obstinate protester of the Intergalactic Military, she forgave the individual. Her publicized response was short. "My love died saving a life. I bear no ill will towards the operative on this matter."

Kameclara toyed with the idea of informing Leera about the conversation with her father; concerning the Pinghe working alongside the Intergalactic Military. It could bring her comfort knowing they'd struck an accord.

After lengthy, internal deliberation, Kameclara decided against it. It wasn't worth the risk of upsetting Leera, to know she could've reconciled with her mother. She'd chosen to leave on a fifty ans mission instead.

Chapter Eleven

Teams rotated warships every few months. For the first rotation, Orareca remained aboard Warship-12. Decks where South Deron teams barracked were unlocked. Powerful ships called drag-alongs—often shortened to "dragons"—pulled them to another warship. Alpha and Beta Teams of North Deron were due to take their place.

Orareca operatives bid farewell to South Deron teams and hung around the central lounge. They were curious of the North Deron operatives. They were seasoned, having been active for seven ans.

"According to South Deron, North Deroners have also trained with Project S-48," Syralise spoke thoughtfully. "They helped the previous South Deron teams develop them." Orareca's teams had seen little progress. They were eager to practice with more experienced counterparts.

The teams chattered distractedly until a beep came from across the hall. Lights framing airlock doors glowed red. Mild clanging came from the other side. Arriving barrack modules were connecting. A moment later, the light flashed green as a hiss filled the room.

The airlock slid open. The first man through flicked snowy hair. He gave a cursory glance around the lounge, eyes not resting anywhere in particular. Youthful operatives of Orareca stretched hands to greet him. He politely, yet solidly brushed passed them as if on a mission.

"Just the way they carry themselves is more sophisticated," Syralise spoke in awe. Streams of North Deroners poured in. Unlike the first man, they stopped and greeted.

Kameclara hung back, smiling politely to those who approached. Syralise flitted about, bubbling with laughter, learning everyone's names. Even Leera opened up, responding to inquiries about her Pinghe heritage.

It wasn't long before Kameclara caught sight of the first man again. Pleasant-faced, he sashayed into mip hall and leaned against the wall opposite from her. He studied Kameclara without a word, a spark in his eye. Fingers commanded stray hairs behind his ear.

Amused, she faced him, waiting for him to speak first. His skin was smooth, save deep creases in the corners of his eyes. He must've seen some things.

"Nice to meet you," a wispy voice cooed. "I've heard a lot about you, Kameclara." He spoke her name deliberately.

"Pleased to meet you too," she gave a serene smile as the two shook hands, "but I'm afraid I haven't heard of you." She couldn't be sure what to make of him.

His fingers gripped longer than comfortable, free hand tenderly clasping her wrist. She forced herself to hold a grin as he stepped into her personal space. The man's eyes darted about her features, analyzing every detail. Though the gaze was tender, guardedness presented in his eyes.

Kameclara firmly removed her hand. He didn't respond, still studying her.

A woman called, "Hayes." He gave Kameclara a wink and excused himself.

"What's that all about?" Syralise approached.

"Dunno… But he's 'heard' of me," Kameclara repeated with a dash of well-intended sarcasm.

"Creep," Leera joked.

"Be nice." Syralise snipped, forever the optimist. "He's probably got a crush on her!"

"I don't think he likes women," Leera smirked.

"How can you tell?"

"I like both, so I got that sense. Remember?"

Syralise laughed, "Logical."

Kameclara sensed there was more to Hayes. "Why would anyone hear of a fresh operative? We haven't accomplished anything worth talking about."

"Was wondering the same," Leera ground her jaw. "Keep an eye on him."

"Whoa, hold on!" Syralise chuckled, "He's not our enemy! We're supposed to be learning from each other!"

Syralise had a point, but Kameclara made a mental note not to drop her guard. Not on Hayes, nor her Captain. She sensed there was much surrounding them that wasn't being said.

~*~

Kameclara immediately noticed Hayes when they reported for duty the next day. He appeared to be at the head of his team, occasionally giving instruction. His Captain didn't appear to mind. A few times he peered her way as if he had something to share, but never approached.

North Deron's specialty resided in Containment. They were consulted across the planet in dealing with sleeper agents. In the event alien threats were detected, they were responsible for preventing communication between the enemy and sleeper agents.

The Captains called an early end to drills and announced direct-combat evaluations were to take place. Teams of each nation were allowed to pick one weapon, set to non-lethal levels.

"Take thirty. Grab chow. Reconvene on Deck Nine," Captain Nanti instructed.

"Kameclara," Hayes called in a tinkling voice as they were dismissed. She faced him, without expectation. Amity oozed in his sway. His shoulders dropped, perpetually relaxed. "Dear," he stepped close, as if they'd been friends for a long time. She didn't know what to make of his congeniality. "You need to breathe through your spine." He patted her there the way a mother patted a child.

His casual touch alarmed her and a flustered noise escaped. Hearing it, Hayes laughed, "Oh honey, I'm no threat to you. I've no interest in women." The comment confirmed Leera's statement and deepened the color of her cheeks. Hayes laughed, embracing Kameclara tightly as if she were a child, "Oh! You're too cute!"

Speechless, Kameclara wasn't accustomed to being called "cute." She stole a look to Syralise and Leera. They studied Hayes with intense curiosity, but remained at a distance, happy to see her squirm.

Hayes apologized, "I let general affection get the best of me!"

Though she didn't appreciate his lack of personal space, Kameclara found him somewhat endearing.

"In all seriousness, I know exercises that might help."

"Sure." She recalled what Syralise said about learning from North Deroners. *I could benefit from being optimistic once in a while.*

Hayes waved Kameclara to a quiet corner of the training room. She had assumed the exercises dealt with motion. Instead, Hayes asked her to sit extremely still. He instructed deep breaths, guiding her to simultaneously direct focus to various parts of the body. He promised the exercises would improve control and balance.

"You should also speak to Leera," he added coyly. "These are Pinghe exercises."

Kameclara tilted her head, "How'd you know?"

"Leera's father trained with us." Sadness flashed through his eyes. It was gone before Kameclara could guess at its cause. Hayes added quickly, "But he trained with many nations."

Hayes lowered himself beside her and sucked in deep breaths. They were long and even as if he were asleep. Kameclara peered to see him in a completely relaxed state. For all she could tell, he could've fallen asleep with eyes open.

Hayes spoke, proving her wrong, "Flow your breath through your muscles and bones. Melt into the ether of the universe. Let it awaken your tissues."

"I'm afraid I don't understand," she sighed, mildly annoyed. "What do you mean by ether?"

"Invisible threads of the universe, tying all energies together," he responded simply.

The explanation didn't register with Kameclara. So she tried slowly relaxing parts of her body. It felt nice, but she didn't feel changed in any way. Hayes must've noticed. He lifted a hand and placed it on her forearm. Kameclara started. "Your palm's burning!" she cried.

"Kame!" Syra trilled, interrupting.

Kameclara pulled away. She excused herself and hurried to Deck Nine with Syralise. There, Leera stretched with others on Alpha Team. She cocked Kameclara an inquisitive brow, "I thought I saw you doing Pinghe exercises with the North Deroner."

"Yeah." Kameclara perked, "You don't know him, do you?"

She thought hard, "Don't think so, why?"

"Said he trained with your father."

Leera wrinkled her nose, "Yeah, I guess he's about the age as the last group my dad worked with."

"What are Pinghe breathing exercises?" Syralise asked.

"There's different kinds," Leera explained, shifting position. "Some are restorative. Others tone muscle. It activates various energies in your body."

"Hmm," Kameclara ran fingers through her hair. "Sounds like something the IM should teach all operatives."

"It's a passive sorta thing though," Syralise commented. "The IM likes measurable results."

"Agreed," Leera nodded, offering, "But I can practice with you two if you want."

"I'd love it!" Syralise perked.

"Hayes' hand was warm…" Kameclara rubbed her chin.

Leera's eyes lit with awe, "He knows the—?"

The Captains sounded a klaxon. The operatives hopped to their feet and entered formation. Hayes arrived a few moments late, but his Captain didn't seem alarmed. They exchanged a few words, and the operative took his position. Kameclara wondered why Hayes had special privileges.

It's likely he's been tapped for an ongoing special assignment.

Captains announced that the fresh-faced Orareca teams were pitted against seasoned North Deroners for evaluative combat. No one made a sound, but Kameclara mentally groaned to herself.

This could get rough!

"Make your selection," a Captain announced. Walls slid open and weapons displayed on racks. Kameclara noticed most North Deron operatives went for Project S-48 gloves.

Leera picked her favorite, the electric staff. Syralise chose simulated crescent blades. They were formed by energy and set to impact everything except flesh.

Kameclara knew weapons were always optional. She went without. One less weapon in her hand was one less to keep track of on the field. She preferred to take an opponent's anyway.

Captain Nanti strode to the center of the arena and held up a slip of paper with two thumb-sized dots. They were sensors. "Each of you will carry two sensors. Your objective is to stick a member of the opposing nation while preventing them from tagging you. Once you've been tagged, the sensors will beep, notifying you you're 'dead.' When it happens, leave the field."

A North Deron Captain smirked. "As always, when you run out, feel free to take another's."

The training hall of Deck Nine was fitted with habbadite clay. The Captains manipulated it into a multi-level terrain.

It was Syralise's turn to command Alpha-Je. When Captain Nanti and the officers stepped off the field, authority over all Orareca teams fell on Syralise. "Beta-Je, take command from me and start in the northwest quadrant," she broke them apart, allowing to cover more ground. She selected high ground as Alpha Team's starting point. "Eyes on targets, southwest sector, A-6," Syralise instructed. Alpha Team used a code to divide the visible field around them.

"Eyes on targets," the team echoed.

"We've got nine eyes on us," Kameclara reported.

"Affirmative. Avoid right flank," Syralise responded.

A horn sounded and the teams leaped into action. Kameclara struggled with experienced operatives immediately in her path. After taking a few hits, she managed to disarm a woman's club. Taking it for herself, she used it to trip a man. She tried to slap a sensor on his back but he rolled away. She dodged his return strike and fought vigorously.

A curved dagger came towards her. The first woman had taken one from Syralise. Biding her time, Kameclara blocked until she saw an opening. A quick jab in a well-placed spot caused her opponent's arm to spasm. The woman dropped her dagger. As she recovered, Kameclara slapped a sensor on her back. There was a beep.

She grabbed the knife and slashed at a man headed for her. Leera was nearby and tripped him as he jumped back. The redhead slapped a sensor on him. He was out.

Kameclara felt an arm brush her shoulder. She leaped away in the nick of time, avoiding a tag. She came face to face with Hayes. "Permission to seek new target!" she asked Syralise.

"Green!"

A grin curled. Kameclara launched towards Hayes, knife swinging. He lifted a gloved hand. Kameclara's stomach lurched as her feet lost the ground. "Gah!" Her ankles swooped over her head. Kameclara braced for a crash landing.

It never came. Hayes kept her dangling.

Kameclara hurled the knife towards him. She dipped a few inches as he ducked. His hand swiped and the wall sped towards Kameclara. She pulled with her core and turned to meet the wall with her feet instead of her face. She pushed, but didn't get far. The wall came towards her again.

"How the…?" her mind raced, trying to find a way to disentangle from his control.

Kameclara caught herself with all fours. It was all she could do to keep herself from being flattened against the wall. Hayes' giggle reached her ear and he calmly slapped a sensor on her back. Kameclara cursed as she heard a beep.

He leaned into her ear, whispering, "Take care dear, I think you'll be leading the charge on Jema."

"Why, because I'm Alpha-Je, like you?" she grumbled, sliding to the ground.

"Sure." His tone changed. Kameclara looked to him in puzzlement, unable to identity its meaning. He immediately giggled again, "And don't forget to breathe!" He strode away, eyes already on another target.

Kameclara sighed dejectedly as she marched off the field. As she plopped onto a bench, she caught a glance from Captain Nanti. The rest of the Captains had kept their eyes glued on the action. Kameclara wondered pessimistically about her special attention.

Should I speak with her? She quickly shook her head. *How would I broach the subject? She's* supposed *to observe us.*

Kameclara did her best to shake thoughts of Captain Nanti. She studied her partners in action. They did well, avoiding multiple tags.

Then she observed Hayes. He dashed swiftly across the field, tagging five more people with sensors he'd stolen. He wielded S-48 confidently, having no problems tossing people in the air. Kameclara frowned. He was leagues stronger with the apparatus than any of the South Deroners.

Soon, time was called. North Deroners won with forty-nine tagged. Orarecans had thirty. Training Captains cited weak and strong tactics, before releasing the operatives to rest.

Syralise moaned, turning to her partners, "I thought we were good, literally 'til today."

"We just need more practice," Leera huffed, refusing to accept defeat. "They've had seven ans on us. We'll catch up."

"Hayes used S-48 on me," Kameclara frowned. She kept her head low, replaying the scenario. "I was virtually helpless."

"I saw!" Syralise exclaimed. "South Deroners couldn't use 'em on people. I figured we had too much mass."

"What'd it feel like?" Leera asked.

"The air grabbed me. I couldn't figure out how to get out of its hold." Her eyes went to Hayes across the training hall. He threw a towel around his neck, laughing with his partners. Catching her glance, he winked. He threw arms around his partners and steered them to Kameclara. They didn't flinch, appearing accustomed to his overly-friendly manner.

"Any bruises?" he asked sweetly.

Kameclara cut to the point, "South Deron can't use S-48 like you. And as far as I've observed, neither could most of your team. Why's that?"

Maralie, Hayes' partner chortled, "He's such a jerk!" Shaking her head, she added, "In all seriousness, he's the most talented S-48 user on Teroma."

"And completely ruthless!" Albera, his other partner rolled her eyes.

"I could tell," Kameclara eased her expression. "But Hayes, you're far past anyone in South Deron, and they invented the gloves."

"Oh! I was definitely going easy on you too," he responded with a hint of spice in his charm. "And it's practice that makes me perfect!" He flopped a hand to his chest.

Albera slapped his arm lightheartedly.

"That's it?" Syralise's spoke with equal admiration and playfulness, "There's hope for me yet?"

He responded brightly, "Use breathing exercises. By clearing your mind and controlling breaths, you can neutralize the hold of S-48."

"The Pinghe Clear Aura Method," Leera's interest piqued. She'd been bored before that moment, as she usually was with casual banter. "It's believed thoughts and intentions send energy out of our bodies. The Clear Aura Method cleanses them… and your body grows warm while it happens…" She popped her hands on her hips, eyeing Hayes incredulously. "It's one of the most difficult to master. Am I supposed to believe you did?"

He ignored her attitude. "Yes dear, I've trained for many long ans. It's brought me great peace and I'll forever hold appreciation for it." He patted her shoulder tenderly, a hand to his heart, "And for the Pinghe."

Leera visibly lowered defenses.

Is this jerk trying to steal my friends? Kameclara thought with a spot of humor. "But how were you able to toss me around?" she challenged.

"The gloves let me grab onto the disturbance around you, created by thoughts," Hayes gave a devilish look. "Strong intentions are like handlebars," he gestured around Kameclara's head, grabbing at nothing. "Syralise told me you couldn't stir enough emotion to use the gloves. I figured you could at least practice the opposite and clear your mind."

Kameclara scoffed, "Sy!"

He is *trying to steal my friends!*

Yet, it was hard to be upset at someone so dangerously beguiling.

"What? I ran into him at breakfast and it came up!" Syralise smiled.

Kameclara turned back to Hayes, "Is there a reason you didn't tell me beforehand that breathing was how to counteract S-48."

Hayes batted his eyes, "Yes. It's not my style. Besides, slamming people into walls is more fun." The group broke into well-natured mirth. As it died down, they headed towards their rooms.

As they went down mip hall, Kameclara realized she forgot to ask Hayes how he'd heard of her. "Go on," she said to her squad-mates, "I'll catch up."

Kameclara jogged back and spotted Hayes trailing behind his team. His usual pleasantness replaced with a stern attitude. He locked eyes with someone on his right. Kameclara slowed, following his gaze. Captain Nanti gave Hayes the slightest of nods. Kameclara stopped in her tracks, stunned.

She shook it off, "Hayes!" she called, jogging to him. Captain Nanti swiftly disappeared around a corner. He waited, greeting with a warm expression. "You know my Captain," Kameclara confronted.

His eyes filled with glumness, the last reaction she expected. "I do," he didn't deny. "We have a day off tomorrow. There's someone I want you to meet."

"Stop diverting. How do you know my Captain?" she demanded firmly.

"Nanti and I grew up together," he spoke disinterestedly. Kameclara detected no ulterior motive. "That's not important. Meet me tomorrow in shuttle bay five."

"Why's this suddenly coming up? Why didn't you ask me right after evaluations? Are you trying to change the conversation to hide something?"

"Not at all! It's something I wasn't sure about until just this moment. I needed to think."

Kameclara wasn't sure if she could accept the answer, but it wasn't why she was there. "Hayes. You said you'd heard of me. How?"

His eyes remained sincere. "From an observer." She opened her mouth, but he interrupted, "That's all I'm going to say. Please give me some credit. I'm not out to get you."

Kameclara knew little about the man before her, who seemed to know quite a bit about her. Yet operatives honored a code to support one another. On this code, she agreed to meet him the next day.

Chapter Twelve

Every now and then, Stanten found his rations stolen. Sometimes it was a snack, other times toiletries. It annoyed him, but the last thing he wanted was trouble, so he kept quiet. Geraldo said he'd been experiencing the same.

One day, Stanten found his tablet missing. A cold knot tightened his stomach. He'd earned reading privileges on it from good behavior. But the tablet needed to be returned in a few days. He didn't know the punishment for losing something of high value.

"Can't be good," he ground his jaw.

The next day, Mardo from two halls down found Stanten. "This said it's assigned to you," he handed him the tablet. They were in the cafeteria. The dingy light made everything gray. Yet for Stanten, the room vivified for a moment.

"Thanks," he sighed in relief.

The elder man took a seat across from him. "It's that Grigol. Watch out for him. He's been takin' everyone's stuff." He shook his head. "I gave him a good wallop and returned a buncha things he stole."

Stanten furrowed his brow, "Dunno 'im."

"Shifty fellow." Mardo nodded to the tablet, changing topic,

"Couldn't help but notice you're readin' the Ia scriptures."

Stanten blushed, "I'm no good at readin'. It's the only book I hearda."

"Well if ya need help, I grew up in a temple of the Goddess. Nuns gave me my education."

"I only went ta primary school," Stanten fidgeted. "Didn' finish."

"No need feelin' bad," Mardo spoke plainly. "One thing I was raised to believe, it's not about where you're from. It's where you're going."

Stanten liked the sound of that. "You hungry? I'd like ta thank you." Offering a meal was all he could do.

Mardo cocked his head, impressed, "A gentleman inmate. And here I thought I was the only one."

"We all need friends." He seldom reached out, but something about Mardo seemed sincere. He had the same kind of face as Geraldo. They didn't want anything from him. Besides, there'd been a few scuffles. Though Stanten hadn't been dragged into any, he'd hate to be alone when he was. So far, Geraldo was his only ally, and he wasn't around all the time.

Stanten used his extra commissary and got Mardo what he wanted. He helped himself to some green fruit he'd grown partial to. "Where'd you think the fresh stuff come from?" Stanten asked. "We've been on the ship forever."

"Beats me. I'm not complaining. They never fed us like this back in Kedba's prison." Stanten gathered Mardo was from the nation Hurwon. Kedba was its largest city.

"I never ate this well my entire life." Normally Stanten would've saved some for his mother. They always looked out for each other.

When thoughts of her came pouring, his throat tightened. Stanten took a deep breath, quashing grief. "You know where were gonna be stationed?" he asked to distract himself.

"They never tell stuff like that to people like us," Mardo took a bite of the protein ration. "Chow's better today. Probably opened a new crate."

"They did. I had kitchen duty yesterday."

"Wonder what the operatives eat. Have you ever seen one?"

Stanten thought for a moment. "I think I passed one on Deck Eleven. There was a spill near a training hall." He had been granted special access to clean during training hours.

"I hear 'em all the frickin' time," Mardo rolled his eyes. "My room must be near them. They're always shouting and banging crap." He took another bite of food. "Never actually seen one though. Guess us undesirables gotta stay hidden."

"I don't mind." Stanten chomped on fruit. He didn't even know what it was called. He just liked it. "You know what this stuff is?"

"It's a pear. You never had one back on Teroma? They're pretty common."

"No."

Mardo leaned sideways and asked matter-of-fact, "So what's your story? How'd ya end up in prison?"

"Killed a guy," he felt embarrassed. "Didn't mean to." Emotions stirred his gut, messing with his appetite. His mother's voice came to mind, telling him to breathe.

"A noble gesture, woefully misplaced." Mardo chuckled dejectedly, "That's what judges always told me. Since I was as young as you." He leaned back, "Our temple was always struggling with funds.

The nuns were always trying to help the down and out. Whenever I'd get angry, I'd rob rich houses."

"Doesn't sound like something you'd earn a life sentence for," Stanten observed. "Unless not everyone on this ship has that."

"We do." Mardo confirmed with a sigh. He folded hands behind his head. "One night, I surprised an old guy while taking some of his crap. His heart wasn't too good." Mardo shook his head, "I called emergency responders and prayed with him, but it was too late."

"They got you for manslaughter?"

"Yeah, was only in for a few ans 'cause I didn't touch 'im. But it got on my record. Coupla ans later, a gang dispute spilled into our temple. I got caught up in the mess and arrested with 'em." Mardo stabbed absentmindedly at his food. "Lotsa my ancestors were missing documentation. You know what happens to people like that."

"First sign of trouble, they lock us away."

"That's if you're lucky." He pointed to the ceiling with his fork, indicating upper decks where operatives were. "Those guys up there. They get called to take you out if you cause serious problems."

"I thought they're supposed to take out aliens." Stanten stiffened as a thought struck him, "What if we're headed into a warzone?"

Mardo shrugged, "It's probable." He added with disgust, "Anything to protect Ia."

"What'd you mean?"

Mardo's face reddened, "It makes me so pissed they go to war in the name of the Goddess. She's about forgiveness." He shook his head obstinately, "She wouldn't want this."

"I thought operatives protected Teroma? What does Ia have to do with it?"

"Way before your time!" He spewed bitterly, "They used to re-cruit people for the Intergalactic Military, telling 'em they're protecting the Goddess if they protected Teroma." He grumbled angrily, "Draggin' Ia's benevolent name into it!" He spat.

A guard leered their way. Stanten calmed Mardo, "How's about you teach me the Goddess scriptures." He pulled the tablet to them. "I'm havin' trouble understandin' some of the star charts."

"All I'm saying is, don't go killin' in the name of peace," Mardo's voice was lower, but he was still worked up.

"This says Ia descends from the heavens? Are the star charts sup-posed to say when and where?"

"She's not real. She's an ideal," Mardo's temper finally leveled. "Ia's the softer side of our personalities."

"If she's only an ideal, why make it a person?"

"It's easier to relate to a person than be preached at." Mardo took another bite of food, chewing agitatedly. "At least, that's how the nuns explained it. I used to think it was a person too when I was a kid. Used to have dreams she'd take me somewhere I wouldn't be miserable."

"For me, this ship's the answer to that," Stanten confessed. "War-dens don't mess with ya. Foods good. Can't ask for much else."

"What about love?" Mardo's voice finally softened. He pushed his empty plate away. Cringing, he appeared to regret saying those words aloud.

Stanten studied his new friend. His eyes seemed lost. "You got someone back home?"

"Not anymore. He's gone." The words were barely a whisper.

Stanten gulped, not sure what to say. "Sorry," he eventually mumbled.

Mardo shrugged quietly, staring at the table.

Stanten considered his question. "I never hoped for love." He never thought anyone could care for him. "I'm good without it."

"We all need some kinda love to truly be alive." Mardo patted him on the back as he stood. "Check out scripture ninety-eight. Talks about universal love." He picked up his plate, "Thanks for the meal kid. Catch ya'round."

Stanten waved as he pulled the tablet towards him. He thumbed through until he found the words. "The world was made livable by the Seed of Life. Love makes the Seed bloom. Love is Life."

Stanten furrowed his brow. "I thought everything in here's 'sposed to be 'bout Ia."

The lights flickered, indicating it was time to clear out. Stanten tucked the tablet under his arm and went to wash his dish. He reached for a cloth to dry it when someone knocked into him. The dish clattered to the ground, but he caught the tablet.

"You got a problem, man?" Tivan growled. He pointed to the dish, "Pick it up."

Stanten recognized the man who had purposely blocked his view when they exited the prison transport back on Teroma. He was older and twice as nasty. "Don't want trouble," he grumbled, fists balling instinctively.

Tivan jerked the front of his shirt. "Whatcha got under your arm?" His other hand grasped the edge of the tablet. Stanten knew some people wanted what they didn't have. It's why he preferred to read in his room.

"Break it up!" a warden barked.

Tivan's eyes narrowed. He already had a strike against him. He calculated if Stanten was worth the trouble of a second.

"Now!" the warden marched towards them.

Tivan shoved him away, "Get outta my sight."

Stanten waited until Tivan was halfway across the room. He relaxed his hands and picked up the dish, washing it again.

The warden hovered until Tivan left the cafeteria. "You should stay away from him. You've got a clean record and he's trouble," he advised.

Stanten nodded.

"Now get to your room."

"Yes, sir."

Don't need to tell me twice.

Chapter Thirteen

As promised, Kameclara met Hayes at shuttle dock five. He waited, standing tall. A green robe from North Deron, with its layered collar enfolding his neck, draped across his shoulders. It appeared formal and she felt underdressed in stretch slacks and a loose shirt.

A waggish grin flashed at her before Hayes offered an arm. Kameclara felt taken aback, not accustomed to old-fashioned gestures. She took it to be polite, intrigued by the novelty. "Where's this mysterious person we're to meet?" she asked.

He smiled discretely, "Civilian ship-2."

Kameclara arched an eyebrow. "We're meeting a civilian?"

"Did you forget some of us have families on this journey?" he mocked gently.

She shrugged, "You didn't strike me as a family person."

"People say that," he shook his head, offended, "but I make time."

When Hayes didn't say more, Kameclara refrained from prying.

On the transport, they exchanged stories of Orareca and North Deron. He was well traveled, but had never been to her home nation. Kameclara shared her favorite parts of Orareca. Hayes appeared relaxed, chatting openly. The roguish part of him she normally sensed seemed to have evaporated. It helped Kameclara lower her guard.

"I really wish I could've visited," his eyes were far away. A hint of a secret on his tone.

She wanted to ask what he meant, but knew by then that if he'd wanted to share, he would do so. If not, she wasn't going to get a straight answer. Instead, she picked his brain. "How dicey can operations go compared to training?"

"Active missions are diverse," Hayes explained, loosening again. "Unless Teroma is under attack, it's unlikely you'll encounter anything more challenging than our training." An upturned hand gestured as he spoke, "Believe it or not, one of my more interesting missions dealt with communications." He faced her, "You know the six comet bases in the outer reaches of the system?"

"Yes."

"They're mostly unmanned. The equipment on them is used to scramble attempted observation from regions beyond. Their secondary function is to detect incoming objects." He flicked a piece of lint from his sleeve. "Whenever a comet passes near the Molta Belt, two technicians and an officer are escorted on site. They're to update and repair equipment and can be left alone for seven to eight ans at a time."

"That's a long time for just three people," Kameclara observed.

"Mmhmm," Hayes nodded vigorously. "Their personalities can be quite interesting when it comes time for retrieval. I was stationed on Molta's section eleven for a bit. Got to be a part of a retrieval team." He let out a snort, "The men decided they didn't need to wear clothes anymore, that living natural was best."

Kameclara chuckled, "That is a bit... cold."

"Oh sweetie, I haven't gotten to the best part! They rambled on and on about a theory they had. The walls of their offices covered with formulas. They claimed to have intercepted alien transmissions from the Archo System. They believed those aliens could travel through a fold in space."

Kameclara's ears perked. "Can't be good. Can you imagine an enemy fleet appearing beside Teroma?" The hairs on her arm stood on end.

"It appeared feasible on paper, but no one's tested the theory," Hayes held his chin.

"Our enemies are from the Maliote System though," Kameclara tried to reason, but she couldn't shake a bad feeling.

Hayes dipped his head. "But galactic drift has brought them closer to the Archo System. There hasn't been proof the two are working together, or anything reason they would be, but…" he trailed, the corners of his eyes creasing. She could tell he felt concerned too. There was always the "what if" question.

"Say, Hayes do you think it's odd Teroma's sending so many operatives to Jema?"

"What do you mean?" his lips pursed, head angling away.

"Well, the IM's primary objective is to protect Teroma from alien invasions. Why're leading teams sent away?" She drew on their conversation, "I mean, we're not diverting time or resources to test the theory of folding space travel. To me, that'd seem like advantageous technology to have."

Hayes balked at her.

Kameclara dropped her voice, "We're deviating from our primary objective. There has to be a more substantial threat than an alien invasion. Am I right? And it must have to do with Seu."

Hayes' face fell into a neutral expression, as smooth as glass. After a moment, a falsely charismatic smile appeared. "You're a clever one. I'm counting that as a blessing."

What the hell's that supposed to mean? It doesn't take a genius to see we're breaking from the IM's core objectives.

Before Kameclara could press, the transport docked onto Civilian Ship-2. Hayes stood quickly and prepared to disembark. Kameclara got the sense he wanted to avoid further questions.

Slightly frustrated, she decided to drop the topic for the time being. *But he knows something I don't.* It solidified her belief that he'd been tapped for a special assignment.

The two were silent as Hayes led Kameclara through the civilian ship. It contrasted greatly to the warship and she felt at home. There were trade stations and playgrounds. A small park with potted trees and a fountain sat in an open area where families played. Aquaponic crops spread across multiple decks and Kameclara recognized the fruit served in her cafeteria.

They continued into residential halls where Hayes stopped before a door. He placed his palm against a panel and it unlocked. As he entered, the sound of giddiness poured out. Kameclara peered curiously over Hayes' shoulder. A light-haired woman spun a blonde girl in the air.

"Come on in," Hayes waved as he swished inside.

As Kameclara stepped through, a little girl bobbled towards Hayes. When she caught sight of Kameclara, she turned and dashed behind the woman.

"Seriously!" the woman scolded, "Where're your manners?"

The little girl sheepishly came out. In cautious steps, she approached Kameclara and offered a hand. The operative felt enchanted and shook it. Afterwards, the child snaked back behind the woman.

"Hello, my name's Ashmarah, I'm Hayes' sister," the woman

introduced herself. "He's told me a lot about you. Kameclara, is it?"

"Yes, pleased to meet you," Kameclara lifted her brows in surprise. She hadn't expected Hayes to talk about her.

"Your name, it's a rare one. It means 'karma cleared' doesn't it?"

She gave a chuckle, "It does."

"And this little lady," Hayes pulled the girl from behind Ashmarah, "Is Isa. Be polite and say 'hello,' sweetie," he kissed her cheek.

"Hi!" the girl peeped. She then buried her face in his neck.

"Isa, a popular name. Variant for Ia," Kameclara shared her limited knowledge of names, mirroring Ashmarah's cordialness.

"She's my daughter," Hayes explained with different kind of smile; mischievousness replaced by protectiveness.

"Oh?" Kameclara couldn't help but startle.

Ashmarah laughed warmly, adding, "*Adopted* daughter."

He shared with a wink, "I'm still waiting for that perfect guy. Until then, this little one," he nuzzled Isa, "fills my heart with love every day." He spoke so tenderly Kameclara saw flashes of her own nurturing mother. She grinned, softening.

"Let's grab a drink from the kitchen," Hayes walked Isa into the next room, "You can pick!"

The girl snuck a bashful peek at Kameclara. When their eyes met, Isa hid her face again.

"I'm really glad to meet you," Ashmarah beamed to Kameclara.

There was an inflection in her tone Kameclara couldn't place. Not sure how to respond, she nodded. "Likewise."

"Come," Ashmarah stepped intimately near and took her hands. Kameclara began to understand Hayes' over friendly mannerisms. Ashmarah oozed the same old-world affability.

The woman seated them on the couch. The fabric was a blend of soft materials, a nice contrast from the warships. Ashmarah spoke guardedly, eyes acute to catch Kameclara's reaction. "I'd like to peer into your soul. May I breathe with you?"

Kameclara kept a straight face, hiding alarm towards the atypical question. "I'm not sure I understand."

Ashmarah smiled reassuringly. "It's an old North Deron tradition," she waved a hand casually. "Some say it's fortune telling, others superstition. But through breathing, I can sense where you've been... And possible roads your life might lead."

"Why would you like to know my future?" she asked, careful to remain pleasant.

"Hayes tells me you're special... For this mission." She made a face, "I just wanna see if he's full of himself." She added in a whisper, "He seems to think he has the same gift as me."

Kameclara questioned Ashmarah's motives. Her words sounded like a poorly concocted excuse. *But to what end?*

Nonetheless, Kameclara sensed no malice. She glanced around the room. It was an ordinary living space. Nothing caused alarm. Some of her father's words came to mind.

Is Ashmarah versed in the forgotten ways of Teroma? More importantly, how much do I really trust Hayes?

He'd seemed genuine most of the ride over. But there was still a moment where she detected secrets.

The warbling laugh of a child with not a care in the world erupted from the kitchen. Hayes' voice cheered, "Master chef, Isa!" Hearing innocent sounds soothed Kameclara's heart.

She lifted her eyes, "Yes."

It's only breathing after all.

Ashmarah touched her chest and bowed in gratitude. "Thank you." She wrapped warm hands, surprisingly strong, around Kameclara's shoulders. "Please close your eyes. I will place my hand over your heart. Just breathe deeply and relax your mind."

Kameclara did as instructed, wondering if this woman used the Clear Aura Method. It would explain her warm hands.

But why would she know Pinghe practices?

When Ashmarah pressed beneath her collarbone, Kameclara felt strangely scintillated, as if she were being inducted in an ancient ceremony. She dropped her shoulders and pulled a breath through her nose. A pleasant hint of fruit danced in the air.

At the peak of her breath, Kameclara exhaled from her core. The hand on her heart grew warmer. Its temperature spread through her, bringing ease.

After a dozen breathes, Kameclara drifted into a trance. Gentle pulses of light flitted through her mind, coming from an indecipherable source. She moved through them weightlessly, soaring for what felt like hours. They circled around her, through her, dancing to their own music. If she were to peer carefully, some streaks held images. Yet they were gone before she could catch details.

When the lights receded, Kameclara grew aware of her body. Weight returned. When she blinked her eyes open, she found herself sprawled across the couch. Her limbs felt like jelly, as they often did after a good night's rest.

A loud sound caused her to jerk upright. She spotted Isa on an armrest, cup in hand. The sound came from the girl's straw, sucking up the last of juice. She hopped down and set her empty cup on a table.

"Here," Isa picked up a full glass and carefully walked it to Kameclara. She seemed to have forgotten her shyness.

"Thanks," Kameclara licked parched lips.

"I think your colors are pretty," Isa said in a small voice.

Kameclara gulped down the juice. "Hmm?"

"Your colors," Isa spoke with increasing boldness. "They were dancing from your heart." Isa beamed, "That's how I know we'll get along!"

Kameclara set down the glass, peering blankly to the child, unable to comprehend the meaning of her words.

"How're you feeling?" Ashmarah asked, emerging from the kitchen. She lifted Isa and they sat beside Kameclara. The girl adjusted herself on her aunt's lap.

"Fine. I didn't mean to fall asleep," Kameclara felt a bit embarrassed.

"No worries," Ashmarah grinned. "It's normal."

"What happened?"

"Most of the time, our souls are… asleep. It's because our conscious mind is always controlling and planning. It acts like a cap on our genuine expressions." Ashmarah beamed, "I merely aided your consciousness mind to sleep, and allowed your soul to shine."

"It makes colors!" Isa chirped.

Ashmarah laughed an easy laugh, "Yes, an awakened soul produces vibrations that some can see as colors."

Kameclara listened with an open mind. She knew Ashmarah believed her words, but Kameclara remained skeptical. "Why do this?"

The aunt grew somber. "I think I'll let Hayes explain."

"He hasn't been the most forthcoming." Annoyance didn't typically plague Kameclara, but she didn't like feeling constantly left out, with secrets dangling just out of reach.

"Dinner's ready!" Hayes called.

The four sat at a modest table. Hayes shared that he had met Isa when she was two ans old. Though he didn't give details, he said he knew he was meant to care for her.

She was now three.

"Ashmarah agreed to come look after her."

I begged Auntie to come too!" Isa cooed.

"Oh, you both know I didn't have a choice!" she chided playfully. Kameclara detected something more behind Ashmarah's words. Perhaps it was Hayes's hesitant chuckle that gave it away.

"Kameclara, I've pulled a favor and reviewed every operatives' file on this mission. I believe you're one of the strongest fighters," Hayes spoke with imploring eyes. Kameclara felt something was coming. "I need to ask for something."

There it is.

"I'll consider," she responded carefully, setting down her fork.

Hayes gulped, stealing a look to Isa. The girl ate in a well-behaved manner. "It's for my daughter. Can you help protect her?" His eyes bore into Kameclara, "Please make sure no harm befalls her whatsoever?"

Kameclara felt taken aback, "I'll do my best to protect all the civilians," she generalized.

"Kameclara," Hayes' voice turned firm but gentle. He laid a hand on her arm. "I know we've just met, and this request must make you feel put upon, but I'm asking sincerely." His eyes glistened, "Should anything happen to me, could you protect her as you would Teroma?"

His mellow expression barely masked a smoldering deep in his eyes. Its cause was difficult to discern; though Kameclara did detect authentic distress. She got the inkling Hayes knew more about the mission than she. Perhaps he even knew the nature of their enemy. The idea intriged her.

Beside him, Isa twirled noodles onto a fork before slurping them down. Kameclara wondered if Hayes had asked his partners to protect his daughter as well. Perhaps Ashmarah also breathed with them to decide if they were trustworthy.

Isa peered to her aunt. Kameclara noticed Ashmarah's eyes begging too.

She turned back to the father. "Hayes, I know details about this mission are purposefully kept from us," Kameclara chose words carefully. "The fact you pulled a favor and viewed all operatives' files shows you're privy to information I'm not. Perhaps you're even on special assignment and you can't tell me." She gazed sternly. "I know there's a reason you're asking me to protect your daughter. It makes me wonder… if you know exactly how dangerous our mission is."

"You're smart, dear," he repeated his words from the transport, still revealing nothing.

Kameclara could easily refuse his request, but something made her take a leap of faith. If Hayes had information, it'd be best to keep on his good side. "If anything should happen to you, I promise, I'll do everything in my power to keep Isa safe. As long as it doesn't compromise my duties," she added firmly.

His face melted with relief and Ashmarah exhaled. "Thank you," he whispered. "You don't know what this means."

"So *Kamawara* gonna be my friend?" Isa grinned ear to ear.

"Yes," Kameclara beamed back.

"I like that," Isa giggled.

The conversation steered in a lighthearted direction. They talked about families left behind. Ashmarah found amusement in Procias. "Really? He shaves one side of the face at a time?" She chuckled. "I would've never imagined…" there was a pause, "that anyone would shave in that manner!" she uttered briskly.

Kameclara smiled politely, passively wondering why Ashmarah was curious about her father.

She didn't stay long after dinner. Hayes walked with her to the dock. He offered to train together when they regrouped. Kameclara accepted. She once more searched Hayes' eyes for more information as the doors closed, but found nothing.

~*~

Hayes returned to his quarters. Isa had fallen asleep in her room. He kissed her forehead as she snuggled deeper into blankets. He smiled. Her safety was more important to him than anything. After lingering over his child, he returned to the seating area. Ashmarah waited at the table.

"So… it was her after all," she referred to Kameclara.

He took the seat across from her. Ashmarah wasn't really Hayes' sister. She was a veteran officer of North Deron. When retired, she became an observer like Kameclara's father. Through the ans she had moved up in ranks and became Procias' supervisor. On the mission to Jema, she was the Commanding Observer.

Hayes was the Supervising Observer. Her second in command.

Ashmarah had worked with Procias for decades and knew his background well. It was the only reason she allowed Kameclara to even meet Isa. However, as she peered into the young woman's soul, an interesting truth came to light. It was something she'd previously dismissed, as paternal pride.

"Her father's suspicions are confirmed." Ashmarah spoke languidly. "There's no doubt in my mind, Kameclara IS the reincarnation of the Princess." Her eyes darted to Hayes, speaking breathily, "I cannot stress how much of an asset she is to our mission."

Hayes shook his head in wonder. "Based on laws of karmic patterns, she has the best chance of bringing down Vesper."

~*~

Orareca 14.236 ans

Procias received a heavily encrypted transmission from Ashmarah. Kameclara fared well, excelling in training. This came as no surprise. He continued to scan the message and paused. He reread the last sentence. Ashmarah confirmed his daughter's soul identity.

The reincarnation of Princess Meliora.

Tears welled in his eyes and his heart ached. A part of him felt glad she contained the karma needed to rival Vesper. Another wept for her tragic death as Meliora.

Procias had spent countless ans observing Ima. It was a humorous twist of fate that the Princess became his daughter.

Watching Kameclara leave for the mission was one of the hardest things he'd ever done. But he had calculated her possible fates countless times. There was nothing he could do when it came to unfinished business.

Meliora was meant to go home.

Chapter Fourteen

"Meliora…" Vesper whispered under her breath. She spoke the name from time to time. She feared if she didn't, it'd revolt and she'd come undone. "Or perhaps I say it to punish myself," the sorceress admitted secretly.

"Your highness. We're in position," a General reported.

She chased away the name, turning to the invasion at hand. "Very good. Hold steady."

Her dragons hovered in Jema's orbit, making her presence known. Within the day, Calio and Songbird had grounded their ships. The marketplaces ceased operation and citizens entered hazard shelters.

She loved how they squirmed.

Seu had been on lockdown long before she arrived. Its large inner walls curving in, closed like petals of a flower, obscuring aerial views. Vesper desired to storm Seu, to rip secrets from its heart and call it her own. Yet, fear planted in her years ago overtook her nerve. She felt certain Seu held a key to her undoing if she were not cautious. So, with an eye and dragons trained on Seu, Vesper made Calio her first target.

Vesper laid claim to Calio's landing ports. Any ship daring to escape was shot down. She then waited until the nation's resources dwindled before descending with her sorcerers. She destroyed iconic landmarks, knowing Calio would beg Seu for help. The sorceress wanted to see how the military kingdom would react.

But Seu remained stalwart, keeping to itself.

Calio surrendered not long after. The action caused fear to infect Songbird. Many of its denizens flocked to Seu. The kingdom's outer walls filled with refugees. To the sorceress disappointment, the inner walls remained firmly shuttered.

~*~

The remaining Masters of Songbird's school of sorcery grew antsy. Ginevra, Heliope, Fervir, and Sessa had been ambitious for power. With their rival Masters gone, they held all sway in Songbird. They were planning to shape the kingdom as they saw fit.

Vesper's appearance was the wildcard none expected. They had only known her as an apprentice years ago. She'd disappeared off Jema after absorbing four Masters.

Coming together in an impromptu meeting, Ginevra, the eldest growled, "We'll need to soon decide if we'll stand by or against her."

They sat in a large instructional hall. She looked about the tawdry space with disdain. Ginevra was accustomed to holding meetings in the Sacred Chamber. With the attrition of Masters, they were unable to access the plane, which took the power of six Masters to open.

Heliope turned to Sessa, the fate seer, "Is there a chance to subdue her? Perhaps in doing so, we can convince Jema to accept us as autocratic leaders." He was opportunistic for power.

Sessa's face hovered over a pool of water. Her breath trembled the stars reflecting from an eye in the ceiling. She performed a cursory reading. A frown creased her lips. "No," the water muddled. "Not even banded together." Slowly she rubbed a temple, brow creasing. "There's something about her lineage," she wheezed. Using her seer powers was exceptionally draining. "Her power can consume us all."

Fervir tossed back his head with a sneer. "Us? Bowing to an apprentice?"

Ginevra spat on the floor.

"It's the only way we survive," Sessa breathed with difficulty. "She detests us for the trials she's endured, and will not hesitate to end us if we give her reason." She sucked in air. "We need to make ourselves useful. Then we'll be revered alongside her."

Heliope rubbed his cheek, lips pressed in discontent. "Sessa's never been wrong."

The rest appeared grim.

~*~

As Vesper took stock of Calio, a messenger brought word from the Master sorcerers in Songbird. They offered allegiance in exchange for a high place in her new world order. To demonstrate their loyalty, they offered to conquer Songbird in her name.

Vesper didn't respond immediately. She waited for things in Calio to quiet. A few refugees escaped here and there by dragons, but she didn't feel concerned. They only had one place to go. Her troops on Ima would take care of things.

Once satisfied with her control over Calio, Vesper turned to Songbird. With dragons in the air and mages on the ground, she marched across the border. Vesper headed straight to the school of sorcery and ordered her massive army to encircle the grounds. "Let them behold my power."

She rode to the front gate and took time stepping down from her chariot. Vesper surveyed the grand building. Stones were chipped and the grounds neglected. It appeared already defeated. A tickle started in her chest and expanded until it burst. She tossed back her head. A cackle filled the air.

She savored this moment.

The ornate grand doors required twenty strong men to open without magic. Menacingly, Vesper lifted a hand. Malevolence in her veins stirred with pleasure as she channeled fury into her fingers. They snapped and the doors flew open, striking the walls with a boom.

A familiar scent, a bit dusty, wafted to greet. For a moment, her knees trembled, recalling her miserable time under Cleodell's control.

No! You're not the same woman.

Renewed confidence lifted her spirits. Vesper entered the dark atrium, glowering.

Kneeling in waiting were Masters Ginevra, Heliope, Fervir, and Sessa. They sensed Vesper's magic and shrank. She was far more powerful than they'd imagined. None could comprehend how an apprentice achieved her level of ability—let alone absorb four Masters.

Vesper snickered, stomping up the steps. Coming to a halt before the Masters, she glowered. Vesper knew despite their impassive demeanors, they were scheming. She had seen them at their worst and knew they only sided with her because they had no other option to survive. "You've made a wise decision," she spoke menacingly.

"Our powers are sincerely at your disposal," Ginevra croaked.

"Serve me well or you'll not live to regret it," she warned.

The once great Masters dropped their heads lower. She basked in satisfaction and a cruel smile appeared. She needed more. "Crawl to me."

The four Masters exchanged a brief look. They carefully lowered onto all fours and slunk. Ginevra, with old bones, moved slowest. Vesper snapped her fingers, sending a shock. With a cry, Ginevra scrambled, half dragging herself.

The Masters congregated at her feet, prostrating. Vesper gave her first command. "Burn Songbird to the ground. Leave only the school of sorcery."

"Yes, your mightiness," they conceded.

~*~

Masters Unadine and Erilph watched with dread as Vesper and her dragons descended into Calio. They pleaded with their adversaries—Cleodell's allies—to help stop her. Ginevra, Heliope, Fervir and Sessa were unwilling to set aside old grudges. Without aid, Unadine and Erilph left for Calio and worked with those citizens to push her back.

Yet, no one anticipated the power and rage the lone sorceress bore. Within weeks, Calio surrendered to Vesper. It was then Masters Unadine and Erilph knew the defeat of Jema was inevitable.

They found themselves amongst a daring group of refugees. The sorcerers assisted them in stealing two dragons from Calio. Using most of their magic, they pushed back hundreds of Vesper's novice mages and temporarily retook a departure port. Hurriedly, they launched from Jema.

They crashed near the eastern border of the Land of the Seraphims on Ima. Many refugees were taken prisoner or killed by Vesper's troops. Even using magic, the Masters saved but a few dozen. They escaped deep into the blue forests of Carpecillero. The Masters knew they would continue to be hunted, so they parted ways with the refugees to keep them safe.

They continued east, as far as possible from Vesper's base in the Land the Seraphims. They settled in a dense area of blue forests, near Priletoria's border.

~*~

"Open…" Vesper whispered at the end of her spell. She eyed aligned stars in the sky. The ground before her glowed as a sphere rose to hover. She stepped through, into the Sacred Chamber. Behind her, four Master sorcerers followed. Ginevra simpered with jealousy at Vesper's ability to access the space unassisted.

"This will be my base of operations," she announced. With twitches of her fingers, Vesper slid tables to form a semicircle. "I want bowls of water covering every inch," she demanded. "I'll be communicating with my mage Generals through illusion spells." As long as there was a sorcery practitioner on the other end to activate a receiving spell, Vesper could communicate through bowls of water.

Vesper's lips pulled into a line. Of course, she had ordered spies into Seu. In an attempt to breach the inner walls—where the secrets were hidden. So far, they'd only been able to access the outer walls and reported heavy patrolling by Seu soldiers.

Patience.

Vesper eyed the four Masters busily crafting bowls. A job meant for apprentices. She grinned at their humiliation. Secretly, Vesper wished they'd oppose her so she would have an excuse to eliminate them.

Nonetheless, having their power on my side is more valuable.

But she didn't trust them, and kept them close.

Water in one of the newly made bowls rippled. Vesper tapped its surface. A General in Calio reported, "We've reports that Masters

Unadine and Erilph escaped Calio on a dragon."

Vesper considered the information. If the two were aggressive, there was a sliver of a chance they could retake Ima. But it wasn't anything that could be accomplished in a short amount of time. "Let them be," she responded. "Given their pacifist nature, I don't foresee a hindrance."

"Yes, your majesty."

She waved and the illusion disappeared.

"That leaves only one Master unaccounted for," Vesper grumbled. "Maza." She turned to the Masters in the Sacred Chamber with a sharp eye. "None of you know where she's hiding, do you?"

"No," they answered.

Vesper studied Ginevra. Her features had flickered for a moment. She strode to the elderly woman. "What do you know of Maza's location?"

Ginevra lowered her head. "Nothing, I swear!" she cried. Vesper sensed the truth.

More bowls rippled. Vesper sighed, tossing a dirty glare towards Ginevra. She turned to the others, "You three," she commanded. "You're charged with finding Maza. There can't be that many places to hide."

They bowed and left, leaving Ginevra alone with the tedious task of fashioning bowls.

Vesper answered the illusion spells. Her mage officers were reporting on the security of Calio and Songbird. "Very good. How are aerial spells working on Seu?"

"None can see into inner walls," came the response. "… And they're too far from the border for distanced attacks."

"It seems as if Seu was always prepared to cut itself off from the rest of the planet," Vesper griped. "Why would they need that much defense? What could they possibly be hiding?"

No answers came. Vesper dismissed her mages.

In all the scrolls and books she had laid eyes upon, it simply stated Seu was a military nation. They also produced food for Jema, making it self-sustaining. "I could easily barge most of your walls," Vesper stared at Seu on a map, "But will I find a trap?" Her greatest fear was Seu having abilities to take magic from her body. She'd be left powerless.

And I've made too many enemies.

Vesper sucked in a breath and considered what she knew.

A part of Songbird was underground. Seu could be the same. Tunneling there could be risky, since they had no underground maps. Excavating near borders had been forbidden by Songbird and Calio as a part of a treaty with Seu.

All she did know was that Seu didn't put up a fight to protect Calio. In fact, she had anticipated it and brought her most powerful forces. Yet, Seu continued to keep to themselves during conflict.

Vesper concluded two possibilities: Either Seu was a farce and they'd crafted the façade of military power, or there was something far more precious hidden inside. It could be a secret terrifying enough to forever change Imans' and Jemans' knowledge of their worlds.

She scoffed at the first.

But the latter drew trepidation.

Chapter Fifteen

Kameclara expanded in a stretch, yawning lazily. A shimmer caught her eye and she arched towards the wall. By pure chance, a few rays of sun peeked in from their slice of a window. It danced across her cheeks, warmer than anything she'd experience before. The serendipity infused Kameclara with a feeling that that day was a bit more special.

She leaned onto an elbow, dark hair curling messily about her shoulders. Her eyes aligned for a better view and caught sight of a star larger than any she'd ever witnessed. Kameclara marveled at their sun. It seemed alive, bursting with magnanimous radiance. She'd never been this close, and it left her breathless.

Kameclara checked the bunk beneath her. Syralise was scrunched into a ball. Her mouth hung open as a soft whistle escaped her nose. Kameclara chuckled. Syralise was often known to burst into song. It was fitting that even in sleep, a note still rose from her.

Silently, Kameclara lowered to the ground and tread to the window. Leaning a shoulder against the curved wall, she caught sight of another valiant orb. It was Oli3. They were leveraging the planet's gravity to pull them deeper into the solar system.

"You're awake," Leera stated gently. She dangled her legs over the edge of the bunk.

"Good mornin'," Kameclara smiled, "Or rather, good awakening. Who knows when morning is anymore?" she pulled her hair away from her face, methodically braiding it above her brow.

"Yeah," Leera scoffed. She glanced at the clock, cracking her joints. "We've got about forty minutes before reporting in."

"I've never seen the sun this bright before," Kameclara turned back to the window.

"I like it," Leera sighed. "Can't explain it, but it makes me feel safe."

"Can you believe we left Teroma two ans ago?" she asked in awe.

"Not really. I've no idea where the time's gone. It feels like we've left only a few weeks ago." She stretched her legs against a wall.

"What do you think it'll be like on Ima?" Kameclara asked in wanderlust.

"Not sure," Leera answered thoughtfully, "But It'll probably be hot. According to videos, there'll be plants everywhere… And when I first saw flowing oceans…" her voice trailed in wonderment.

"Yeah, to be able to sail across the planet, instead of merely diving underground rivers…"

Leera breathed, "You think we'll have time to do that after the mission's completed? Or will we head straight back to Teroma?" Her eyes grew lost.

Kameclara recognized the look. "Miss your mom?"

Leera's eyes drooped. "I wish we didn't leave things the way we did."

"Why don't you help me with one of those Pinghe breathing exercises to take your mind off? Maybe the one Hayes was talking about. The Clear Aura Method."

Leera flashed a grin. "I'd like that."

She joined Kameclara by the window. Together, they sat tall. "The important aspect with this exercise is to release anything preventing peace. Replace it with acceptance."

Kameclara didn't feel at peace about hiding information from Leera. She grappled with not telling her about the Pinghe stepping up in the Intergalactic Military's absence. As her body filled with breath, Kameclara questioned why she still even kept it secret. Originally, it was so Leera wouldn't be tortured by deciding to leave on a lengthy mission. Now, she wasn't certain.

Yet, if Kameclara told now, it would be for selfish reasons. She would be alleviating herself of guilt.

A feather-light grasp landed on her shoulder. "I can sense your erratic vibes," Leera spoke soothingly. "Let it all go. Imagine time a thousand ans from now. Whatever's plaguing you, it'll no longer matter."

Kameclara did as instructed. True. In a thousand ans, Leera would no longer care. Their time in this existence merely a blink in history.

Kameclara's limbs relaxed until they felt faded. She continued pulling air in and out, allowing herself to accept her situation as complete.

Soon, the only thing she became aware of was her chest heaving. From there, she sensed the air around her. There was a pale, silvery mist—the hum of the ship. In the thick of it, a tender energy vibrated before her. It took Kameclara a few breaths to realize it was Leera's aura. Her partner's energy glowed a magenta and amber, assured and lively.

Is this how Ashmarah saw things when I breathed with her?

The clock's alarm went off. Syralise snorted as her body lurched awake. Instinctively, the three jumped to their feet. Syralise slammed the sensor and the alarm silenced. They moved in unison without a word, dressing quickly. The calm of her breathing exercise energized Kameclara, and her she couldn't help but notice her skin had grown warm.

After grooming, they left their room and grabbed a quick meal.

"Good work this morning," Leera snuck a compliment as they started their day.

"Thanks!"

On Warship-23, they paired with the country Mantipas. They were one of the few nations that didn't rank their operatives into teams. Rather, they maintained a single fleet of one-hundred-and-forty-seven fighter pilots. Mantipas' specialties included long distance aerial tactics and intricate flight patterns. Since their crew was large in number, they divided into two rotations. Orareca's Alpha and Beta Teams trained with their operatives numbered one through seventy-two.

"We've been doing this for weeks!" Syralise exclaimed, climbing into a flight simulator. Specials formations were adapted for Orareca's teams of thirty-six. "When are we going to test the real crafts?"

Kameclara shared her partner's sentiment. They'd been achieving high marks during evaluations. She powered on her simulation.

"Until there's no chance to get it wrong," Captain Nanti responded.

Leera nodded, strapping herself in. "Alright then, let's do this."

~*~

After a long day of simulated battles, Syralise and Leera were ready to turn in. "I'm feeling restless," Kameclara informed them. "I wanna work on the Clear Aura Method. I felt I was getting in a grove this morning."

"Alright, come get me if you have questions," Leera offered.

"Will do."

Syralise yawned and waved.

They parted ways and Kameclara found herself on the warship's viewing deck, a separate lounge provided for morale. Low-back seats were arranged in semicircles. Potted plants scattered about and a beverage station protruded from a wall. During days off, snacks were often set out. But the best part was the windowed wall, granting a splendid view of the stars.

Kameclara greeted a half-dozen Mantipas operatives as she entered. "Good work today."

After selecting a light beverage, she made her way to a quiet corner. Kameclara seated on the ground and folded her legs. She pulled breaths into her body, wanting to continue the exercise from that morning.

Yet, her mind grew restless and her thoughts drifted.

"Is it true Pinghe practices are meant to stimulate the nevino sequence?" She recalled Hayes once asking Leera.

Kameclara's partner had nodded, "We call it our divinity link. We practice to feel a bond with transcendent energies."

Kameclara recollected the first time she felt divinity. Procias had taken her to a frozen ocean shortly before her graduation. It was just the two of them. She noticed her father had walked slowly; his steps defined. He valued every movement. She kept pace in consideration for his age.

She chuckled to remember that in early youth, she had huffed to keep up with his swift steps. The spikes in her shoes often caught in the ice and she'd have to shake her boot loose. Their roles had reversed.

When she peered into his face, Kameclara observed contentment. "Father, why're you so happy?"

"How can you tell I'm happy?"

"You're quiet in a certain way."

Procias smiled. "It takes one to know one. I'm glad to be alive and still visiting the oceans with my daughter."

No more words were spoken, but in her heart Kameclara understood his satisfaction. Life was a gift. No one could know what death brings, but as long as breath existed, so could things like choices, love, and beauty. She felt grateful to the Goddess for having given her life. It was in that gratitude she felt a connection to the divine.

Memories of the broad, sweeping ocean brought Kameclara tranquility. Her mind calmed and after a few deep breaths, she was no longer aware of the viewing deck. Receding into a warm blur, thoughts carried her along.

A pleasant sensation surfaced from an obscure source. It felt as if a warm breeze caressed her shoulders, and the memory of a laugh tinkled somewhere behind her oldest recollections. In her mind's eye, Kameclara turned to look. The image of the frozen ocean returned momentarily, before transforming into rolling green plains. Overhead, an enormous sun blazed. Its sheer size took her breath away.

The feeling of divinity remained.

A voice called. Kameclara felt herself turning, as if reliving a memory. She saw a young man dashing, arms outstretched. Joyful sounds bubbled from her chest as he wrapped them around her. Long, snowy hair tickled her cheek and joy as bright as the gargantuan sun flooded every iota of her being.

"You're here!" she heard herself exclaim in the Jeman dialect, but with an Iman accent. Her voice sounded unfamiliar. Lyrical. Yet, somehow it still felt like her own.

Scratching reached her ears, cutting through the strange vision. The sun faded, as did the youth with white hair. Her eyes opened and Kameclara found herself alone. The timer on the viewing deck lights had run out. Only the glow of the stars illuminated the space. Her eyes drifted towards the clock. She'd been in the lounge for hours.

Yet, Kameclara didn't wish to move. The deck sat strangely beautiful in silence. Warm starlight pulsed on the objects, making them seem alive. She felt as if the universe kept her a secret, hidden in the dark.

Her hand swiped at loose hair and brushed her lips by accident. A shudder ensued. The sensation of a kiss lingered, filling her with fondness. Before Kameclara could make sense of it, scuffling came from the far end of the deck. It was the same noise that had stirred her from her reverie. She briefly wondered it if could be a critter.

"Can't," she whispered. The ships were scanned and free of vermin before they took off.

She climbed to her feet to investigate. Her body moved loose and comfortable, short carpet muffling steps. Around the edge of the room, hard flooring was arranged in a decorative pattern. As she approached, Kameclara observed a floorboard shaking near the window. A moment later, it descended into the ground.

Intrigue settled upon her. Kameclara lowered onto her stomach and peered into the hole. Through a mess of wires, light shined from another room. Gazing through was a pair of startled eyes.

"Hi," she chuckled with amusement. The sense of warmth from

her breathing exercise persisted, putting her in a pleasant mood.

"Hey," a male voice responded tentatively.

"What're you doing down there?" she asked.

The eyes held her gaze with guardedness; as if he were prepared to run any second. After a moment, he responded, "I like the view of the stars." Then added, "Please don't tell anyone."

"Why don't you come up here to see 'em?"

"Not allowed."

She heard shame in his voice. He must be an inmate. Kameclara giggled affably, "Then how do you know you can see the stars from your angle?"

"Mopped a spill there once." The distrust in his eyes decreased a bit. Kameclara caught a spark in them. Her chest responded with a soft tug. She blinked in confusion.

Where have I felt this sensation before?

"Hmm," She lowered her face to the opening. "Do I know you from somewhere?"

"Don't think so." He gulped. "I gotta go." His eyes grew impassive. A hand fumbled around the hole and a piece of floorboard started to eclipse the light.

"Wait!" Kameclara wasn't ready for their interaction to end. "I'm almost certain I've seen you before." The tug in her chest grew stronger.

The floorboard ceased moving. Dark eyes studied her cautiously. Then, as the corners softened, he muttered sheepishly, "I feel the same."

She blinked and took a breath to calm the churning in her stomach. A playful thought struck. "Well, I spilled some water. I think you'd better get that mop."

The eyes widened, processing her words. Then they creased into a smile. "Be right there." The man hesitated for a moment, studying her. A moment later, the flooring went back into place.

Kameclara pulled herself to her feet and stretched her arms. Eagerness coursed through her veins, leaving her imbalanced. She felt as if invisible winds whipped her around a vortex. "This won't do."

Positioning herself gingerly on the edge of a seat, she closed her eyes and attempted to calm her racing heart.

~*~

Stanten shut the hatch. He stood for a moment with his forehead against the wall. He heavily questioned his sanity and what he was about to do. Every ounce of his being wanted to see the woman, but knew it was a dumb idea.

"She must be an operative. Too young to be an officer." Not that it'd make a difference. If she were to accuse him of anything, even irritation, he risked being jettisoned. He'd already skirted trouble once, and should avoid any chance of conflict.

Yet as her warm gaze flashed in mind, he felt boundlessly uplifted. Something he rarely experienced. The soothing voice from minutes ago sent tremors through his core. Stanten hadn't even planned on being in the laundry room that night, a place he often went to be alone. He was supposed to play cards with Mardo. But a feeling had pulled him there. A tug in his chest.

Stanten pushed from the wall with his mind made up. He needed to see her, no matter what.

He locked up the laundry room. Light strips lit his way along the floor. As he turned a corner, Stanten slowed, noticing an open door. A retina scanner was mounted on the wall. It meant only officers with clearance could enter. An eerie feeling traveled down his spine. To his recollection, he'd never seen the door open before.

Stanten peered in cautiously as he tiptoed past, wondering if he'd catch an officer or two. He had permissions for the level, but perhaps he might've missed a message to keep out that night. If that were the case, he didn't want to get caught.

But why are the lights dimmed?

Something didn't feel right.

A silhouette tangled in wires cursed. Alarmed, Stanten's foot knocked the doorframe. The man jerked up. A pale screen in the silhouette's hand illuminated his face. Stanten recognized Tivan's beady eyes.

Stanten didn't want a fight. Tivan wasn't an officer, and he wasn't going to report Stanten if he was doing something wrong himself. Stanten hurried away, choosing to ignore what he'd seen. He had some place to be.

He hurried up metal steps leading to the viewing deck. He'd taken them many times, but this time, his knees wobbled. In part due to seeing Tivan. Mostly because of the green-eyed woman.

Too soon, he found himself standing outside swinging doors. Stanten paused, doubts revisiting. He took a shaky breath and before he could turn away, pushed through. He peered about warily, feeling a bit silly.

Why am I nervous? Do I expect her to attack me?

The room sat in dimness. A large window to his left framed an enchanting sight of the stars. It was more beautiful than from his obscured viewing place. He swept his eyes to the piece of flooring he usually removed. Seated nearby was the woman; her eyes closed.

Stanten approached gingerly. Crystal light cascaded over her form, making her glow like a mirage. Stanten was careful not to disturb her. If she were an illusion, any agitation might make her disappear.

A smile played on her lips as he lowered beside her. Her eyes blinked opened. "Hello."

"Hi." He commanded his shoulders to relax, but they refused. He felt like a golem.

"My name's Kameclara, what's yours?"

His heart drummed fast. "Stanten."

"Nice to meet you." Her voice sounded like a lover rather than a stranger. Something he wasn't used to, and it sent prickles down his arms. "So, you also believe we've met before?" He could feel the smile in her voice as it swished around him.

"I dunno. I'm sure I woulda remembered you."

"That's too bad." The honesty in her voice made him blush. Good thing it was dark.

She reached for his hand and he turned up his palm. When they touched, Stanten felt a jolt run through his body. The pull returned to his chest. The same that brought him to the laundry room. The same he felt the night he entered the prison, across the snowfield. This time, he clearly knew it pointed to her.

Braving a look to her face, he observed a startled expression. She exhaled sharply, fingers lightly touching her chest.

Did she feel the same pull?

Her hand moved. He watched entranced, as it floated to his face. Calloused palms caressed his cheek. But they were warm. Warmer than anything he'd ever felt before; in a way that encapsulated emotion. It stirred the pull in his chest.

Is this the love Mardo spoke of?

Maybe it was his imagination, but it seemed as if their hearts beat as one.

When he couldn't bear it any longer, Stanten braved a kiss on her thumb. To his awe, Kameclara leaned in. The hue of green in her eyes instantly became his favorite. Soft lips touched his cheek, so near his mouth it made him tremble. Instinctively, they locked arms.

"Doesn't matter if we can't recall a previous acquaintance," she breathed. "It feels as if I've known you a long time."

Forgetting all insecurities, he brought his lips to hers.

Chapter Sixteen

Warship- 23 14.238 ans

Kameclara awoke on the viewing deck, flabbergasted at the time. She rushed straight for the showers and doused herself. Hurrying to her locker, she saw her partners already lacing up their shoes.

"Where were you last night?" Leera asked absentmindedly.

"Breathing on the viewing deck. Fell asleep." Kameclara pulled a spare training uniform from her locker. She wasn't ready to tell them about Stanten. In part, she wasn't even sure if last night was real. There would also be too many questions, and there was no time.

"Awesome," Leera nodded, "Hopefully it'll give you an edge today."

"I'm happy for you dear!" Syralise mimicked Hayes' voice. The jest made them guffaw.

Kameclara grabbed an energy bar before they headed into their morning drills. After working up a good sweat, they only had a few minutes to get cleaned up. Afterwards, they moved to their language course. That day, to enhance proficiency, the instructor gave a history lecture in Jeman.

He pulled up satellite images of Ima. "The planet enjoyed peace and prosperity for over eight hundred ans. That changed their year 2188, our 14.211 ans. Priletoria attacked."

He zoomed in on the lush kingdom of Brisea. Endless acres of fresh crops were seen. "We're not sure what incentivized the maneuver, but it couldn't have been scarcity. Ima is a fertile planet and all kingdoms were prosperous."

As the officer lectured, Kameclara's focus slipped. Thoughts of Stanten arose, with the previous night nestled in a soft haze. They had embraced for a long time. He eventually pulled away. Apologizing, he said it was time for him to check-in with his warden.

After he withdrew, she returned to her corner and resumed breathing exercises. True to what she had told her partners, Kameclara fell asleep.

She sat up straight, realizing Stanten could very well have been a dream. Kameclara felt embarrassed to admit, but she'd felt euphoric in his arms. With her personality, only in a dream could emotions overwhelm.

"Two monarchs made a stand against Vesper, but were unsuccessful." The officer displayed images, side by side. "Queen Meliora and King Jedrek lost their lives."

Something in Kameclara pitched violently. The profile of a young woman with soft brown hair felt intimate, as if she'd studied those features at length. "We haven't seen these two before, have we?" she whispered to Syralise. She lifted a hand to her throat where it tickled.

Her partner shook her head. "She has your eyes though... and the boy's kinda cute."

Kameclara couldn't pry her gaze away as unfamiliar sensations stirred deep. Last night, she could've sworn she'd met Stanten before. Though after a conversation, they discovered they'd never been to each other's neighborhoods.

Now, a couple deceased before she even knew of their planet's existence elicited similar feelings.

She could hardly look at the snow-haired boy without waves of melancholy. When she did peek, *He... looks like the young man from my vision last night!*

Kameclara shook herself, lowering her head. It was impossible. She must be mistaken.

~*~

Syralise peeked at Kameclara. "You look pale." Their language course had ended and they gathered their things.

She rubbed her cheeks, "Feelin' kinda worn." Images of the deceased Iman couple seared in her brain.

"Well suck it up," Leera whooped energetically, "We're supposed to be doing live flights soon!"

"That's right!" Syralise joined in. The two expressed their enthusiasm with a giddy dance.

Kameclara mustered a smile. Mantipas operatives had helped Orareca's Alpha and Beta Teams devise dozens of attack plans. Any day now, they were to take their custom-engineered fighter crafts on a first spin. She'd been excited too.

Now, all she wished was to find a moment to process her wellspring of new emotions. If not, they might interfere at an inconvenient time.

A siren blared, ripping through Kameclara's skull. Her body galvanized on instinct. Alpha Team headed to the nearest gear station with blood thundering in their veins.

"It's alert four!" Syralise shouted above the screech. It indicated a fast-approaching enemy. Leera and Syralise grabbed combat boots and side arms as Kameclara laid out battle uniforms. In record time, they suited up.

As Alpha Team raced towards lower levels, they slapped on com-helmets. It notified them to report to Hangar-7. There, on-duty officers prepped type-a13 fighter crafts. They were designed especially for Orareca operatives.

Each hopped nimbly aboard his or her sleek craft, identified by their insignia. They secured themselves with crisscross straps. Their com-helmets synced. Auto-targeting and weapons-lock detection were basic features of the helmet. The craft expanded its range.

Kameclara reached forward and two control rods shot from the dashboard. They snapped to the inside of her gloves and holograms arched around her knuckles. The left was for targeting and firing, the right for cockpit maneuvering. The vehicle itself was a clear ball in which the seat was cradled. Two rounded fins encircled on either side, ending in points. The rims tapered to a razor-thin edge.

Kameclara wriggled her left and right wrists. The fins toggled. They were omnidirectional, as was the highly sensitive craft. Beneath her feet sat the velocity pedal.

She and her partners were first to complete preparation. The rest of the team wasn't far behind. They waited for further orders.

Captain Nanti's voice came over the com-helmets. "Drill complete, five minutes forty-six seconds."

Leera spat out a cuss. "Sixteen seconds over!" She smacked the dashboard. "Are we Alpha Team or not?" This was the closest they'd come to reaching their target preparation time. As each country cross-trained with Mantipas, they needed to earn the green light for advanced combat piloting. Drills testing preparation was one element. It came at all hours, sometimes in the middle of sleep cycles.

"Cool it, Lee. We're supposed to support each other," Kameclara radioed.

Leera grumbled incoherently, but agreed.

Syralise sounded disappointed, "I guess we're not green-lit to fly these yet."

Captain Nanti's voice continued smoothly, "Alpha Team, prepare to launch. Formation keta-sim with Beta Team."

Kameclara peered to Syralise. Even through tempered glass, she could tell her partner's expression brightened.

"Mantipas operatives will be running interference," Captain Nanti added. "First nation to have all operatives circle Warship-1 and return to their dock, wins."

The officers cleared out. A buzzer sounded and hangar doors opened. It was Syralise's lead. She wasted no time gliding out of the warship. Kameclara and Leera followed close on her heels.

In the vacuum, they took formation. From a nearby hangar, Mantipas operatives appeared in various assault crafts. They scattered quickly, most disappearing behind warships.

"They're trying to sneak up on us," Leera commented in amusement.

"Follow keta-sim," Syralise reminded Alpha and Beta Teams. The formation required operatives to spread over a wide field. It was a defensive maneuver.

A blue cross careened across the clear orb of Kameclara's cockpit. It locked onto Warship-1 and blinked confirmation. She marveled at the ease her craft propelled—exactly like the simulator. She gave her right wrist a twist, firing engines. A fin changed direction and her craft swirled. Kameclara drifted past the viewing deck of Warship-35.

Operatives were pressed to the windows, cheering them on.

Syralise commanded they increase velocity. Pulling up feed from a rear-facing camera, Kameclara saw Mantipas fighters closing in. "I've got a suggestion," Kameclara radioed.

"Speak," Syralise responded.

"Captain Nanti's back on Warship-23, so you've got command here. I recommend ditching keta-sim. Mantipas knows it too well. Do something to show we're from Orareca!"

"Was thinking the same!" came the response. There was a soft click as Syralise opened coms. She spoke heatedly, barely able to contain excitement. "Beta-Je," she radioed. Their squad leader responded. "Take Beta Team at top speed and head to the far side of Warship-1. Request permission to dock in Hangar-3 and wait for my command."

"We're breaking Captains' orders?"

A smile could be heard in Syralise's voice, "Captain isn't here."

"Confirmed," the leader spoke. Beta Team took off, leaving Alpha Team behind. Mantipas was nearly upon them.

"Alpha-I, stay with us," Syralise hoped two squads would be enough to delay Mantipas fighters.

Verniv was Alpha-I's leader that mission. She radioed back, "Got it."

Syralise then ordered Alpha-phen, the third ranked squad of Alpha Team, "Lead the rest of Alpha Team to circle Warship-1. We'll hold opponents here. On your return, engage aggressively." Weapons were set to tracers. Strikes would cause their ships to internally disable by degrees, but deal no real damage.

"Received." Alpha-phen sped off behind Beta Team.

"Engage in combat," Syralise commanded Alpha-Je and Alpha-I. No sooner did she speak, Syralise twirled her ship into an oncoming swarm of Mantipas fighters. She fired liberally.

"There's only twenty crafts," Leera announced of the swarm. No sooner did she speak, a dozen Mantipas fighters appeared from behind nearby Warships. They headed Alpha-Je off at a sharp angle. Leera let out a laugh and baited them to follow.

"Hold them off until the rest of Alpha Team returns," Syralise ordered. "Mantipas fighters are offensive. They'll be focused on preventing us from completing the mission. Use it to our advantage."

"Got it. Give them the chase of their lives," Leera whooped.

"There's forty Mantipas fighters unaccounted for," Kameclara observed.

"Let's flush them out," Verniv voiced. Her squad broke away, drawing a handful of crafts. They disappeared behind Warship-9, and reappeared with opponents on their tail. They continued looping behind other warships.

Syralise spiraled in a difficult maneuver. Her ship slowed in its controlled tumbled. "I'm hit! My left fin is down ten percent." She narrowly evaded further damage, wobbling away.

"I can't shake any of them!" Kameclara grunted. Five Mantipas fighters were upon her. It took every ounce of creativity to avoid being struck.

"And I haven't hit a single target!" Leera griped. The three danced nervously in their orbs.

"Docking permission granted by Warship-1," the leader of Beta Team radioed. "We're in position."

"Finally, some good news," Syralise breathed. She hadn't been sure if the warship would give permission. Now Beta Team could lie in wait. "Hold position."

"I see the rest of Alpha Team," Leera announced. "They're coming around Warship-1."

Ten squads of Alpha Team raced towards them, firing in support of Alpha-Je and Alpha-I. Kameclara ordered her craft, "Count enemy." It reported back within seconds. "Still fifteen enemy crafts unaccounted for," she shared.

"Alpha-Je, Alpha-I, circle Warship-1," Syralise commanded. "Then head for the finish."

Kameclara and Leera drew near their partner's maimed craft, offering defensive fire. They whipped around Warship-1 close behind Alpha-I. Two dozen Mantipas fighters pursued.

"Beta Team, enemies are on our tail. Exit and fire from behind," Syralise commanded coolly. She then added, "No one's seen the remaining fifteen, have they?"

"Negative," came replies.

Alpha-I had cleared the blind spots of about one third of the warships. But there were still plenty of places for the remaining fighters to secret.

"They must be waiting to ambush near the finish. Remain diligent on your return to Warship-23." Syralise closed coms to all but her partners, "I believe they're hiding behind Warship-23. My ship can't make it, but you two, flush them out. I'll hold off the others."

"Roger," Leera and Kameclara responded in unison.

They flew into a firefight. Orareca and Mantipas attacked each other mercilessly. Kameclara's right wing lost five percent functionality. The pursuing Mantipas ships were slowed by Beta Team chasing from behind. Leera must've observed the same, "Kame, a clearing!" she shouted.

Kameclara burned her nevite engines and followed Leera. They spiraled to avoid fire, with three Mantipas fighters on their heels. They slid to the far side of Warship-23. There, the remaining fifteen waited.

"Their weapons are trained on us!" Kameclara shouted. She knew what Leera was thinking. There were no other objects nearby, therefore it was the best option. The two swung their propulsion fields towards each other. They fired engines and pushed away at high velocity, narrowly evading damage.

They arced back around Warship-23 at recklessly high speeds, laying fire as they went. They struck a few Mantipas crafts in their path. The confusion caused the fifteen ships to scatter.

"All Mantipas ships accounted for," Kameclara reported.

"Thirteen Mantipas ships have taken heavy damage," Syralise announced. "So have twenty-two of ours."

"Alpha-phen and squads below have completed the mission," their leader reported. "We've returned to Hangar-7 of Warship-23."

"Great! Now re-exit and offer assistance," Syralise commanded.

"Are we… allowed?" the Alpha-phen leader questioned.

"Hurry up before an officer commands you otherwise!" Syralise barked.

Orareca's Alpha and Beta Teams' ships reappeared. The last fifteen operatives of Mantipas gave up assaulting Kameclara and Leera. They headed to slingshot Warship 1, noticing how close their opponents came to completing the race.

Kameclara noticed Syralise's ship less responsive than before. "Damage report, Sy?"

"I'm down forty percent in my left fin," she replied. In that instant, she took two rapid hits. Syralise cussed. "Twenty percent ability in both fins! My alarms are going crazy!" She groaned in aggravation as she opened coms to Alpha and Beta Teams. "Passing command to Leera. I'm heading to finish and staying."

Mantipas copied Orareca's tactic. Those who had crossed to finish also re-exited into combat. Their final fifteen didn't take long to circle Warship-1. They raced towards Warship-23, recognizing it would be a tight competition.

Syralise's handicapped ship struggled to approach Hangar-7. Mantipas crafts harassed it, constantly knocking her off course. It wasn't looking positive for Orareca.

"The last fifteen are almost back!" Kameclara alerted Leera. She fired her engines and swiveled around a Mantipas craft, inadvertently clipping its wing.

"Great idea, Kame!" Leera twisted sharply between two enemy ships and angled her fins towards a third. The sharp edge cut through the shielding of a Mantipas wing, physically disabling it.

"Lee! What did you do?" Syralise laughed nervously. It was implicitly known not to damage their cutting-edge ships.

Leera shifted direction and nudged Syralise, sending her partner within a few yards of the finish. She took heavy fire, and cut across Kameclara's dogfight. "Kame, get Sy across."

"Done."

With Leera creating distractions, Kameclara found an opening. She rammed her ship into Syralise and they tumbled into the hangar. Kameclara looked back to see Leera's fin slice through a Mantipas engine. Leera tumbled, gaining control seconds before she slid into Hangar-7. She was the last of their teams to finish.

The lone damaged Mantipas ship floated helplessly in space, unable to return on its own.

Orareca erupted into shouts of celebration.

The cheers were short lived. Hangar doors clamped shut and sour-faced Majors appeared. Alpha-Je was admonished for their reckless use of ships. "This behavior has caused a huge disruption in your training schedule. This impacts South Deron as well! We'll need to bring their engineers on board to repair the Mantipas crafts!"

Another grumbled about the Orareca operatives being the young-est and lacking maturity.

Alpha-Je stood tall, withstanding the verbal lashing. They knew they had done wrong. Despite it, they tried their hardest to keep from vibrating with joy. They were the first team to win against Mantipas.

The Majors punished the women with maintenance duty. "You three are to clean and repair all hangars for the remainder of your time aboard Warship-23!"

Alpha-Je saluted in acceptance.

When the Majors left, Captain Nanti and other training captains entered. She dismissed Alpha Team, holding back the punished. "I shouldn't be encouraging your demonstration, but I'm impressed. It was clever use of your ship, Leera."

The redhead saluted.

"But, don't try anything like it again, unless it's a dire situation," her eyes warned. "With limited resources, we can't repair crafts indefi-nitely."

"Understood!"

The Captain shook her head, but didn't appear displeased.

Chapter Seventeen

Despite their defeat, the Mantipas operatives were in high spirits. They invited the Orarecans to socialize on their off day. They were going to show a film from their nation.

Alpha-Je couldn't join. All looked to them sympathetically as they marched towards Hangar-7.

Syralise tied a rag over her hair and whistled as they waited for instructions. Leera wandered to where damaged Mantipas ships were parked. "They have more weapons," she observed.

"We're auxiliary flight combat," Kameclara reminded.

"Yeah, but wouldn't I love to fly one of their ships," she ran a hand over a grip. "To feel how it handles."

A hangar door slid open and footsteps approached. A man dressed in a dark uniform appeared with a half-dozen poorly postured men in jumpsuits. Alpha-Je drifted into formation, out of habit. Uncertain of his uniform, they didn't salute.

"I'm warden Cashu. Are you..." he squinted at a tablet. "Alpha-Je of Orareca?"

"Yes," Kameclara responded. None of them had seen a warden before. They kept out of sight, like the inmates.

"May I ask your names?" he addressed politely.

The women responded.

When Kameclara said her name, a man in the group twitched. Her eyes darted in his direction. She immediately recognized Stanten and her heart skipped a beat.

So it wasn't a dream.

When Stanten caught her eyes, he dropped his head. All the excitement of winning against Mantipas drained away. Disorientation settled back in.

"Very good, where would you like to start?" the warden asked her, simply because Kameclara stood closest. She didn't hear him, stunned. She hadn't expected to see Stanten again, and so soon.

Syralise gave her a nudge. "Huh? Sorry, what?" Kameclara turned back to the warden, eloquence evaporating.

"I was told you needed instruction on janitorial services. Where would you like to start?"

Kameclara tried to process the words, but all she heard in her head was a whir.

Leera stepped up. "The floors will be fine."

The warden turned on his heel and shouted to the inmates. Stanten and two others shuffled forward. The warden instructed them to bring Alpha-Je to the cleaning equipment.

Stanten led the way. They went to a door and he entered a code. It slid open, revealing a large storage area. He showed them to a machine that waxed the floors. It was large enough to ride. Syralise felt tickled and called dibs, hopping onto the seat. "Hey, you think this handles like a type-a13 craft?" she snorted.

"You gotta sweep up debris before usin' it," Stanten pointed to long brooms, head still lowered. Leera grabbed one and tossed another to Kameclara. "But the floor's damaged, so you gotta patch it first."

Kameclara and Leera peered over their shoulders. The Mantipas ship Leera had sliced showed an awkward protrusion. It had carved a deep groove in the floor. Leera gulped. "How'd you do that?"

Stanten shrugged. "Haven't done it before." He picked up a can from a shelf. "I think we gotta use this." He tossed it to Leera. "I wonder what asshole did that."

Syralise sputtered into a guffaw. Kameclara couldn't help but join as Leera made an annoyed face. "Screw you!" she snapped at Stanten. Exhaling sharply, she exited the storage area, reading instructions on the can. The other inmates followed her, carrying more cans and a toolkit.

"How fitting, the 'asshole' gets to patch her own handiwork," Syralise snickered.

"It was her?" Stanten's eyes grew wide.

"Mm hmm, and you shoulda seen her in action!" Kameclara said with a little too much familiarity.

Syralise caught it immediately. "Do you… two know each other?" she asked, intrigued.

Stanten and Kameclara locked eyes for a second. Then quickly glanced away. Kameclara cleared her throat, feeling her cheeks warm. As she searched for an appropriate response, his finger accidently brushed against her hand. Kameclara shuddered, losing all grasp on words.

It was Stanten who replied, "Met once."

Syralise propped her chin with her hand and studied the two with a puckish expression. "Just once, eh?"

Leera's voice boomed from the distance, "Are you two gonna

help or not?"

Syralise snickered, "The 'asshole' summons."

Kameclara and Syralise grabbed brooms and started sweeping metal scraps from around the damaged ship. The putrid odor of sealant filled their nostrils and they breathed shallowly. Syralise lowered her hair rag over her nose and mouth. Kameclara felt grateful it made them less inclined to speak. With the looks Syralise tossed her, she couldn't be sure what questions awaited.

The other inmates hosed down the fighter ships. After they dried, they applied a clear spray. Kameclara studied the substance. It didn't appear heavy like the protective coatings she was familiar with. She sniffed, but couldn't identify a scent over the floor sealant.

"What's this stuff?" she asked the warden.

"Manico oil. I'm told it helps prevent damage from... space radiation?"

The main door to the hangar slid open and Captain Nanti entered. Alpha-Je quickly stood in line and saluted. The warden followed suit. The Captain took her time marching to their location. Her eyes were keen on observing the inmates spraying manico oil. She appeared satisfied.

"How're they doing?" she turned to the warden, nodding at Alpha-Je.

"Very well, sir."

"Good," Captain Nanti nodded. "As you were."

Kameclara and Syralise scooped the debris into a wheeled bin. Leera tested the sealant and declared it was dry. As they went to dump trash, a soft warning tone alerted that the outer hangar doors were opening. When they returned, the inner hangar doors lifted and a dozen

South Deron engineers appeared.

"Who did this?" Damas cried in exasperation, hands gripping his head, sinking to his knees. "Our masterpieces!"

Comically, Syralise pointed to Leera, not bothering to hide a grin on her face. "This 'asshole.' And it was awesome. Oh! And there's another!" She pointed to a ship parked across. Its wing also clipped by Leera.

"Maybe your team wasn't ready for live flights," Damas grumbled.

Leera shrank.

"Hey, but we won," Kameclara gave a playful simper. She caught Stanten stealing a glance at her.

"I thought Orareca's specialty was to be subtle!" Damas stomped to scrutinize the damage.

"We're adapting!" Syralise sang as she carted off the last load of metal scraps, skipping merrily.

Captain Nanti spoke with the South Deroners, explaining the situation. Once they had all the information, she left. Her eyes trailed once more over the manico oil. This time, they appeared hopeful.

~*~

Captain Nanti marched swiftly through the halls. She had a video call with Hayes. Kameclara showed progress. Ideally, the operative should've had much more field experience before this mission. Yet, the fates must've held something else in store.

She entered her office and locked the door. Taking a seat, Captain Nanti dialed Hayes. He answered from his and Ashmarah's apartment. He asked they speak quietly.

Isa was sleeping.

Captain Nanti gave her report, and finished with her usual recommendation, "I believe the operatives should be informed on the existence of magic."

Hayes sighed. "You know Hegemon General Theol's orders."

"It's a gamble not to," she gulped. "Though to be fair, I can understand why he ordained it."

Magic was commanded two ways, by emotional manipulation, or dissolution of desire. The first led down a path to dark magic. The second required an inordinate amount of discipline. There simply wasn't adequate time to train the operatives on the latter. It often took half a lifetime. As compromise, the Hegemon Generals reluctantly allowed Project S-48. Its purpose was to expose operatives to limited magic and gain a basic understanding of its nature.

"I'm glad the output of S-48 is regulated," Hayes rubbed his chin. "Using emotional manipulation to command ethereal flow is dangerous."

"It's too bad we couldn't have started training operatives decades ago on the Clear Aura Method. It's abundantly more effective," Captain Nanti sighed. "As you demonstrate."

"We couldn't have known. I learned out of my own interest." Hayes had elected to study Pinghe breathing techniques of his own accord in his youth. It greatly aided in the dissolution of desire.

"It's why we need Meliora—or rather in her incarnation," she added.

"Due to Meliora's end at Vesper's hand, the woman is heavily indebted to her. Ashmarah believes the natural resolution of their karma would give us the upper hand. "

"I'll continue to keep tabs," Captain Nanti reported. "You know I have my reservations about her too."

Hayes gave a short laugh, "I know you do, but try to act a little less suspicious. She's already confronted me about being acquainted with you."

"What's the harm in knowing you?" Nanti asked, genuinely confused.

"Nothing. But she probably feels you're hiding something. It might prevent her from trusting you fully," he explained. "I told her the truth. That you're an old friend. But she definitely senses there's more going on."

"She doesn't know we've worked with her father?"

"No," he shook his head, "and Procias doesn't want her to know. He wants her to focus on the mission, on Ima and Jema. Not Teroma."

Captain Nanti felt chills. They knew the dangers of leaving Teroma exposed. Even with the Pinghe stepping up. "Understood."

They ended their communication.

Captain Nanti leaned back, sighing agitatedly. She excelled when they focused on strategy. However, she struggled with identifying emotional cues. Perhaps her actions had been alienating Kameclara. She deliberated on a way to alleviate potential discord, without showing favoritism.

~*~

"Ah, my arms!" Leera griped, pulling herself from bed. "Who knew positioning a new engine would be so straining!" They'd assisted South Deron with repairs. A portable crane had been used to lift the engine, but help was needed to keep it in place.

"… And we've got more repairs tomorrow," Syralise groaned.

She dramatically flopped off her low bunk onto the floor.

"Worth it!" Kameclara laughed. Her shoulders also ached. "Watching Leera slice through that ship was legendary!"

Her partner blushed.

"I'm glad tomorrow's mostly reconnecting nevite crystals to the engine," Syralise rubbed her neck.

"Then back to training the day after that," Leera reminded, downcast. "I'm going to be a pile of mush."

The three sluggishly dressed for the day and stopped in the cafeteria for food. They were swarmed by Orarecan and Mantipas operatives alike. They inquired Alpha-Je of their first day of punishment.

"Damas was NOT thrilled," Syralise spoke animatedly.

The Mantipas operatives marveled at Leera's use of the ship's fins. "They were designed for defense," one said.

Another added, "Wait 'til you fly other assault models. We wanna see what you can do!"

Frobe, a lead fighter from Mantipas exclaimed, "You should have seen Bashwick's face when they towed his damaged craft to the hangar! It was like this!" Frobe clenched his jaw and squinted his eyes.

"I thought you were going to be permanently benched, for sure!" Bashwick patted Leera on the back. "But I feel better knowing we've got a flyer like you! Enemies won't stand a chance!"

"Yeah, too bad you weren't assigned to the Mantipas branch," Frobe added, "You would've been a great fit!"

Bashwick laughed, "Don't think the officers would agree after yesterday!"

Leera bantered with the operatives. With all attention on her, Syralise pulled Kameclara aside. "Who was that guy in the hangar? How did you meet?" she asked of Stanten.

"I—," Kameclara felt tongue-tied, "I dunno. It was by chance. We just... hung out."

Her partner appeared skeptical. "You two seemed *really* comfortable. I could tell by your body language." Syralise giggled, "Are you two regularly seeing each other?"

"No! Nothing like that!" Kameclara tried to put jumbled thoughts into words. She wasn't used to feeling out of control of her emotions. "I dunno," she repeated. "I felt different around him. But I barely know him. I only met him once!"

Syralise chewed her lip, thinking. After a moment, she grabbed Kameclara's hand, "Let's go!" The two skirted out the cafeteria. She waved to Leera, indicating they'd be back. Their partner nodded, busy with fellow operatives.

"I think... I've seen janitors coming off of this elevator before," Syralise took them around a tucked corner and faced a set of doors. In an adjacent storage room, an inmate was organizing a shelf. "Excuse me, on what level do you guys congregate?" she asked the man.

He blinked, baffled. "You mean where we take our grub?"

"Yah, sure!"

"Sub-deck three," he scratched his head.

"Thanks!" Syralise called the elevator.

"What are you doing?" Kameclara hissed.

"Let's find your friend."

"Um..." Kameclara's skin prickled. "I don't know if that's the best idea." There were difficult feelings about him she had yet to resolve. She felt the furthest thing from ready to see him again.

"Oh come on, just look at you," Syralise scanned her up and

down. "I've NEVER seen you like this!"

The elevator arrived. Syralise pulled her in. The man stepped into the hall, "Hey, I dunno if you're allowed down there. I mean, we're not allowed up here unless we have a pass."

"We're already in trouble anyway!" Syralise called as the doors closed.

"I met Stanten two nights ago," Kameclara explained, palms sweating. It was a reaction she didn't feel accustomed to. What happened to her usual calm? Perhaps Syralise was right. She needed to have a conversation with him, to sort it all out. Perhaps then she could mitigate these unwelcome reactions.

"Hey, if you click, you click," Syralise sounded supportive. "I knew right away I liked Nolram," she spoke of her boyfriend.

The doors opened slowly. A warden stationed outside turned with a grimace. Seeing the two women, he reeled. "May I help you?" he asked in alarm.

"We're looking for an inmate. Stanten?"

"Who are you?" he demanded.

Syralise unbuttoned the top of her cleaner's jumpsuit, flashing her standard issue operative gear. "Alpha-Je of Orareca."

The warden blinked in bafflement. "I don't know 'im, but I don't guard all shifts. If you're filing a complaint, I can take you to my CO."

"Not a complaint. We just want to talk," Kameclara spoke assertively, powering through a tumultuous stomach. Perhaps she came off too aggressive. The warden appeared even more taken aback. He called down the hall to a fellow warden. The second man strode over.

"Hey, you know a Stanten?"

"Cafeteria," he pointed to an open door at the end of the hall. "But why're you lookin' for him? Did he give you a problem?" he asked. "Doesn't sound like something he'd do."

"We're not here for trouble," Kameclara assured as Syralise dragged her away. She wondered if this Stanten was the right man. There could be another.

The moment they stepped into the cafeteria, the room immediately went silent. Syralise leaned in whispering, "When do you think was the last time any of them saw a woman?"

"Excuse me," a stern voice came from behind. Alpha-Je turned to see a commanding warden. His uniform had an extra stripe. "I must ask you to leave."

"We're not doing anything wrong," Syralise explained.

"True," the warden pulled them into the hall. "But it's been a long journey and the inmates are restless. We don't want them picking fights with operatives out of boredom."

"We understand," Kameclara cut in before her partner could respond. She grabbed her arm, "Let's go."

"Wait," Syralise stood her ground. Thinking on her feet, she added, "We were ordered to perform janitorial duties as punishment. We wanted to request Stanten to assist her," she nodded to Kameclara.

The warden wrinkled his nose, "Oh, you're of those three."

"Never mind if it's too much of a problem," Kameclara spoke. She didn't want to cause an issue.

"My next shift is laundry. I don't mind showing her," a voice came from the doorway. The three turned to see Stanten. His cheeks were deep red. Kameclara felt her palms sweat even more.

The warden tugged at his collar, thinking uncomfortably. "I suppose if you two can arrange it, but you'll be alone with him."

"Even better," Syralise whispered so only Kameclara could hear. She added in a bright voice, "Then it'd be easy for Kameclara to take him down if he tries anything!"

The warden rolled his eyes. "Try to keep it quiet. I'm only allowing this because Stanten's behavior has been exemplary. Please note it's highly against my advisement to have operatives and inmates working together without a warden."

"Noted," Syralise gave a playful salute.

The warden looked them over from the corner of his eye before marching away. Syralise waited until he was out of earshot. "What's with his attitude? Don't we outrank him on this ship?

"Yes," Stanten mumbled. A brief smirk appeared on his lips.

Syralise caught it. "Hmm... I think I like you."

Kameclara cleared her throat, "So, laundry...?"

"Yeah, I can meet you at the entrance to sub-deck one in an hour."

"Works for me," Kameclara was warming to the idea.

As she and Syralise returned to the elevator, Kameclara breathed a sigh of relief. "What were you thinking?" she asked when they were alone in the car.

Syralise nudged her. "Just doin' ya favor."

"What if Captain Nanti doesn't approve the shift in procedure? We're supposed to scrub the hangars."

"Then poor Stanten'll have to do laundry alone. But at least I tried!"

Chapter Eighteen

"You're seeing a primitive, simian beast?" Leera's eyes bugged.

"It was just laundry," Kameclara defended. They were back in their rooms after a long day. Syralise had filled Leera in about Stanten.

"Not the way you were acting," Syralise teased.

"What's gotten into you, Kame," Leera grimaced. "It's kinda… beneath you."

"Hey, she likes him, and that's alright!" Syralise defended.

Leera ran a hand through her hair, "Maybe it's just a phase?"

"I don't know what it is, and I'd appreciate it if you'd let me figure it out!" Kameclara spoke sharply.

Shame filled Leera's eyes. "Sorry. I know you're free to do what you want, but you're important to me. I just don't wanna see you doing something I'd regret if it were me."

"Thanks Lee, but you're not me," Kameclara spoke flatly.

"Whoa, we're all just havin' fun here, aren't we?" Syralise tried to ameliorate the situation.

Leera and Kameclara locked eyes. Circles of worry sat beneath the redhead's gaze. Kameclara recognized this was the woman who had fought by her side and would continue to stand by her. Leera only held her best interests at heart.

"Sorry I snapped." Kameclara couldn't explain it. She wasn't certain why she even felt the need to defend Stanten in the first place. He was the stranger, not Leera.

But it feels so much more than that.

"I'm sorry too. It's just… I dunno know anything about this guy except he's a criminal." Leera added sincerely, "But I'm sure you can look out for yourself. I didn't mean to imply otherwise."

Kameclara didn't know how to respond. She would've likely reacted the same had their positions been switched. "I appreciate your concern." She meant it.

"We should all get some sleep. We gotta help with more ship repairs tomorrow," Syralise said. The others agreed and turned in for the night.

As Kameclara curled on her bunk, her thoughts drifted to events early that day. She had gone to ask Captain Nanti for permission to change her chores to laundry. The Captain cocked an eyebrow and agreed. Then asked Kameclara to take a seat in her office.

"I'm afraid we didn't get off on the right foot," Captain Nanti explained. "Hayes informed me you were suspicious of my friendship with him."

Kameclara's shoulders tightened. "Yes, sir," she spoke honestly. "And I've noticed you observing me more than others."

Captain Nanti played with the rim of her mug. "I'm going to break a personal promise," she sighed. "In doing so, I want to build trust with you. I value you as an operative under my command. I fear your distrust of me could weaken teamwork."

"Sir?"

"I'm a low-class observer," she continued. "I've worked with your father. Hence I'm intensely curious about you." Captain Nanti went on to explain, "Procias has asked me not to speak to you of our connection. He wanted you to focus on the mission."

"Sounds like him."

"I can tell by your tone you're not satisfied." Captain Nanti set down her mug. "Your father spoke highly of you for this mission. When I was selected as Captain for your team, he called me personally and asked me to keep an eye on you."

"Captain Nanti, may I speak freely?"

"Yes."

"All operatives have noticed that officers aren't answering basic questions about this mission. Hayes seems to know more. He said he's pulled strings to get information. Did you help him?"

Her Captain's eyes widened for a moment before returning to their stoic glaze. "I did not provide Hayes with any information he wasn't already privy to. He has many friends." Her nostrils flared. "I follow military orders. I will answer any question within the clearance you've been granted."

"I see," Kameclara understood. The orders for the mission's silence must have come from high up. Possibly even the Hegemon General.

Kameclara considered her next questions carefully. "Captain. Does magic exist? Are we protecting the Goddess?" If Captain Nanti knew her father and was an observer, they must hold similar beliefs.

Captain Nanti's expression didn't change. Silence hung in the air for a long while. Finally, in a soft voice she responded, "I'm not at liberty to say."

Kameclara gulped. "I-is the Goddess on Jema now?"

"Alpha-Je," she addressed Kameclara in a professional tone, rising slowly. "I must forbid you from further questions down this path."

"Yes, sir."

In the following moments, the two shared a look that spoke volumes. Kameclara knew then, her Captain was on her side.

~*~

Stanten paced his cell, a foolish grin on his face. He'd never liked doing laundry as much as he did that day. He thought back to when he had pushed a cart of clothes off the elevator. Kameclara was leaning against the wall, waiting. He'd froze, speechless. When he found his voice, Stanten asked her to follow him. He'd checked over his shoulders many times to see if she was truly there.

For a while the two stood silently, folding towels. She seemed preoccupied by something on her mind. He tried a few times to work up the nerve and speak with her, maybe liven up spirits. Yet a lump lodged firmly in his throat.

In his jumpiness prepping the second load, he dropped an industrial-sized detergent container. It spilled across half the floor. As Stanten stooped to pick it up, he slipped. Kameclara caught his arm, but her foot had been covered in the soapy fluid. They both crashed to the ground.

Stanten froze. Terrified he'd scared her off for good.

Tinkling filled the air as Kameclara burst into laughter. The sound infected him and Stanten felt a chuckle rising.

He helped her off the ground. Kameclara then devised a game where they slid around the floor, racing to see who'd finish organizing their stack of laundry first. They zipped about, dropping items into appropriate carts.

He let her win. She probably knew, but by the way she smiled, Kameclara didn't care.

Afterwards, they cleaned up their mess. Kameclara found some of her training gear in the laundry. She created a makeshift screen with a sheet and changed. Stanten did the same. If he were back in Pudyo, some of the boys would have goaded him to peek. But he couldn't do that. Not if he wanted her to stick around.

They delivered the clean laundry to the locker rooms. Kameclara played a prank on some members of her team. She purposely placed uniforms on the wrong shelves.

"I could get in trouble for that," Stanten chuckled nervously.

"I'll make sure they know it was me," she patted his arm.

Her touch sent flashes through his body. Stanten braced himself as his legs weakened. He told himself it was because he wasn't used to attention from women.

Once everything was in order, Stanten had a few spare minutes before his shift ended. They stood idly in the laundry room. He leaned against a table and cleared his throat. "So uh... you know where we're goin' on this ship?"

"Yes," her voice didn't indicate emotion, "but I can't tell you."

He nodded, "That's fair."

There was a pause before she asked, "Can I ask why you're here?"

"You mean how I ended up with my sentence?"

"Yeah."

Stanten gripped the edge of the table. "I hurt someone real bad. They'd broke into my place... beat my mom."

"Is she alright?" Kameclara asked sympathetically. She pictured her own mother and grew upset.

Stanten shook his head, voice dropping. "Neither was the guy."

Speaking was a mistake. Years of dampened frustrations broke through, clouding his eyes with tears. Head lowered, Stanten squeezed them shut, breathing deep. He kicked himself, ashamed to appear weak before Kameclara.

Warm hands cupped his face. The tenderness felt foreign, and he lost control. Kameclara cradled him as he sputtered. For the first time, Stanten felt safe.

Chapter Nineteen

Gossip of Kameclara and Syralise asking for Stanten spread across Warship-23's lower decks. Prisoners tossed prurient comments at him. Stanten brushed them aside. The moments he shared with Kameclara were nothing he could make them understand. There was no point trying to explain.

When she spoke, Kameclara addressed a deeper part of him that'd been asleep all his life. Though Stanten had great friends like Geraldo and Mardo, they only knew him as a prisoner. Kameclara treated Stanten as if she saw him for the person he wanted to be.

With a heavy heart, he met her for one last round of laundry duty. It was nearing time for Kameclara's rotation. They'd agreed to end contact once she left.

"I really wanna thank you," Stanten spoke wholeheartedly. There was more he wanted to say, but courage escaped. It wasn't easy to find the right words. Yet he didn't want to part without at least trying to express what she meant to him.

"Oh please, your formality's making me blush," she teased.

"You're not red one bit," he spoke with sincerity. "And it's not your style."

"In that case, I need to thank you too," she mellowed. "I feel as if a part of me has been complete these last few months." She set aside a sheet. "I just want you to know, even if we never cross paths again, I'll remember you fondly."

Her words made him whole. The two worked for a while in contented silence. He was never going to feel disdain for laundry again.

"Stanten?" Kameclara asked.

"Yeah?"

"All joking aside, why'd you think we've met?" her voice took on a silvery quality and the question caught him off guard. Something about her had changed.

Stanten fathomed she felt the racing of his heart. He pondered for a moment as he studied her face. There was something earnest, as if the most vulnerable part of her had asked the question. He needed to be careful with his response and searched for something inspiring he could leave with her.

Stanten's thoughts went to a phrase Mardo shared from the Temple of Ia. "All I can say is what I've come to believe. As living, breathing creatures, we all strive for meaningful connections." He stopped folding. "Ya know, 'cause people forget what it's like to be seen."

"Yeah… I know what you mean," she took his hand in response.

The warmth made him brave. Stanten added truthfully, "I can't speak for you, but I've seen ugly things that people do. It's hard for me to hold onto hope for the future." He gulped. "But meeting you. I think I feel the meaningful connection people search for. I thought I'd never have that." His voice grew soft. "If I were to die tomorrow, I'd be happy, simply because you've seen me."

Kameclara placed a hand behind his neck and pulled him close.

"I'll never forget you either."

His cheeks warmed as he lowered his head. There were three words he desperately wished to say, but they snared in his throat. Stanten wanted to open up completely, but didn't know how. As her fingers stroked the back of her neck, he could only hope Kameclara sensed what he felt.

"I..." he tried anyway, *love you...*

Courage failed. is b

"I'll miss you," he spoke instead.

Her breath swept across his cheek, "Me too." She gently wiped his tears before pulling away. "Keep on making meaningful connections."

Their shift ended soon after. She was to transfer in a few days, but had served her punishment. She wasn't going to be doing laundry anymore.

Stanten saw her off. She entered the elevator and turned to face him. Hands clasped before her, Kameclara's eyes flash longingly as the doors closed.

Stanten locked up the laundry room and trudged to his cell. He wanted to replay their meeting and let the pleasant feelings linger.

To his surprise, there was a message waiting on his communications panel. He wondered if there was a special assignment. It happened sometimes when there weren't enough on-duty inmates to handle a task. Those with a clean record were awarded commissary for assisting.

He opened the message without much thought. "Hey Stanten," a grating voice filled his room. "I wanna start off by apologizing 'bout the run-in in the cafeteria. I was only testing ya... to see if you grew into a tough bastard."

Stanten blinked in confusion before resentment set in. This wasn't a message assigning him a chore. The voice belonged to Tivan. He must've hacked into the communications system.

"Anyway, forget the whole thing. I just want you to know you're my son and I'm proud of ya. I hope to see you around once we get to where we're going."

Stanten deleted the message. His pleasant mood soured as Tivan's words repeated in his mind.

"I don't have a father..." Angrily, he punched a wall, leaving a dent. He'll get in trouble for that, but didn't care.

Stanten knew he looked very little like his mother. It meant he must look like his father. He and Tivan were as different as could be.

He paced restlessly. Once he reached the far wall, he walked back and punched the same place. His knuckles bled.

"I don't have a Goddess-damned father!" he shouted.

~*~

Alpha-Je lounged in their room after a long day of cleaning. Curious over Stanten, Syralise threw a slew of questions, most pertaining to his background. Kameclara answered the non-personal ones the best she could. It was the least she could do since she chose to serve her punishment with him instead of her partners.

Leera felt uncomfortable to hear he was convicted of manslaughter. She didn't approve of how Stanten lost control.

"But his mother, Lee!" Syralise defended. "I might've done the same. Besides, we're trained to kill people too. Does it make us wrong?"

"We protect Teroma," Leera said.

"Yes, to protect our *home*," Syralise said in a compelling voice. "He was doing the same."

"He went overboard. He didn't stop," Leera argued.

"We're not supposed to stop either until our mission's complete." Operatives were trained to adapt infinitely until success or ordered to cease.

"But we're calculating. His was a crime of passion."

"I wouldn't worry about it," Kameclara cut in. "I won't see him again. There's no future for us," she unsuccessfully tried to hide gloominess. The words were more for her than her partners.

Syralise and Leera exchanged a look. They hadn't noticed Kameclara growing upset. It rarely happened.

Leera hopped onto her bunk and gave an apologetic squeeze. Syralise sat on the other side and draped an arm around her shoulders. Kameclara gave a tired smile. She felt conflicted. There was a mission before her. She never had a problem prioritizing over emotions before.

"I think you two really shared something," Syralise spoke tenderly.

Kameclara gave a lopsided grin. "Good to know. Now if only I can process this … Maybe power through it…"

"Well, we've got a few ans," Leera moved a piece of Kameclara's hair from her eyes.

"Let's get some rest," Kameclara said. "At least when we rotate to Warship 24, we won't be punished with janitorial duties anymore."

Syralise chuckled, playfully shoving Leera, "Unless this one gets more ideas!"

~*~

On a regular day, Stanten finished a long shift and went to grab food at the ration station. After making his selection, he walked towards an empty seat, minding his own business.

Tivan and his gang cut off his path. Stanten felt his muscles stiffen. His eyes swept side to side and saw no allies. His hand clutched the tray tight, ready to turn it into a weapon if needed.

Four men surrounded him. Stanten's eyes hardened, preparing for trouble.

"Where's your girlfriend? The one you've been actin' all high and mighty 'bout?" Tivan stepped to him. His gray beard shook as he spoke, belittling Stanten.

"Don't want any trouble," Stanten's teeth clenched. He took deep breaths to keep his rage under wraps. The last thing he needed was a fight to mar his record.

"Trouble?" Tivan laughed tauntingly.

It dawned on Stanten he'd once seen Tivan in a forbidden area, near the laundry room. He hadn't thought about the incident in a while. It would give Tivan motive to silence him. Stanten hadn't responded to his claim to being his son, clearly a move to manipulate him under Tivan's control. The man could mean to kill him today.

Tivan shoved Stanten's shoulder. "When you admit to being my bitch of son and do what I say, there won't be any."

Stanten growled, "I don't have a father."

One of Tivan's friends brought down his fist, knocking Stanten's tray out of his hands. It clattered, causing food to go up in a colorful spray. There was a taut moment as the cafeteria went silent. All eyes trained on them. Stanten focused on pulling his breath deep into his gut. It helped control the urge to knock out Tivan's teeth.

The man stepped close, "How's about it, SON?"

Tivan stood an inch away. Stanten stopped breathing to avoid his rotten breath.

The older man's lip curled, "We both know what has to happen today… Just take it like the little bitch you are."

If Stanten would've taken breaths against the putrid odor, perhaps he could've soothed himself. Instead, his anger flashed. His hands moved before he could stop them, shoving Tivan.

The large man stumbled, eyes filling with a crazed look. He shrugged, laughing. After a moment, Tivan straightened himself and turned as if to walk away.

Stanten tightened his fists, knowing better than to drop his guard.

Tivan spun abruptly, fist launching at Stanten. The younger man caught the punch and returned it. People in the cafeteria crowded to cheer. Tivan reared from the unexpected slug. He stood for a moment, rubbing his chin. Stanten brought his fists to guard his face, highly aware of the three men surrounding him.

"Whoa, cool it!" Mardo appeared beside Stanten. "None of us want this."

"Yeah we do!" someone crowed.

"Seriously, let's just walk away," Mardo held out his hands amicably.

Without warning, one of Tivan's men slashed. Mardo pulled Stanten back as the edge of an object narrowly missed his eye. They meant to kill him.

Stanten felt cornered and refused to go down without a fight. He charged the closest man. The sharp object came at him again. Stanten grabbed the wrist and twisted, popping the joint. The weapon clattered to the ground as the man howled in pain.

There was a mess of arms and legs as Stanten found himself restrained by Tivan's other two men. One tall, one short. He tried to jerk his limbs loose and charge Tivan.

Mardo punched the tall man in the face, allowing Stanten's fist to find an opening. It struck Tivan in the chin. It'd been ans since Stanten's last fight, but the skills he'd honed on the streets of Pudyo never left.

Stanten landed a second punch into Tivan's mouth and felt blood gushing over his knuckles.

A hand grabbed Stanten's shoulder and he instinctively found the thumb. Turning, Stanten used the movement to unlock the grip and whip the attacker's arm. It resulted in a dislocated shoulder. A squeal followed as the short man fell away.

Mardo grappled against the man with a broken wrist. He seemed to be doing well. The tall crony had Stanten's arms pinned to his side. Tivan picked up the sharp object and lurched to strike.

Stanten was ready. His foot flew into Tivan's face and followed with another to his throat. Using the same foot, he swung back, striking the knee of his restrainer. The tall man dropped with a whelp. Stanten silenced the cry with a fist to his nose. The tall man flew backwards. Where he landed, he stayed down.

Stanten rolled his shoulders and cracked his joints. He recalled the thugs of Pudyo complaining about him being fast. Looked like it still came in handy.

Stanten marched to where Tivan sprawled on the ground. He grabbed him by the collar and shook him. Tivan's limbs bounced like a rag doll. "Leave me alone. You mess with me or any of my friends, I'll KILL you."

Fear seeped Tivan's eyes as he stared back. His jaw bulged in defiance, but his head bobbed the slightest of nods. Stanten held for a moment longer to get his point across, then released Tivan's collar.

As he rose, Stanten felt his body spasm. The room spun as his cheek planted to the ground. From his position, he saw two sets of wardens' boots. Dangling beside one was the rod of an electroshock weapon. Stanten felt his hands tied behind him and a prick entered his neck. He lost consciousness.

~*~

Stanten awoke in a dark, narrow cell. He sputtered a sigh of relief to discover he was alive. The fight with Tivan was the worst act of violence that'd occurred on the ship. They could've jettisoned him while he was out.

No sound reached his ears, but that didn't bother him. Stanten never minded silence or loneliness.

The tight cell allowed for minimal movement. It must've been an isolation room. He'd heard about them. Stanten eased to seated position, rubbing the gunshot scar on his torso. It felt tender, probably from the shock.

Leaning against the wall, his feet found themselves near the toilet, which was little more than a hole. Emotions he couldn't comprehend coursed through him. He wasn't sure if he should be grateful or cynical. If they were planning to jettison him, he would've preferred it to happen while he was unconscious. Finding himself alive allowed for shaky hope. That was torturous.

Time seemed to slow. The only indication of its passage were the meals he was served. With next to no light, Stanten couldn't tell if he was awake or dreaming most of the time.

It was around the ninth or tenth meal when he felt he was losing his mind. Stanten beat the walls, begging to be let out… even if it meant death. He couldn't take it anymore.

No one came.

He fell into a haze. Often dragging his head along the walls to pass the time.

Then, he began banging it. Just so he could feel something.

Perhaps he'd thrashed his skull too hard. Stanten started to hear a voice.

It rose like a memory, long forgotten. Sometimes it trilled a song. Other times it spoke methodically, as if detailing difficult decisions. Mostly, it spoke openly, confessing feelings.

Stanten covered his ears, but the voice continued.

"Have I lost it?" he asked.

There was no answer. Only the voice, seemingly belonging to a young woman.

He learned she loved wistra flowers—something he'd never heard of. Her favorite gown was blue, and herbs could be used to heal most ailments. She missed her mother too, and had no idea if she were alive.

Sometime after meal twenty, there was a creak. As light cascaded over Stanten, the voice withdrew. He kept his head down, ears covered, attempting to hold onto his invisible companion.

A nudge came at his side. "You're free ta go."

We could spend eternity together…

Then, nothing. No more whispers of wistra flowers.

"Hey you!" a warden barked. "Get outta here!"

Stanten blinked, finally gazing up. The door was open. He rose on rubbery legs and stepped into the hall. Cuffs were placed on his wrists as he was led down turn after turn.

A heavy door opened before him. Dazed, Stanten entered and found himself before the head warden. He struggled to process his surroundings.

The surly man scrolled through documents on a tablet. Without looking at Stanten, head warden Groum lectured, "I've read every inmate's record at last three times and know everything there's to know about you all aboard this ship." He shook a finger, "You, I'm surprised with. I didn't peg you for a troublemaker."

Groum set aside his reading and folded his hands. "We conducted an investigation. Nearly everyone in the cafeteria vouched for you. Said Tivan started the fight." The warden huffed. "Either you've got a lot of friends, or lotta people hate Tivan." He faced Stanten squarely, "Or... they liked the way you fight and want to see it again."

Stanten gulped. Sweat beaded his brow.

The head warden's eyes narrowed, "Make sure you don't."

"Yes, sir." His stomach voiced its opinion with a growl.

Groum picked up his tablet again. "I'm gonna let you get back to your duties with a warning, but I'm only going to say this once," The warden's eyes flickered at Stanten, "If I ever catch you in any kind of trouble again, I'm gonna kick you off this ship... like I did with the other four sorry asses. Is that understood?"

"Th- thank you sir," he mumbled, blood draining from his face.

"Now get back to work!" Groum waved.

Stanten stumbled out of the office, hardly noticing the other warden taking off his cuffs.

He made his way towards his room to check for assignments.

His legs trembled and he needed to rest against a wall. His mind raced, wondering if Groum meant Tivan and his gang were jettisoned. If that were the case, Stanten had come close to being executed too.

"Stanten!" a familiar voice called.

It was Geraldo. "Hey man, how are ya?"

"You okay? You're white as a ghost!"

"Yeah. Did you hear what happened with Tivan and his gang?" Stanten asked.

"Oh yeah, they had it coming. They were causin' trouble with all sorts of other people too. It was only a matter of time before they were sent to another ship," Geraldo informed.

Stanten stared in confusion, "They weren't jettisoned?"

"Nah, these warships need workers. They'd have to do some really bad things to be jettisoned," Geraldo said. "Their gang got split up."

Stanten blinked through cold sweat, feeling stupid.

"Hey, but you're on Warden Groum's watch list now," Geraldo said with urgency. "You'd better keep your head down."

Stanten nodded, rubbing a sleeve over his face. The knots in his stomach didn't ease. He searched for the soothing voice.

I'm here, it emerged for a moment before receding back into the fog of distant memories. It was enough. Stanten's nerves steadied.

Chapter Twenty

Kameclara knocked aside a chunk of habbadite clay with the tip of her assault rifle. A familiar sizzle came from behind, raising her hairs. Her foot pivoted and she rolled left, quickly recovering to her feet. A bolt of electricity struck where she stood a second before. Two West Jebbun operatives peered from behind a boulder. Project S-48 gloved their hands.

A loose rock levitated. "Look out!" Kameclara shoved Syralise. A rock nicked her partner's shoulder, leaving a scratch.

Kameclara aimed her rifle at the opponents as Alpha-Je moved through their formation. It was her lead, and Kameclara had chosen offensive strategy zeta-mip. Leera was getting into position.

She fired two stun rounds. The second opponent motioned his arms in a circle and a shield formed around him. Kameclara's shots struck the shield and fizzled. She uttered a curse, but remained optimistic. They were merely creating a diversion.

Leera soundlessly approached the opponents from behind. She dropped low and tripped them with a swipe. As one fell, she kicked him in the back. He tumbled down the slope as Syralise stabbed the other with a simulated blade. His vest glowed red. Critical hit.

Kameclara threw her virtual knife as the tumbling man caught himself. Too late for him. His gear lit up as well.

The eliminated dropped their weapons and exited the field. They were training in direct combat. The Captains encouraged the use of S-48, but Alpha-Je preferred conventional tools of war.

Syralise pulled out dual handguns, rushing towards an oncoming West Jebbun operative. He waved his hands. A gust of wind propelled forth. Syralise slid to the ground, avoiding the attack. She fired upwards, striking her target.

Three West Jebbun operatives charged, generating shields with S-48. Leera pulled out a cane, a foot in length. She snapped it against her leg and it grew to seven feet. It was her favorite weapon, the electric staff. With it in raised, she met the opponents head-on. Kameclara followed, adhering to their predetermined attack strategy. She narrowed her eyes, observing West Jebbun's behavior.

Leera dashed left as Syralise went right. The three zigzagged uphill, giving fire. They met their opponents in the middle. Leera slid and shot electricity from her staff. It hit a shield at a narrow angle. The electricity snaked through and stunned the operative. He fell, eliminated.

Shots do sometimes make it past the S-48 deflectors. Perhaps it's the angle of entry. If a ship doesn't approach an atmosphere correctly, it'd bounce off or burn up.

Kameclara tested her theory, firing at a West Jebbuner. She watched her stuns fizzle. Syralise came from the side and fired from two different degrees. The second shot made it through and the opponent lit up.

"We've gotta find the right angles to get through the shield," Kameclara radioed.

"Copy," her partners responded in unison.

More West Jebbuners appeared and Alpha-Je scattered, dividing their attention. Kameclara took a leap from a boulder.

Instead of landing, her feet flew into the air.

"Breathe dear!" she heard a dove-like voice.

She craned her neck to see a familiar form donning a mischievous grin. Dauntless, Hayes stood amidst the melee without protective gear. A palm faced Kameclara, controlling her body. He dropped his hand and she rushed to the ground. Kameclara landed in a tumble and nearly lost her rifle.

She reeled. Never before had her grip loosened on her weapon. "I'm taking Hayes!" Kameclara radioed. "Sy, take command."

"Roger," Syralise responded.

"What's he doing here?" Leera mumbled.

Hayes reminded sweetly, "The only way to beat me is to clear your mind." He raised his hand and Kameclara felt herself rising from the ground. Seeking options, she aimed her rifle down and fired. She hoped its propulsion would jerk her from his hold.

It didn't work. Instead she tumbled awkwardly, stopping a few feet from the ground.

A large rock flew through the air. Kameclara took the opportunity and fired against it. The force pushed her about fifteen feet from Hayes. She banked on increased distance weakening his hold.

But his grip didn't falter. She couldn't get her feet on the ground.

Hayes appeared wide open. Kameclara pulled the trigger. A smile crept across his lips. A deflection shield arced between them and her stun rounds were ineffective.

"Dammit!" she moaned under her breath. "Gotta find the right angle."

Her body snapped sideways as he tossed her. Kameclara landed hard. Scrambling to her feet, she saw Hayes closing in. His shield gleamed, larger than any she'd seen. "It's at least a twenty feet radius," she commented with awe.

Kameclara pushed off the ground, sprinting sideways before he could grab hold again. To her dismay, she realized he hadn't even tried to attack. If Hayes went on the offensive, he could easily eliminate her.

Still on the move, Kameclara angled her weapon, finding the degree a hunch told her Syralise used earlier. With determination, she squeezed the trigger.

She held her breath, watching the round pierce Hayes' shield. Kameclara felt a cheer rise in her throat.

It quickly evaporated as she slid to a halt behind a boulder. She'd been dashing, so she couldn't be sure. But Kameclara swore Hayes emitted a fuzzy glow, then streaked sideways. His form returned to focus about a foot to the left; eyes heavier, stance weaker.

"Impossible! Teleportation's impossible!" she exclaimed. Before Kameclara could wrap her head around what she'd witnessed, she found herself in the air.

When the ground rushed towards her, Kameclara didn't tuck and brace. Perhaps it was the shock of what she'd witnessed, but she instinctively sucked in a lung-full of air. Closing her eyes, she focused breathing through her lower spine. A tingle traveled through her body as she warmed.

"Good," Hayes called, his voice raspy with exhaustion.

Leera's voice came to mind as Kameclara recalled Pinghe breathing exercises. "Your breath is your relationship with your body, and a link to the nevino sequence." Kameclara wondered how the nevino sequence was supposed to help her in this situation. So little was known about it.

Air swished rebelliously against her skin. Kameclara opened her eyes a crack to see Hayes waiting patiently. She grappled with remaining relaxed. With each inhale, a gentle hum pressed through her body.

Closing her eyes again, Kameclara shut out sounds of battle. She did something counterintuitive to an operative's training: She let go of the need to win.

Breath after breath washed through her, and the world fell away.

Something hard touched the bottom of her feet. She gazed down and gasped in pleasant surprise. She stood on the ground.

"Time!" Captain Nanti called. The sounds of weapons and shattering rocks ceased. Opposing teams pulled each other off of the ground.

Kameclara peered to Hayes with inquisitiveness. "What're you doing here?"

He stuck out a leg in a svelte brace. "Ankle injury. I'm barred from physical training for a few days." He approached, hobbling. "I thought I'd visit my favorite operative!" he draped an arm across her shoulders. Exhaling sharply, he appeared spent.

"You're allowed to show up during a battle session? No questions asked?" Kameclara scoffed, "Who are you, Hayes?"

"Relax," he rolled his eyes. "I told you, Nanti and I go way back. Since Orareca is training against S-48, she figured it'd be nice if I helped."

They exited the field and Hayes saluted Captain Nanti. The woman's eyes showed of knowing. Kameclara could only guess at what. She wanted to ask Hayes about him appearing to teleport, but though better of it. It could've been an optical illusion as her round pieced his shield.

Leera and Syralise joined them. "That… was different," Syralise's eyes were wide. "I don't recall North Deroners having so much control with S-48." They'd witnessed Kameclara's skirmish.

"It's because I'm the best," Hayes beamed with pride, "*And* I know how to clear my mind."

"If I tried to force anything, you'd get control," Kameclara surmised.

"You used the Clear Aura Method?" Leera asked Kameclara.

"Yes."

She appeared proud, "The Pinghe also call it 'Stillness in the Storm.'"

Hayes clapped, "I love hearing it from the source!" His eyes flicked sadly to Leera for a moment. Kameclara couldn't decipher its meaning.

The redhead didn't catch it, going on to explain, "Thoughts naturally emit vibrations. They go into your aura. The Stillness in the Storm helps you alleviate them."

Hayes held up his hands and flexed his fingers. "With S-48, we can manipulate thick auras."

"But when you lost control of me…" Kameclara started.

"You successfully cleared your energy," Leera grinned.

"It's about self-mastery," Hayes added. "No matter what chaos is bombarding you outside, inwardly you're able to keep cool." He patted her shoulder. "When Syralise told me how you're perpetually level-headed, I knew it was a matter of time before you'd get it!"

Kameclara listened with keen interest. She cocked her head at Hayes, "Is S-48 hinting at the nature of the opponent we'll face on

Jema? You said you pulled a favor to view operatives' files. I've been wondering… what if you'd found out more?"

Hayes' lips puckered indignantly, staring with affront.

Kameclara didn't back down.

He turned to Syralise and Leera. Their eyes also hungered for information. He weighed his words carefully. "Yes… but I trust your discretion." He glowered, "All three of you."

The women nodded, exchanging unsatisfied looks. Kameclara debated whether to push for more. In the end, she decided against it. For now.

The teams retreated, done for the day. Alpha-Je waited until they were back in their room to discuss Hayes' words. "Kameclara, what do you think about Hayes?" Syralise asked.

"I think there's more than meets the eye." She paused. "But I believe his intentions can be trusted."

Syralise nodded, "He didn't have to say anything. I'm glad he did. I wonder how much he knows."

"He said he grew up with Captain Nanti," Kameclara recalled.

Syralise frowned. "Nanti doesn't strike me as an officer who'd mingle with an operative."

Leera chimed in, "Maybe he's not who he says he is. Maybe Hayes' is a high-ranking officer, assessing us undercover."

"Perhaps," Syralise didn't appear convinced. "Though the few times I hung out with him, I didn't get that vibe."

"I had a short conversation with our Captain on Warship-23. I flat out asked her about our mission." Kameclara didn't mention her questions about magic, or the Goddess. Mostly out of the promise to her father.

"Oh?" Leera appeared intrigued.

"Yeah, but to sum it up, she indicated she wasn't allowed to tell us anything," Kameclara sighed.

"I think silence is very telling," Syralise chewed her lip.

Kameclara pondered her meeting with Ashmarah. There was also the promise to protect Isa. "Remember when Hayes brought me to meet his sister?" Kameclara asked.

"Yeah," Syralise responded.

"He asked me to look after his daughter, should anything happen to him. Either he's overly cautious or he's hinting something about the challenges on the inner planets."

Leera shook her head, "All this speculation's giving me a headache. Let's focus on facts." She sat up, "Our mission is to secure Seu and bring down Vesper and her army."

"… She took over a planet," Kameclara rubbed her cheek. "I know we're planet defenders and all, but the fact is, we've never gone on the offensive."

"I'm sick of conjecture too. We're Alpha-Je," Syralise cut in with no-nonsense. "We can excel at this mission because we don't need all the facts. Operatives are trained to expect anything and everything." Her stomach grumbled. "Here's a fact. I'm hungry. Let's go eat."

~*~

Orareca 14.241 ans

With a heavy heart, Procias encoded his last transmission to Ashmarah. He was giving a final update of Teroma's situation. After he hit the "send" button, he gazed out his window. The sun was rising. Pale blue washed into the black expanse of starlit sky.

He sighed. Teroman sunrises were truly beautiful. Since the planet was a great distance from its sun, it never became too light. The brightest stars could be seen at all times, and they danced in a perpetual watercolor sky.

This was the last sunrise he'd see for a while. Procias took a moment and committed it to memory.

After shutting down his computer for the last time, he flicked "the switch." All information became permanently lost.

He gathered a few personal belongings and joined his wife and sons in the living room.

Before long, a car arrived. They piled in and left for a top-secret, deep underground military facility.

Chapter Twenty-One

Three years passed since Vesper's acquisition of Calio and Songbird. Since then, she'd scoured every morsel of information she could lay her eyes on, concerning Seu. Their farming practices and ecological priorities she'd learned inside and out. But regarding the knowledge she sought—their military and technological advances—she uncovered nothing.

Vesper's desperation climbed to new heights when startling information reached her.

Her communications council's usual duties were to relay airwave messages to and from Ima. Sometimes, they caught stray transmissions from Seu, but nothing of value. Recently, they intercepted a heavily coded message. When the information was finally extracted, it hinted at a flotilla of ships en route to Ima. They reported it immediately.

Vesper marched briskly into the Sacred Chamber. Master sorcerers and her Generals followed, tripping over themselves not to be caught in the closing portal. Vesper had summoned them urgently. She didn't wait for her subjects to be seated before roaring, "What's the meaning of this?"

Her Generals and Master sorcerers tugged at their collars. The room grew sultry as Vesper emanated fury.

"Where did they come from?" Her hands quivered. "Somebody has to know something!"

One of the Generals stood, "They could've been launched from Seu before the invasion of Jema."

"There's no record of a launch this magnitude! Fifty ships! Someone in Calio and Songbird must've seen something and reported it!" she fumed. Her communications council had scoured records.

The General fearfully took his seat.

Sessa stood, gripping the table. "I can do an in-depth reading," she spoke reluctantly. She didn't look forward to being bedridden for weeks. It was a result of using her seer abilities to the fullest.

"What are you waiting for?" Vesper snapped. She sat heavily into her chair.

Sessa steeled herself. Pulling a breath deep into her body, a thumb lifted methodically to her teeth. She drew blood. No one dared twitch as she drew a symbol on her forehead. It was a fork facing right. A long tail trailed left, indicating life comes from one direction, but could go many.

Her hand drifted back to the table. Sessa shut her eyes and the air around her froze. A wispy chant dripped from her lips. It snaked throughout the room, discovering every crevice. Syncopated words increased in volume and onlookers gawked at her rare gift.

Sessa's body stiffened as she tapped into an esoteric source. The chant ended abruptly.

The air thinned. Time seemed to stand still. The Master commanded, "Show me what's the be!"

Without warning, her hands clawed the table, leaving long marks. Sessa's head dipped sharply, nearly smacking her nose. Her angular shoulders poked high. "My connection's weak," she rasped.

Sessa pushed violently from the table. Her body pitched sharply to the side, seizing as her shriek shattered the room. Her chair fell backwards, her tumbling beside it. "I see them," a hollow voice moaned. The Master writhed in agony. "These ships… are like nothing we've… encountered before."

Sessa's chest heaved rapidly, as if they couldn't fill with air. "They're not from Jema… not from Ima. They come… from the stars…" Her body contorted. "A region we've never traversed. They're trouble."

"What nature of attack do they have?" Vesper barked.

A guttural sound emitted. Sessa's eyes rolled back, "Nothing we've ever seen."

Vesper growled, "It must be a terrible secret of Seu." It was the only kingdom outside her control. "In memories I've consumed, I've caught glimpses of protected knowledge behind their walls."

The room remained still as Vesper slouched. Wary of her foul mood, no one wished to become the brunt of her rage. A hand shielded her eyes as a vein throbbed.

"How long until these ships arrive?" Vesper finally demanded.

"No sooner than a year, no later than two," Sessa's throat tightened. She scrunched into another position, nearly bending in half. "Can't… hold… longer." A lasting wail escaped as Sessa's limbs stretch taunt. As the sound diminished to a rattle, her body fell limp. She breathed unsteadily, eyes fluttering.

Vesper turned to her Generals, "Ready the troops and dragons. We attack Seu in three weeks."

"Yes, your highness," they spoke in unison. The Generals discretely exchanged apprehensive expressions. The sorceress ordered them to lay siege on the oldest kingdom of Jema. They had no affirmed knowledge of its strengths or weaknesses. It appeared a suicide mission.

Vesper waved disdainfully at Sessa, "Get her out of here."

Three Master sorcerers moved to Sessa's decrepit form. Fervir used a spell and the unconscious woman levitated.

"Dismissed," Vesper circled her arms and the portal flew open.

She waited until her council left before sealing herself in the Sacred Chamber.

Vesper stormed to an entrance hidden by shadows. It was a portal to her workshop. The door snapped open, nearly ripping from its hinges. Vesper's heavy aura pushed against torches, nearly putting them out. She drifted to the center of the room, groaning. Her eyes swept around. The workshop was a replica of her former one in the palace of Priletoria. She'd even salvaged some of her old tools from the wreckage. It was her place of retreat, to be alone with her thoughts and gain perspective.

"What's the point of all this? Am I only pushing forward because I've come so far?" A hopelessness lingered at the edge of her senses.

Vesper approached her worktable. She kept a simple bench where she could have opted for a throne. It allowed her to move about freely. She seated herself. "These people headed to Ima," she shook her head, "What're they planning?"

She considered Sessa's words. "What if it's a lie? Sessa could be working with Seu to divert my attention." It was why Vesper had ordered the siege on Seu in three weeks. If Seu hoped she was going to be distracted by newcomers, they were wrong. It merely forced her hand against them.

"And if these strangers aren't a fabrication, the more reason to take Seu. I must find their secret. If it's a weapon, I'll need it at my disposal." Vesper leaned her elbows on the table. The soft glow of candlelight caused shadows to dance. They flickered at the mercy of disturbances in the air. Vesper related to the flames. She wasn't amused by her current situation, at the mercy of uncontrolled elements.

Anger flashed and her arm swiped across her table, knocking vials and powders to the ground. A sudden throbbing set behind her eyes. She eased the palm of her hand to her forehead.

"Just one more kingdom stands between my control of two worlds. These ships are nothing compared to that." Yet as she spoke those words, doubt crept forward. Vesper trembled, struggling to keep it at bay.

~*~

Carpecillero- 2216 Iman Year

Unadine and Erilph's camp nestled deep in the blue forests of Carpecillero. A barrier spell concealed them. The abandoned East Palace sat to the south, overgrown and hidden. The only indication that a large structure once stood was by the trees. They were younger than their surrounding growth.

The two sorcerers scavenged deep into the palace to find usable implements. It was an exhausting task. Refugees who'd escaped Vesper's reign had already picked the site clean. Only using covert magic were they able to come up with anything for cooking and basic needs.

Maza stayed with them. She had hidden herself in commoners' robes and boarded the same escape dragon. Unadine and Erilph had sensed magic aboard. They didn't immediately investigate, being preoccupied with protecting the flight from Vesper's attacks. It wasn't until they had crashed on Ima and were swarmed by Vesper's soldiers, did Maza reveal herself. She aided Unadine and Erilph in pushing back aggressors. Together, the three Masters fled into the blue forests of Carpecillero.

Maza seemed particularly perturbed. Once they had constructed a makeshift safe haven, she made a request. Maza asked Unadine and Erilph to guard her as she placed herself under a sleeping spell. They felt put off by the irregular wish. However, they agreed.

"She's Vesper's mother," Unadine informed Erilph as they enclosed Maza's body in a shell. It allowed light to pass through, becoming invisible.

"Vesper's magical signature does remind me of her." They lifted their palms and the shell rose into the trees, hovering safely from accidental discovery. "Bruno must've been the father. He was extremely talented as well."

"Do you think Maza's distress stems from the knowledge of what her daughter's done?"

Erilph pondered the question at length. "I would feel conflicted in her shoes, so yes." He frowned, "If I weren't afraid of pushing her too far, I'd've tried to convince Maza to stand against Vesper."

"Agreed," Unadine took a seat by the fire. They'd built a small, open-faced oven. "She must come to a conclusion on her own."

"Let's hope she awakens to stand against her daughter." Erilph's sighed weakly.

Unadine stared into crackling flames. "What if she decides the opposite?"

Erilph lowered across from her. "We both know how strong
she is." His brow furrowed, peering into the branches. "Unnaturally
strong."

"Just like her daughter. Should they come to battle, I don't think
any of us would fare well."

Erilph appeared disturbed, "Then if it should come down to it,
let's hope the remaining Masters side with us." Then added, "Though
the younger ones probably don't know of their relation."

"I'm fairly certain Ginevra does," Unadine commented. "She was
a Master when the Maza's probationary hearing came around… about
her relationship with Bruno."

Erilph shook his head. "But even with six of us… We don't stand
a chance against the two of them."

A rustling in the leaves startled Unadine and Erilph. "Who's
there," Erilph challenged. He rose to his feet, slower than he would've
liked. He exchanged a fearful glance with Unadine. "How did anyone
get past the barrier?"

"You can relax, Erilph! It's just little old me," a voice chuckled. A
shriveled man dropped down from a tree and landed before them.

Erilph startled, arm raised, "H-how do you know my name?" he
eyed the visitor suspiciously.

"Well, young man, that's no way to greet an elder," he teased, rat-
tling a finger.

Erilph felt taken aback. Nearly ninety years old, to be called
"young" was as uncommon as it was absurd.

"Oh, relax!" the old man waved his cane playfully, "You might've
heard of me. My name's Ottokip."

Erilph and Unadine gasped. "Grandmaster Ottokip was a terrible man who nearly destroyed the school of sorcery! He consumed half the Masters and was banished," Unadine informed curtly.

"I don't understand how we're to relax if you claim to be him," Erilph braced for the unexpected.

"Besides, that was hundreds of years ago," Unadine grumbled skeptically.

The old man's innocent expression melted into one of despondency. "Is that what they're saying of me?" He reached into a satchel he took from his back. Unadine and Erilph tensed as they prepared for a showdown. To their surprise, the old man produced pears. "Let's eat and I'll tell my story."

Disarmed by the gesture, Unadine and Erilph sat cautiously. Ottokip joined them by the fire. Slowly, each accepted a fruit from him, but didn't eat. They watched as he took a hearty bite through orange skin. "Oh my! So crisp!" he giggled and rolled his head. Juice dripped from his mouth into his beard.

Erilph and Unadine waited as the strange man finished eating. He tossed the core in to the air and snapped his fingers. It vanished in a puff of smoke. Ottokip glanced around for a moment with a dazed look in his eyes. "Where am I?"

Unadine and Erilph weren't sure how to respond. Unadine eventually said, "You're in the blue forests of Carpecillero."

"Oh! Yes, yes!" he chuckled, slapping his knee. "I was going to tell you my story!" Ottokip settled comfortably and folded his hands deep in his robes. In a hypnotic voice, he explained the foundations of Jeman magic instead. "It's a gift from the Seed of Life. The Seed changed spirals in our body. It allowed souls to tap into the ethereal."

He noticed an insect on his sleeve. Ottokip allowed it to crawl onto his fingers. "The gift was meant to help us adapt to difficult conditions. We could survive icy regions and scorching ones. Then, some people discovered they could change the elements around them. That is, if they'd spent a lifetime becoming one with their surroundings."

"Yes, and incantations help focus that power through repeating waves of sound." Erilph grew irate. "We know all this. Tell us YOUR story."

Ottokip blinked, "Wasn't I doing so?"

Erilph felt unsure how to respond.

Ottokip didn't notice. "People were growing ill on Jema. The Seed of Life made a single return and gave a greater degree of her breath to twenty-four people who could connect with their surroundings. They became the Master sorcerers." He yawned. "They could reach across realms and, in a limited manner, channel energy not found in our worlds."

"We became unrivaled in the world of mortals," Unadine sighed, hurrying him along. She looked to Erilph guardedly. What Ottokip spoke was accurate. If only they could identify his motive for appearing.

"Unfortunately, after the Seed receded from Jema, some Masters grew corrupt." Tears beaded as Ottokip sputtered pitifully, "If I hadn't absorbed all of those Masters hundreds of years ago, Songbird would've fallen into an age of despair. Jema would've disappeared altogether." His lips quivered, "Maybe Seu too."

"If you are Ottokip, tell us what happened next." Erilph demanded.

"Believe me when I say I didn't take the task lightly," Ottokip sniffed. His insect friend flew away, and he waved his finger as he spoke. "The mages of Songbird recognized that my friends and I had the best intentions for magic. For many years they begged us to act against the dark sorcerers. To my regret, we hesitated, wishing for the issue to resolve itself." He hung his head. "We all know it didn't."

The three sat in silence. Each reminisced on their knowledge of Jeman history. A low mumble emerged from Ottokip's messy beard. "Dark sorcerers experimenting with new spells created a hole in the fabric of our existence. It tore through realms, opening a portal to a dark place." his head trembled sadly, "The portal contained a tremendous pull, and it absorbed a large piece of Songbird."

"THE forbidden spell…" Erilph murmured. There were many forbidden spells with ties to dark magic. But with one, even dark mages didn't tamper.

"Before we could seal it off, many people were gone in an instant, vanished into an endless abyss." Ottokip appeared exhausted. "We tried to hold the sorcerers accountable, but they denied allegations. We were on the brink of civil war. A war that would be fought with sorcery!" Lucidity flashed in his eyes. "Because of the it, my friends and I ultimately decided the dark sorcerers must be stopped. Since I was the strongest, they selected me to be the recipient." The elder shivered. "They chanted the spell that sacrificed their lives to me. They allowed me to absorb their power as they passed from the world of the living. It was only then, could I conquer the dark sorcerers."

Unadine and Erilph sat entranced as Ottokip scratched dejectedly, "In the end, I absorbed them all and relieved Jema of tyranny." He sighed. "I paid the price. For a long time, I was tormented by furious souls inside me."

The three sat in silence, ruminating Jema's dark history.

In a hoarse voice, Ottokip continued, "I left Songbird to start anew, barely containing the darkness trapped inside. I came to Ima where no one recognized me." He breathed through his nose. "I hid away. And for these last two hundred years, I purified my body and soul's vibrations… seeking stillness in the storm. The peace I've found in these forests was crucial, purifying and purging the consumed from my body."

He sighed, gazing around. "I sense a vague hint of the Seed in the blueness of the trees." He beamed, "Perhaps she's once blessed this place."

"But why are you here now?" Unadine asked, still undecided about Ottokip.

He spoke gently, "For a long time, I've felt ready to leave the world of the living. But my time in these peaceful forests afforded me a strong connection to the other side. I began having vivid dreams. They told me of things to come. I knew you three you would be here, and there is much more for me to do." Ottokip's expression grew solemn.

Unadine and Erilph waited for him to say more. When it became apparent Ottokip's words were finished, Erilph ventured softly. "Grandmaster, if you were here when Vesper took Ima, why did you not stop her?"

He shook his head, "I could not. She is stronger than me—*far* stronger," he wailed. "There's periods when I lose mental clarity. If she were to capture me during those times, she could coerce information that's best left unknown." He shifted his head, wet cheeks reflecting campfire. "I felt such an invalid… a helpless fool. All my magic, and I couldn't save the people of this planet from her cruel hands." Ottokip's mood grew despondent as he shifted about. Unadine and Erilph wished to comfort him, but were lost in their own misery.

"Thank you for your companionship," the old man eventually

crowed, climbing to his feet, "I'll need your help in the near future."

"To do what?" Unadine inquired, though she had a clue.

"To take liberate Jema from Vesper," his voice found firmness.

"How do you plan to accomplish that?" Erilph recalled the trouble Vesper had dealt them in Calio.

"With the aid of Meliora and Jedrek," Ottokip answered simply.

"Who?" Unadine had never heard the names before.

Ottokip peered to the sky. "They should be here in about... two years."

Unadine and Erilph followed his line of sight. They saw nothing through the canopy of trees. When their eyes returned to where Ottokip had stood, he'd disappeared.

Chapter Twenty-Two

Civilian Ship-2 14.242 ans

Ashmarah's computer blinked, calling her away from Isa piecing a puzzle on the floor. She opened the transmission and read Procias' final report. The words struck her heart with grief. Ashmarah uttered a silent prayer for Teroma.

Agent 47,

Preparations in Orareca are complete. I'll be leaving to go underground. Our worst fears have been confirmed. Habbada and Lib forces have teamed with the Ressogureys once again. It's likely a final flotilla from the Archo system will join too. It will not be long before they attack Teroma in a coordinated assault like none in the history of our planet.

I pray for your mission to be a success, not only for the sake of our existence, but also for my daughter. I know it's against protocol, but please look after Kameclara the best you can. I can only hope to see her again in another life.

Regards,

Agent 39

Ashmarah deleted the message and shut off her computer. She sat quietly for a moment, absorbing what it meant for Teroma. All top officers and observers knew the journey to Jema absolutely could not fail. Not only did the survival of their species depend upon it, but it was also unlikely they'd have a home to return to.

Hands quaked as Ashmarah clutched them over her chest. The Pinghe teaming up with the few remaining Intergalactic Military teams on Teroma were not going to be enough. Countless trillions would lose their lives. The miserable truth remained that it was the better of two dire options. The Teromans were backed into a corner this time. Their current mission to the inner planets was the last resort.

She glanced to Isa who was unaware of her aunt's change in mood. "Ia, please protect us all," she prayed under her breath.

~*~

Warship-17 14.243 ans

Captain Nanti finished her work and slid the pullout desk into the wall of her office, trading for legroom. Her emotionless gray walls were soundproof, providing a sense of security. Having survived countless risky missions, the feeling of security was something she didn't take for granted.

Fingers tapped lightly on her favorite mug as her thoughts dwelled on that morning's briefing. The warships were on schedule, expected to enter Ima's orbit within a few months. Activity on the planet showed they'd been preparing for the Teromans' arrival. Though Iman technology and magic couldn't match the Teroman fleet's firepower, the sheer number of soldiers and civilians caused concern.

Vesper had taken Calio and Songbird five and four years ago, respectively. Seu had been under siege for two. Their defenses held without fail, as they were designed to do, but even they couldn't last forever under Vesper's brutal magic.

Captain Nanti dragged a hand along her cheek, breathing a flustered sigh. Upon the Teroman's arrival to Ima, Jema would be on the opposite side of the sun. Their original plan had always been to land on Ima before heading to Seu. There had been slim hopes of subduing Vesper before she reached Jema.

Now they resorted to the alternate plan. Seu would continue to hold their own as the Teromans disabled her troops on Ima.

Some Generals argued to set Ima free from Vesper's rule. It was a high-risk, time-consuming option. The soldiers of Ima had trained for Vesper at an early age. They were loyal to her. Many would see it as treason to follow any rule except hers.

After much deliberation, the Intergalactic Military decided time was of the essence. Control needed to be obtained swiftly. The Teromans would force Iman troops into surrender. Captain Nanti didn't particularly appreciate the idea, but admitted it was the most efficient.

Warships would land in Brisea and cut off food supply. Hunger was the quickest way to ascertain control. Additional warships would establish a presence in other parts of Ima to manage uprisings. It would also give the operatives a chance to adapt to environmental differences.

Some ships would stay in orbit of course, remaining battle-ready should Vesper's troops return. The plan was to rotate Teroman warships to the surface every few days; giving all the operatives a chance to acclimatize—something that should only take days.

There were still a handful of officers who opposed Iman domination, stating it made the Teromans no different from Vesper. The commander of the mission, Hegemon General Theol gave the ultimate word. He made all final decisions. Whatever he determined, was law.

He decided Ima needed to be controlled expediently, through whatever methods necessary.

On Teroma, the Intergalactic Military assigned a Hegemon General to each continent. Because Hegemon General Theol was one of the most experienced, he was given to the Jema mission.

Beneath Hegemon Generals were standard Generals. A dozen were assigned in each nation on Teroma. One from each left with their mission. Answering to the Generals were the Majors, followed by the Wyzenkors. The Wyzenkors commanded the Captains, who directed operatives.

"We're not here to show we're better than the despot," Hegemon General Theol proclaimed. "We're here to secure Seu. The best we can do is minimize collateral. To do that we need to demonstrate we cannot be contested."

Grimly, the others accepted the plan. It was true, there was more at stake than lives of all the Imans. It was all Jemans and Teromans too.

As she considered the details of her latest briefing, Captain Nanti glanced at her watch. She sprung from her seat in alarm and grabbed her beret. It was five minutes later than expected. An important meeting demanded her presence.

Captain Nanti jogged from her office and turned briskly down the hall. She passed a transport dock as its doors opened. A shuttle had just arrived. She slowed her pace upon seeing Hayes disembark. He stepped in rhythm beside her as they rushed to the same destination.

The two appeared minutes before the meeting. They saluted a

room mixed with operatives and officers. Hegemon General Theol stood at the head. A distinguished scar ran from his left ear to his nose. His jaw was firm as he nodded to Hayes and Nanti. They found a seat and waited for the remaining attendees to dial in.

Captain Nanti studied the Hegemon General. He held the reputation of being a hard man, one with an inquisitive mind. None dared let him down, even those who knew him outside the Intergalactic Military. Captain Nanti was an observer and because of it, had seen the Hegemon General with his inner circle. He was kind. From time to time, even a jokester. But that side of him would not peek out on a mission of this magnitude.

Their present meeting was classified. It steered the entirety of the mission to Jema. There were thirty-eight observers traveling amongst operatives and civilians. Like Procias, they'd observed Jema's history and were privy to top-secret intelligence.

The thirty-eight observers reported directly to Ashmarah. She ranked just below the Hegemon General, but operated in secret.

Ashmarah also oversaw a very special element of the mission.

Observers held critical information. As a precaution, only twenty of them attended the meeting in person. Another eighteen communicated via transmission. Should an attack ever occur, it made it difficult to target them all.

Once everyone was present and dialed in, Hegemon General Theol spoke, "I'll once more express the importance of the next few months. Plans have been made to neutralize Ima. We will use it as a base to replenish resources and train on variant gravity before heading to Jema." Large fingers massaged his jaw, sore from being perpetually clenched. "Jema is volatile. Vesper could easily barge into Seu and take everything but the citadel. It's only her doubt that keeps her at bay."

He tapped a screen on the table. The wall behind him lit with a view of Seu's citadel—a sight no civilian on Jema nor Ima ever had the privilege of viewing. Most Teroman officers weren't even cleared to see the citadel.

"We need to calculate our deployment and keep her from entering Seu. Unlike a mad beast that could easily be felled, she's cold and calculating with a significant degree of sorcery. There's also reports of her psychological imbalance, making her unpredictable." Hegemon General Theol's nostrils flared. "Her magic is on a scale unknown to any on Teroma. As discussed before, Songbird amplifies that power further." His scar darkened. "This is unfortunate because it lies in close proximity to Project S.E.U.- Scion Endeavor Unit."

His jaw returned to its clenched state. "S.E.U. is our last hope if the aliens ever discover and reach Jema."

Captain Nanti felt the words strike her body as if physical blows. They were all observers or high-ranking officers in the room. Only they knew what was about to happen to Teroma. She didn't fear much, but Nanti feared for her people.

But if the aliens ever learned of Jema, it could be the end to all life in their solar system.

General Theol cleared his throat. "Vesper's presently holed inside Songbird where her magic is most powerful. It will be difficult—but not impossible to take her down."

He swiped the screen. The image of the citadel disappeared. "Now, some of you have suggested we inform the troops of their enemy's ability to wield magic. I've been considering this heavily since we've left Teroma." He lifted his chin. "Here's my conclusion. It's best to continue to NOT inform the operatives."

Disenchanted expressions scattered throughout the room. He continued, "Proliferate practice with Project S-48 was intended to subconsciously expose our troops to the nature of magic."

A Major spoke, "Permission to speak."

"Granted."

"The primary weapon our troops will face is magic. Without complete knowledge of its effects, can we truly be at our best? The power of the Master sorcerers is infinite compared to Project S-48."

"They're excellent strategists and combatants," General Theol spoke through his teeth. "Their training allows them to take situations in the blind. I've complete faith they can prevail." His head shook. "What I don't wish is to have widely spread that the legend of the Goddess is more than just legend. We all know the ancient scriptures of Ia stated she gave us magic. The existence of one can easy lead to the assumption of the other."

His voice lowered, "Operatives will hold their tongues, but say a perceptive civilian takes notice. A careless comment and panic could be incited. Or worse," his fists tightened, "if by some stroke of bad luck, a stray transmission gets past our communications blackout and reaches Teroma. It could end up in the hands of a sleeper agent." His eyes grew dark as faces around the room tightened. "We all know what that could mean. Especially with the enemy en route."

Captain Nanti felt a chill as the Hegemon General allowed the room to run with their imaginations. Faces wore mixed expressions.

There was more the Hegemon General didn't say. Captain Nanti knew there was great fear that came with magic. To be able to learn to wield it in a short amount of time meant dabbling in impure methods. It was unwise to have operatives running such a crucial mission with an unchecked path to dark magic.

That was the true danger.

Ashmarah's voice came through the radio, "Hegemon General Theol, permission to speak?"

"Granted."

"I respect your decision to withhold the magical nature of the Imans and Jemans. May I suggest an exception? Form a task force with select operatives and officers. We could select them based upon their effectiveness against Project S-48. More importantly, based on limited relations aboard civilian ships."

"What would be their purpose?" Hegemon General Theol respected Ashmarah deeply. He patiently awaited her thoughts.

"Share with them the magical nature of the enemy. Since their numbers would be small, this allows for control. They'd be sworn to secrecy of course. Yet, because they have this knowledge, it can increase their adaptability on the field. Without the need to reveal why, they can suggest effective counterstrikes."

"I second that," Hayes immediately voiced. Others, including Captain Nanti offered support as well.

Hegemon General Theol bobbed his head, a rough hand running over his knuckles. If Ashmarah suggested this tactic, she must've considered it thoroughly. "I trust your judgment," Hegemon General Theol finally spoke, "Approved."

Ashmarah's voice floated over the speaker, "Hayes is my second in command and he's trained directly with all operatives in some fashion. I will leave it to him to formulate the task force. Please assign someone to assist."

Captain Nanti raised her hand, "I volunteer."

"I'm willing to accept," Hayes answered. They looked to the Hegemon General.

"It's settled," Hegemon General Theol confirmed. He gave Hayes a tempered glance. He didn't feel a man too young to make officer could handle such a task. He believed it was chance, not merit that made Hayes Ashmarah's second-in-command.

Captain Nanti caught the glance and knew the Hegemon General thought Hayes was unworthy. Yet she held faith in her friend. She'd known him since he was nine ans old, and she fourteen. Their mothers were Majors.

Nanti's family was visiting North Deron when the two discovered how much they had in common. The most important was that they both believed the legend of the Goddess to be true. Their earliest bonding consisted of commiseration. Both were teased at school for believing in the tale of the Goddess. It was a relief for them to finally meet another who shared their views. They'd spent hours talking over minutia of the story and how they imagined the Goddess to be if they ever met.

Throughout the ans, they'd kept casual contact. Nanti followed her mother's steps to become an operative. Later, recruited as an observer like her father. As per observers' regulation, she kept information about Jema and the aliens from everyone, including Hayes. A part of her had always wanted to tell him, to let him know the fairytales were legitimate.

A few ans after serving, Nanti discovered Hayes' name on the observers' roster. She felt comfort knowing her oldest friend was in the loop.

Incidentally, seeing her name was a pleasant surprise for Hayes as well. He meant to reach out, but found heavy responsibilities on his plate. It came with the territory of being Ashmarah's second.

It wasn't until the Jema mission did Hayes contact Nanti. Ashmarah had wanted eyes on a potential asset in Orareca. Hayes couldn't think of anyone better.

Until the Jema mission, Nanti didn't know much about Ashmarah except she was a Commanding Observer. One of the highest ranked. Once she finally got together with Hayes, he told her in confidence the elder woman was also a sibyl and geneticist.

"Ashmarah lives alone and keeps many of her projects secret, even from me," he'd confessed. "She's a part of a clandestine coalition that trains in divination arts. Their sole purpose is to calculate the Goddess' reappearance."

For the present mission, Ashmarah went above the call. Not only did she calculate the Goddess' return, consulting with equally talented seers across the planet, but she also sought souls with karmic ties to Jema. She had tracked down a handful of operatives and officers. They were referred to as assets.

Ashmarah shared this information with her trusted protégé. It was up to Hayes to keep tabs on them. Some were reincarnated Generals of Vesper. Others had crossed paths with her incidentally. A gem of hope came when one of Ashmarah's subordinates shared suspicions about his daughter. Procias believed his daughter's soul was Vesper's deceased child. Even better, the young woman had already entered the Intergalactic Military. It seemed as if destiny played on their side.

~*~

When Hayes and Nanti sat down to vet operative files for the task force, Kameclara was first on the list. They also included other souls divined by Ashmarah. They combed over every detail, seeking sixty tight-lipped individuals.

It took them two weeks to finalize.

"You haven't said any of the reservations I KNOW you have," Hayes commented as they submitted the list for Ashmarah and Hegemon General Theol to review.

"Just wondering. What if the karmic ties don't swing in our favor? What if their unfinished business leads them to assist the enemy?"

Hayes grunted. "There's always that risk. No one knows exactly how fate'll play out. Just that they will meet like two waves crashing."

Captain Nanti straightened her beret. "I was taught fate is inevitable, like celestial bodies on a collision course. Karma in comparison, affects attributes such as velocity, angle… Yet, a larger body will surely demolish a smaller one. We have no way of knowing which souls would translate to the larger in this realm."

Hayes felt a lump in his throat. "Oh Nanti. I can always appreciate you to be a realist. Even if I don't like what you have to say." He sighed. "It just makes me worry about Isa even more."

Chapter Twenty-Three

Captain Nanti entered the gymnasium. It was a free-training day and the operatives exercised independently. Her eyes scanned rows of equipment, catching a glimpse of dark hair on the peg wall. "Kame-clara!" she called.

"Sir!" drifted across the space. Her subordinate appeared by her side in an instant.

"Marcello!" Captain Nanti hollered. A young man from Beta-team appeared just as quickly.

"Follow," she turned on her heel and marched towards Major Galmone's office. The Major was an observer like her. He was selected to notify operatives they were to be incorporated into the task force, Protocol Phen. Hearing the command from a higher officer enforced the importance of the task force.

Captain Nanti's boots clicked on the metal floor as her heart drummed. Though she was an avid supporter of spreading the knowledge of magic, a lot could go wrong. Disposition for good and evil existed in each soul. Magic behaved like an amplifier. Whichever nature resounded stronger could take over, even beyond the control of the soul. On Ima or Jema, an operative could find a way to permanently take magic into their bodies. All it took was a wavering of control to turn good soldiers.

She stopped before Major Galmone's door. As she rang, Captain Nanti stole a glance at Kameclara. The operative gazed back. The Captain hoped the reincarnated princess held a virtuous soul. Ashmarah believed Kameclara displayed benevolent qualities. Captain Nanti instinctively liked her too. Yet, there was no telling for certain. Should Ashamarah's intuition prove wrong, Nanti would be forced to take out Kameclara.

The door slid open and Nanti saluted. "Sir!" Behind her, the operatives did the same.

Major Galmone waved them in and sealed his door. He didn't mess around, speaking as he leaned against his desk, "As of this moment, the two of you are active in a top-secret task force, Protocol Phen. The information I'm about to share is not to be disclosed it to anyone. Not even your partners."

"Yes, sir!"

He used a steely tone. "You've all been briefed on Vesper. No doubt you've questioned the technology behind her attacks." He didn't wait for the operatives' reactions. "It's sorcery," he announced plainly. "Magic exists and that's what we're up against on Jema and Ima."

Kameclara's ears rang. Did she hear correctly? An officer confirmed the existence of something Teroma thought to be make-believe. It still came as a shock, even though her father had already told her that the Goddess was real. And he was one of the most logical people she knew.

Kameclara forced a breath as her palms sweat. She didn't feel equipped to accept perceived irrationalities as fact. Yet, she had no choice. The Major's words were law.

"We have a sibyl," Major Galmone continued. "She calculated that the two of you have fates tied with the planets Jema and Ima. We're entrusting you with classified information… in hopes you'll make effective decisions." He puffed, arms folding, "And to call upon you should we need special operations."

"Fates, sir?" Marcello asked to make sure he'd heard his officer correctly.

"Yes," Major Galmone answered, as if it were perfectly natural.

Kameclara spoke, "What of the rest of the IM? How are they to defend against magic attacks if they have no knowledge of it?"

"Your training is your best defense," he parroted. "Use it."

"And Project S-48?" Kameclara asked. "Is that magic?"

The Major nodded to Captain Nanti.

She explained, "Yes and no. It taps the surface level of the nevino sequence using electrical frequency. The sorcerers you'll encounter have the sequence fully awakened."

"Any more questions?" The Major barked.

"I have no further questions," Kameclara spoke clearly.

"No further questions," Marcello echoed hesitantly.

"If you do, come see me," Captain Nanti ordered.

Major Galmone explained duties for Kameclara and Marcello. "You're to operate as usual. If Protocol Phen is enacted, an officer will contact you directly via your com-helmet."

Kameclara and Marcello saluted to accept the order. The Major dismissed them.

Kameclara marched back to the training hall with Marcello. "Holy shit," he wheezed. "We've been tapped for a special mission! I was expecting some unconventional explanation to Vesper's power but… not sorcery. I dunno what to think right now!"

Kameclara grunted, "I need to process too."

They parted ways.

~*~

Captain Nanti returned to her office. After the door slid shut, she tried relaxing her shoulders, to no avail. Across all warships, officers were notifying subordinates of their recruitment into Protocol Phen.

Kicking her feet onto her desk, she let out a long exhale. Captain Nanti replayed the looks on the operatives' faces when she told them about magic. Marcello appeared dumbfounded, but Kameclara's eyes sharpened. Captain Nanti imagined thoughts flying around the operative's head. She couldn't get a read on their tune. The Captain sincerely hoped Kameclara played out as valuable as they'd hoped. If not…

She uttered absentmindedly, "May the blessed Goddess protect us." A moment later she chuckled, "Well actually… we're protecting the Goddess."

Chapter Twenty-Four

Kameclara neatly folded her things, chatting with Syralise and Leera. In less than an hour, they were to rotate warships. They liked to clean their space before each transport. She kept the conversation lighthearted, but in the back of her mind, Kameclara pondered Protocol Phen. It made her uncomfortable to keep it from Syralise and Leera.

That would be two secrets. She also kept the conversation with her father private. Squad-mates were encouraged to be open and accepting of one another. It generated the strongest of bonds, leading to enhanced cooperation on the field. The past seven ans were mixed with laughter, disappointments, and triumph. Through it all, they had each other.

Would my withholding behavior seep into other areas of our lives, causing a rift?

Their fleet neared the inner planets. After two more rotations, they'd enter Ima's orbit. The eight-ans journey was reaching its end. The true purpose of their mission would begin.

Kameclara felt relieved. As much as they cared for each other, being together nearly every day aboard a warship had grown tiresome. Regular psych evaluations kept them on track, but everyone couldn't wait to get off the ships for a bit.

The last items she sorted were her civilian clothes. Kameclara noticed a rolled shirt wedged in the back. It was a gift from her mother, with a design she didn't particularly care for. Missing her, she unrolled it to reminisce.

A small box dropped onto her bunk. Kameclara recognized the case her father had given her. She'd completely forgotten about it.

Kameclara lovingly refolded the shirt and stored it away. Her eyes never left the case. She picked it up gingerly and peered inside. Vials of fluid glimmered subtly, speaking of mystery. She recalled her father saying he could only get two vials. One of her partners would have to do without. Kameclara opened her mouth to tell them about the substance, but loud rapping interrupted.

"Five minutes!" Captain Nanti alerted.

Kameclara shoved the case into her drawer. It'd have to wait. An unscheduled briefing was taking place. If the Captain was at their door, then most of the other operatives must've already gathered.

The three marched into their common area and met with the rest of Alpha Team. Captain Nanti conversed with a Major. Her mannerisms were too informal with someone of the Major's rank. Kameclara wondered how connected her Captain was with other officers.

The two nodded in agreement. Captain Nanti turned to her team. "Listen up! There's a change in rotation. For now, we'll progress to Warship-31, as planned. But on our last rotation, Orareca's teams will be assigned to Warship-23 again, instead of Warship-27. We'll be first to land in the Priletoria sector of Ima."

"Psst, Kame," Syralise whispered, "Isn't that your boyfriend's ship?"

Kameclara didn't know how to respond. She'd never expected to see Stanten again.

~*~

Teppa Nevo knew his parents had been selected based upon the purity of their nevino sequence. He wasn't the only one. There were a dozen other children birthed by screened contributors. The fathers were donors; the in-vitro mothers well compensated. They were taken from birth and raised in preparation to become the autocrat of Seu.

A title only one would earn.

The autocrat managed the kingdom, such as maintaining self-sufficiency. He or she also oversaw vital communication with Teroma. All of it was in support for their primary duty—to protect the ultimate secret of Jema.

As children, potential autocrats went through Pinghe training, coupled with Teroman Intergalactic Military tactics. Should war find its way to Jema, they'd be prepared. Counter sorcery measures were also instructed. A precaution, should sorcerers turn against Seu.

Teppa Nevo straightened his collar. "The safeguards mitigate Vesper's power, but it's not enough to stop her indefinitely."

Teppa Nevo was seventy years old. Though healthy and agile in mind, he felt wearied. He thought he would continue with Seu support duties like the autocrats before. It'd been thousands of years since they'd been activated for their primary duty.

The new autocrats-in-training were around age sixteen. They would've been ready in about ten years. One would be selected to succeed him, and Teppa Nevo could've retired.

However, the true purpose of Seu was now being called upon. Teppa Nevo would be tested not only on his training, but his fate.

Sitting beneath the citadel, the autocrat relayed messages to troops at outer walls. There, they held back Vesper's army of mages. Almost two years had passed since her minions first attacked. Her magic was brutal and Seu lost many good people. But the outer walls held.

Seu couldn't deploy fighter crafts often. The technology relied on a giant nevite crystal at the planet's core to recharge. If they depleted it, all was lost.

He chuckled at the situation. It was also this crystal that enhanced sorcerers' power in Songbird. Underground rivers carried fragments close to the surface, beneath the school of sorcery.

For a time, Teppa Nevo had anticipated naval attacks. Seu's outer wall began at the borders of Songbird and Calio. It ended where it reached the oceans. The coastline was jagged. Seu's navy had long provided food for Jema with fishing. What else was there to do in times of peace? It resulted in them holding unparalleled knowledge of the oceans. None in Calio or Songbird could out-maneuver Seu boats and Vesper had lost many to the sea. She quickly gave up that route.

Cutting off resources was not advantageous for Vesper. Seu was built to self-sustain through isolation. Teppa Nevo felt confident they could withstand until the Teromans arrived.

Despite Vesper's malicious, she wasn't his greatest concern.

The autocrat reread the latest transmission from Teroma. It was a stray message, not meant for Seu. It didn't come from any observer. They'd all gone underground. He could only speculate it was sent by a sleeper agent. To someone not aboard the Teroman fleet.

Ia has incarnated, but left Teroma. They're hiding her elsewhere. A fleet of fifty launched year 65\897.

The date format matched the Habliban calendar, used by two

races of enemy aliens, the Habbadans and Libans.

Teppa Nevo rubbed his neck. "Our ancestors anticipated this… but we've never seen such dire circumstances."

Chapter Twenty-Five

More than thirty thousand years before life existed on Teroma, an angelic soul crossed into the corporeal realm. Fleeing from a demonic soul, Ia incarnated on the planet Habbada. "Habba" meant "Gray." The indigenous humanoids displayed skin tinted gray, and silvery hair.

The Habbadans accepted Ia warmly. In gratitude, she aided their civilization. She guided technology, medicine, and spirituality. They worshipped her for the gifts she bestowed.

With Ia assisting their advancement, they soon achieved space travel. Ia journeyed with them to a neighboring planet. Its name was Lib, which meant "Blue." The people of Lib had powdery blue skin. Their dark hair shimmered with luminescent undertones. They were becoming industrialized, but had yet to achieve space travel.

The Libans had long viewed Habbada through their telescopes and were in awe of them having a Goddess. Once Ia traveled to Lib, they welcomed both her and the Habbadans. Ia continued to bless people on both planets. For one thousand years, there was peace and harmony. The people intermingled into a single race.

Near the end of the thousand years, the demonic soul named Pem arrived. He'd tracked the Goddess from the ethereal realm and incarnated on Lib. After a struggle, he captured Ia, and prepared to bring her back to the nether realm.

Ia's loyal worshippers, the Pinghe, broke her from confinement. They stole a ship and flew her to Habbada. They hid for a while, but Pem was swift to chase.

The Pinghe left Habbada and Lib behind. Without a destination in mind, they traversed endless space with only hope.

Their daring rescue touched Ia's heart. Using abilities as a celestial soul, she bent realities of space. Safely, she brought her people to the next star system. They arrived famished and exhausted on a large, frozen planet.

Ia wished to take them further, but her powers had grown weak. Her exertion to change the corporeal world thinned her connection to it.

The Pinghe tried their best to survive on the planet, but the environment proved harsh. They were dying from cold, and poor nourishment.

Ia took the crystals powering their ship and embedded them into the planet's core. They contained residual energy from her younger days. It heated the planet via underground rivers. Caves warmed enough to grow tough species of crops, with artificial light.

Yet many remained ill. The journey had been grueling. With unpredictable weather, the future of the Pinghe appeared bleak.

Summoning fading strength, Ia gave one last gift. She enhanced the genetic structure of her followers. The people became hardy and were quick to adapt, allowing them to survive in a wide range of environments. In doing so, she tied the fate of all those with the genetic sequence to her. Their existence became hinged upon Ia's wellbe-

ing. If she were harmed in the mortal realm, the effect would spread through their genetic sequence. All their descendants would perish.

With her last breath drawing near, Ia made two promises. Each time she was to incarnate, it would only be with them. She handed down information on how to estimate her return. When celestial bodies aligned, they produced triangulations of gravity that allowed a soul's easy passage to a destination.

Next, she promised while in the ethereal realm, she would find a way to bar Pem from incarnating in their solar system. If he was to pursue her into the corporeal realm, the nearest he could incarnate was Habbada or Lib.

When Ia finished addressing her people, light left her eyes. Her followers laid her to rest in the icy earth and erected a temple. They grew to love the planet she had altered for their survival. They named the planet "earth mother," Teroma.

Chapter Twenty-Six

Warship-31 14.244 ans

Orareca's Alpha and Beta Teams settled in on Warship-31. They were given a three-day break to celebrate Orareca's Founding Day, the day their nation established sovereignty. The operatives busied themselves, preparing.

Syralise finished her share as quickly as possible. She had made arrangements to spend well-needed time with her boyfriend, Nolram. Dressed in civilian clothes, she shuttled to Warship-7. Stepping casually to his door, she sighed, looking forward to idle time. Nolram had asked his squad-mates for privacy. They found other places to be.

Syralise knocked and waited. A moment later Nolram answered. Without a word, her arms found their way around his neck. She missed the taste of his lips. They giggled in private as his hand stroked her shoulders.

Hours later, they were fast asleep, limbs entangled.

After some time, Syralise opened a lazy eye. A tickling breath stirred the base of her neck. Around her midsection, she felt Nolram's arm. Syralise gently trailed a finger along his hand. He grunted, pulling her closer.

For the next hours, she wanted to pretend she'd chosen another life. Syralise wanted to imagine she was happily married, like her parents. There was no mission. No pressure. Life was easy and good.

Tranquility swathed her as she drifted back to sleep.

Syralise awoke to lips on her neck. She turned and they reengaged their intimate vacation. She didn't hold back. Syralise wanted to soak in every moment of joy and connection. Her life wasn't guaranteed. There was no knowing when danger would strike. For now, she wanted to feel free and loved, nothing else.

In the heat of the moment, Nolram buried his face in her hair, "I love you." The words were soft, barely audible, but she'd heard them.

Syralise pulled away, careful not to be cruel. Many ans ago, when they first started seeing each other, they'd agreed not to let it get serious. How she wished he'd kept those words sealed away.

Syralise kicked herself too, for indulging in earlier fantasies. It broke her own rule never let anything get in the way of her dedication to the Intergalactic Military. Reservations of any kind proved dangerous.

But at least, she'd kept those whims to herself.

Nolram sensed her change. "What's the matter?" Apprehension scrawled on his face.

If she were honest, Syralise felt for him too. Yet, she needed to do what was necessary. What they'd agreed upon. She peered steadily to him. "We can't see each other anymore. It's for our own good."

"I—," he began. Nolram's eyes drooped, understanding. Though his expression switched to stoicism, Syralise sensed his spirit crushing. Hers crashed too.

A part of her wanted to say, "I'm sorry," and she was, but it'd only make matters worse. They both understood the choices they'd made. There was no apologizing for taking the greatest oath of a Teroman. The one of an operative.

Syralise dressed silently and stood to leave. He showed a moment of frailty and pulled her close. Syralise didn't let her body respond. Even as Nolram's arms tightened and her heart melted.

"Just stay a little longer," he asked, on the verge of tears. "I promise, tomorrow we'll call it quits." He stroked her hair. "Don't tell me you don't feel something too."

"No," Syralise pulled away, looking him firm in the eye. She took every bit of affection in that heart her partners called oversized, and pushed it to the furthest corners of her being. It was no easy feat. "As Alpha-Je, I'm ordering you to stand down." She accessed her soldier mentality.

After a moment of stunned silence, Nolram stepped back and gathered himself. He faced her with a salute. His eyes accepted her command.

Without another word, Syralise left.

As she trudged towards the dock, she let out an aggravated grunt. It was either get angry or cry. She didn't like either emotion, but tears were harder to control.

Truth was, she and Nolram should've ended things long ago. It was her innate desire to bond that had prevented it. He was the same.

"I do score exceedingly high on emotional awareness," she grumbled, rationalizing. It was a good thing, normally. It allowed her to detect psychological weaknesses in an opponent. It also meant she held a proclivity to connect deeply. Not the most convenient for an operative.

"Wish I were a bit like Kameclara. She senses others' emotions too, but unlike me, doesn't get entangled."

Syralise stopped short. "But what about that inmate from Warship-23?" She'd never seen her partner fall for a guy. Ever. Yet, something about Kameclara had been different around Stanten. The thought distracted her from her heartache. Syralise contemplated what it could mean.

~*~

Leera served the letti, a heavy dessert cake from Orareca. Founding Day celebrations were underway. Her teammates had sighed in relief to receive extended time from training. Leera knew them well though. How could she not? Having lived the past seven-and-a-half ans in closer proximity than any operatives in Teroma's past. Many would hit the gym in a few hours anyway.

Syralise had gone to see Nolram. Kameclara helped organize the obstacle course. The prize was a handshake and photo with Hegemon General Theol. Leera wanted to try her skill on the course too. Not only because few got to meet a Hegemon General in their lifetime. Kameclara was known to be creative with her runs.

Leera's eyes drifted to the far end of the habbadite cavern. There, away from food and socializing, Kameclara clutched a communicator. She radioed to operatives and officers in the control room, putting finishing touches on the course. A block of habbadite rose beneath Kameclara's feet. Leera observed, enamored as hairs danced across her partner's face. How she envied those strands.

"Did you make the letti?" Hendran from Delta Team seemed to materialize before her.

Leera peeled her eyes away. "Huh? No," she scrunched her nose, "If you ate my cooking, you'd be in sick bay."

They shared a laugh, "I'm grateful then!"

Leera served him a large helping. "Syralise made this yesterday. Her dad's a chef! She's picked up a few things."

Hendran raised a brow, "Didn't know! Can't wait to try this," he shoved a bite in his mouth. "Where is she, by the way?"

"Hanging out with Nolram," Leera gave a mischievous smile.

"I see," Hendran grinned bashfully. "Um... well, have you ever thought about getting together with anyone?" His cheeks deepened and he cleared his throat clumsily.

She grew nervous, fearing he'd caught her glances towards Kameclara. "Why do you..." Leera trailed, realizing suddenly why he'd asked. She placed a hand comfortingly on his arm. "I'm flattered, but I like women. Only." It wasn't true, but it was easier for Hendran if he believed so.

"Oh! I didn't know," his face glowed.

"It's alright. I don't publicize my preferences," she spoke graciously. "So... how's the letti?

Appreciative of the change in topic, Hendran responded, "It's amazing!"

The door to the cavern slid open. Syralise entered. "There's the chef now," Leera nodded over.

"I should pay my compliments!"

Leera observed her partner's slumped posture. "Hmm... maybe I should speak with her first."

Hendran detected something was off. "Sure, give my regards."

"Mind taking over here?" she gestured to the trays of letti with a grin.

"Not at all!"

Leera stepped from behind the table and made her way to Syralise. "You're back early. Didn't expect to see you for a few days."

Syralise's face hung sorrowfully. Without a word, she walked into Leera's arms.

"You wanna talk about it?" she returned the hug. Funny. This partner didn't stir the same emotions as Kameclara.

Syralise shook her head. "Maybe later."

Leera knew Syralise and Nolram had been growing close. She assumed they'd decided to do what was best for the mission and end things.

Leera glanced to Kameclara. She understood on a level how Syralise felt. Leera needed to keep her emotions in check, or be transferred. Teammates were not allowed to see each other romantically. If anyone discovered her feelings for Kameclara, she would be moved to another team, or another nation altogether.

Leera had joined the Intergalactic Military to feel close to her father. It wasn't so much that she searched for answers. He'd communicated clearly with her and her mother. Leera understood how passionately he'd felt about assisting the planet's primary defense forces. She wanted to be a part of something he'd held of high importance. It kept her memory of him alive.

It's true, she could accomplish that with any branch of the Intergalactic Military. But Alpha-Je of Orareca had always felt a perfect fit.

Leera gazed forlornly at Kameclara. Having the feelings she did was something the redhead never expected. She mentally shook herself and averted her gaze.

"I know what'll cheer you up," Leera beamed to Syralise. "Kame's about done setting up the obstacle course. Wanna chance to meet the Hegemon General?"

Syralise's eyes flashed, "You're doin' it too, right?"

"'Course!"

Signups for the obstacle course opened. Syralise perked a bit, but Leera still noted her woefulness. For a moment, she considered letting her partner win.

Leera quickly shook her head. Syralise didn't need a fake win. She needed to blow off steam. Besides, she'd be upset if she discovered Leera didn't go full out.

They took their positions as signup closed. When the klaxon sounded, a few dozen operatives leapt into action. They dashed through changing terrain, some fighting through, others finding a way around. Leera nearly lost her step as a piece of habbadite launched towards her. She regained balance and nimbly charged on.

Before the finish line, Kameclara and other volunteers waited. Leera smirked, ready to spar. She kept her eye on Kameclara. Few people tested her as well as her partners. She questioned if she should choose the hardest route, or the swiftest towards the finish. One meant going through Kameclara.

Syralise chose for her. She lunged past Leera, with a kick aimed for Kameclara. "Looks like you've got some Nolram issues to work out," Leera commented to herself. She felt relieved.

It'd started about an ans or two ago, Leera couldn't be sure. She'd discovered she held an inclination towards Kameclara. It grew gradually, day by day. In recent months, it sometimes got difficult to keep her feelings in check. Like now. She was getting worked up.

Leera used a breathing technique. It cleared her mind, and with it, her emotions. She reminded herself the first thing a Pinghe mastered was him or herself.

It'd been growing increasing difficult to clear her affections for Kameclara.

Buer from Beta Team confronted her and she easily slipped past. Leera crossed the finish line without much thought.

Cheers erupted from the other operatives. Sweeping her gaze, Leera noticed she'd finished first. Pride swelled as her shoulders lifted high. "What a surprise!" she murmured.

The doors to the arena slid open, and an elderly man entered. The air fell silent and everyone saluted. Leera quickly dropped to the ground and did the same. Her knees wobbled at the sight of Hegemon General Theol.

"As you were!" he announced. The room hesitantly stirred back to life. All eyes followed him as whispers filled the air.

Leera's feet felt latched to the ground as he lumbered towards her. She stared. Not that she would've been able to look away if she wanted. He held a demanding presence.

The Hegemon General's eyes glowed with pride as he reached out a hand.

Leera accepted.

There was a flash as they shook.

"Congratulations." The word sounded more like a command than a blessing.

"Th-thank you, sir!" Before she could say more, he turned and left the arena. The door slid tightly shut behind him.

The honor seeped slowly through her as operatives swarmed, offering similar sentiments.

Leera breathed in awe, "I just met the Hegemon General…" Exhilarated tingles went through her, and she wanted to kiss someone.

Before she knew it, her eyes fell on Kameclara. Her partner cheered, still perched on an outcropping.

Someone handed Leera a tablet. It was a photo of her, dumb-struck, shaking hands with Hegemon General Theol. That day, she was the number one operative. It reminded her it was her prerogative in life.

With priorities re-centered, Leera held up the image to show her partners. Kameclara and Syralise beamed to her. One of them made her heart flutter. Leera breathed deep, composing herself once more.

Chapter Twenty-Seven

Final rotations took place a week before arrival to Iman orbit. The Orareca teams found themselves aboard Warship-23 with North Deron again. Hayes made time to greet Kameclara. Their cordial conversation remained brief. He excused himself, saying he had other business to attend.

After settling in, Kameclara and her partners visited the observation deck. They wanted to catch a glimpse of the planet. As she stepped foot into the familiar room, her heart raced. Kameclara looked to the corner where she'd met Stanten. She half expected to see him gazing through the floorboard.

What's wrong with me? Was I secretly hoping he'd be there?

Yet, she knew he was on board, somewhere. The awareness screamed in the back of her mind.

Kameclara had debated heavily whether to seek out Stanten. They'd said final goodbyes ans ago. He could've forgotten her.

"It doesn't matter," she murmured. Alpha Team wouldn't have any more days off until they landed on Ima. By then, they'll be little chance to interact. "Not worth the trouble." Yet as the words left her lips, a knot of resistance formed.

"Wow, all that green!" Syralise gasped in wonder, peering through a scope. "Ima's so beautiful!" Kameclara turned her attention to the view. To the naked eye, the planet appeared the size of a pinprick.

"I'm glad they did gradual climate adjustments aboard the warships these past ans," Leera sighed. "I'm not looking forward to the extreme heat." She took the scope from Syralise and studied their target.

"Yeah, otherwise it'd render us ineffective for a week or two," Kameclara added. She gulped, trying hard not to think of Stanten. It felt as if the air in the observation deck held a memory of their encounter. It taunted her every second.

"The sun… it's so bright," Leera admired. She handed the scope to Kameclara. "You can catch some solar activity even at this distance." They had recently entered the corona. Leera cracked her joints, "Can't wait to land. You know they'll have us take some of that gear out for a spin! I've been dying to handle a bike on new terrain."

"I wanna taste warm air." Syralise's eyes brightened. "I hear you can smell flowers in the wind. Not just the stuff they grow in the biodomes back home, but unknown species that give off natural fragrances!"

"I wanna eat real food," Kameclara laughed, "Cooking from powders is really becoming awful!"

Syralise made a twisted face, "Yeah, I really miss my dad's food."

"I second that!" Leera added. "It's too bad we can't have Founding Day food every day!"

"Wonder if we'll be allowed to hunt wildlife," Syralise asked with intrigue. "I wanna feel like a native, sit by a fire… roasting the leg of whatever animal we find!"

They women broke into guffaws, picturing Syralise's words. It would certainly be an interesting experience. Meat was rare on Teroma.

They mostly subsisted on a vegetarian diet, supplemented with fish.

"Alright, we should probably be getting ready for the briefing," Leera sighed.

The three exited the viewing deck. Kameclara's eyes lingered over the space one last time.

~*~

Priletoria- 2221 Iman Year

Unadine and Erilph watched in awe as an enormous space whale landed near ruins of the Priletoria palace. It appeared to be made of metals, ceramics, and materials they couldn't determine.

Massive doors opened and people dressed in strange garb emerged. They rushed about, some commanding others. It was a militia.

The Masters waited until nightfall. As most of the strangers rested, they cast an invisibility spell upon themselves. They approached cautiously for observation. Listening to speech, the dialect of the people sounded unfamiliar. Some phrases were close to Jeman, but carried different intonations.

Vesper's name was whispered a few times, making the Master's uneasy.

Unadine tightened defensively, "Where did Vesper find them?"

Erilph responded, "What if they don't serve her?"

"Then they should be facing her on Jema," Unadine spoke sharply.

"Hello?" a man nearby peered in the direction of Unadine and Erilph. He'd heard hushed voices, but saw no one.

"Let's go," Unadine covered her mouth with a hand.

She and Erilph hurried back into the blue forests. Once they were safely at their camp, they debated what should be done.

Ultimately, they decided to gather more information. "We can at least perceive their capabilities," Erilph concluded.

"Do you think Ottokip knows who they are?" Unadine asked. After their first meeting, he hadn't returned. Unadine and Erilph had multitudes of questions left unanswered.

Erilph shook his head sadly, "I'm not certain. But he did mention a Meliora and Jedrek arriving. Could they be the strangers?"

Unadine scrunched her face. "Uncertain."

The Masters kept hidden behind their barrier spell. A few days after the strangers' arrival, refugees flooded the forest from Carpecillero. The sorcerers overhead they were pushed by Vesper's troops, advancing from the west. The troops were sent to investigate the large ship in Priletoria.

Once Vesper's soldiers reached the strangers, Unadine and Erilph felt explosions rocking the forests. They were kept awake all hours of the night. Secretly, they casted a protective shield in the canopy of tall trees. It protected the refugees too.

Some of those refugees dared venture to the border of the blue forests. Upon their return, Unadine and Erilph heard talk about horrible weapons. The refugees spoke fearfully, marveling at foreign carriages traveling faster than any in Calio, and sticks shooting lighting instead of bullets. Even Vesper's mages were hardly a match.

Unadine and Erilph exchanged mixed expressions. At least the strangers weren't on Vesper's side. Yet, the motivation behind their arrival remained to be seen.

~*~

Vesper's Iman troops received a transmission from an invading fleet, demanding surrender. Their response was to shut off landing ports in the Land of the Seraphims. They assumed the ships would be struck in orbit.

To their infinite bafflement, ten warships gracefully touched down. Four landed in Brisea, two in the Land of the Seraphims; the last four in other kingdoms around the planet. With uncontested power, the fleet took control of military bases.

Vesper's troops fought back. Stricken by strange weapons and coordination, they laid down arms within days. Those who refused to surrender left controlled populations and rallied in the forests. Every now and then, they rose against the newcomers' ships. They were driven back expediently. The large warships were impregnable and their operatives demonstrated strength and strategy beyond their wildest imaginations.

On the eight-ans journey, the warships had maintained Teroman gravity levels. Lesser gravity on Ima allowed the operatives to be faster and deadlier.

The Teromans viewed the rebels as a nuisance, not a threat. The real trouble came from Iman sorcerers. Though only Vesper's beginner apprentices and a handful of mages remained on the planet, they were able to combine powers and cast large spells.

The Intergalactic Military required time adjusting to defense against magic. Windstorms started randomly. Lightning struck without a cloud in the sky. Sometimes operatives were thrown into the air without warning.

The strange occurrences were explained to the operatives as weather patterns. Many appeared skeptical, but accepted the explanations as part of command. Inmate workers were ordered to build temporary shelters out of stone to protect equipment. A proliferate white berry called manico was found to have mild neutralizing effects against "weather," and its oil was sprayed on everything.

As operatives dealt with rebels, Hegemon General Theol coordinated plans for Jema. Teppa Nevo had informed him the outer wall of Seu still held. They agreed there was time, and it would be advantageous for all operatives to experience Ima. Environmental controls aboard the warships were set to gradually mimic Jeman temperatures, but none had basked in direct sunlight.

Warships weren't the only ones landing on Ima. Two civilian ships lowered alongside each rotation. They remained in less populated areas of the planet. This way, they could replenish supplies while remaining protected. It also gave the citizens a chance to stretch their legs.

Children like Isa couldn't wait to get into trouble.

Chapter Twenty-Eight

Warship-23 landed in Priletoria and scanned the area. Civilian Ship-2 followed after the perimeter was deemed secure. But before citizens were allowed to exit, the operatives were to perform a manual sweep.

As they disembarked, intense heat struck Kameclara. She grimaced, "Ugh." The sun was just rising. It was only going to grow hotter.

"It's to be expected," Syralise tried to convince herself the discomfort was acceptable. "We are SO much closer to the sun."

Their uniforms were climate controlled, but mostly against frigid weather. It only cooled them a smidge. To their relief, officers granted them the option to strip down to their basic gear. "Only after you've cleared the area."

After their task was complete, Alpha-Je peeled off top layers and tied them about their waist. A gust of wind swept across the plains, making tall grass dance. It sopped heat off their skin like a dry sponge.

"That's better." Syralise pulled off her com-helmet, sniffing, "Don't smell any flowers though."

"Are you kidding? That's all you're thinking about? There's millions of scents in the air!" Leera exclaimed in wonder. She inhaled deeply. "I never thought such aromas existed!"

Kameclara sniffed delicately, her visor up. Something about the place stirred a sense of nostalgia. It threatened to carry her away. Her eyes darted to a distant row of blue. She'd never seen trees that tall before. They called out to her.

Alpha-Je wasn't too far from Warship-23. Kameclara noticed prisoners unloading. She scanned briefly for Stanten before chiding herself. "It's over." She turned her eyes away.

Captain Nanti whistled and Alpha Team moved into formation. Her collared, long-sleeved uniform remained buttoned to her throat. The officer's impassiveness appeared unaffected by sweltering heat. She announced a training exercise, holding up two flags. Exuberant murmurs were heard.

"You'll be divided into two groups. First group to take the opponent's flag, wins. Losers take first shift on watch."

All vehicles were at their disposal. The Captains warned to prevent damage, glaring at Leera. The operative chuckled nervously.

Orareca's Alpha Team paired with North Deron's Beta Team. They chose their starting position behind a hill in the forest. Their field was limited to a five-mile radius. They could return to the ship expediently, should there be a need.

It was Kameclara's lead. She displayed a virtual map of the terrain, projected from her com-helmet. "The dense forests of the northwest are a great place to lose them." She fought a longing to lose herself in the trees. It seemed as if she could imagine their smell.

That's silly. No Teroman's been here in millennia.

The flag went to Syralise and she hid it in a pocket.

"Let's break into squads and scatter," Kameclara ordered. "It'll divide the enemy's efforts. Stay on coms and keep a sharp lookout for their flag."

A green flare went into the air to signal start.

Vehicles lurched forward as members of Kameclara's group separated. Her squad headed northwest with the intent to keep Syralise hidden.

~*~

Kameclara felt woozy, as if underwater for too long. She fought to surface, alertness eluding at every attempt.

After what felt like ages, her eyes dragged open. She discovered herself on her side. She kept calm and scoped her environment. Light dancing on a tree trunk hinted at a fire nearby. She was still in the woods, surrounded by enormous trees. They must be someplace deep in the northwest. It was dim, reminding of daytime on Teroma.

Minimizing head movement, she peered to her hips. Her weapons were no longer strapped. Kameclara's eyes hunted for them and located her sidearm dangling from a branch. Her legs felt fine. She wanted to jump and grab for them, but her ankles were immobilized by rope. A scratchy material bound her wrists too.

She sniffed. A savory odor wafted to her nostrils. A rich, sweet odor permeated the background. The smell of unfrozen earth.

Kameclara wanted to bask in the overwhelming new sensations, but she needed to focus. How she became unconsciousness remained a mystery. She furrowed her brow, searching her memory. The last thing she recalled was positioning with her partners in the blue forests. They were defending against the other team from capturing their flag. Her eyes and ears constantly scanned their surroundings, as did her helmet and bike's redundant sensors. Nothing should've gotten past.

She studied her weapons again to see if there was some way to knock them down. Perhaps a well-placed kick against the tree trunk. She subtly tugged at the rope around her wrists. They didn't seem to budge. Strange. Knots weren't usually difficult for her.

A fluttering in the branches caught her eye. A tattered cloth stirred an odd emotion. It felt as if she knew it deeply somehow.

Impossible. It looks like it's been here for centuries.

Yet, Kameclara couldn't avert her gaze. A longing built in her chest. One she'd never felt before.

A gust lifted the cloth and she saw "Priletoria" scrawled across in a flowery script. Plants and flowers were embroidered along what was left of the edges. It was an old flag.

The flag!

Realization that they were in the middle of a training exercise shoved sentiments aside. Discretely, she scoped a wider range. Syralise and Leera were tied on the ground nearby. Both slept peacefully, appearing unharmed.

Kameclara tried the knots again. The rope seemed to resist any amount of tugging.

There had been soft rustling behind her, by the fire. Soft tinkling as someone worked leisurely, perhaps cooking. It would explain the odor. Kameclara kept her movements minimal, careful not to alert the people that she was awake.

"We know you're awake," someone croaked.

Kameclara froze, trying to identify the voice. Far off, faint droning of Teroman vehicles reached her ears. The hunt for flags must still be in progress. She pondered if refugees could've taken her. Most were reported harmless, but nothing could be certain on this foreign planet.

Kameclara chose to face her captors. She pulled herself to a seated position and turned to see an elderly couple. She swept her eyes around, trying to detect if there were more people hiding in the brush.

Nothing.

She should be careful though. This type of terrain was new to her, and she could easily miss signs.

She directed her attention back to the man and woman. They huddled with guarded expressions. A spoon stirred the pot before them. On its own.

Kameclara gulped. *Magic.*

They appeared as wary of her as she was of them. She shifted her legs to the front. In doing so, she nudged Leera and Syralise with her toes. Kameclara hoped it would wake them, but they continued breathing deeply, undisturbed.

"They'll not wake," the old woman spoke in Jeman dialect, having noticed Kameclara's disguised action. She was keen. "Please be patient. We've made food to share. It'll be ready soon."

"What am I doing here?" Kameclara demanded in the Jeman tongue, feeling grateful to have had ans of practice.

"We're hoping you could tell us," the old woman's eyebrows lifted slightly, impressed Kameclara spoke their language. "Why did you invade this planet and quash Vesper's troops?"

Kameclara took in details of the two. She recalled a Protocol Phen meeting. The robes on these strangers matched the description of sorcerers. They could've casted a sleeping spell on her and her partners. She could try to take them, but with Leera and Syralise asleep, she risked them unnecessary harm. It'd be best to bide her time and see what they wanted.

"We didn't invade. We came to liberate Ima from Vesper," Kameclara proclaimed cautiously. These could also be secret agents of Vesper. The operatives had done a thorough sweep, but with magic, it's possible a mage or two could've gotten through.

The old man and woman exchanged fretted looks. They chattered amongst themselves. Kameclara overheard "The Seed of Life."

Her brow crinkled. She had seen the term once before, but couldn't place exactly when and where. An obscure text on the Goddess flirted at the edges of her mind, along with the scent of her father's office.

The two shifted their gaze to her. "Are you... Jedrek and Meliora?" Even as the man said those words, he gave a slight roll to his eyes.

"I don't know what you mean."

The woman sighed, smug. Apparently, she'd won a debate. "Then, are you from the stars?" she asked hurriedly.

Kameclara blinked slowly, trying to anticipate how much they knew. "The stars are unreachable," she said. She waited to see how they'd respond.

The old woman appeared annoyed. "Are you from Teroma?" There was doubt in her voice as her shoulders tightened.

"Guardians of Seu?" the man added. "We've heard things in our youthful days."

Kameclara bore her eyes into them and calculated. Even if they were sorcerers of Vesper's, they wouldn't leave the forest alive. Not with the number of operatives nearby. She swallowed, taking a measured risk. "Yes."

The old couple deliberated some more. The man excitedly; the woman with reservations. Eventually, her eyes showed sway. The old man turned to Kameclara, "May I study your eyes?"

Kameclara wondered if he meant harm. He could be scheming to cast a spell. She couldn't see past his guarded demeanor. With her weapons in the tree, she would have no way to defend herself. "Why would you like to study my eyes?" she asked plainly.

"I sensed something usual about your aural vibration. It's why we chose to bring you and your friends to our camp." His eyes wavered for a moment. She caught a flash of fear. "We have many questions for your people, but right now, I suspect you may be the return of a certain immortal." Slim hope broke his voice.

Kameclara laughed heartily. She couldn't believe it. Immortal. The fairytale of the Goddess was prevalent even on Ima. It must be the "Seed" they were talking about.

How would I have reacted if my father hadn't spoken to me before the mission?

"Sure. But only if you answer my questions first," she negotiated.

The two nodded, slowly.

"Who are you and what do you want? It can't just be to study my eyes."

"My name is Unadine," the woman introduced guardedly.

"And I'm Erilph," the man a bit more cordial. "We're Master sorcerers, formerly from the renowned school of sorcery in Songbird." They exchanged a wearied glance. "Due to unfortunate events, we've come to Ima. We mean you and your friends no harm. However, your weapons are terrifying and we wished to be careful. We wanted to know your purpose, and if you are our enemy."

Kameclara sensed he spoke with veracity. Yet knowing they were sorcerers kept her defensive. *Master* sorcerers nonetheless. She didn't know much about magic, but a Master must mean they were more formidable.

"Vesper is a great imbalance," Kameclara admitted. "You know of Seu. Her threat to it is of interest to us. If you don't wish to harm us, I don't see why we're enemies."

"Why're you victimizing the people of Ima?" Unadine demanded with indignation, standing to a looming height. "The refugees are terrified."

"I cannot speak to how they feel about us. We're here to subdue Vesper's people."

Unadine and Erilph considered Kameclara's words. They conversed quietly and bobbed their heads. They seemed to accept her explanation. "May I please see your eyes now?" Erilph asked.

Kameclara nodded as a show of good faith. *How different could it be from my experience with Ashmarah?*

The old man climbed to his feet and hobbled on creaky knees. He leaned into Kameclara and delicately grasped her chin. Dry hands were careful not to force as he moved her head side to side. His brow furrowed as Kameclara felt pulsing from his skin. It was warm, and she felt intrigued.

After a long moment, he spoke over his shoulder, "Well, it's not her. She's not immortal. However, I'm reading something else... I can't determine why, but her soul's responding to the land."

"It doesn't matter," Unadine spoke dismissively. "I didn't believe she'd be 'The Seed of Life.' Regardless, we can untie the others."

My soul's responding to the land? What does that mean? Does it explain why I've been hyper-sensitive? Kameclara tried to find meaning.

As Erilph shuffled back to Unadine, he spoke in a low voice so only his cohort could hear, "It seems their aims align with ours. We should work with them concerning Jema."

Unadine lowered into her seat, "Yes, well they say they're here to liberate, but they're starving the people of Ima. I'm not sure how much they're willing to sacrifice for their beliefs of what's good."

"Unadine, you know Vesper trained the people of Ima to live and die for her. It would take drastic measures to defeat her influence," he rationalized. "They must know this too."

"Perhaps," she grumbled. But her eyes softened.

As he lowered, Erilph waved a hand in the direction of Leera and Syralise. He informed Kameclara her friends would awaken soon. He snapped his fingers and the rope tying her wrists and ankles loosened. Kameclara finally pulled them off. They had been charmed.

She moved to sit protectively before her partners. The Teroman watched keenly as Erilph grabbed the self-stirring spoon. He lifted an old bowl with a small chip, and scooped a large serving of stew. He shuffled back to Kameclara and stretched out an arm.

Bewildered by the gesture, she didn't accept the food right away. Not sure what to do, she studied Erilph and Unadine once more. They waited, regarding her with equal cautiousness. Kameclara took the bowl with uncertainty. Only after she watched the two eat did she sample the food.

As the spoon hit her tongue, there was only one word to describe the mixture of flavors: enchanted. Her taste buds danced with joy. The spicy stew contained solid meat, something she hadn't tasted since she was a child. Chunks of vegetables were strewn plentifully, and herbs unknown to her enhanced their flavor.

She hated to admit it, but it was even better than the food Syralise's father made.

Yet as food scavenged from local earth filled her, what was most startling was Kameclara felt as if she'd returned to a place she longed.

But why would my soul respond to this land?

Chapter Twenty-Nine

Priletoria- 2221 Iman Year

Syralise rubbed her eyes, grunting. She stared at the trees, on her back. She blinked a few times then sprung to her feet, alert. She immediately saw the elderly couple as her hand went to her pocket and pulled out the flag. She sighed in relief.

Beside her, Leera's head shot up. A hand brushed loose hair from her face. "Who are those two?" She growled to Kameclara. Leera eyed their weapons in the tree.

"From what I figured, refugees."

"How'd we get here?" Syralise questioned.

"Where are we?" Leera demanded.

"Have some soup," Erilph strutted over with two more bowls. Syralise and Leera exchanged confused expressions.

Kameclara introduced Unadine and Erilph in the Jeman dialect. She explained they had escaped from Jema and had been living on Ima for the last few years. Her tone indicated she still felt unsure how much they could trust them. She purposefully left out they were sorcerers.

"Yes, we're Master sorcerers. Using our powers, we helped commandeer dragons to come here," Erilph explained.

Kameclara felt her body tense as Syralise and Leera exchanged an alarmed look. Each precariously clutched their bowl of stew.

"Is this guy for real?" Syralise asked under her breath in Teroman. "A sorcerer?"

"Illogical," Leera frowned.

Kameclara kept silent. Had she not been sworn to secrecy by Protocol Phen, she'd be speculating alongside her partners. A part of her surreptitiously hoped Erilph would tell them more.

"Please, enjoy the food while you're here," Erilph spoke graciously. "We've learned what we need for now. I didn't sense you were lying when you confessed your purpose on Ima." He waved his hands lyrically. "I have lifted the cloaking spell. You're free to leave whenever you wish."

Unadine added in her flat manner, "I understand you'll need to speak with your elders about this encounter. I request you take us with you when you leave for Jema. We'd like to also defeat Vesper and restore peace." She spoke with confidence, as if there was no doubt in her mind the Teromans would require her aid. "I'm sure you'll have room for us on your giant ships."

Alpha-Je gazed at each other, unsure how to respond.

Before a word could leave their mouths, operatives dropped from trees and surrounded the camp. One grabbed for the flag in Syralise's lap. She snatched it back, instinctively punching the assailant. He blocked and the two locked in a struggle. More flag seekers appeared and Orareca's Alpha-Je was drawn into combat.

Without warning, bright light filled the forests. All but Alpha-Je flew backwards. The three women turned to see Erilph winding his arms. An orb of blue energy formed between his hands. He thrust and a burst of wind as powerful as a jet engine emanated from his palms. It cast flag seekers far from Kameclara and her partners.

"Cease!" Kameclara shouted in Jeman.

Erilph paused, confused.

"It's game! They allies, don't hurt!" Kameclara explained in a rush, tripping over her Jeman.

Erilph and Unadine appeared perplexed. "We don't treat our friends like that."

"What a barbaric game," Unadine frowned. "I'm still uncertain if I'll take to you people."

Nervously, Kameclara glided her gaze over the scene. Operatives were pulling themselves off of the ground. Syralise took the opportunity and grabbed the opponents' flag. She then jumped into the tree and pulled down her com-helmet. She radioed Captain Nanti with delight. "Group two claims group one's flag!"

The flag seekers groaned in disappointment, marveling at the trap they'd walked into. "How'd you set up that blast?" one asked. "What'd you use?"

"It must've been some type of concentrated S-48 energy," another speculated.

Kameclara sighed with relief. They didn't catch sight of Erilph casting the spell. "It's a secret," she tried to laugh, but it came out nervously.

Leera and Syralise stared down Kameclara. Hundreds of questions waited on the tips of their tongues.

"And who're they?" A North Deroner asked of Unadine and Erilph.

Kameclara gulped. "Refugees."

"Why're they with you?"

Kameclara gulped again. "We asked to camp with them for cover."

"Well played!"

The Captains radioed for return to the Warship-23. The flag seekers complied, hopping upwards through trees. Hovering jets waited above the canopy. Alpha-Je hung back, uncertain where their bikes were.

For Leera and Syralise, they mostly wanted answers.

Kameclara retrieved her com-helmet and set a private line to Captain Nanti. "This is Kameclara. We have a situation."

"Speak."

She lowered her voice. "Meet at my coordinates. It involves a certain protocol…"

"Roger that," Captain Nanti's voice remained apathetic. If she felt concern over the exposure of magic, she didn't show it.

Syralise strode to Kameclara. "Magic, huh? That's what the big secret's all about?" Erilph's confession of being a sorcerer remained fresh on her mind.

Leera furrowed her brow. "Preposterous! There's gotta be a scientific explanation!"

"Don't tell me you know something about this?" Syralise drilled Kameclara. The dark-haired operative couldn't meet her friend's eyes. "You knew!" Syralise exclaimed. "Why didn't you tell us?" she pushed, upset.

"It can't be magic!" Leera echoed. "It's not rational."

"I cannot confirm nor deny anything," Kameclara pulled off her helmet.

Syralise's face softened, taking a step back. "I get it, you couldn't tell us. This must mean officers commanded it." A hand propped crossly on her hip. "Why'd they pick just you to give this info to? We're a squad. Why didn't they include all three of us?"

"Enough!" Captain Nanti's voice cut through the air. She hopped over monstrous, gnarled roots as if they were nothing. A second figure followed close by her side.

"Why's Hayes here?" Kameclara blurted. It was true Hayes was another operative of Protocol Phen; but he wasn't from Orareca like the rest of them.

As Captain Nanti approached, she eyed the two sorcerers. They'd gone back to tending their fire, ignoring the Teromans' commotion. The Captain froze as fleeting hope danced across her usually imperturbable face.

Hayes saw them too. He grasped her shoulder tightly as they whimpered. The two dropped a knee to the ground.

"Honored Masters! You've survived!" Captain Nanti spoke with reverence. It was the most emotion Alpha-Je had ever observed from their Captain.

"What the hell?" Syralise whispered.

"Should we kneel too?" Leera asked under her breath.

Syralise raised her shoulders. After consideration, she awkwardly lowered to the ground. Leera and Kameclara sunk behind her.

"And who are you?" Unadine asked the Captain, chin in the air.

"Please rise, you're making me uncomfortable," Erilph chided.

Captain Nanti straightened herself and spoke respectfully, "I am Captain Nanti. This is Hayes and we're from the planet Teroma, at the edge of our system."

Kameclara gawked at how readily her Captain spewed information.

"We knew much of the twelve Masters sorcerers until a few years ago. Sadly, it was believed you two had perished at the hands of Vesper." Captain Nanti exchanged a look with Hayes.

He knew what she wanted to ask. As Ashmarah's second in command, he held the power to approve. He nodded.

Captain Nanti puffed her chest and approached Erilph. Unadine hung back, appearing sour. "Before your disappearance, it was our hope to have you allied with us against Vesper. I beseech you, on behalf of Teroma's Intergalactic Military, please assist us in restoring Jema."

Does our Captain have the power to speak on behalf of the IM? Kameclara stared at the woman with fresh wonder. *You continue to surprise me, Captain.*

"Couldn't have said it better myself!" Unadine's disdainful wrinkles finally disappeared.

"There is one caveat," Captain Nanti added, "You're welcome to stay in our camp. However, we've kept the knowledge of magic a secret from our people. We ask you to please be discrete about your abilities."

"Kept the knowledge of magic a secret?" Unadine shot to her feet, offended. It was her life's work. "Why?"

"Where we're from, the use of magic has faded from common knowledge..." Captain Nanti began to explain.

"Say nothing more," Erilph flicked his hand, interrupting with a grin. "We're elderly and prefer to keep to ourselves. We're more comfortable in our cloaked camp. Fetch us when you leave for Jema."

The true reason Erilph agreed so quickly was Maza. They couldn't leave her behind. She slept in a hidden cocoon high in the branches.

"Thank you," Captain Nanti bowed reverently. Kameclara thought she noticed moist eyes.

"… Our Captain just confirmed the existence of magic…" Leera choked in disbelief.

Chapter Thirty

On the eastern border of the blue forests, miles from Warship-23, Captain Nanti stopped Alpha-Je. They had left Unadine and Erilph with a radio. It didn't take long to instruct them on its operation. They'd used similar contraptions from Calio.

The Captain made sure they were out of earshot from any who might listen. She placed herself between Kameclara and her partners. Addressing the two, she asked, "What do you think you've witnessed?"

Hayes hung back, a haughty expression on his face. Kameclara tried to fathom why he was present, but no clear explanation came to mind.

Syralise saluted. "The elder gentleman explained his abilities as magic. We heard you refer to him and his companion as Master sorcerers, Sir!"

Leera stepped stiffly, "I believe we witnessed a weapon we have yet to find an explanation for, Sir!" She flicked eyes to Kameclara. "Permission to speak."

"Granted."

"Why is Kameclara not being questioned?"

"I'll tell you why," Hayes folded his arms, striding casually towards the group. "She's been recruited for a secret protocol. One I believe you two might be a good fit for."

Kameclara saluted her Captain. She couldn't hold her tongue anymore, "Permission to speak." Her officer nodded. "Why is Hayes here?"

"If you partake of this knowledge, you must swear never to speak of it to anyone, despite country or rank," Captain Nanti specified. "Are you willing to take that vow of silence?"

"Yes, Sir!"

The officer glared at the other members of Alpha-Je. "Yes, Sir!" they echoed.

Captain Nanti held out a hand to Hayes, inviting him to explain. He swayed casually, propping a hand to his chin. "You've all heard of observers. Truth is, we do far more than watch the skies. We're a covert operation, seeded into every level of the IM. We're keepers of Teroma's oldest secret, and guide to the Hegemon Generals." His eyes glistened, a hand moving to his chest. "I am a high-ranking observer."

Kameclara felt a lump in her throat. His account clarified many of her suspicions. *But he's so young.*

"What is that secret?" she asked bravely, not expecting an answer. It was likely above her clearance.

Hayes and Captain Nanti stiffened. Kameclara caught a hint of doubt skittering in his eyes. "When the time comes, you'll find out."

Kameclara tried to bite back her next question, but it burst before she could hold it back. "Is it about the Goddess?"

Her partners looked to her in alarm.

"Dammit Procias," Hayes chuckled, rubbing his brow. He sighed, peering devilishly at Kameclara. "He told you, didn't he?"

Kameclara felt uncertain how to respond. She wasn't an observer.

Hayes' rank in the organization meant nothing to her. As an operative, they were equals. Even more so, she felt speechless at Hayes' reaction. It affirmed all her father had imparted.

"That's not what we're here to talk about," Captain Nanti saved her. She gave Hayes an admonishing look. She tipped her head to Syralise and Leera.

He clapped his hands, rubbing palms together. "Alright. Let's talk about Protocol Phen."

~*~

Kameclara trudged silently through the forests. She needed time to clear her head. Or rather, finally give her head a chance to process the true elements of their mission. Having won the flag game, the other teams were on watch. She wouldn't need to report back for hours.

Something about the blue forests felt soothing. She sensed much joy had been shared in them in the past. Their scent soaked through her pores and lifted her spirits.

"Sorcerers exist. Magic is real." The words didn't feel real to say.

She recalled the bewildered expression on her partners' faces when Hayes swore them into Protocol Phen. They were all unique in the way they dealt with stress. And the new information certainly was stressful. Leera hit the gym. Syralise slept on it. Kameclara went on her stroll.

As she trekked through undergrowth, Kameclara became aware of a fragrance. It tickled deliciously and she swung her head around. Inhaling deep, the sweet scent lit a tender flame in her chest. She followed, searching for its source, hunting for a buried memory.

Kameclara came to an area overgrown by thick vines. They twisted around decaying logs, lifting some into the air. She shifted her footing, sliding along a crooked trunk. Something snapped loose, and curtains of vines cascaded to the ground. In the opening, Kameclara caught sight of an untamed bush, crowding out a small clearing.

Her feet came to rest as she naturally found balance. She'd never seen such a plant before, yet its scent brought waves of wistfulness. The blooms grew in bunches, hanging against each other amorously.

Kameclara studied the bush's tiny blue buds with intrigue. Their soft shape stood in contrast to surrounding thick bark and thorn-heavy climbing plants. Those competed for meager sunlight, whereas the tiny petals blossomed from a power within.

The operatives were required to study many plant databases as part of training for Ima and Jema. Mostly so they knew which poisonous ones to avoid. There were quite a few Kameclara committed to memory for their beauty. "These are wistras," her voice quivered. Seeing them in person stirred her profoundly. The written description had detailed the scent as sweet, but tasting the fragrance brought a different dimension to the experience.

Inhaling deep, her heart quickened for a moment. Euphoria pulsed. "What was that?" she murmured, startled by the strange sensation.

Kameclara stole one last sniff, then turned to continue her walk.

After a few hours of exploring, she returned to the clearing, unable to shake it from her mind. Kameclara stepped into the ubiquitous petals. As their softness caressed her cheek, a tear dripped from her eyes. She buried her face and breathed deep. Love washed through her being.

"I'm home," she called out.

A piece of her soul waited for a response. A tinkling laughter of welcome, perhaps.

Nothing came. Yet, standing amongst the wistra, Kameclara did not feel alone.

~*~

Hayes reported to Ashmarah all that transpired with the Master sorcerers. Her eyes lit with relief at the mention of the Unadine and Erilph. He also informed her of his decision to indoctrinate Kameclara's partners into Protocol Phen.

Ashmarah responded curtly, "I was surprised they weren't on your original list. Leera's a Pinghe warrior, and Syralise has an open mind—easy to accept the existence of magic."

"Those were the reasons I didn't put them on my list," he sighed. "The Pinghe were the ones to initiate the phasing out of magic. Open mindedness can lead to being manipulated."

"The Pinghe were the original holders of magic," Ashmarah corrected gently. "And Syralise is loyal to her partners. Besides, as an Alpha-Je yourself, you should know she's not weak-willed."

"Noted. Truthfully, they did make my auxiliary list." He pulled his lips into a line. "Is Hegemon General Theol going to berate me for the two additions?"

Ashmarah patted his shoulder. "I'll explain to him."

Hayes grinned. "Wish I could get some of that respect he gives you."

Chapter Thirty-One

The hum aboard Warship-23 changed for a few days. Rumor had it they were idling in orbit. Stanten asked Geraldo if he knew where they were.

"Prolly someplace 'round Molta. We've been onboard for eight ans after all," his friend responded. "Molta's the furthest we've ever gone."

They continued chores for a few days. On the morning of the ninth, the head warden announced they were to return to their rooms and brace for landing.

Stanten's fear of flying had long since dissipated and he sat calmly in his chair. It'd grown threadbare over the ans, but more comfortable. He'd spent many hours reading on it. He found books soothing as they opened his mind to new possibilities. In words, he found freedom, knowing there were better ways to live.

The ride was bumpy as they entered the atmosphere. When the perpetual hum of the warship ceased, silence enveloped. Stanten basked in stillness, not realizing how much noise surrounded him at all times before.

It wasn't long until his door opened. A warden held a pair of shackles and Stanten allowed his ankles to be cuffed. In the hall, inmates were being marched in the same direction. Stanten followed them to the lowest deck. There, he found Geraldo and Mardo. "How cold ya think it's gonna be out there?" he mumbled.

"Molta orbits outside Teroma," Geraldo frowned. "Wish they'd give us thicker clothes. I ain't gonna like this." His rolled his shoulders.

A hiss reached their ears. Sealed lower doors of the warship were opening for the first time in eight ans. Stanten braced for frigid air.

Instead, blinding light seared his eyes. Heat as torrid as a burning star struck him, making it troublesome to breathe.

Geraldo immediately took off his shirt and Stanten followed suit. Even then, sweat poured from their skin. A few people hyperventilated, collapsing to the ground. Others screamed, hugging the walls, praying for Ia to save them.

"Where the hell're we?" a man shouted in panic.

"Oh my Goddess, we're being jettisoned into the sun!" one shrieked.

Hysteria started to spread.

"Calm down!" The head warden demanded. His words didn't pacify. He turned to his subordinates. "Get 'em off the ship. They'll see soon enough it's fine."

A warden strolled down the gangway, disappearing into brightness. Seeing his action abated some panic.

A sharp object pushed Stanten between his shoulders. His skin prickled as he stumbled into the light. Stanten lifted a hand to shield his eyes. His feet clumsily found a ramp. Dread hung around him as he waited for death, unsure what form it would take.

It didn't come. As he carefully peered between his fingers, Stanten's breath caught in his chest. Eyes wide, he stumbled in a circle, unable to comprehend the sight before him. Stretching for an eternity, fields of green danced in sultry wind. Far in the distance, a line of what could only be trees stood in greeting.

He'd never seen so many in one place! And they were huge!

"Move along!" a warden shouted.

Huffing from shock, Stanten lumbered to where he was told. There was canvas and piping dumped haphazardly on the ground. They were put to work, setting up tents.

A few inmates were called back on board. They appeared moments later with coolers of water. During break, Stanten chugged a large cup to quench his never-ending thirst. He returned to work, staking tents into the ground.

When they finished, a warden called out lackadaisically, "Hang out here for a while" gesturing under the tents. He tugged at his long-sleeved uniform, eyes squinting. "Don't do anything stupid. This place is dangerous. The environment can kill you." Exhaling uncomfortably, he added, "You'll get used to the heat in a few days." The words seemed more for himself.

Most prisoners stripped down to their underwear and sprawled uncomfortably in the shade. Stanten joined them and miserably tried not to move. The scorch bore down despite the tents, and he couldn't think straight.

Is this their idea of torture? How long are we to stay here?

"Ya think this is our final destination?" Mardo asked as he plopped beside him.

"Hope not," Stanten growled.

Too hot for conversation, they drifted into an uneasy nap.

When night came, it cooled considerably, but was still too hot for

Teromans. The prisoners stayed under the tents and an occasional cooling breeze brought relief. Stanten used his shirt and wiped sweat from his face. Unable to rest in sweltering temperatures, he walked to the edge of their camp and admired the landscape. "Never thought I'd see something like this!" he exclaimed, mood improving.

In the distant north, an enormous pile of rubble formed a tall hill. Trunks of young trees poked towards the sky at awkward angles. To the east there was a mountain range. Stanten could see snow on its peaks. Compared to Teroma, it was mere trace amounts. He cursed. "Why couldn't we have landed there?"

He contemplated his life and its unique turn. A decade ago, he would never have anticipated sitting in a tranquil green field. It was a far cry from the dark, cramped alleys of Pudyo. Despite chains around his ankles, he felt free.

Stanten sucked in sweet air. For the first time in his life, he felt peace. He never believed much in fate, but as Stanten sat there, it seemed as if it were all meant to be.

He reclined in the grass, marveling at how it tickled. Peering at the stars, he realized he couldn't pick out any constellations from the books he'd read. Stanten gulped. Perhaps they were just that far from Teroma.

A bright green star caught his eye and Stanten's heart quickened. The color reminded of Kameclara's eyes.

If fate were real, was I destined to meet her?

It seemed like an outrageous notion, but he wanted to believe.

Immediately, Stanten chided himself. He didn't want to lose touch with reality. Whatever he and Kameclara had shared was over. Dash what he hoped was meant to be. The last time they'd spoke, she said she wouldn't be back to Warship-23 for the rest of her mission. He'd accepted he'd never see her again.

Stanten tried to force his thoughts elsewhere.

It didn't work.

The more he guided his notions from Kameclara, the louder her name played in his head.

Cautiously, he allowed himself to reminisce, just a little. Memories surfaced of their embrace on the viewing deck. Something in him had awakened.

It wasn't until long after Kameclara had left Warship-23, did he fully realize the depth of the love he carried for her.

It was so foreign he'd ignored it at first. He'd assumed it was moodiness. Stanten had never felt strongly towards anyone, let alone a woman. He wished things were simpler. Emotions were complex. And annoying.

Though if he needed to find a word to describe the way he felt towards Kameclara, it would be "beautiful." That is, if beautiful things were meant for someone like him.

He told himself that even if he did confess his feelings, she couldn't have accepted them. He would've only embarrassed himself. He didn't need that.

Lying on the grass, he lifted a hand and reached towards the green star. The twinkling was as far to him as Kameclara. He knew in that moment he was hopeless. Stanten could never forget her.

~*~

As days dragged on, prisoners' shackles were removed. The wardens weren't concerned with escape. They had no place to go and heat made them sluggish.

Stanten appreciated the added freedom. He went off to explore, not feeling a bit concerned about the unfamiliar terrain. Somehow, it felt enticing.

The forest to the west intensely drew his inquisitiveness. They carried a majestic blue hue.

"Be careful out there," Geraldo warned.

"I'll be fine," he waved. Stanten filled his pockets with provisions before venturing into the forest.

The scent of earth tasted sweet and his heart thumped wildly. He loved the feel of bark against his hands as he leveraged branches to climb. He continued with no destination in mind, simply reveling in the exotic environment.

He must've traveled quite far. The sounds of camp faded and the trees towered far over his head. The roots were large and entangled to form patterns. He found a nook and paused to rest, leaning against a trunk many times his size. Stray animal calls reached his ears, but the forest was otherwise serene.

A soft thump came from behind.

Stanten's ears burned. He scrambled for a weapon, hands finding a large stick. Guardedly, he circled the trunk.

An orange sphere rolled before him. Stanten looked up.

Did it fall from the tree?

He felt a bit silly and lowered his weapon. He inspected the sphere and noticed it smelled like his favorite green snack. He wiped the skin and took a bite. "Mmm," he grunted. It tasted much sweeter than its green cousin, the pear. The juice helped quench his thirst too.

Stanten found a few more pears nestled amongst the roots. He collected them before continuing on his way. He thought he heard a chuckle in the trees. When he craned his neck to search, he didn't see anyone. Regardless, he couldn't shake the feeling of being watched. He hurried back to camp.

When he returned, it was the middle of the night. A few inmates stood around conversing. Geraldo and Mardo hovered near the water cooler. Stanten went over. They were discussing their location.

"I think it's a planet," Geraldo ventured. "I heard there's an ocean to the south."

"Makes sense," Mardo joined. "There's mountains," he nodded east. "Too bad they're too far to reach on foot. I'd like to check 'em out."

"Who do you think lived here?" Geraldo asked.

"What makes you think people lived here?" Mardo responded.

Geraldo pointed north with his chin. "Some o' the guys said the hill there useta be a building." Stanten eyed the odd-shaped mound.

"Hmm," Mardo rubbed his chin. "Ya think this was a Teroman colony?"

Geraldo's shoulders tightened, "Maybe we're in enemy territory, gettin' ready for a war."

Mardo's expression fell, "Hope not."

Stanten's vision drifted north. In his mind's eye, he saw a castle rising against the sky. "No, not enemy territory. Not a place this beautiful."

~*~

The next day, the inmates were put to work, building structures. They dug large stones from the earth. Some were already cut into cubes. It fed Geraldo's belief the location was previously inhabited. "These rocks look like they coulda been a part of a home," he commented.

The Intergalactic Military stored their gear in the buildings as soon as they were constructed. The operatives weren't around much, always running around. Stanten liked watching the jets take off. They arched far into the sky until they couldn't be seen. Then they'd roar back from a different direction.

It wasn't until all the structures were finished did Stanten find an opportunity to explore north. He wandered off early one morning, making sure to bring water. By midday, he neared the odd hill. The ground sloped and he saw shards of colored glass. He felt a rush. Glass meant buildings.

Where the slope grew steep, sandy colored stones jutted out. Stanten started to climb, hoping the top held a nice view.

Somewhere in the middle of the hill, he came upon decorated megaliths. There was no longer any doubt in his mind this place was once inhabited. The megaliths had crashed onto their sides and were partially buried by years of weathering. Devastating cracks covered most of its surface. He moved towards a slope of pebbles, not wishing to disturb the fractures.

Stanten lost his footing. "Dammit!" The pebbles rushed downwards and brought Stanten with them. They took him between the two large slabs, and the ground gave way. He landed on his back and heard a crack. He cursed loudly. Pain emanated from his gunshot scar, and he waited for it to subside.

As he rested, Stanten stared at the gash in the earth. The megaliths formed a cavern beneath them. It'd protected fabric lining the sides. They were embroidered with plants.

Once the pain dulled, Stanten carefully climbed to his feet. After some stretching, nothing felt broken. He reached high and ran fingers over the fabric. The texture kicked up a dust of emotions. His heart palpitated with yearning.

Frightened by his innate reaction, he withdrew his hand. "Gotta get outta this place." He didn't like having feelings. Especially ones he couldn't explain. Made him vulnerable.

He found secure footing and pulled himself up. In doing so, something came loose, clattering into the hole. It caught a ray of sun, shining it in his eyes. Stanten peered down to see a circular object encrusted with jewels. It was a golden insignia with swords. Perhaps the crest of an old nation. It elicited the same yearning as the fabric.

Stanten quickened his climb, exiting the cavern.

Continuing upwards, a sparkle in the air caught his attention. It was followed by the sound of a splash. It seemed out of place in the peaceful afternoon. Stanten vigilantly proceeded up, eager to investigate.

He soon found himself below a vertical drop, twice his height. He looked around and couldn't find footholds. Stanten took a step back and darted forward to push against the wall. His hand grasped the edge and he managed to pull himself up.

As his left arm reached over, he felt wetness. Something slimy made it difficult to grip. He kicked his feet hard. Moments later, Stanten rolled over the edge and splashed into shallow water. Stunned, he looked around to see a shimmering pool. The sliminess was rich growth at the bottom of the pond.

Another glimmer caught his eye. In the distance, a purple fish splashed. It drew his attention beyond the edge of the suspended pond. The canopy of the blue forests danced to the touch of wind. They seemed to be waving in greeting. Stanten sucked in a lungful of air, a chuckle rising from within. He really liked it there.

He took his time wading towards dry stones. Little creatures darted from his every step. Some hopped, most swam. He'd seen a fishery once, but rivers in Teroma held no such life.

Stanten wondered again where they were.

And why does it feel so much like home?

As he climbed from the pond, he came upon a dented shield. It bore the same insignia as the crest he'd discovered. Stanten drew a finger across the object and a fleeting sentiment soared in his heart, disappearing as quickly as it had come.

He took a step back with dubiety. A strange attachment to the stones beneath his feet manifested, and the wound in his torso burned. It woke mourning into his heart.

Stanten swept his gaze across the staggering landscape. Once, there was a great palace here. He could feel it in his bones. Something terrible had happened.

His earlier sense of ease became replaced by crushing sadness he couldn't comprehend. He shook his head. "Gotta get outta here."

Chapter Thirty-Two

Isa danced in anticipation when she learned their ship was to land. Civilians were allowed to disembark for a whole nine days. Weeks before, she had made plans with her friends to explore. Secretly, she hoped the place would be warm. Many times during their journey, she'd dreamt about a big sun.

More than anything, Isa hoped there would be a pond or a lake. She'd read about swimming and wanted to try it. She'd talked to Aunt Ashmarah about their destination, but the woman didn't seem interested.

Isa chewed the inside of her cheek. "Are you feeling okay, Auntie? You're the only person I know who's not overjoyed!"

"Oh, when you get to my age, you've pretty much seen it all," she sighed, not looking away from her computer.

The ship was abuzz with excitement and Isa shared it with other civilians. A list of precautions was sent to every family. Mostly it warned not to wander far from the ships; and a list local flora and fauna to avoid.

None knew where they were headed, but no one minded. They felt safe, knowing an enormous Teroman fleet accompanied them.

Once they drew closer, live images of a green place streamed onto monitors in common areas. Isa wriggled impatiently. Green meant lots of sun. "I knew it would be warm!" There was a channel on their home screen that displayed select video clips, taken at high altitude. Isa nearly screamed with joy to see a vast expanse of water in one. "Swim-ming!"

Aunt Ashmarah ignored her. She hadn't left her computer in days.

~*~

On landing day, Isa awoke early. It was a surprise she'd slept at all. She dressed herself in her favorite outfit and rushed to the common area where her neighbors gathered. There, they watched short videos of warships on the ground. The operatives landed first to make sure everything was safe.

The clips were limited, as the Intergalactic Military was secre-tive. But Isa didn't care for most of the ships. She waited for shots of Warship-23. That was the ship they were to land beside. She busily searched the backdrop for a place to swim.

The humming of their ship changed as a message on-screen an-nounced they were initiating landing procedures. Isa grabbed her friend Lorae's arm and squealed. The two bounced on their toes, joined by many others. The message asked the citizens to return to their homes and find a seat for safety. Isa and Lorae promised to find each other after disembarking.

Isa wanted to sit still and be good for Aunt Ashmarah, she truly did. But her elation refused to be contained. She ran around their living room in circles. She was too old to play with some of her toys, but she still picked up Mr. Frimples and squeezed.

The floor suddenly felt strange and Isa crumpled to the ground. "Hey, what's going on?"

"You're used to the ship moving," Ashmarah explained. "Your body's astounded that it's stopped."

Isa hopped back onto her legs. She laughed as she wobbled. After a few minutes, the peculiar sensation went away. Ashmarah stood without trouble.

"Auntie, can you walk so normal because you used to be an operative like Dad?" Isa asked.

Ashmarah pet her niece's head, "Yes, dear. I was on all kinds of ships."

Isa did a cartwheel, landing awkwardly. "I wanna be an operative too, when I grow up!"

Her aunt chuckled heartedly, "Is that so? You know it's lots of hard work."

"Don't care!" she zoomed about, "I wanna protect people!" A sad look entered her aunt's eyes. Isa stopped in her tracks. "Did I say something wrong?"

"No, dear. I think it's wonderful you want to protect people." She walked to the couch and patted the seat next to her. Isa flopped down. "It's just… I have some bad news." Isa's eyes grew big. Ashmarah decided it was best to rip the bandage off. "Sweetie, you know how I'm working all the time?"

"Uh huh."

"Well, outside the ship is dangerous. You can only leave when you're with me, or your father. Do you understand?"

"Yeah!" Isa didn't see the problem. "We can go soon though, right? I made plans with Lorae."

"…And because I'm working all the time, and so's your father, you won't be outside as much as the other kids." All civilians traveling with the fleet were assigned jobs. Most tended to crops, some cleaned, and others educated children. Ashmarah's cover was budgeting resources, such as water and food. Truthfully, a program did it for her, giving her time to command observers.

Isa shrugged, "I can come back early and help with dinner and stuff."

"Isa, sweetie. You can only go outside for two to three hours a day. That's all your father and I can spare."

Isa's face grew long, "But the other kids get to go whenever they want!"

"Well, honey, you're not other kids. You're our responsibility." It pained Ashmarah to see the child's spirit plummet.

"What about Talda's dad? He watches me sometimes. Why can't he watch me outside?"

"Because Talda's dad can't protect you if something goes wrong. He never had the same training as me or your father."

"Nothing's gonna go wrong!" Isa covered her face and flopped into the couch's cushions. "This is SO unfair!" she wept.

Ashmarah patted her leg. Isa pushed her away, curling into a ball. "I just wanna be normal. You're too overprotective," she whined. "What makes me different from the other kids?"

"It's because I care about you," Ashmarah soothed.

"Noooo…"

"Well, you can stay here and cry, or we can disembark right now," Ashmarah's tone grew firm.

Isa considered for a moment. She really did want to see the new place. Still fuming, she dragged a sleeve over her eyes. "Ok, fine! Let's go."

"That's my sweet girl," Ashmarah pulled her close and kissed her head. Isa groaned, but accepted her affection.

People were exiting Civilian Ship-2 in long lines. Isa found Talda and Lorae and they strolled down the ramp with arms linked. Aunt Ashmarah hovered closely.

The civilians spread out. Many sought shade in erected tents. Others went to explore a line of trees far in the distance. Isa frowned. She couldn't see any bodies of water.

"Where do you wanna go first?" Lorae asked.

To Isa's dismay, her aunt cut in, "Sorry ladies. Isa isn't allowed to leave camp."

Isa's jaw dropped. "But there's only sweaty operatives here! I wanna find a place to swim!"

"Just appreciate the fresh air and pick some flowers," Aunt Ashmarah smiled. She appeared uncomfortable in the heat. Isa noticed her friends wilting too. They cupped their hands over their eyes as if hiding. She didn't think it was that warm.

Isa tried to sway her aunt with sweet talk, but her usual tactics failed. Lorae and Talda expressed their sympathies before running off. They promised to bring her something interesting.

With nothing better to do, Isa found herself seated on a log. She pouted openly, sore with disappointment. She stared at the operatives running drills all day. They never did anything fun. Isa questioned her earlier desire to become one.

"There's gotta be other ways to protect people," she puttered, "And what's Aunt Ashmarah doing, talking to them that much anyway? Can't she budget their resources from any computer?" She pulled a piece of tall grass and poked the dirt with it, bored out of her mind.

That evening, her friends brought home a treasure trove of findings. Strange looking seeds and little critters filled their pockets. They shared them with Isa and she felt delighted, but only briefly. It wasn't the same as striking out on her own.

At dinner, she whined and begged her aunt to change her mind. When her father showed up, she tried to convince him as well.

"No sweetie, we need to keep an eye on you," Ashmarah stood firm. "Besides, there's dangerous rebels about," she added in an attempt to scare Isa.

"You can come with me to run errands tomorrow," her father added, trying to cheer her.

"No. That's okay, daddy," Isa sulked, "I'll just get in your way. I'll be good." A lump formed in her throat. She might never get the chance to swim. Not that her friends reported there to be water nearby anyway.

Isa hoped and hoped that her caregivers would change their minds and let her explore on her own. Yet as the end of the nine days drew near, they continued to deny her pleas.

Soon, their last day rolled around and Isa hung her head low.

Depressed, she exited the ship for the last time with Aunt Ashmarah. She slumped on a log by some workers. Her father stood near too, talking to an operative. Isa stuck out a tongue at their backs.

As a laborer walked by, a breeze knocked off his hat. She saw his hands were full, so Isa offered to place it back on his head. He leaned down and she pulled it tightly over his ears. He grumbled a solitary word of gratitude and walked off.

Isa tilted her head and watched him strut. Something about him seemed familiar, but she couldn't quite grasp what.

She went back to her log and sat for most of her allowed two hours. Then, an idea struck her.

She hopped to her feet and found Ashmarah. "Auntie, I'm going back to the ship now," she said. "The sun's too hot out here." It was a white lie. She didn't understand why everyone was sweating. She felt perfectly fine.

"Okay, dear," Ashmarah beamed. She felt badly the eleven-ans-old couldn't play with her friends, but it was too risky. Isa must've finally resigned herself, knowing they were lifting off at dawn. Ashmarah watched intensely to make sure the girl reached her destination.

Isa trudged onto Civilian Ship-2. Ashmarah sighed, turning attention back to her tablet. There was a new transmission from Hegemon General Theol.

Isa grabbed a hat from her room and tucked her hair underneath. She changed her clothes and went back outside. She held her body bent and tried to walk with a different gait. She snuck past her aunt and ducked behind water coolers.

Once she felt certain no one would notice, she strolled off camp as casually as possible. Isa set her sights towards a tall hill and fought the urge to glance over her shoulder. She didn't want to accidentally lock eyes with anyone.

When she couldn't hear sounds of camp anymore, Isa allowed herself to peek back. People were tending to their business, working like robots. No one noticed her.

She turned and let loose, running as fast as her legs could carry. The soft grass gave bounce and when she leaped, Isa soared through the air. She cried out in joy. For now, the world belonged to her and she belonged to it. She wondered what secrets it held in store.

Chapter Thirty-Three

Ashmarah didn't return to her quarters until late that evening. There was much to coordinate and she needed to do it all under the guise of a civilian. Isa's door sat closed so she left the girl alone. She seated herself at the kitchen table and scrutinized a checklist of preparations for lift off.

Once completed, Ashmarah made a quick dinner with fresh greens. She hummed a tune as she set the table for two. She knocked on Isa's door. "Sweetie, it's dinner time." There was no response. "Isa?" Ashmarah frowned and tried the handle. It was unlocked.

The room sat dark. Perhaps Isa had fallen asleep. Ashmarah turned on a soft desk lamp and saw an empty bed. A bead of terror formed inside her as she quickly flicked on the ceiling light. "Isa, this isn't funny, where are you?" she called.

There was no response.

Ashmarah checked the closets and under the beds. Nothing. She took a few deep breaths before calling all of Isa's friends. But the girl wasn't with any of them.

"Isa's never disobeyed before," She thought aloud. Isa was an easy child to care for. It was unlike her to run off. "Did someone kidnap her?" Ashmarah fretted. "No, why would they?" There'd been talk of adding security for the children, but some felt it would raise suspicion.

Ashmarah sent a message to Hayes and paced about her living room. After a few lines back and forth, she forced herself to sit and remain calm. Ashmarah analyzed the situation. Isa was at the age when children pushed boundaries. Perhaps she merely went off to explore. She could return any moment. There was no reason to assume something more was wrong.

"Oh, but what if she doesn't?" Ashmarah vexed, leaping to her feet again. She was deemed an expert on many things, but parenting was never one of them.

"I got your message!" Hayes burst in. Face distraught.

"Do we dispatch Protocol Phen?" Ashmarah ditched all rationale from her decades of training. In that moment, she was only an anxious guardian.

Hayes kept cool, despite paling. He thought for a moment and shook his head, "If we dispatch them, we'll need to concoct a reason. Let's send a camp wide message first and see if she turns up."

Ashmarah agreed.

A description of Isa was sent to every family on board the civilian ship. It was also shared with the troops. Ashmarah and Hayes waited impatiently inside their apartment. After much pacing and calling, dusk deepened into night. No one came forth with information.

Ashmarah cried desperately to Hayes, "It's all my fault…"

"Don't do this to yourself."

He couldn't disguise the worry in his voice, and Ashmarah weakened, "I'm sending out Protocol Phen."

He nodded with surrender. "It's late and we can't take chances."

Ashmarah pulled out her communication device and contacted the officers of Protocol Phen. An order went out to the operatives to search for a girl by Isa's appearance. She and Hayes exited the ship to wait.

"Sir!" a warden approached Hayes, "I have information about the missing girl. Your daughter, I believe?"

Hayes perked, though astounded to hear from a warden. "Speak."

Ashmarah turned intently.

"This inmate remembers seeing her," he gestured to a man a few paces behind.

"When did you see her?" Ashmarah demanded, rushing to him.

"I saw an orange dress running past the north hill sometime after lunch," Stanten reported. "She turned around and I recognized her. She helped me pick up my hat today."

"Oh goodness! She must've changed her clothes! Our description's wrong!" Ashmarah wrung her hands. She pulled out her radio. In a low voice she updated orders to Protocol Phen.

Hayes dashed to a vehicle. Ashmarah watched him go. The inmate looked like he had more to say, but the warden dismissed him. Too consumed with worry, Ashmarah didn't give it much thought.

~*~

Captain Nanti summoned Unadine and met her at the edge of the forest with Ashmarah. They explained to the Master sorceress they were searching for a missing child. They were worried about her safety with rebels scattered about. They pleaded for her to cast a tracking spell.

Unadine seemed annoyed to be asked such a trivial task. She did comply as a show of good faith. The spell would show Isa's footsteps from the last four hours. Captain Nanti then instructed Protocol Phen to search for glowing tracks.

Isa was last seen six hours ago. There was no telling where they'd find the last of her tracks.

~*~

"What's magic, really?" Syralise speculated to her partners over their com-helmets. The three stood a few hundred yards apart, facing east towards the mountain range. Alpha Team was keeping watch that shift. The rebels learned days ago not to challenge their perimeter. It left lots of time for idle chatter.

"Probably some experiment gone awry," Leera dismissed.

"Yeah, but why keep it a secret," Syralise added. "I mean, I wouldn't think it'd have anything to do with this mission except for those two weirdoes we met in the forest."

"That old man did push back the operatives quite easily." A frown was heard in Leera's voice.

"It can really make this mission suck," Syralise sighed. "Kame, what'd you think?"

"You mean besides it being like a more advanced Project S-48? I think we'd need a geneticist to take a look at the nevino sequence to explain magic."

Syralise smacked her lips. "You think the higher ups did that already, and secretly know how to stop it?"

"Doubt it," Kameclara speculated. "We're told to treat magic as an unconventional weapon. If they had a way to stop it, they'd give it us… also disguised as an unconventional weapon."

"I don't like blind spots," Leera spoke firmly, "and this mission has plenty."

Kameclara listened to her partners banter as her eyes scanned the distance. With her visor up, she caught a whiff of Iman air. The scent made her feel alive. She wished she could bottle some and take it with her.

Captain Nanti's voice cut through their conversation with a code to activate Protocol Phen. A photograph blinked onto their visors. "Search and retrieve, unharmed."

Kameclara slapped her visor down and eyed the familiar face. "That's Hayes' kid. What's goin' on?" she wondered to her partners.

Captain Nanti continued, "A spell has been cast to show target's footsteps in the last four hours. If engaged by hostiles, permission granted to neutralize."

Alpha-Je accepted the command.

"Brock," Leera radioed.

"Here," the Alph-I member responded immediately.

"We got called away. Take command and spread Alpha Team to cover our position."

"You got it, Boss."

It was Leera's lead. She turned to her partners. "Now. Where should we start searching?"

Chapter Thirty-Four

Carpecillero- 2221 Iman Year

Isa awoke to soft sounds of an animal chittering. She rubbed her eyes and yawned. She sat up with a start. It was dark! "I'm gonna be in sooo much trouble!"

She didn't mean to fall asleep. It was just so peaceful in the blue forests. Well, that peacefulness was over now. Aunt Ashmarah was going to kill her.

Carefully, she climbed down from the niche in the tree trunk where she'd napped. Strange markings had drawn her to it, and she realized it was a road sign. She had spent most of the afternoon marveling at the care it took to carve the beautiful script. Aunt Ashmarah had taught her something called the "Jeman dialect" on their journey. This was it.

Her hat fell as she stumbled. When Isa reached for it, she saw her feet. The bottoms glowed. Isa peered around nervously. "Did I step in something?" She hoped she didn't squish an innocent creature.

"Who's there!" a voice called angrily.

Isa ducked behind a large rock and froze. She peeked and saw a torch. Beneath it bobbled a mean looking face. He had a mole on his nose. Isa shrank away, trying to hide between the rock and a tree, but her glowing steps gave her away.

"You're from those ships aren't you!" the mole-nosed man loomed over her. She lied, shaking her head in fright. It didn't work. "Your clothes aren't from around here!" The man grabbed her arm and jerked her to her feet.

Isa let out a cry.

"You lost?" another man jeered, joining his friend. She whimpered as they crowed, "Well today's your lucky day! We'll take care of ya." She didn't like the sound of that.

He called into the distance. A third torch appeared, illuminating an equally sour expression. This one had a scar.

"This is perfect," Mole-nose said. "We can use her to negotiate. She looks well fed. Must be a kid of someone important."

The scarred man spoke up, "I knew it was a great idea to bivouac here. There're plenty of places near the old palace to hide. And now we find this bargaining piece!"

The three dragged Isa away. She dug in her heels and hammered at the fingers around her wrist. Her small fist didn't affect the rebel's grip. Flustered, she let out a wail, "Heeelp!"

No sooner did she cry out, the scarred man let out a grunt. He fell over, dropping his torch. The other two turned. One called, "Show yourself."

Trembling, Isa searched the dark too, but saw nothing.

There was rustling nearby. A large branch came out of nowhere and swung towards Mole-nose. It nearly clipped him. He jumped back at the last second and held out his torch in defense. A shadowy figure ducked behind trees.

The second rebel pulled out a gun and carefully peered behind a wide trunk. A rock flew into his face and he fell back, gun firing into the air. The shadowy figure tackled the gunman and knocked the weapon away. After a brief struggle, the man in shadows slammed the gunman's head into the ground. He stopped moving and Isa shrieked.

The scarred man had picked himself off the ground and came up behind the shadowy figure. He socked him in the jaw. The dark figure didn't buckle. Instead he twisted, hitting the scarred man with an elbow. The scarred man wheezed, bending to the ground.

The dark figure brought his fists together. He jumped, slamming into the scarred man's head. He fell to the side, unconscious.

The dark figure turned to Mole-nose, the last one standing.

"That's close enough," Mole-nose held a knife at Isa's neck.

Tears streamed down her face as she eyed the gleaming blade. "I'm scared," she whimpered.

"Take one step closer, she dies," Mole-nose warned.

The dark figure tensed; his ugly scowl illuminated by torchlight. Yet, Isa didn't feel frightened. She knew this person was good. She sensed brightness in his eyes, though it'd been buried under layers of misfortune.

Dozens of angry people swarmed, brandishing weapons. When they caught sight of their defeated friends, they beat the stranger to the ground. Isa screamed for them to stop, and found a rag in her mouth.

They subdued his hands and forced him to march.

"The girl!" a rebel pointed, "Her feet are glowing! Someone must've put a tracking spell on her. These strangers know magic too!" Someone griped it might be too dangerous to take them back to their camp.

Mole-nose waved his hand and said an incantation. The glow dimmed, but was still visible. "What in the…" his face scrunched and he uttered the same incantation. "It's receding too slowly. Whoever cast it has strong magic." His cheeks reddened in vexation.

After many repetitions, the light from Isa's steps eventually faded. Mole-nose appeared exhausted.

They dragged Isa and the man who attempted to rescue her through the trees. Her feet blistered by the time they stopped. The rebels forced them to sit on a log, and tied them side-by-side. She saw haphazard structures thrown together with misshapen stones and rough-cut panels. A few small fires burned in low pits. This must be their camp.

The scent of copper reached her nose. Isa peered timidly to the bloodied man beside her. Though his face was swollen and even uglier than before, she recognized him. He was the laborer from earlier that day. She'd assisted him with his hat. "Thank you for helping me," she spoke meekly.

He grunted, "'Lotta good it did."

"Are you scared?" she asked.

His head shook. "Don't get scared. 'Sides, there's people looking for ya. They should be here soon, 'specially after that gun goin' off." He lisped a little. A front tooth hung loosely in his gums. Isa wanted to push it back in.

"If you knew there were people coming, why'd you help me?" she asked, still shaken. She should've listened to Aunt Ashmarah. Then she wouldn't have caused so much trouble for everyone.

"Was gonna offer my help lookin' for ya anyway," he stared at the ground. "I come into these forests almos' ev'ry night. I didn' plan on gettin' in a fight, but you were callin' fer help."

Isa took a shaky breath, "I really am thankful. My name's Isa. What's yours?"

"Stant'n," he replied, the tooth getting in the way.

Isa started to nod, but stopped short. Her eyes glazed and a familiar tickle entered the back of her head. She got a feeling sometimes. It was always unexpected and it showed her things others didn't know. The tickle brushed over her brain, whispering another name. She turned and carefully studied his bruised face. "No…" she said slowly, "It's not."

"What d'ya mean?" he asked lamely. "A person knows his name."

"Well," Isa explained, "My Auntie tells me I have a gift. Sometimes I sense things. Your name isn't Stanten. At least, not to these forests." She squeezed her eyes, trying to draw on the tingle. Isa coaxed its little voice until it spoke. "Your name here… it's Jedrek."

Stanten shrugged, "Call me what ya want." He didn't seem to care.

"Alright," she smiled sweetly and leaned back. "Jedrek," she repeated in a sing-song voice. "That name's important. It belongs here, to this land. Is that why you're here? I know I'm supposed to be here too, but not sure why."

"Kid, I've no idea what you're talkin' about," Stanten sighed, "I come to the forests to be alone. This's the first time I've run into anyone."

"Quiet!" Mole-nose shouted.

The two fell silent. Through the leaves, early rays of sun peered over the horizon. "Oh drat!" Isa whispered under her breath, "The ships launch at dawn and I'm gonna miss it!"

"Don't worry, there's always the next one," Stanten said.

"Yeah, but my dad and aunt are gonna KILL me!" she nearly wept in exasperation.

"Then you shouldn't have run off," Stanten spoke plainly.

Isa frowned, trying to think of something smart to say, but knew he was right.

"By the way, who are you? Why're operatives searchin' for ya?" Stanten asked.

Isa crinkled her brow, "I don't know what you mean."

Before Stanten could utter a response, bright lights flooded the camp. Rebels scrambled like startled animals, tumbling over each other. A loud voice boomed overhead. "You are surrounded. Hand over the girl unharmed and we'll let you live!"

With weapons in hand and hiding, the rebels blinked against the light. Suddenly, Mole-nose let out a laugh. "Boys!" he shouted, stepping into the clearing. "Relax! There's only three of 'em!"

The rebels followed to where he pointed. Three women stood high in the branches. They wore helmets and fitted jumpsuits in red, purple, and blue. The rebels joined their leader in guffaws.

"Don't laugh!" Isa shouted defiantly. "I've watched them train, because that's all they do," she rolled her eyes. "Just you wait! One of them can take all of you!"

"Oh yeah? Let's see," a rebel sneered. They aimed their weapons and fired.

The woman in red retrieved a baton. She aimed at the group. Electricity shot out, forming a net. It hit half the group, disabling them.

The woman in purple jumped down and fought her way to Isa as the one in blue ran interference. They moved fast and felled many before the enemy had a chance to react. Isa gawked at the trail of battered men. The woman in purple slashed Isa's restraints and lifted the girl onto her shoulder.

"Wait! You have to help my friend!" Isa shouted. The woman in purple looked to Stanten. Spikes of white hair peaked from beneath her helmet. Isa added, "He's from Teroma like us, and tried to save me!"

The woman tilted her head, "Stanten?"

"Do I know you?" he hunched defensively.

The operative bent down and cut his ropes. Stanten leapt to his feet and tackled a rebel who charged them, joining the melee.

The woman in red pulled out a stun rifle. She took out rebels from her position on high ground. In less than a minute, the rebels were subdued.

In measured stride, the woman in blue made her way to Mole-nose. He was clearly in charge. When they had radioed in the situation before apprehending, it was commanded he be brought in for questioning. He geared up to cast a spell. As he chanted, the woman in blue changed posture, pulling in a deep breath. The wind spell hit her and she glided back a few feet, undaunted.

The leader stared anxiously, not sure what to do. "The strangers are impervious to spells," he whispered to himself.

Seeing Mole-nose's hesitation, the operative charged, black hair whipping. Administering a series of swift kicks, the woman in blue knocked him to his back. She rolled him onto his stomach and secured his hands before he could react. The operative in purple threw a bag over his head. When he thrashed, she punched him once, just enough to daze him.

The rebels who pulled themselves off the ground retreated north. The woman in red watched through the scope of her rifle, in case any should decide to turn back. Beneath her, Isa shouted challenging remarks at her receding captors.

Golden rays of sun splashed through the branches onto five Tero-mans. The woman in purple pulled off her helmet. Stanten recognized Syralise. She gave her hair a tousle. The one in red raised her visor, scowling and refusing to meet Stanten's gaze. It was Leera.

That could mean one thing.

Stanten's mouth went dry. He turned to the third woman as she marched to him. Kameclara slowly removed her helmet and beamed. Her green eyes stirred something in the depths of his soul and his breath stopped.

"Hi Stanten," she spoke in a collected voice, unruffled from the skirmish.

He felt relief, joy, horror all at once. Unable to overcome shock, he averted his eyes, wishing he could melt away. Seeing his bloody knuckles, Stanten remembered his disfigured face. Pride got the best of him and for the first time since he could remember, Stanten felt embarrassed. He didn't want Kameclara to see him battered and think less of him. His earlier thought that he held his own pretty well was forgotten. Never before had he felt the need to prove himself. "Why'd you have to be here?" Humiliated, he shut down.

Kameclara didn't respond.

"Command, come in," Leera radioed.

"Speak," Captain Nanti's voice replied, a hint of urgency behind her coolness.

"The situation's been neutralized. We've acquired the target and two others. We're on our way back."

"Let me speak with Isa," another woman demanded breathily.

Leera hesitated for a moment, then realized the channel was to her commanding officer. Therefore, whoever made the request had clearance. "Roger." She pulled off her helmet and handed it to the girl. "Someone wants to talk to you."

Isa covered her face in embarrassment. Obediently she took the com-helmet from Leera and put it on. Alpha-Je exchanged looks of curiosity.

"Sorry Auntie Ashmarah," the girl said.

An alarm rang in Kameclara's mind, but she kept silent. Ashmarah being connected with Protocol Phen was the last thing she expected. There were ethical questions involved.

Is Hayes using it for personal reasons?

"Isa, are you hurt?" Ashmarah demanded.

"No..." she braced for a scolding.

"Good," Ashmarah sighed with relief, "Come back immediately and listen to the operatives."

"Yes, Auntie," Isa said dejectedly. *Maybe yelling will come later.*

Alpha-Je had taken motorbikes to maneuver swiftly through the trees. Syralise shared a vehicle with Isa as they'd previously decided. Kameclara had custody of the rebel leader, which left Stanten to ride with Leera.

At first, he offered to return on foot, wanting to avoid awkwardness. The operatives insisted he return with them. He needed to be questioned expediently by an officer, concerning the incident.

The woman in red gave him a cold look, probably because he'd called her an asshole before. Uncomfortably, Stanten climbed behind her. Neither preferred the situation. Together, the six rode back.

Kameclara eyed Stanten through her helmet. To be near him made her ecstatic. She couldn't remember for the life of her why she'd considered never seeing him again. She'd hoped he would be happy to see her too. Unfortunately, his demeanor remained sullen. He'd questioned why she was there. Perhaps what they'd shared was over.

The thought stung.

Perhaps it'd just been a bad day.

As they bumped over the rocky ground, Kameclara thought of him defending Isa. Admiration warmed her cheeks.

Chapter Thirty-Five

Before Syralise's motorbike came to a full stop, Isa was plucked from her seat and ushered towards her aunt. Ashmarah had ordered a break in procedure to delay their ship's launch. She would have a lot of explaining to do to Hegemon General Theol; not to mention the suspicions that'd arise. Normally if a person missed their ship, they'd be forced to wait for the next one. Ships' schedules were not to be interrupted.

But this was an extenuating circumstance.

Once word arrived that Isa was found, officers initiated the civilian ship's take off sequence. Civilian ships were not as advanced as warships. Their engines could take up to two hours to warm up. Warship-23 had already left for orbit. Ashmarah couldn't delay the launch of two ships.

Tears streaming, Isa rushed into Ashmarah's arms. "I'm sorry!"

"Hush now," Ashmarah felt too relieved to be upset. Clasping Isa's hand, she headed towards Civilian Ship-2.

Before she reached the ramp, a buzzing approached the Teroman camp. It built swiftly to a howl as loose objects were tossed about. The workers on the west side of camp peered in confusion as the sky darkened.

Then, panicked shouts fill the air.

Isa turned to see a dark funnel descending from the sky. It rushed in their direction as workers scrambled out of its path. Their feet barely touched the ground.

Ashmarah's instincts kicked in. She released Isa's hand and grabbed the nearest operative, who happened to be Meliora's incarnation. She ordered Kameclara to escort the girl on board, trusting the operative to do as told.

Ashmarah raced to contend with the cyclone. She steeled herself, clearing her mind. She pulled in a deep breath and chanted. Warmth expanded through her extremities. She felt it build, and when the cyclone was almost upon them, she released her spell.

Ashmarah felt every cell in her body ignite as a blast from her palms met the swirling pillar. The large funnel quivered and slowed. She whispered a chant to boost her spell. The funnel shook, growing wispy.

Ashmarah marveled at her ability to cast. She'd studied as many spells as she could get her hands on, but seldom had the opportunity to practice such powerful ones. She'd always thought it was a pity Teroma only retained records of battle spells. Practical ones, like tracking, were lost in time.

Around her, operatives of Protocol Phen busily secured equipment that'd been dragged around.

Ashmarah uttered one last boost and the dark clouds dissipated. Exhausted, she sank to the ground. It'd been a long time since she'd used any spell. She flexed her hands, thanking the stars it came back easily.

Before the Teromans could relax, a battle cry was heard. The cyclone was merely cover. Vesper's rebel troops had charged behind the windstorm and entered camp.

~*~

Kameclara didn't question why Ashmarah was giving orders. It was a consensus that a child of Teroma be protected. She lifted Isa and ran with her on board the civilian ship. She turned down a hall and opened the first door she found. It was a utility room. Kameclara stowed the girl carefully. She knelt and pulled off her com-helmet.

"Isa, look at me."

The disorientated girl found her eyes.

"I need you to stay here, okay? Don't go anywhere."

"Where's my father?" Isa pleaded.

"I don't know, but he'll want you to stay put. Can you promise me you won't leave this ship?"

The girl trembled, nodding. She wasn't going to break any more rules. Not after last night.

Kameclara gave Isa's shoulder a squeeze. With com-helmet in hand, she dashed to the doors of the ship as they were sealing. Kameclara slipped through, hopping to the ground. Shouts came from behind. She whirled to see Syralise and Leera running towards her. The doors shut, separating them.

Kameclara put on her helmet, "Why're you on the ship?"

"We followed you! Squads stay together!" Leera exclaimed. "What the hell were you doing with your com-helmet off? We've been trying to radio you!" Once doors of a civilian ship were shut during launch sequence, they couldn't be reopened.

"I was engaging with Isa. Thought she'd listen better if she could see my face."

"Kame, be safe," worry saturated Syralise's voice.

"It'll be alright. See you on Warship-23."

"You'd better," Leera grumbled.

Murderous shouts reached Kameclara's ears. She scoped the situation as nevite engines roared. The shadow of Civilian Ship-2 lifted behind her as Alpha-Je was separated.

Only a few operatives of Protocol Phen remained in camp. They were taking down rebel troops despite being outrageously outnumbered. Kameclara estimated sixty assailants to the five operatives. "We have the advantage of equipment and training," she reminded herself.

As she rushed to find a weapon, Kameclara caught sight of Ashmarah lifting her arms. The woman's hands wove intricately, fingers dictating a pattern. The air a few yards before her shimmered. A dozen rebels smashed into the shield as they charged.

"Why don't I feel surprised to see Ashmarah wielding magic?" Kameclara wondered aloud.

She ducked from a swing and took down two rebels, grabbing a large blade from one. Kameclara wielded the archaic weapon as she searched for an upper hand. Her eyes locked onto a four-wheeled vehicle with a distance-weapon mounted. It was her best option.

Kameclara passed Ashmarah, eying the woman's ferocity. She lashed out with attack spell after attack spell. All more powerful than any Kameclara had witnessed with Project S-48.

Even stronger than Hayes.

She couldn't help but notice Ashmarah's form was excellent. She appeared a natural. Kameclara's scalp tingled.

Is she a sorceress? A Teroman *sorceress?*

A flash of lighting hit Kameclara in the ribs. She convulsed, dropping a knee to the ground. Luckily, she'd been sprayed with manico oil. After a split-second to catch her breath, she jumped to her feet and continued her sprint towards her chosen vehicle. She slid to the ground while grabbing a rifle from the clutches of a rebel. Rolling under the carriage, she escaped a fireball. It singed the tip of her hair.

Kameclara braced herself and using manual aiming, fired. The rebel fell. A second later, her helmet synced with the weapon. Kameclara rolled from under cover and tried the door. It was stuck. Using the long blade still in her hand, she pried it open.

Kameclara threw the rifle over her shoulder and pulled herself into the driver's seat. The vehicle had guided lasers that could be set to target anyone or anything within a range.

She tossed the blade aside and spoke the code to start the vehicle. Her com-helmet verified her identity through a retina scan, and linked with onboard systems. She hit the pedal and the vehicle launched to life. She steered towards a wave of rebels as she verbally ordered weapons to power up.

"Will be ready in six seconds," the vehicle reported.

Meanwhile, she took shots from her rifle through the window, her helmet auto-aiming.

"Weapons armed," the vehicle projected specs onto her visor.

"Fire in a twenty-feet radius," Kameclara commanded, after ascertaining no Teromans were in that range. The vehicle easily neutralized rebels near the slowly-lifting civilian ship. She then swung around and headed the opposite direction.

Kameclara only made it a few yards before the ground quaked. The earth curled from underneath and encapsulated her vehicle. She let out a cry as she flipped. Swallowed by darkness, the only visibility came from the light on her com-helmet. Kameclara felt herself being pulled deeper as dirt rushed past on all sides. She was being buried alive. "I need assistance!" she radioed on all channels.

"Coming," a feathery voice floated. It was Hayes.

The vehicle shuddered. Kameclara held onto the frame as it pitched violently to one side. She could no longer follow which direction the dirt moved, but hoped she was heading up. The windows fractured from pressure. Kameclara propped her foot on the dashboard in hopes to push back should it try to crush her.

The vehicle lurched left, then right as if two children fought for its possession. Ignoring a bruised shoulder, Kameclara adjusted her position accordingly.

The shaking worsened before the vehicle burst through the earth. Sunlight pierced her eyes as it sailed, landing roughly. It leaned to one side as if it were going to tip. She scrambled to the far end. The vehicle swung back, settling solidly on four wheels.

Hayes stood nearby, his hands in the air; one pointed at her, the other towards a swarm of rebels. His visor was up and he gave a wink. She saluted in appreciation.

Kameclara tried the vehicle. The engine ran smooth. She let out a whoop as she ordered a systems-check. It reported permanent damage to automatic weapons. She cursed.

A few bullets hit the vehicle. Kameclara grabbed her rifle and returned fire. Flooring the pedal, she whipped the car into a pack of scattering rebels. Shooting from the driver's seat, she took out as many as she could.

Kameclara frowned. This was taking too long. There had to be a better way. She scanned her surroundings for a solution.

A familiar figure caught her eye. It was Stanten. He wrestled with a rebel. When he found an opening, he gave a hard punch, sending his assailant backwards. Another grabbed him from behind.

Kameclara placed her rifle on the dashboard. Shooting out the window, she fired. Stanten's attacker fell away. She pulled the vehicle beside him. "Can you drive?" she shouted above the noise.

"Yah!" He hollered.

"Alright," she moved from the driver's seat. "I'll shoot!"

He clambered in and studied the vehicle. Stanten wasn't sure if he'd know how to operate it, but didn't want to be out in the open. Fortunately, the gears were the same as some of the cleaning equipment. He shifted controls and pressed the pedal. They shot forward at breakneck speed. Stanten's head hit the back of the seat.

This vehicle went much faster than the cleaning equipment.

He stole a glance. Kameclara braced a leg on the dashboard, unleashing a rain of calculated fire. A few rebels managed to deflect her bullets with translucent shields. Stanten had no idea how those worked. They seemed to come out of thin air.

In the mirror, Stanten sighted a cluster of rebels. He put the vehicle in reverse and backed recklessly towards them. Kameclara saw them too and adjusted her rifle's setting. It took a few seconds to charge. She leaned out the window and squeezed the trigger. A ball of fury exploded forward. It caught the rebels and they flew through the air.

A blast to their right caught her attention. Kameclara watched as Hayes put the palms of his hands together. As he opened them, rays of light appeared. Some magic-wielding rebels deflected the attack, while others were knocked back.

Watching his six, Kameclara spotted a rebel gearing a spell. His lips moved ominously. Switching her rifle to standard mode, Kame-clara took aim and fired. The rebel fell back, still.

"We're even now," she radioed Hayes.

The rebel troops thinned and were forced to retreat. Kameclara shouted for Stanten to give chase. She fired behind them to discourage return as they sped through tall grass.

They stopped at the ruins of the old palace. Their vehicle idled as they surveyed men scattering. Kameclara fired one last warning shot. Its thunder ricocheted across the plains.

When the last rebel disappeared into distant trees, she let out an exhilarated cry. Stanten shared a victory shout.

Kameclara tore off her helmet. A spark in her chest grew to overtake. Unable to contain herself, she grabbed Stanten's hands and clutched them tight. "May I kiss you?" she breathed hungrily against his lips.

His body responded as they pressed together. Any doubt he'd ever felt melted in that moment. Kameclara was in his arms. It was all that mattered.

They didn't relish long in their reunion. Their camp was still vulnerable. They rode back with smiles plastered. Stanten took her hand, and she didn't pull away. His palm pulsed steadfast against hers, a direct line to her heart.

Pleasantness dried away once camp came into view. Dead bodies littered the grass, tarnishing it red. Stanten gulped, recognizing some to be fellow inmates.

In the distance, the civilian ship continued its slow ascent, safely away from Iman weapons.

Hayes was easy to spot, his silvery hair catching morning light.

He knelt on the ground over a woman in yellow. Her body convulsed as half of her outfit showed a dark stain. It was Ashmarah.

"There!" Kameclara pointed.

Stanten guided the vehicle to where Kameclara directed. She hopped out before he could stop and dashed to her friends. Stanten stayed in his seat.

Ashmarah sputtered, peering frantically to Hayes. When she spotted Kameclara, she reached for her weakly. The operative dropped and took her hand. "Isa's aboard the civilian ship," Kameclara spoke comfortingly.

She smiled with gratitude, "Procias…" Ashmarah wheezed, "…sends his love."

"You knew my father?" Kameclara asked in a small voice.

Ashmarah nodded. She opened her mouth to speak, but blood choked her words. She forced herself to swallow. "You need to know… I snuck him two vials. He should've given them to you… It's a pr-prototype." Pain contorted her face. Ashmarah's grasp weakened. She was fading, but her eyes blazed on. "U-Use them. W-worked on me… and Hayes."

"I have them," Kameclara squeezed her hand. She had no doubt Ashmarah referred to the vials of milky fluid her father had given her. It was starting to be clear what they were for. Kameclara hadn't witnessed any other Teroman besides Hayes and Ashmarah wield magic to their degree.

Another fact clicked. The reason Ashmarah gave orders to Protocol Phen was because she was an observer; like Hayes and her father. It tickled at another question in the back of her mind. Kameclara wanted to ask about Isa, and why Protocol Phen was ordered to find her.

But now was not the time.

More blood leaked from Ashmarah's lips. She pleaded to Hayes, "Isa'll blame herself," she gurgled. "Tell her... it's not... her fault," she gasped between words.

"I will," Hayes spoke tenderly. His eyes were steadfast as he cradled her head, "Goddess-speed."

Ashmarah grimaced as wrinkled eyelids fluttered shut. Her breathing grew labored as she fought against final throes. Hayes and Kameclara stayed by her side until her chest ceased to heave.

Her body let out a final shudder.

Hayes sniffed as hair fell over his eyes. Kameclara compassionately placed a hand upon his shoulder. "She was my mentor and like a real sister," he sobbed, "She taught me so much. Why do the best teachers leave so soon?"

"I'm sorry," Kameclara spoke, knowing no words would be the right ones.

The hot sun glared ruthlessly until a dark shadow cast itself upon the mourners. It was the next warship arriving. Kameclara gazed up and whispered, "If only you were here an hour earlier."

Stanten watched sympathetically. Kameclara and another operative hovered over a dying woman. Overhead, a warship prepared to land. Stanten glanced around with apprehension. He hoped Mardo and Geraldo were safe. He hadn't see any signs of them.

Chapter Thirty-Six

Hegemon General Theol boiled as he counted all the things that went wrong. Ashmarah should've kept a better eye on Isa. The child should've never been out of her sight. Then, Ashmarah was killed. Their tactical strategy for Jema hadn't even begun and they lost their Commanding Observer. Not to mention, more operatives than ever were asking about the Imans' "special abilities." It was growing difficult to rationalize magic.

He smashed a fist onto his desk. After catching the Teromans off guard, the rebels would likely develop an inflated sense of power. It could lead to further assault attempts. This simply could not be allowed. The more they faced off with Imans, the more resources would be taken from the Jema mission.

Hegemon General Theol shook his head in disappointment. There was no choice but to change his stance to an aggressive one.

He wasted no time calling all Generals into a videoconference. He addressed the recent attack and summed up their losses. He then informed of their next move. "All rebel troops within a five-hundred-mile radius to our ships are to be exterminated. After the disaster at the Priletoria site, we don't want word to reach Jema we're soft."

Four Generals voiced their concerns, namely backlash from

Iman citizens.

Hegemon General Theol scowled and repeated his command, adding, "We've lost Ashmarah. It's a crippling blow. We cannot risk any more."

They saw he was firm. The Generals saluted and went to carry out his order.

Hegemon General Theol ended the transmission and leaned into his hands. The scar on his cheek burned from annoyance. They should've tightened control when they first arrived, but he had compromised and chosen a softer path. He should've remembered this wasn't a diplomatic mission.

This was war.

The Hegemon General picked up his tablet and reviewed the timeline for upcoming weeks. He didn't really need to. He'd already memorized it a thousand times over. He did it to soothe his nerves.

There were presently ten warships on Ima's surface. After their allotted time, they were to return to orbit. The last twelve warships and civilian ships would then descend. Thirty warships in orbit would prepare for battle. They were to head to Jema as the twelve on the surface held Ima. When they left, all civilian ships would return to Iman orbit, where it was safe.

A notification appeared on his tablet. The Hegemon General tapped it and a message sprawled across his desk. It was an update from Teppa Nevo. Vesper's troops had started heavy attacks against Seu's third outer wall. If the severity didn't decrease, the autocrat estimated it would only hold for four weeks.

Hegemon General Theol sighed. It was well time to mobilize.

~*~

"You shouldn't have gone off on your own, Kame," Syralise scolded. "We followed you aboard the civilian ship to stay together."

"Seriously, what were you thinking? You took off your com-helmet!" Leera added.

"I honestly thought you were both still on the ground," Kameclara felt taken aback. Here partners weren't this protective, if at all. She felt touched, despite their biting tone. "My instinct was to guard the ship so I rushed back to deal with the oncoming attack. It didn't even occur to me that you'd followed me on board." She found herself apologizing, baffled.

"Well," Syralise sang sweetly, "We were worried, but apology accepted."

"Yeah, don't leave us out of the fight next time," Leera smirked. "It's the first real action we've seen in eight ans."

"By the way, why did you follow me onboard? Protocol was to stay and fight."

Syralise and Leera exchanged a look. Hayes had told them to keep something a secret. Kameclara was an asset to the mission. She didn't know it, but they were to keep an extra eye on her.

"Oh, by the way!" Syralise dodged the question, "the official report said you and Stanten were in a vehicle, taking out half of the rebels! Tell us more!" She jumped onto Kameclara's bunk and hugged a pillow. "Was it romantic?"

"What?" Kameclara's face grew hot. Memories of their kiss flashed through her mind.

"Oh, that inmate," Leera rolled her eyes. "I still don't approve," she forced her posture to relax. She didn't feel sure of this conversational direction. She clasped her hands to keep them from shaking.

"Hey now," Syralise teased, "You're just mad because he called you an asshole."

"Am not!" Leera sniffed nonchalantly.

"Are too!" Syralise tackled Leera. Kameclara took her pillow and hit the two girls as they rolled into her with laughter.

"It was nice to see him!" she giggled. "But we're back to agreeing it's best not to keep in touch."

"Why?" Syralise asked as the three settled down.

"Yeah?" Leera could hardly breathe.

"Well," Kameclara gulped. "For one thing, I learned the workers are staying on Ima. They're not coming to Jema."

"Hmm," Syralise grunted sadly. "That's too bad."

"Yeah," Kameclara felt her throat tighten. She cleared it, changing the topic. "What do you think Hayes' daughter has to do with all this?" she spoke the question on everyone's mind.

Leera and Syralise exchanged a glance. "You're the one who's buddies with him. Don't you know?"

Kameclara frowned. "Unfortunately not."

~*~

Civilian Ship-2 14.244 ans

Hayes received clearance to fly a jet from Warship-6, stationed in Priletoria. He took off as soon as allowed and docked on Warship-23. From there, he shuttled to Civilian Ship-2—to evade suspicion. Kameclara had told him where she hid Isa.

When he found her, hours had passed. Sad and droopy, Isa pulled back a bit, unable to gauge her father's mood. She expected him to be angry.

Hayes knelt and tenderly pulled her against his chest. Thin arms squeezed his neck as she sobbed. He sighed in relief. Isa was safe. That was all that mattered.

She stiffened, looking up at him. Something in her eyes darkened as she asked in a small voice, "Where's Auntie?"

"Let's go home first," Hayes instructed.

At those words, a wail escaped the girl. Hayes guided her past prying eyes to their quarters. Seated on their couch, he told her the truth about Ashmarah. Isa grew inconsolable, wracked with guilt over Ashmarah's death. "If I hadn't run off, trouble would never have happened..." she howled.

Hayes tried his best to calm her, but she wouldn't have any of it. Isa dropped to her knees and clenched her hands in prayer. She shouted to the heavens, bargaining with the Goddess for her aunt's return.

Hayes shook his head, gritting his teeth against tears. "What irony," he whispered to himself.

There was an astounding secret he and Ashmarah had kept from the eleven-ans-old. It was also the truth of their mission. Only a few high-ranking observers, and Hegemon Generals knew.

Isa is the reincarnation of the Goddess.

Only this time, Ia incarnated without memories. And no one knew why. They could only deduce something had gone wrong in the ethereal realm.

Ashmarah decided knowledge of Isa's identity was too much for a child to handle. They would allow her to awaken in her own time. If at all.

"Isa, honey it doesn't work like that," he gently pulled her to her feet. Isa threw her face into her father's chest and wept miserably.

Hayes stroked her hair and let her cry for both of them. He needed to remain collected. Ashmarah had been the grounding force in their lives. Hayes often felt overwhelmed with duties as an operative and observer. He hadn't been ready to be promoted as high as he was.

Ashmarah kept things orderly for them. And she was teaching him magic, bit by bit. The positive kind. With the weight now on his chest, he didn't dare practice, lest his nature awaken dark magic.

The two remained huddled for hours. When Isa finally tired, she fell asleep. Hayes scooped up the girl and carried her to her room. He laid her gently in bed and took off her shoes. Grabbing a cold towel, he wiped her tears.

She awoke briefly. Through puffy eyes, she asked, "Who'll stay with me now? Can you?"

"I'm sorry, dear. I wish with all my heart that I can," he confessed. "But you know I'm an operative and have a lot of work." He sighed. "I can make arrangements with your friends and their families."

Hayes knew it couldn't be a permanent solution. Ashmarah was a retired operative who had the abilities to defend Isa if needed. With fluency in the basics of light magic, she worked closely with the Goddess to awaken her powers as well. Ashmarah's shoes would be difficult to fill. Staying with civilians would only do for now.

"No," Isa shook her head. "They wouldn't understand how I'm feeling." Her eyes veered to the side as a thought struck. She asked out of the blue, "Can Jedrek stay with me? He's sad too. And he tried to save me. I feel safe with him."

"Jedrek…? Who's he?" Hayes' brow tightened with suspicion. The Goddess was supposed to have limited exposure to people. All civilians aboard her ship were hand-picked and thoroughly vetted. Hayes knew the names to every single one. Most were observers and their families.

This name was new. A security threat.

"He's somebody that'd help me. I can sense it when I look at him," Isa responded.

"I'll see what I can do," Hayes kissed her head sweetly. In the back of his mind, he panicked. *How did this person get through?*

"Promise you'll look for 'im?" Isa half sat up and grasped her father's hand. The look of intensity made Hayes realize that this wasn't something she'd easily drop. His heart melted.

"Promise," he patted her hand.

Isa gave the tiniest of smiles. "Thank you." She shut her eyes and was soon back asleep.

Hayes posted an observer in his apartment, a civilian from their ship. For the rest of the day, he searched high and low for the person named Jedrek. He held reservations, but a promise was a promise. After all, Isa was the Goddess.

If she sensed someone wants to help her, who am I to contradict?

After an exhausting search, Hayes only discovered a young boy by that name. He was merely an infant. Wearily, he returned to Isa to give her the bad news. *So much for the Goddess' instincts.*

"Oh, right," she smacked her forehead. "He said his name was something else. What was it again?" A finger tapped her head.

"Why would you tell me his name is Jedrek when you knew his name is something else?" Hayes asked in exasperation.

"It's because of that thing. You know when I sense things other people can't?" Isa exhaled shakily. "Auntie Ashmarah said to trust it."

Isa wiped tears from her eyes at the mention of her aunt. She continued bravely. "His name in this place is Jedrek, and it really suits him much better than his Teroman name. So I forgot his Teroman name." Isa scrunched her nose and thought hard. "I… I'm trying but I really can't remember his other name…"

"Then how am I to find him, silly?" Hayes tickled Isa. She gave a weak smile and brushed his hands away.

"I know! Ask Kameclara. When they rescued me, Kameclara recognized him! She'll remember!"

Hayes sighed. This mission of his daughter's was more tedious than things down on Ima. "Okay, I'll find Kameclara. Meanwhile, I asked Elover's mom to let you have dinner with his family. She'll look after you for the time being. Want me to walk over there with you?" he asked.

Isa nodded and scooted to her feet. She took Hayes' hand and they set out. After Hayes made sure Isa was safe, he made arrangements to have an observer pick her up from Elover's later.

He rushed back to his apartment and took care of tasks he'd been putting off. As promised, Hayes left a message for Kameclara to meet aboard Warship-23.

Sure enough, as his transport docked, she was there. "How is she?" Kameclara asked of Isa.

"Upset," Hayes answered solemnly.

"How're you?"

Hayes shrugged. He wished to mourn, but there was work to be done. Training allowed him to put emotions aside.

"So, what did you need?"

Hayes put on his business face as the two walked towards a

lounge. "Isa desperately wants to see a person who tried to save her. The problem is, she can't remember his name. It's why I've called you."

"Oh?"

"Yes. She said when your squad saved her, he was there and you knew him. Does that ring a bell?"

"Yeah, it's Stanten. I'd like to think he's a good friend." She immediately regretted the second sentence.

"Like to think...?" Hayes lifted an eyebrow. He'd picked up on her subtle undertone. His business face receded as his mischievous nature reared its head.

"Well," Kameclara fought the heat rising to her cheeks. "I don't see him often. And I can't see him anymore. So... he's just a friend." She coughed to stop herself from rambling. She wanted to kick herself. This was unlike her.

Hayes gasped, "Pining away are we? Is this a love interest for our dear Kameclara?" His mood improved as he teased her.

"No!" Kameclara shot back, "It's not like that!"

Hayes shoved his face close and sniffed. "You stink of lies. Just take me to him," Hayes commanded in a steamy voice. "I'll let you know if he's worthy."

"I can't," she shied away.

"Why's that?" Hayes smirked.

"Well," she bit her lip. "He has to stay on Ima."

Hayes stopped, agape. He studied her for a moment with hands on his hips, piecing together her words. "How did you meet an inmate?" he figured, "and long enough to develop feelings?"

"I—," Kameclara turned her face away, "I don't care!" she shrugged.

Hayes gave a devilish grin. He threw an arm around her neck and pulled her close. He whispered slyly, "Don't care huh? I just got you to admit you have feelings for 'im."

Kameclara's face radiated heat.

~*~

Civilian Ship-2 14.244 ans

The rebel leader Kameclara had taken into custody snuck aboard Civilian Ship-2 during the attack in Priletoria. He stole Tero-man clothes and found a place to hide. He scratched at the mole on his nose, trying not to gawk at the outlandish technology.

He only needed to bide his time. The ships would be headed to Jema sooner or later. Meanwhile, he'd gather information for Vesper.

Chapter Thirty-Seven

Hayes was one of the few operatives who simultaneously served as an observer.

Two ans before launching from Teroma, his North Deron team was given a mission. The Captain in charge informed them it was a standard sweep.

His supervisor, Ashmarah, told him the truth. He might be recovering the Goddess.

"Seers around Teroma and I have been constantly performing readings. We need to predict when and where the Goddess will appear," she explained. "We know it's soon. We've deduced seventy-nine possible locations and times."

The Intergalactic Military had been systematically sent to each.

The location Hayes' team was about to sweep held a forty-two percent chance of containing the objective.

The mission would've been simple. Except sleeper agents were on site first.

Thousands of ans ago, enemies from the Maliote system had made surface contact with Teroma. The Intergalactic Military were able to drive most off the planet. Those left behind were small in number. Genetically similar, their descendants embedded into Teroman society.

Centuries after the incident, it was discovered many descendants maintained a pact to capture or kill the Goddess. As time went on, more and more secret societies were revealed. Some disgruntled Teromans had joined too. They felt it unfair of the Goddess to place burden upon them to protect her.

The Teroman governments of the time saw a difficult task before them. They decided to fade the belief of the Goddess into myth. The best way to protect her would be to deny her existence.

Next, they needed to identify sleeper agents without sacrificing the rights and privacy of their citizens. Keeping birth records only did so much. Ultimately, the North Deron Teams of the Intergalactic Military were tasked to identify and control sleeper threats.

On the day Hayes met Isa, North Deron's Alpha Team arrived to investigate a housing complex. They were undercover. All except for Hayes believed it was merely to hone their skills.

Squads of three spread throughout the complex. Uniforms and weapons were strapped beneath oversized coats. A sleeker model of com-helmets was used. A unit sat at the base of their necks, hidden by scarves or high collars. When activated, plated metal expanded over their heads.

North Deron's Alpha Team had explored most of the blocks without incident. As they approached the last area, unknown assailants opened fire. Two operatives sustained minor injuries, and the situation quickly escalated. Dozens more shooters appeared, aiming to be rid of the operatives.

"Exterminate," the Captain of the mission instructed.

Hayes and his team pushed through, expediently taking control. Mercy wasn't shown. Remaining sleeper agents laid down arms in return for their lives. The site was soon secure.

The operatives moved through homes to ascertain citizens' safety. To Hayes' horror, he discovered nearly all had been murdered. His senses heightened when he realized what it could mean.

In the last home, he found two adult bodies matching the description of potential parents for the Goddess. There didn't appear to be a child's body. Hayes sighed in relief. Perhaps the Goddess didn't incarnate at this site.

The relief was short lived when he noticed an infant in many of the photos. Hayes' skin tingled. He hoped the child was visiting friends or relatives.

The Captain of the mission had left to escort some of the arrested. Hayes was highest ranked on site. He ordered the team to check all bodies in the last block.

To his relief, none reported a child matching the photographs.

But it wasn't over. Not until they had located the missing child. Even if there was less than a one-percent possibility she was the Goddess, he needed to be sure.

Hayes marched into the square where the second transport prepared to take away the remaining arrested. He questioned the sleeper agents. They denied knowledge about the child.

He scowled, "I'm not satisfied with your responses."

One spat on Hayes' boot.

His eyes clouded over.

One by one, Hayes dragged them into the nearest home and closed the door. Away from the eyes of his teammates, he used more persuasive techniques. It was a side of him he thought he'd left behind.

After thoroughly "questioning" them all, Hayes felt confident the sleeper agents truly didn't know the whereabouts of the Goddess. He released the arrested to the transporters. Many wept in relief.

Hayes went to the potential Goddess' home and focused his com-helmet on a photo. He snapped a picture and sent a message to his team. "We're not leaving until we locate this child. Search known contacts and reach out."

Hayes' partners privately questioned his action. It deviated from protocol. He made an excuse that they'd have a lot of paperwork if a citizen remained unaccounted for. Of course, he couldn't tell them they were searching for the Goddess. They'd think he was crazy. To them, the Goddess was only legend.

Squad Alpha-Shech-I eventually radioed that a toddler had come out of a closet. There was a well-hidden panel accessing a cubbyhole.

Hayes jogged quickly to the location. He entered the bedroom with trepidation. A terrified girl, partially covered in blood, wailed as hot tears rolled down her face.

"She's frightened because she can't see our faces," Hayes retracted his com-helmet. The girl ceased screaming once she saw he was a person. Withdrawing into her hiding place, her tiny shoulders trembled. "Hi there," Hayes leaned in.

The back of his neck tingled. This child before him could very well be the Goddess. He fought the urge to bow in exaltation. His priority should be to coax her out of the closet and check if she was injured. Slowly, Hayes reached out a hand.

The girl shook her head profusely. "Mama?" she cried, following with a hiccup.

"Mama isn't here," Hayes gulped. How does one explain to a child she was now alone in the world?

"MAMA!" she shouted. The girl buried her head in her arms and screamed again.

Behind him, Hayes' teammates grew annoyed. They didn't understand why they were wasting their time with a fitful child. It was a job for the local police.

One of Hayes' partners ordered the team to wrap up the mission. They left, but Hayes' squad-mates remained behind. He let them be, speaking soothingly to the scared girl.

"Hayes, you coming?" one of his partners barked.

"In a minute," he called. He had a more important mission at hand.

Hayes set aside his weapon and crawled into the closet. Sitting beside the girl, he spoke, "I'm Hayes."

She eyed him suspiciously, clutching her sleeves. He reached for her again and she kicked him away. By her movements he could tell she didn't have serious injuries. Hayes reached around flailing fists and gently pulled her to his chest. "Shh, it's okay," he cooed.

She thrashed about, tiny knuckles pounding his face. Hayes didn't flinch. He kept his arms steady and reassured her. The girl bit his arm as hard as she could, jaw quivering. He grunted, but his uniform protected him. He continued speaking softly, promising everything was going to be alright.

Even if it's not. I'll do my best to make it better.

He felt his heart bending for the child.

She seemed to sense the change in him. She peered at him guardedly as trust seeped into her eyes. She'd been brutal and all he returned was kindness. Her wails petered into sniffles and the girl slumped against him. She soon fell asleep.

"Seriously Hayes, it's time to go," his partner, Albera peered into the closet.

"Shh, she just fell asleep," Hayes said in a tender voice.

Maralie, his other squad-mate scoffed, "Never saw you as the motherly type." She paused before asking, "What're we gonna do with her?"

"I'll take her to child services," he responded. "I'll meet the rest of you at base for debrief."

Albera nodded, "She seems to like you."

Hayes grinned nervously, unsure if the child was the Goddess. Forty-two percent was kind of low. He could've been wasting his time.

But as he peered at her face, all he felt was the need to protect her.

He carried the tiny person out of the residential block. She slept in his arms during the trip to Ashmarah's lab.

His supervisor studied the girl as she snoozed.

"Her registered name's Demitorra. She was born two ans ago," Hayes scrutinized the fact sheet that loaded from her print scan. He considered her name. "Do you think her parents knew she's Ia? Demitorra is an antiquated term for demiurge."

"It's likely. I've very little doubt this child's none other than the Goddess," Ashmarah announced. "But it's still possible our calculations are off by a few ans. It's kind of a blessing. The Goddess did this to make it difficult for her pursuers too."

Ashmarah took a blood sample from the child by the prick of a finger. Demitorra groaned but didn't wake, worn after the ruckus. Hayes watched as Ashmarah smeared the sample on a specially formulated crystal dish. Next, she inserted it into a large instrument. She put in commands to bombard the substance with concentrated nevite radiation.

Every Teroman carried the nevino sequence. Nevite radiation

burned up all cellular material, but attached to the nevino sequence. The Goddess would not carry the sequence because she didn't need it. And no mortal could survive Teroma without it.

"Her aural vibrations match that of the Goddess, but I want to be one hundred percent sure," Ashmarah studied instruments attached to the child. "I detected a mark of darkness on her soul," she tapped a dip on the readings. "Which means there's a chance this child is sent by the Great Evil to confound us. She may not be the Goddess."

"A mark of darkness?"

"Yes," she brushed stray hair from her eyes, "it can be caused by a few things. If she's the Goddess, then she was affected by an enormous amount of dark energy before incarnating. If she's not the Goddess, she'll be a troublemaking soul, touched by a demonic entity and sent to foil us."

"If she's the Goddess, and carries this mark of darkness, what does it mean?"

"Trouble. It can affect her many ways," Ashmarah bit her lip. "One of the most devastating is that she won't have knowledge of who she is." Ashmarah checked the machine before turning to Hayes. "Normally, a soul like hers would begin to achieve awareness around her present age. If she cannot, then she'll be vulnerable, unable to protect herself." She sucked in a breath. "The burden'll be placed solely upon Teromans to keep her from harm." Ashmarah shook her head sadly, "And we're mere mortals."

Hayes eyed the blinking lights of the nevite radiation machine. "The future of Teroma will be determined by this single test result," he said somberly.

Ashmarah glanced at the clock. "You'll need to return to your base for debrief soon," her voice lingered at the end. Hayes nodded, but didn't really want to go. Ashmarah sensed it. "You want to be here when the analysis is complete?"

He blinked slowly, "Wouldn't we all, if we knew what it meant?"

The child stirred. She sobbed lightly as she opened her eyes. Ashmarah walked over and spoke in a gentle voice. When Demitorra saw the stranger, she cried out. Little hands waved for Ashmarah to leave. The woman glanced over her shoulder to Hayes for assistance.

When Demitorra saw Hayes, her eyes sparked with hope. She turned onto her belly and slid over the side of the stretcher. She landed uneasily and slapped at Ashmarah's hand when the woman offered to help.

The toddler stumbled to Hayes. She wrapped arms tightly around his leg. Her sobs ceased as she buried her face in his knee.

If Hayes' heart was soft before, it now completed melted. He reached down and picked her up. The girl hid her face in his neck. "Demitorra, are you hurt? Do you want water?"

She shook her head avidly and pulled away to give Hayes an angry face. A finger pointed at her cheek and one word came out. "Isa!"

"You're not Demitorra?" Hayes asked.

She nodded to confirm that was her given name. Then immediately followed with a shake of her head. "Isa," she repeated, still pointing to herself.

"You want me to call you Isa?" Hayes asked. It was a common name on Teroma, a variation of "Ia."

The child nodded.

"You think she knows?" Hayes asked Ashmarah. "Despite a mark of darkness?"

She sighed. "Perhaps. Or her parents taught her." Ashmarah frowned and reminded, "Or she's sent to cause this confusion."

Hayes felt the girl's heart beat against his chest. "A name is something hard to forget. It's the last thing I'd hold onto if I were fighting to keep my identity…"

Ashmarah's instrument beeped loudly. Frightened, Isa buried her face back into Hayes' neck. Her entire form trembled. He didn't know what horrors she'd experienced, but hoped they didn't leave her scarred.

Hayes placed a blanket around her and she settled a bit.

"Done so soon?" Ashmarah marveled, approaching her instrument. "It normally takes twice as long." She slid open a door and retrieved the blue crystal.

Hayes watched her body freeze. Bit by bit, Ashmarah turned and stared at Isa. She tilted the dish for Hayes to see. The plasma was completely gone. It confirmed that the child in Hayes' arms was none other than the Goddess.

"No," he breathed. His arms turned to jelly and Isa seemed to grow infinitely more precious. It took every ounce of control not to drop her.

Ashmarah's astonishment transformed into a beam. "It looks like the Goddess has chosen you as her caretaker."

In the following days, Ashmarah pulled strings and Hayes became Isa's adoptive father. She also took him on to be her second in command so both could remain near the Goddess. They were to work as a team and ascertain the effects of the mark of darkness.

Meanwhile, with sleeper agents on Teroman, Isa's safety was of grave concern. When the conflict on Ima with Vesper intensified, a decision was made. The best operatives of the Intergalactic Military would escort the Goddess to her safe haven on Jema. In Seu, they could securely work with her. The operatives would also eradicate the threat known as Vesper.

Little did they know, troubles were to soon appear from the Maliote system. It seemed fate was against the Teromans this time.

Chapter Thirty-Eight

Hegemon General Theol met with Hayes for the report on Ashmarah's death. He tried his best to tame his foul mood. Yet with every word leaving Hayes' mouth, he felt a vein in his neck throb.

"Thank you, Hayes," he said when the operative finished. "It's difficult for all of us. The severity of losing Ashmarah is especially felt." He took a breath, forcing himself to set judgments of Hayes aside. "Having been her second in command, you're promoted to her position. And as Demitorra's father, it's natural you'll continue to help awaken her powers."

Ashmarah had long ago dictated her command would go to Hayes should she be compromised. Hegemon General Theol didn't think that day would come—hoped it wouldn't come. Hayes was far less experienced, and had demonstrated questionable behavior in his past.

Uneasily, he added, "Captain Nanti shall assume your former role as the observers' second in command, due to her proximity to the asset—codename 'Meliora.'" At least Nanti was an officer.

"Yes, sir," Hayes saluted.

Hegemon General Theol read from a tablet, eager to move the meeting along. "Now, if I understand correctly, during your last rotation, you were fortunate to meet two Master sorcerers?"

"Yes, Unadine and Erilph. Two of the missing from Jema. They reportedly fought against Vesper in Calio."

"This is good," Hegemon General Theol raised an eyebrow. "They will be familiar with the Master sorcerers working for Vesper. They may have crucial information on their weaknesses."

"Shall I bring them to meet you, sir?" Hayes asked.

"Expediently," Hegemon General Theol responded.

Hayes saluted and exited the Hegemon General's office. He contacted members of Protocol Phen in Priletoria. They reached out to the Master Sorcerers and escorted them to a chartered war jet.

They arrived shortly aboard Warship-1. Hayes bowed politely in greeting. The Masters thinly veiled wonderment as they wandered about the hangar. Hayes identified hope in their eyes.

"Our planet has known conflict for millennia," he explained of the war machines.

"I see," Unadine responded without emotion.

Hayes understood. Though impressed, the Masters could effortlessly disable their warship. It only meant Vesper was even more formidable.

"This way please, your honors," Hayes led them towards a hall.

The Hegemon General's chambers were deep in the ship. Hayes took them down a less traveled route. The Masters in robes drew a few skeptical glances, but the operatives they passed didn't ask questions.

When Hayes and his guests approached their destination, heavy doors opened. The Hegemon General gave a traditional Seu greeting. He folded fingers against his chest and bent at the waist. The Masters returned the gesture before sitting.

Unadine and Erilph's eyes swept around the room. Large screens displayed letters and characters they didn't recognize. Tiny lights blinked in erratic patterns. They felt as if their every action were being watched.

"Great Masters, it blesses me to be in your presence," The Hegemon General spoke reverently.

"And it relieves me to learn your stance on Vesper," Erilph responded.

Unadine shared her mind, "General, we've learned that you've not informed your soldiers on the existence of magic. We think this is a mistake."

The Hegemon General frowned. "This wasn't a simple decision. On our planet, sorcery is a security risk." He didn't mention sleeper agents—people of the Great Evil—should it trigger dissidence from the Masters.

"I don't understand," Unadine furrowed her brow.

The Hegemon General shared a look with Hayes. It was one of the few times they were in agreement. Teroma was once similar to Ima before Vesper's takeover, simple and benevolent. Except, with magic too. The sleeper agents' greatest damage was corrupting Teroman culture. It introduced discordant behaviors—paths to dark magic. To eliminate the chance of it destroying Teroma, sorcery was abandoned. Then, all attempts were made to erase magic from the public's knowledge.

Hegemon General Theol sat tall. "Acknowledging magic is a risk we cannot take."

Unadine didn't like his response, but knew it was futile to argue. He was from a different world. "Alright then," she conceded. "How can we be of assistance?"

"I would like to discuss the four Master sorcerers assisting Vesper. What are their weaknesses? How can we contain them?"

"If you're seeking to kill a Master, it simply cannot be done," Erilph frowned. "The magic in our bodies protect us from mortal harm."

Hegemon General knew this, but listened politely.

Unadine followed, "There are only two ways to defeat a Master that is not detrimental to all of existence." She peered around the room. "Since we're allies, and none of you are our peers in magic, I'll share this information."

"If I may," the Hegemon General spoke politely, "We've learned a Master must willingly relinquish power to another through death. Or engage in an energy battle, in which the soul is ripped from the defeated."

"...Yes," Unadine appeared impressed.

"We are in contact with Seu. They know more about Masters than they care to let on. I don't mean to come off belittling," Hegemon General Theol wanted to keep their relationship amicable, "but in the interest of time, perhaps I'll cut to the point. Is there a way to restrain a Master's magic?"

"There's a few ways," Erilph agreed hesitantly, "But when it comes to a Master, it's never a permanent solution."

"I give my word. We won't use these methods against you as long as you're allied with us. Would you be willing to instruct us how?"

Erilph and Unadine knew they had little choice if they wished to liberate Jema. "Yes."

"Your generosity is infinitely appreciated," the Hegemon General spoke truthfully. "Also, I need to ask: What of the missing Master Maza? Do you have an idea on her whereabouts?"

Erilph and Unadine exchanged a look. Unadine sighed, resigning.

"She is with us. But unable to assist."

"Why is that?" Hegemon General Theol asked with suspicion.

Unadine answered in an abated tone, "She has no wish to be involved." She didn't share that Maza was Vesper's mother. They couldn't be sure how the Teromans would react.

Hegemon General Theol accepted the answer for now, but could sense the Masters were hiding something. He asked them once more to swear their allegiance.

Erilph did so on the grounds they help return Jema to harmony. Unadine asked they eliminate Vesper as a threat.

Hegemon General Theol wasn't satisfied. The words were superfluous to show they shared the same goals. He didn't completely trust their answer concerning Maza. However, the Intergalactic Military and Seu needed them on their side. He swallowed the lump in his throat. "Alright then."

Erilph appeared equally uncomfortable. "Let's get started."

Chapter Thirty-Nine

Captain Nanti asked the Beta Team Captain to cover for her. She needed a few days to take care of observer business. She noticed Kameclara studying her as she entered Warship-23's hangar. Despite her cautious nature, Nanti wished she could share more information with the operative.

But protocols exist for a reason.

On a bright note, she now felt confident Kameclara's fate genuinely fell to their favor. After her performance in Priletoria, there was little doubt.

Nanti took a war jet down to Priletoria. She radioed Hayes upon landing. He had just escorted the Master sorcerers back to the forest.

Nanti felt a swell in her chest. Having the Masters allied was an incredible advantage. Yet, her vigilance stirred too. "Let's hope Unadine and Erilph remain as righteous as their profiles indicate." She shuddered to think of the catastrophe should they switch allegiance.

She waited around the Teroman camp, greeting fellow officers. Some asked why she was there. "Official business," she cleared her throat.

When he returned, Hayes greeted with a sagging face. "Thanks for joining me."

"What's the problem?"

"Isa," he rubbed his chin. "She's requesting to see a man named Jedrek, whose real name's Stanten."

Captain Nanti gave a rare grin. "Isa's up to her quirks, I see." As an observer on the mission, she'd spent her share of time caring for the girl. "I hope it means she's feeling better."

Hayes sighed, "Jedrek's likely a former name of his, or a future one. Isa can't usually tell. Goodness knows I can't. Ashmarah…" his voice quivered. Captain Nanti gave him a sympathetic gaze. Hayes continued, "Ashmarah would've been able to tell," he finished with difficulty.

Captain Nanti's thoughts turned inward, "The name Jedrek does sound familiar. Where have I heard it before?" They strolled at the borders of camp.

He shook his head. "It's not a common name. Of all registered passengers, only an infant was named Jedrek," he answered.

"I wonder why the parents chose it."

"It's Lobash's kid. He was an observer under Ashmarah's command too."

Captain Nanti's eyes lit up. "So he watched the inner planets. The name, I think it's an inner planet name."

Hayes scrunched his face, "I believe he was a Prince or something."

The thought hit Hayes and Captain Nanti at the same time. They exclaimed simultaneously, "Prince Jedrek of Carpecillero!"

"Why didn't I think of it sooner! This makes sense," Hayes spoke in a rush, "I mean, Ashmarah deciphered that Kameclara is Meliora. What if Jedrek also incarnated because of unfinished business with

Vesper?"

"This could help our odds against her!" Captain Nanti's excitement overrode her conservatism.

"Let's hurry and locate this man." Hayes smirked to his friend, "Unless you have doubts about his loyalty too."

She sniffed, "Always. But I'll take the chance."

~*~

Stanten and the inmates who survived the rebel attack were ordered to clean up camp. Progress was hindered since their numbers were low. More inmates were due to arrive in a few days, sent down with warships on rotation. Until then, Stanten and the others did the best they could.

Geraldo and Mardo were missing. No one had seen them and no corpses matched their descriptions. Stanten searched for them during his breaks. He hoped they weren't caught up with rebels. It could be dangerous since the operatives were performing sweeps. He'd overheard that any rebels refusing to leave the area were to be killed.

Stanten's problems multiplied when the next warship arrived. Tivan was amongst the new inmates. "Son of a…" Stanten muttered to himself. He had forgotten about the man. Stanten clenched his fists when Tivan waved, and did his best to disregard him.

"Hello, *son*," Tivan approached during their first break together.

Stanten sauntered to the water station. He got himself a cold drink, ignoring him.

Tivan followed. "How ya been?" he asked.

Stanten didn't respond.

"I hear you got to see your girlfriend again. That pretty operative."

Stanten's nails dug into his palm. He took a breath and crunched his cup. Tossing it, he walked away.

Tivan's laugh followed. "You two are an odd couple, but I'm happy for you. What d'ya talk about? Did she tell you what this place is?"

Stanten continued to sulk.

"Forget words, what's it like to be with one of them high and mighty?"

Stanten felt a vein in his neck pop, "Don't talk about her," he spat over his shoulder. He quickened his pace, trying not to get drawn into Tivan's bullshit.

"Whoa," Tivan held up his hands. "I was just trying to get to know my son," he said sleazily.

"I'm not your damn son!" Despite his attempts to keep cool, Tivan got under his skin. Stanten marched back and pushed a finger into his chest. "You stay the hell away from me," he growled.

"What's going on here?" a warden demanded.

"Nothing, sir," Tivan took a step back, hands lifted. He eyed Stanten with amusement, "Just a father and his son exchanging words, s'all."

"Get back to work!" the warden growled.

"Yes, sir!" Tivan left, casting a sick glare.

Stanten lowered his head, trying to erase "son" from his mind. He went back to clearing camp. Anger drove him to work twice as fast.

When his free day came around, Stanten went into the blue forests to get away from Tivan. The man was overly supportive of Stanten's love interest and kept asking about Kameclara. Just to hear Tivan say her name made Stanten's blood boil. He knew if he didn't get away, he'd start a fight.

Stanten went much further into the forests than usual, and came upon refugees. The Teromans had left them alone since they were mostly unarmed women and children. Sitting amongst them, dressed like locals, were Geraldo and Mardo. They embraced Stanten, relieved to see each other safe.

"Don't go back," Geraldo persuaded. "Stay with us. You can start a new life."

Stanten fell quiet. He weighed Geraldo's words heavily. It'd allow him to avoid Tivan and that greatly appealed to him.

"I can't..." Stanten replied after a long hesitation. His lips still burned from the memory of Kameclara's kiss.

Mardo studied his face for long a time. "It's her, isn't it?" he asked softly.

"Yeah." Stanten sniffed. "Saw her again."

"Then you know what Ia says," he advised kindly. "It's meant to be."

Geraldo slapped his friend heartily on the back. "Ever since you started telling me about this woman, something about you's been different. It's like you're optimistic for once."

A part of Stanten wanted to stay in the forests, because reasonably, nothing with Kameclara could ever work. Yet, his friends' words gave him encouragement. He wanted to see her one last time. Somehow.

Stanten hung around a bit longer. They talked about problems, such as Tivan. Geraldo rolled his eyes and warned Stanten to watch his back. Tivan clearly wanted something. "And he's the type to stop at nothing to get it."

When the sun began to set, the forest grew dim. "The trees are beautiful," Mardo sighed. "They say Ia's home is just as lovely."

"Maybe that's where we are," Geraldo beamed.

"Where do you think we are?" Stanten asked.

No one knew the answer.

He grinned. It didn't matter. They've found peace.

"Carpecillero," a refugee nearby answered in a heavy accent. "Sorree, nidn't meana eavesdrop," the middle-aged woman added.

"Capa-what now? The hell's that?" Geraldo asked with a laugh, "It's gibberish!" He turned to Stanten, groaning, "I can only understand every other word these people say."

"Planeet Eema, uv'kerse," the woman sassed back. "Where fwom yoo'n cha friends'alls cooms?"

"Teroma."

The woman crinkled her brow. "Heh. Now tat's jeeboorish." She puffed her chest, "Carpecillero noble-like Priletoria. Petra's m'called," she introduced herself. Her eyes lit for a moment before dimming. "Mi once bestie a Princess gone."

"Princess?" Stanten thought the word only existed in fairytales.

"Aye, noble-kind."

"Where's she now?" Mardo asked.

Petra's eyes cast to the side. Her head wobbled slowly. "Gret'Evil. Sorce-mageness."

Geraldo shook his head and whispered, "See. Not making sense. They complain about sorcery and magic stuff all the time!"

"Probably folklore," Mardo reasoned.

Stanten didn't know what to make of Petra's words. He thought about the attack at camp. Some of the rebels looked like they could've been wielding magic. He didn't understand it, so he tried to block it out.

"It's getting dark," Stanten said to his friends. They bid each other farewell and he started back. As he hiked, the woman's words repeated in his mind.

This place is Carpecillero.

Though he had no clue where it was in relation to Teroma, it was a start. He clung onto the name because it gave him a sense of purpose. It was a point of stillness in the spinning chaos of no information.

As he neared the edge of the forest, Stanten heard his name being called on a speaker. He jogged to a warden, "Here!"

"You've got people looking for you," he announced gruffly. "What'd you do?" he asked as he sent a message on his communicator.

Stanten shrugged, "Dunno."

"I know what he did!" a creaky voice came from behind.

Stanten and the warden jumped. From a high tree branch, an old man dropped. He landed lightly as if floating. He strolled towards them with a puerile grin. "Nice to see you," the old man said to Stanten. Dressed in tattered clothes, he stroked his lengthy beard. "I told you we'd meet again," he used the Teroman dialect, lilting in a rich Iman accent. "Did you like the pears I left?" His eyes widened in earnest.

Stanten took a step back. "I've never met him before," he informed the warden nervously.

"Oh, rubbish!" the old man spat. "I've watched you grow up yonder," he gestured into the blue forests. Stanten and the warden exchanged a skeptical look.

Stanten held up his hands. "I think he has me confused with someone else."

"Sir, please evacuate the premises. Go home," the warden spoke impatiently.

"Well, I am home," the old man struck the earth with his cane. "Everywhere there is this ground, I'm home!" he exclaimed in laughter.

Before the warden or Stanten could respond, a Captain and operative approached. "Is this the man?" the Captain nodded to Stanten. The warden answered affirmatively.

The operative in green uniform studied Stanten with ardent curiosity. Deviousness radiated from every pore. Stanten knew the man was sizing him up, but couldn't be sure why. It made him sweat. Stanten felt as if he were on trial again.

Or worse, about to be pulled into something he couldn't refuse.

"Who's this gentleman?" the Captain asked of the old man.

"I'm a friend of Jedrek's," the old man shuffled beside Stanten. He nudged the inmate in a chummy manner.

Stanten smelled forest on his cloak. The scent relaxed him. "Why does everyone call me that?" Stanten muttered.

"Because that's who you are!" the old man exclaimed and slapped his knee.

"You may be excused," the Captain dismissed the warden in a rush. She'd tensed at the name "Jedrek."

The warden saluted and walked away, stealing a baffled glance over his shoulder.

The Captain waited until he was out of earshot before turning to the elderly man. "I'm Captain Nanti. May I ask your business?"

"I've promised to help Jedrek." He placed a hand on Stanten's elbow. "He's got an important duty."

"There's that name again!" Stanten exasperated, jerking away.

The operative folded his arms. "Sir, what *is your* name?" There was forced pleasantness in his tone.

"My name?" the old man scratched his head, "I… forgot. Sometimes I forget things."

"I swear I've never met him before," Stanten repeated. "The warden already asked him to leave, but he refused. I don't want trouble!"

"It's alright," the operative waved dismissively. He studied the old man for a long time. "Is there something we can do to help you remember your name?" he asked.

"It doesn't matter," he waved his arms, "What matters is Jedrek needs to care for the 'Seed of Life' until Meliora's ready!" he raved.

The Captain and operative shushed the old man in a hurry. They peered around to make sure no one had heard. Stanten grew increasingly uncomfortable. He opened his mouth to ask permission to leave, but the operative spoke first.

"How does he know all this?" he hissed, face reddening.

"We need to get someplace secure. Where there's no chance of prying ears." The Captain looked around nervously.

"You, come with us," Hayes commanded the inmate.

Stanten's stomach tightened. He didn't like where this was going.

Chapter Forty

Stanten found himself aboard a warship with a Captain, an operative, and the peculiar old man. The old man needed to be guided there
firmly, as he nearly wandered away a few times. They'd squeezed into
a tiny office. Stanten didn't know any of their names, and it made him
sweat.

"Stanten," the Captain asked, "Are you familiar with the name
Jedrek?"

He had two names, apparently.

"The kid you guys were looking for called me that. Otherwise
I've never heard it 'til this old guy today."

"So, you've never *asked* anyone to call you Jedrek?" she wanted
to be clear.

Stanten felt the urge to roll his eyes, but thought better of it. "No.
Why would I?"

"I believe him," the operative said. He stuck out his hand in introduction, "Hayes." Then added humorously, "As far as I know, that's
my only name." He jerked his thumb, "This's Captain Nanti. But right
now, I'm more interested in this gentleman," Hayes poked his chin
towards the pile of rags. "You know where he came from? He seems
to know you."

"Dunno. He appeared from the forest just b'fore you showed up."

Faded fabric shuffled as the old man's arms relaxed. His eyes drooped, on the verge of sleep. Stanten watched as the look on Hayes' face changed. "Stanten, you were there for the rebel attack, right?" Hayes asked slowly. "You saw what they could do with the elements?"

"Yeah. Figured it was a local thing."

Captain Nanti eyed her friend, wondering what he was up to. Hayes didn't say more. Without warning, the operative flicked his hands. A ball of lightning hurled towards the old man. Captain Nanti and Stanten jerked in alarm, lifting arms to their faces.

The old man's eyes remained half-closed. He lifted a finger and caught the ball of lightning. It instantaneously fizzled to nothing.

"Just as I thought," Hayes sounded thrilled. "You're a Master sorcerer, aren't you?"

The old man snorted awake, "Am I?" He scratched his head, eyes searching the room. "What's my name...?" His brow crinkled, thinking as hard as he could.

"Master," Hayes gave a slight bow, "Who are your allies? Cleodell? Or Reynoro?" He gazed intently, waiting for an answer.

Stanten didn't understand the questions. He wanted to dash off the ship. He didn't like being in the presence of someone who could throw electricity. Or whatever the hell that was.

"I...um..." the old man trailed. "I don't recall those names," he shrugged uneasily. "I'm here to assist Jedrek and Meliora. I remind myself everyday so I don't forget."

"You are CERTAIN this man is Jedrek?" Hayes pointed to Stanten.

Stanten squirmed. He didn't want to be Jedrek. It sounded like Jedrek had something they wanted.

"Yes, no doubt!" the elder jumped to his feet, "I met with him and Meliora before they passed on. I recognize the chords of his soul." The old man's eyes widen, a sincere expression on his face. "I can feel it deep in the forests all the time!"

The spark of light in the old man's expression died all of a sudden. He glanced about in confusion. "Where am I?"

Captain Nanti and Hayes exchanged a guarded look.

Stanten couldn't be sure if he was in trouble. "Can I go?" he finally asked clumsily.

"My apologies," Hayes straightened himself. He eyed the old man, who snored lightly in his chair. They weren't getting answers from him at present. He turned to Stanten. "We wanted to know if the girl told you why she called you Jedrek."

Stanten exclaimed nervously, "Look, I didn't do anything wrong! All she said was the name suits me better!"

"Hmm," Hayes considered his words. "Do you have experience babysitting?" He asked out of the blue. He appeared uncomfortable, as a hand rubbed his cheek.

"W—What?" Stanten couldn't be sure he heard correctly, feeling equally prickled.

"Hayes, you're not thinking…?" Nanti wasn't sure what her friend was thinking.

"I've reviewed your record. Manslaughter." Hayes' tone was difficult to place. "But if you're Jedrek like my daughter and this Master says… I can…" he gulped, "maybe make an exception."

"I—I don't…" Stanten didn't understand. He scrunched his face, "What do you want from me?" He struggled to keep obedient.

Captain Nanti whispered to Hayes, "Are you certain this old man isn't somehow working a ploy to get Stanten near Isa?"

Hayes spoke discretely, "I trust Isa in recognizing what she needs." He turned back to Stanten. "Your file says you were imprisoned for killing the person who assaulted your mother?"

Before Stanten could respond, the old man leapt to his feet. "AH YES!" he announced, startling the Teromans, "MY—NAME—IS—OTTOKIP!" He dropped back and slapped his knee, laughing. "How could I have forgotten? Of course! I am a light sorcerer with wishes to stop Vesper!"

Hayes' eyes flashed as he recognized the name. "*Grandmaster Ottokip?*" he asked with incredulity. He'd heard stories from Ashmarah about a man by that name. He was largely undocumented by Teromans, having disappeared hundreds of years ago. If he were somehow still alive, it would make sense he'd be a little senile.

"Some used to call me that," the old man shrugged, "but you just call me Ottokip." He patted the operative on the shoulder.

Hayes tested him, "How many masters are on the sorcery council?"

"Twenty-four, of course," Ottokip answered sensibly. His expression changed to a sullen one as he recalled. "No… not anymore. There are only twelve now."

Hayes' heart skipped a beat. Not many citizens of Jema and Ima knew there were once twenty-four Masters sorcerers. He took a leap of faith. "I choose to believe him," Hayes said to Captain Nanti. "Between him and Isa, there's little doubt in my mind Stanten's the reincarnation of Jedrek."

"I've never heard of an Ottokip. You have?" she asked, distraught.

Hayes nodded. "Ashmarah's clearance gave her information on him. She shared it with me."

"What if this guy's impersonating Ottokip?" she always sought the worst scenario.

Hayes shook his head. "The attack I cast towards him is powerful. Only a Master sorcerer could contend with it as easily as he did. The only other Master unaccounted for is Maza. Her personality profile states she'd be unlikely to disguise herself as someone like him."

"I'm still unsure of this," Captain Nanti expressed.

"You," Ottokip pointed to Captain Nanti, "You're doubting me. I see it in your aura." He moved closer with a serene expression. "You retired a year early from being a soldier because of an injury in your back. It's been your regret you didn't finish your service. You've been trying to compensate ever since."

"Nanti?" Hayes turned to her with a sympathetic eye. They'd always been close. Hayes felt surprised she didn't share this with him. It must have been a great disappointment in her life.

Captain Nanti hardened, "Just shy of an an. It wasn't a permanent injury."

"I have no proof I am who I say I am," Ottokip continued with clarity. "But I speak from my heart when I say I wish to help Jedrek," he placed a hand on Stanten. The worker flinched.

"Stanten?" Hayes faced him too, "Please answer my question from before this exciting interruption. Did you kill a man?" Hayes had already gone over Stanten's file. He wanted to hear the inmate admit to what he did. There was a lot Hayes could tell by the way someone answered a difficult question.

"Yeah. I killed 'im," his voice cracked, "It's why I'm here." His eyes showed he still felt ashamed.

"This was your only crime?"

"I stole, fought. It's how we survive Pudyo," he grumbled. "No one comin' from where I did's innocent."

Hayes nodded. "And if you were given all you needed?"

"I've been real okay the last eight ans. Plenty to eat and good bed. Only time I fought was when someone tried to off me."

Hayes sensed Stanten wasn't deceptive with his answers. Yet he also knew he would never feel completely comfortable with him around Isa. He'd decided it when she first said his name.

However, Isa's instincts were never wrong. Even if she can't yet see the future, she often asked for things, or people, that became relevant. He needed to take a leap of faith.

"King Jedrek," Hayes chuckled into his hand as he thought of the observers' stories. He knew the odds were infinitesimally small that Jedrek was here. Fate *must* be on their side. His expression filled with admiration, despite Hayes staring down the man. He turned towards Captain Nanti, "Will you support my decision if I ask him to stay with Isa?"

She mulled for a long while, her features contorting with every scenario that played in her head. Finally, "Yes, but let's not tell Hegemon General Theol right away."

Hayes grunted in agreement. "He won't like it."

"She's legally your daughter."

"Right." Hayes took a seat across from Stanten. "Let's get down to business. He sighed. "We need you to care for a child."

"Sure, I can watch a child," Ottokip answered the question with a yawn. His eyes grew drowsy.

"Grandmaster, we have more questions for you later, but right now Jedrek has an offer we need to discuss," Hayes spoke respectfully.

"Babysit?" Stanten repeated, profoundly puzzled.

The operative explained to Stanten that he would be assigned to protect the girl he had met in the forest.

Stanten asked if there was anything else he needed to do. He didn't want unexpected commands sprung on him because he didn't ask for clarity.

"We just need you to keep the girl safe to the best of your ability." There was some hesitance in Hayes' voice. Something about the girl must be special.

"Sounds like a tall order," Stanten gulped.

"You'll be relieved of your inmate duties indefinitely," the Captain added.

Stanten looked around the room. There was definitely much more they weren't saying. But… he'd be able to get away from Tivan. Not doing back-breaking work didn't sound so bad either. "Alright," his voice shook with uncertainty. He wasn't sure why this was being asked of him in particular.

And why does everyone call me Jedrek?

Hayes and Captain Nanti nodded to each other.

The Captain stayed with the one named Ottokip. Hayes asked Stanten to follow him. They left the cramped office.

Making their way through multiple decks, a few operatives tossed Stanten curious glances. It made him twitch. After twists and turns, they arrived in a hangar. Hayes pointed to a craft, armed to the teeth with weapons. "Strap in." He said little else.

Stanten climbed the steps and peered inside. There were four seats behind the cockpit. He wondered if Kameclara flew something like this. He could picture her at the controls. The thought warmed him.

As he found a seat, Hayes gave Stanten yet another probing glance. It seemed as if he knew things about him. By whatever pleasure, Hayes didn't say a word.

Hayes pulled on a helmet as he entered the cockpit. "Hang on," he warned.

Stanten tightened his crossed straps.

Hayes spoke a few words, muffled by the sound of his helmet. Then, Stanten heard, "Green," as hangar doors opened. A moment later, an extraordinary forced flattened him.

They glided swiftly into a bank of clouds. Thick condensation broke to either side. The ride was bumpy, and Stanten wanted to squeeze his eyes shut. But he didn't, afraid what might happen should he not keep his wits.

As cloud cover fell away, Stanten saw blue fading. They were riding into a dark expanse. Stanten swallowed to ease discomfort. His fear of heights returned. Fighting it with every ounce of strength, he stole a glance down. The curvature of a planet spread beneath. "Oh my Goddess!"

He never imagined they were on a planet. An artificial colony in the Molta Belt, maybe, but never a planet. The beauty distracted him from inquiring where they were in relation to Teroma.

Before long, they approached a ship marked "2." It was the one that had landed in Priletoria, with normal people. Ones who weren't operatives.

The transport docked gracefully and they disembarked. Hayes guided Stanten through winding halls. The décor seemed luxurious, not simple and efficient like the warship. Definitely not like the crummy homes in Pudyo. It made Stanten feel out of place.

A few civilians greeted Hayes, and nodded to Stanten with a smile. Not accustomed to the attention, Stanten trudged diffidently behind the operative. Life experiences didn't prepare him for this type of interaction. Inmate quarters and streets of Pudyo were filled with scowling faces.

Stanten flicked his eyes to Hayes. He felt exceedingly uncomfortable around the man. Mostly resulting from those looks Hayes kept tossing his way, but also because the operative could summon electricity. Stanten had never seen a weapon like that before.

What if I don't do this job right? Hayes can end me in a snap.

Stanten knew he didn't have a whole lot of good options in life. Babysitting would likely keep him away from war, and rebels. Because what civilian—especially a child—would be headed into a battle zone?

They stopped in front of a door and Hayes scanned to enter. Inside, a person in regular clothes greeted them. Stanten wondered if he was an operative too. The man's eyes hesitated when he saw Stanten. Hayes said some words in a low voice and he nodded, quietly leaving the apartment.

"Isa," Hayes called, "I brought someone here to see you!"

Footsteps plodded. A door flew open and a girl peered out with guarded eyes. When they fell on Stanten, an enormous grin spread across her face. "Jedrek!" she dashed forward. There was a hop and suddenly her arms squeezed Stanten's neck. She remained there, dangling and laughing. Stanten didn't know what to do, so he kept his arms at his side. She clung tightly as if she were seeing an old friend after a long time. "How's your tooth?" she asked.

Stanten ran his tongue over his gums. "Popped it back in. Seems to be stayin'."

"Manners, Isa," Hayes scolded gently, "get down." He felt relieved to see his daughter smiling again.

Stanten felt sadness tugging at his heart. His mother used to warn him about manners. He softened a bit and met the child's gaze as she slid to the ground. She was genuinely thrilled. Stanten wasn't accustomed to people being happy to see him.

"Thank you, daddy!" she said sweetly. "Jedrek's here to help. I just know it somehow!"

"She's really your daughter?" Stanten asked in bewilderment.

"Yep, and you better treat her like the lil' Goddess she is!" Hayes warned.

So much for clarity. If he messed up, Hayes would definitely have him killed. Stanten's shoulders broke into cold sweat.

Chapter Forty-One

Isa continued to advocate that Stanten's name was Jedrek. He grew accustomed answering to it. He was given a small apartment in the same sector as Isa. His identity as a former inmate remained hidden. The civilians were told Stanten was an operative permanently injured from a rebel attack. He was instructed to speak as little as possible about himself.

Each day, Isa was allowed a six-hour block of time to spend time with Stanten. Usually, another person accompanied them. Mostly she chatted away, and he listened. She talked about her friends and the games they'd play. Sometimes, she talked about her aunt, and how losing her was sad.

It took Stanten a while to piece it together. Isa's aunt was the dying woman Kameclara had rushed to after the rebel attack. Stanten couldn't tell from a distance at the time, but the man there was Hayes. He wondered if Kameclara was related to the child too.

One day, Isa's eyes grew big. "I knew you'd understand how I feel about Auntie." Stanten hadn't said anything aloud. But inside, he'd been reflecting on painful memories. "You've lost two people you cared about before their time. I can feel hurt inside you just like mine."

Stanten couldn't figure out the second person Isa said he'd lost. His mother was the only one he'd cared for.

After the girl mentioned it a few more times, he finally asked.

Isa gazed into the distance, scratching her head, "Her name is M... Meliora?"

"You must be mistaken. Dunno know that name." Though... he thought the old guy in rags might've mentioned it. Stanten couldn't be sure.

Isa pouted. "Auntie used to say my words don't always make sense right away... but they will. Just wait and see."

Stanten wasn't sure what to say to that. He knew even less about how to behave around a child. It took him a while to grow comfortable, usually doing whatever she asked. He wanted to keep his easy new life. He went as far as allowing her to draw on him with a pink marker.

In time, Isa's inherent cleverness and sociability lowered his guard. He found himself looking forward to daily games and stories. She was well educated and he learned a lot sitting with her through lessons. He wondered what he could've been on Teroma with studies like hers at a young age. His schools were more about who bullied the most.

Outside of time with Isa, Stanten found difficulty adjusting. He was allowed to sleep whenever he wanted, and could leave his room without reporting in. He often lost track of time. He spent much of it on a small viewing deck. It wasn't as nice as the one on Warship-23, but he could still see the stars. And he didn't need to hide.

With many hours to himself, his thoughts often drifted to Kameclara. There was something about her eyes he could never block out. It made him feel a certain way. It was different from anything he'd felt in his waking life. In his dreams, sometimes her voice called, eliciting a now-familiar sensation in his chest.

On dreary days, he found himself sickened by the realization they were apart. "You gotta let her go," he told himself over and over, to no avail. "You're just a passing fancy to her."

Yet, from time to time, another voice spoke louder from deep inside. It told him it didn't matter how out of reach Kameclara seemed, they belonged together. He sighed. "Why can't I stop these thoughts? I'll never see her again."

~*~

Warship-23 14.244 ans

"Kameclara," Captain Nanti called her to the edge of the training pit. Alpha Team was running morning drills.

"Sir!" she hopped over the edge.

"Hayes would like to see you in my office," she commanded, giving her a look that asked for discretion.

Kameclara saluted. Turning on her heel, she left.

In Captain Nanti's office, Hayes sat on a desk, chatting with an old man. When Kameclara entered, the bushy eyebrows of the elder danced with exuberance. He raced to her and grabbed her hands. To Kameclara's shock, the grip of his fingers was quite firm. "Meliora, it's you!" He exclaimed in celebration. "I was worried you wouldn't find your way back!"

Kameclara cocked an eyebrow. Hayes sat with a roguish smile, observing.

And here I thought he couldn't surprise me anymore.

She turned to the elderly man. "Excuse me, I think you have the wrong person," she took her hands back. "My name's Kameclara."

"Kameclara, Kameschmera," he spoke sarcastically, jowls shaking, "you're nobody but Meliora!" He struck his forehead unexpectedly. "Oh, I forgot, you cannot remember." He looked eagerly to Hayes, "What's my name again? I seem to have forgotten that too, but I believe I told you earlier."

"Your name's Ottokip. You're a Grandmaster of light sorcery from Jema," Hayes recited.

Ottokip nodded as he absorbed the words. He turned back to Kameclara, "Please, have a seat." He led her by the hand to a chair, brushing Hayes out of the way. "General Guyak was telling me about your friend."

"General?" Kameclara asked Hayes. There was no officer on the mission by that name.

"According to our dear Grandmaster Ottokip, I am the reincarnation of a General Guyak, and you are the rebirth of my former Queen, Meliora," Hayes elucidated. He'd taken quite a liking to Ottokip. He added with a chuckle, "Perhaps I should be answering to *you*, Meliora." He crossed his legs in amusement as he found a new seat.

Hayes wasn't shocked to learn of his previous life from the Grandmaster. Ashmarah had hinted to a similar thing, telling Hayes he was crucial to the mission. In Hayes' mind, it only affirmed Ottokip's identity. Still, he wanted to be sure about the Grandmaster, so he invited Kameclara. Sure enough, the old man recognized her as Meliora without provocation. Something Ashmarah had already confirmed.

Hayes couldn't help but wonder if it was his karma to lose mentors prematurely. It would certainly be a result of his previous life. Records indicated General Guyak was in the midst of training Jedrek and guiding Meliora when he was struck down.

He shook himself and turned attention back to the two in the room.

"Now, this is very important," Ottokip gazed into Kameclara's eyes, "When you are with Jedrek, how do you feel?"

"I don't know a Jedrek," Kameclara tried to grasp the peculiar situation. Ottokip didn't appear connected to the observers or Protocol Phen. Hayes was no help—offering no explanations. He'd seemed satisfied letting her figure things out on her own. She shot him a disgruntled glare.

But Hayes suddenly sat up with alarm. "How do you know she's met Jedrek?" There was no longer any doubt in his mind about the Grandmaster. The old man knew more than any outsider could possibly discover.

"I read it in your eyes you were going to invite an old friend to meet me," Ottokip shook a finger at Hayes. "I didn't know it was Meliora! I'm overjoyed! She is here, and Jedrek is here. The two spend all their time together, I presume! Their connection is like none other. It's of the essence that holds the universe together!"

Hayes didn't know how to respond. Kameclara and Stanten were from two different worlds. She had a duty, and him… not so much. There was often debate in those versed in Teroma's old ways, of which should hold more importance: the present life, or strong karma from a past one. Hayes gulped. A consensus had never been reached.

Hayes said slowly to Kameclara, "I'm going to ask you some personal questions."

"Alright," she didn't sound so sure. "I reserve the right to not answer."

"When you're with Stanten, have you ever felt … unusual?" He couldn't find a better word. "Ottokip and I had a laborious conversation before you arrived. Apparently, you and Stanten share a karmic bond that's extremely powerful. Sometimes when this happens, it can shadow your present consciousness."

Kameclara prepared to dismiss the question. Then, memories of the viewing deck surfaced. Her eyes lowered as she relived the moments. It was true, it seemed as if they were remembering emotions they'd never shared. Even now, he was often in her thoughts and she couldn't find a rational explanation.

She blushed.

"I take that as a yes!" Ottokip chuckled sheepishly. His cheeks dusted pink, as if he were a maiden in love. "This is excellent indeed! The fates are on our side!" He scratched his head as bubbling laughter filled the room. He stopped abruptly and his tone became serious, "But wait… if Jedrek and Meliora cannot connect with their past, they won't have a good chance to stop Vesper."

"Kamecl-, I mean Meliora and Jedrek are only precautions," Hayes started to explain.

"No, no!" Ottokip cut in. "Do NOT underestimate Vesper! Even she doesn't realize it yet, but that Nevo descendant has the ability to wipe out your entire fleet!" he huffed. "All other Masters cannot come close to surpassing her, even combining their efforts!"

"What are you saying?" Hayes frowned. There'd been concerns that Vesper had yet to show the full force of her power. It was impossible to tell the upper bounds of a Nevo's abilities.

Half Nevo, he corrected. Seu soldiers had taken her residual DNA from Songbird and tested it.

"She could be considered a Grandmaster because she's absorbed enough Masters' powers to equal one." Ottokip shook his head. "However, she lacks the control that comes with decades of proper training. And she has no mentor to bring out her full potential." Ottokip's scratching grew vigorous. "There is only one person who can defeat her at full force, but she'll never raise a hand against Vesper. Luckily, neither does she have an interest in stopping your fleet."

Hayes frowned, "Another Grandmaster? I thought you were the only one?"

"The woman I speak of is not a Grandmaster per se, because she has not the experience in multiple masteries. But her natural ability is overpoweringly strong." He leaned back, eyes darkening. "She is an *original* Nevo. That person is Vesper's mother."

"You're speaking of another Nevo wielding magic?" Hayes' skin prickled. This was bad. They didn't have information on Vesper's biological mother. She was an orphan. If her parent was truly a full-blooded Nevo, the implications were harrowing.

Kameclara sat patiently, following the conversation to the best of her knowledge. A lot of information came to light, but she still couldn't clearly see how she fell into the scheme of things.

"Yes, yes," Ottokip spoke breathily. "Before Vesper's mother was a sorceress, she was a Nevo. THE Nevo that had been selected to become autocrat." The old man shrank, "But an injury left her for dead, so the position went to Teppa. The injured girl's caretaker, oblivious to her identity, took pity and snuck the child to Songbird for healing."

"What are you saying?" Hayes couldn't breathe.

"I'm saying, the injury was to the girl's head. She recalled nothing of being a Nevo. The caretakers are never told they are caring for Nevos either."

Hayes choked, piecing it together, "And that's how she could learn sorcery."

"Yes. And if anyone had known what she was—or if she could've remembered herself—it would've been stopped. The 'Seed of Life' strictly forbade Nevos to wield sorcery."

Hayes clutched his head.

"Explain," Kameclara demanded, sensing foreboding in Hayes' change. He'd paled considerably.

There were dark circles underneath his eyes as Hayes turned to Kameclara. "Ia has had families in the past. 'Nevo' means 'divine.' Nevos are direct blood descendants to the Goddess." He swallowed, whispering, "Their connection to the source of magic is thousands of times stronger."

Kameclara felt her mouth go dry. "How do you know this?" she asked the old man.

He blinked large eyes. "Because I am Ottokip," he replied innocently.

Hayes placed a hand on his chin, contemplating, "Can we ask Vesper's mother to convince her to stop?"

Ottokip shook his head, "Vesper never knew her birth mother, so there is no emotional connection." He shrugged, "Besides, Vesper's behavior has little to do with how she feels loss or sorrow. Not even the turmoil of battling souls in Vesper's body is the dominating factor. Those are all indirect consequences that drive her present mad state."

"Meaning?" Hayes narrowed his eyes.

Ottokip waved a finger. "You need to understand the larger scheme, the universal one. Vesper is the way she is, simply because her soul is young. She has very little karmic entanglement so there's not much guiding her destiny." He spread his hands. "As a result, the fates have little to restrain her, and karmic debt is created left and right!

Every single one of us," Ottokip pointed around the room, "are here because of karmic cycles. We're bound into existence to resolve its debt."

"What does this have to do with me?" Kameclara cut in.

"Because she's indebted to you. And by a great deal," Ottokip responded as if the answer were obvious. "I need you to spend time with
me and Jedrek to reconnect with your previous lives. You must understand, you cannot tell anyone who you really are." His eyes roamed the
walls. "I sense spies and loose lips on your ships. No one must know."

"What do you mean?" Hayes aggressively leapt to his feet. "Everyone was vetted thoroughly!"

"No person vital to your mission," Ottokip spoke dismissively.
"But make sure you don't speak carelessly…"

"Do you have names?" Hayes stuck his face into Ottokip's with
urgency. A vein in his neck throbbed. His North Deron instincts were on
high alert. "I can't allow a single sleeper agent to get by!"

Ottokip's eyes changed. Ignoring Hayes' question, he spoke,
"Your service as General Guyak was cut short in your previous life by
Vesper. But as her General, your life always belonged to her… So, her
debt to you is weak." His eyes started to gloss, mumbling, "All you can
do is train Meliora and Jedrek to face her."

"The spies…" Hayes' face turned red. "I need to find them."

"I cannot tell you more, other than I sense ulterior motives," Ottokip sighed. "Though inconvenient, your troops can easily contend
with them." The light in the old man's eyes dimmed, and he fumbled
aimlessly with his robes.

Hayes recognized that Ottokip knew no more and gave up for the
moment. His face returned to a normal color, but the vein didn't recede.
His eyes narrowed as they scanned the walls, anticipating who was

beyond them.

Ottokip turned to Kameclara. His eyes flashed with a momentary return of lucidity. "Your father gave you a gift before you left home. It's two objects of fluid. One is for you. The other—you wondered long and hard which of your friends you'd choose." His voice intensified, "I am telling you now, give it to Jedrek. General Guyak will train the both of you to use magic. It's *imperative*."

Kameclara pulled away. She tried to hide alarm at the mention of her father. "How did you know about the vials?" She'd told no one, not even Leera or Syralise.

Ottokip now spoke to Hayes, "I will take Ashmarah's role, and train the young Goddess. This is my destiny." He gave a bow.

At the mention of the Goddess, Hayes stepped forward, "How do you know this?" his voice grew ominous as paternal instinct kicked in.

"How do you know my father?" Kameclara demanded as they towered over the shriveled old man.

Ottokip scratched his head. A dull expression clouded his eyes again. He responded in a childlike manner, "Because I am Ottokip." There was a long silence before he mumbled as if not comprehending his own words, "The universe shows me information in dreams. This life is one of my last karmic resolutions as a seedling soul. I'm on the brink of ascension."

"What does that mean?" Hayes hissed. He wished with his whole heart Ashmarah was still around. There was so much he had yet to learn.

Ottokip shrugged, "I don't know." He pointed upwards, "Ask the universe. I do."

Kameclara and Hayes exchanged a look, "Nothing that was

spoken here leaves this room. Not even to Protocol Phen," Hayes commanded strictly. Too much classified information had been blurted by the Grandmaster. It was information Hayes couldn't have anticipated him knowing.

"Of course," she nodded firmly. Kameclara reflected for a moment as Hayes wrung his hands. "The serum my father gave me. Did you and Ashmarah take it too?"

"What?" Hayes seemed distracted.

"You and Ashmarah. You wielded magic like the locals," Kameclara confronted. "Ashmarah told me she snuck vials to my father. Does the serum allow one to use magic without S-48?"

Hayes spoke intently, "Kameclara, to keep you focused as an operative, we keep information from you. Why do you always need to know more?"

She crossed her arms stubbornly, "You're an operative too, and you know much more than me." She stressed, "Besides, what's the point of being Protocol Phen if you can't tell me?"

Hayes cackled in amusement. "Alright then. Yes. The serum does permanently activate the nevino sequence, allowing one to tap into the ethereal realm and use magic."

"Why hasn't it been distributed to all operatives on this mission?" she contended. A snore reached their ears. Ottokip had fallen asleep. "Is he...?" she asked.

"He's fine. He does that sometimes." Hayes turned back to her. "The serum hasn't been thoroughly tested. Ashmarah and I were the only trials. Furthermore, we couldn't predict how it'll change the IM's operations."

Kameclara felt bewildered. "This is hardly the time to be conservative!"

Hayes sniffed. "When you become a Hegemon General, you can call the shots. Besides," he tossed his head, "you got the serum, didn't you?"

He didn't feel comfortable telling her about dark magic. It was a slippery slope that could start with innocent experimentation. He barely trusted himself to keep his abilities in check. He didn't want to burden her with its possibilities.

He redirected with a smirk, "Speaking of which, how have those breathing exercises been going?" Besides neutralizing spells, the Clear Aura Method was the foundation of light magic.

"Fine," she pulled her lips into a line. Kameclara learned to recognize when Hayes purposefully withhold information. She didn't know why, but knew he his reasons weren't to harm her. She didn't push the issue.

Chapter Forty-Two

Stanten pranced with Isa on his shoulders. She had made paper flowers and showered them around the room, singing a tune. He chuckled at his own ridiculousness. He would've never done anything like this back in Pudyo. The kid's nonjudgmental disposition made him feel safe enough to be goofy.

Stanten glanced to the operative stationed with them. She kept an eye trained on him and the girl as she read on a tablet.

Once Isa was out of petals, she slid down his shoulders and asked for a drink. Stanten went into the kitchen and poured her a glass of juice. Isa asked for another and gave it to the operative. She thanked the girl and continued to ignore Stanten. He wasn't sure if it was a good thing. It could indicate Stanten was trusted around Isa. He'd been looking after her for some time now.

"Or maybe she thinks I'm beneath her," Stanten mumbled to himself. He also couldn't help but notice today's chaperone had a weapon strapped.

"Jedrek?" Isa asked when returning the glasses, "are you sure you don't remember anything about yourself?"

Isa felt convinced he'd incarnated near their present location before. When Stanten first heard the wild theory, he wasn't certain how to respond. Even more surprising was how the child knew about reincarnation. It wasn't commonly discussed on Teroma.

"I'm sure," he responded.

The sound of a door sliding made his steps slow as they returned to the living room. On guard, he ushered Isa behind him. The operative rose from her seat, hand on weapon.

Isa's father and the eccentric old man, Ottokip entered. Stanten breathed a sigh of relief.

Until Kameclara appeared in the doorframe.

All air escaped his body. Stanten lowered his eyes. His tongue felt heavy as blood thumped through his ears. He realized he got his wish: One last chance to look into her eyes.

Then why does this feel so difficult?

Kameclara nodded to the operative in Hayes' home. "Thanks, Ablon," Hayes dismissed her politely.

After Ablon left, Kameclara turned her attention to Stanten. She had no clue he'd be present. Kameclara quickly did away with consternation. With a smile, she approached him in a light step. She paused a few paces away, uncertain how to greet him.

After consideration, she decided it was best to shake hands. "I see you've been promoted," she joked.

"Yeah, to babysitter," Stanten mumbled. The warmth of her hand filled him with unspeakable joy.

"Jedrek is very important," Isa said in a serious expression. "Just as important as Aunt Ashmarah said you are." A grown-up expression plastered her dainty face. "I can feel it. His soul is awakened to his fate, but his mind is still asleep."

"Oh no, not another Ottokip," Kameclara giggled.

Ottokip was introduced to Isa and the two immediately became friends. They chattered about things that seemed like nonsense to the others.

Hayes sighed in relief. Bringing Ottokip to Isa was a calculated risk. However, he needed to see his daughter's reaction to him—to see how much the Grandmaster could be trusted. It was why he'd brought Kameclara along. Albon was secretly waiting in the hall too.

Hayes sent him a message to let Ablon know she could leave.

"Hayes," Kameclara moved to stand beside him. Isa had pulled Stanten aside.

"Yes?" Putting his messaging device away, he kept his eye on his daughter.

"Is there something about Isa I should know?" Theories had been brewing in her mind. Kameclara's voice lowered until it came barely as a breath in his ear. "Is she the Goddess?"

Hayes purposefully changed the topic, "Well Kameclara, is there something about you and Stanten I should know?" he moved away. Hayes spoke deviously, "Because if you're not interested, I might be."

Kameclara felt heat rise to her cheeks. She didn't dare look in Stanten's direction. It wasn't like her to be bashful, but Hayes had a way of getting to her. Or maybe it was Stanten's presence. "Hayes, I'm serious," Kameclara composed herself. "With so many once unbelievable things now accepted as facts of the mission, is it crazy of me to ask that question?"

Something inside of Hayes sounded an alarm. He tilted his head mechanically and studied Kameclara. His hip shifted to one side and a hand supported his chin. He felt irked. Yet, he knew he was responsible. Ashmarah had always told him he had a really big mouth around people he liked. "Really, Kameclara," he sighed, "You're too smart for your own good. You're lucky I believe you're Meliora or you'd be in hot water."

"So, I'm correct in my assumption?" she pressed, hairs rising.

He paused and considered whether to deny or confirm Kameclara's theory. He could be in trouble for revealing tightly classified information.

Yet, Ottokip had already done that. He weighed whether to write it off as ramblings of a bizarre man.

Hayes trusted his gut. He brushed his lips against Kameclara's ear so his words wouldn't carry. "One hundred percent." He added in a threatening tone, clutching her shoulder, "I don't need to remind you the importance of keeping this confidential."

"Of course," Kameclara gripped his arm back in response. "I already made the vow to look after her, didn't I?"

Before Hayes could speak, Isa walked to Kameclara and pulled her away. She gave the woman a tight hug. Kameclara's breath caught in her chest and she felt faint, having just learned Isa's secret.

"I'm sorry... I didn't know you were Meliora. Ottokip just told me." Isa pulled back, large eyes staring into Kameclara's soul. "I knew I liked you because your colors are pretty. It's because you're caring. But yours were extra bright, because you're supposed to be here."

"Um...Th-thank you," Kameclara swooned. She couldn't take her eyes off of Isa, absorbing every iota of detail.

So this is what the Goddess looks like. Does she always incarnate to this appearance? Her mind wondered over random questions. *What's her favorite color? Food?*

Isa grew emotional. "It's because of your traumas that you aren't awakened to your fate. I'm sorry you've suffered." Her eyes watered and Kameclara felt taken aback. "Pain from past lives can force memories to hide. Ottokip says Jedrek can help you to remember. The two of you need to connect to who you once were."

"Yes, child," Ottokip spoke to Kameclara. "I sense you and Jedrek are like me. You're nearing the end of your days as seedling souls. This allows deeper perceptions to the past."

Isa ran a sleeve over her eyes, grinning hopefully, "Ottokip and I think it will be a good idea if you two go on a date!"

Hayes overheard, "Aha! My daughter reveals our true plan!" He took her hand, "Let's play on the viewing deck. They can have privacy here." He ushered Isa and Ottokip out of his home, promising treats. Isa and Ottokip squealed with joy.

"Hayes, I don't think—," Kameclara began. The door shut on her words. She rolled her eyes. He was worse than her mother when it came to setting her up.

Kameclara took a moment to absorb the information she'd just learned about Isa. Her hands trembled as she stared at the door where the Goddess had left.

Stanten moved beside her and took her fingers. The quivering stopped.

"So, how've you been?" he asked sheepishly.

"Strange," she bobbled her head with unspoken frustration.

He chuckled nervously, "Tell me about it!" They stood silently, trying to think of things to say. Yet, they didn't need words. The space between them filled with velvety emotion, seeping from unseen memories.

Kameclara channeled her annoyance with Hayes. "Wanna see if

there's drinks to steal in the kitchen?"

"Sure," he smiled, gazing into her eyes. Time disappeared. Neither moved. "I've missed you," he braved a whisper. "I hated not seeing you."

"D-do you believe all the things they're saying, about our past lives?" Her hand tightened in his. A hope she didn't recognize gripped her chest.

"I dunno," he drowned in the green of her eyes.

"I think… I might…"

Stanten blinked as the words made his heart accelerate. Frightened by the intensity, he released her hand and marched to the kitchen. He was only able to locate a few juice boxes.

"I hope these are alright." They each took one and sat at the kitchen table. The small activity helped Stanten relax.

Kameclara made a comment about their daring chase after the rebels. Stanten laughed. It didn't take long to delve into a comfortable flow of conversation.

"You haven't changed in seven ans," she commented.

"Neither've you."

"I bet we're different from Meliora and Jedrek," she gave a lopsided grin. "I wonder how they died."

Silence followed. Then, "Do you really wanna know?" Stanten's voice wavered. He had struck a friendly conversation with one of Isa's guardians. The woman had heard Isa call him Jedrek. She seemed to know quite a bit about him. She'd named her newborn Jedrek.

Kameclara flashed a look of curiosity. "I 'spose it couldn't hurt."

Stanten wasn't sure. It'd hurt him. He spoke carefully, gaging her reaction. "Jedrek committed suicide after losing Meliora. She died at the hands of Vesper." It felt surreal, speaking of his death in a former life. Even if he wasn't sure if he believed.

He left out how Meliora had traded her life for Vesper to spare Jedrek. He felt ashamed Jedrek didn't do more with her sacrifice.

"Oh," Kameclara breathed.

He couldn't place her tone. Taking a gamble, he took her hand again. This could be the last time they saw each other. "I feel ridiculous sometimes," he confessed.

There were three words inside him that needed to be vocalized, but he struggled to find courage. "I care about you and I can't explain it. I wanna protect you." He worked up bravery, "It's dumb because you're an operative, but I lo-," at the last second, Stanten shied away.

Instead, he said, "I know you can take care of yourself."

Kameclara lowered her head with a lump in her throat. She knew what he was trying to say. The truth was, she felt the same.

Kameclara loved him too.

A part of her felt relieved he didn't say those words. If they were to proclaim their feelings, it would complicate things. The pull between them would inextricably connect, and he would become a priority to her. It's something Kameclara couldn't afford. Not if she took her Teroman oath seriously.

Maybe when the Jema mission was over, they could sort things out. Until then, those words needed to remain unspoken.

"I appreciate the sentiment," she managed awkwardly.

Stanten glanced away, clearing his throat.

Perhaps her speechlessness was coming off as aloof. Apologetically, she stroked his hand.

"I don't know much about past lives," he said, and wanted to add, *but I know I must've loved you more than life.* However, those words remained locked away. "I'm happy to be here with you now," he spoke achingly instead.

"Me too." It was all the emotion she'd allow herself.

Hayes eyed Ottokip. He had given the old man clothes from his civilian wardrobe. It hung loosely as the Grandmaster flitted about. Isa told him something and he laughed. Hayes flexed his wrists. With a deep breath, he felt power humming in his cells. War on Jema was coming. His body and mind were ready.

He lowered his arms. But not his heart. He didn't *feel* ready.

"You're prepared to unleash far more powerful spells," Ashmarah had told him on multiple occasions. He'd kept his abilities subdued, secretly terrified of the arcane potential in his blood. He used to have nightmares about becoming Vesper.

Another voice came to mind from before he had met Ashmarah. Grandmaster Hegmin had complimented him, "Your breathing control is excellent. You would make a fine Pinghe warrior." Those who studied arcane knowledge knew Pinghe breathing exercises were the true path to light magic. Hayes took it as the greatest compliment.

Hayes sighed, resting his eyes for a moment. Meeting Leera had been difficult. She looked so much like her father, Grandmaster Hegmin. Hayes had wanted to say something to her, but each time, his nerve failed.

Hayes owed Grandmaster Hegmin his life. Not only because he'd saved Hayes from the training accident, but he gave Hayes direction as well.

Before working with Grandmaster Hegmin, Hayes was a different person. A ruthless person. He had no peace, and besides the satisfaction of besting others in combat, no purpose. He had done countless things he wasn't proud of; all to prove superiority.

He looked to his hands again. Ashmarah and Grandmaster Hegmin had faith in him. Faith he lacked.

Perhaps, what I fear is my inherent dark nature.

A shiver ran down his spine.

Chapter Forty-Three

Kameclara lurched awake, kicking blankets from her limbs. She gasped heavily with her dream fresh in mind. She closed her eyes and shuddered as sensations returned. The touch of Stanten's hands made her flesh turn to fire. His fingers had traced between her shoulders, finding their way lower.

Kameclara pushed the image away, jumping from her bunk. She landed clumsily and made her way to the bathroom. Shutting the door, she flicked on the light. Hoping to drive away disorientation, she ran icy water over her head. She squeezed her eyes against the memory of Stanten's lips on her collarbone. "Gotta keep my head clear."

No matter how many times she tried to push him from her thoughts, there he was. Now, even in her dreams.

"You alright?" Kameclara heard through water.

Startled, she lifted her head and bumped into the faucet. "Oomph."

As she came away, Syralise tossed her a towel. Kameclara dried herself as she shut off the tap. Syralise gave an inquisitive look; curly locks tousled high on her head.

Kameclara blinked as her friend's hair color evoked an image of a boy with long, silvery hair. A scent filled her nostrils. It took her a moment to recall where she had whiffed it before. There was an over-grown bush of wistra flowers on Ima. The fragrance had riled her.

And the boy…

It was Jedrek—one of the monarchs that stood against Vesper. The person Isa said reincarnated as Stanten.

"What's up?" Syralise waved a hand in front of Kameclara's face.

She realized she'd been staring off. "Did I wake you?"

"Landing like a sack of bricks? How could I sleep?" her partner teased.

"Sorry," Kameclara croaked.

Catching her partner's expression, Syralise's face turned serious, "What's the matter?" She folded her arms across her chest. The harsh light contoured her muscles, reminding Kameclara of her own as she had clutched Stanten in her dream.

She squeezed her eyes, vigorously rubbing her face with the towel. "Nothing. Just had an intense dream."

"Hmph," Syralise snorted, "Must've been some dream. Was it about Stanten?" Kameclara dropped her head. Her partner laughed and ran her hands through her hair. "No way! It was?" she snickered, "is that why you're so hot and bothered?"

"It's probably just that thing my mom talks about. That biological clock," Kameclara grumbled.

"Probably. But why're you upset? If I had a dream like that, I'd be pretty satisfied," she tossed her head in amusement.

"But I'm not actually seeing him," Kameclara bit her lip.

"You mean you haven't—," Syralise began to ask.

Kameclara shook her head adamantly. Droplets of water scattered about. "I don't even let myself think about it. Not with him! He's been such a distraction! I can't let it go further!" The towel twisted in her hands.

Yet, as she said those words, Kameclara knew things with Stanten were outside her control.

Syralise leaned against the wall. "Can I say something?" Her voice grew contemplative.

"Sure."

"I don't think you should try to control the way you feel about 'im," she shrugged.

Kameclara raised a brow. Her partner's eyes sparkled a sad hue, making their golden tone dimmer. Something must have happened recently. Final training was pushing them to their limits and the girls spent most of their off days sleeping. They hadn't found a lot of time to catch up with each other.

Kameclara felt a surge of guilt. She'd been wrapped up with her own issues and hadn't noticed her partner being less bouncy.

Syralise continued, "When you talk about Stanten, something about you's different. It's never happened when you were with other guys."

"Yeah, but that's why I've gotta cut him out. It's just… a lot harder than I thought it'd be."

"I bet," Syralise spoke tenderly, "I think it's because you've found real love." Kameclara opened her mouth to protest but Syralise held up a hand. "Now, I know it's a platitude and all, so before you huff and tell me you don't believe in that kinda stuff, shut up and think." Her eyes sparkled, "On a deep level, you know what you're feeling is important. Mere crushes can't sway you. What else can distract you like this but true love?"

"Yeah, but…I can't…" They needed to protect the Goddess.

"I believe true love is the one thing in the universe that cracks you open and forces you to face yourself."

Kameclara nodded solemnly. "You mean I'm compromised."

"Nah," Syralise shrugged. "You're having a hard time right now because these deeper emotions are new to you. It can be tricky getting a handle on 'em." She nudged Kameclara. "But I know you. You'll get your shit together when you need to. It's who you are. It's who WE operatives are." Syralise laughed. "So, don't avoid him. Accept how you feel. He's not an operative, so it doesn't matter to the mission. Love away!"

Kameclara found comfort in Syralise's words.

Still. Stanten scared her more than any enemy could. The way she felt when they were together seemed dangerous. When Kameclara neared him, she felt balanced, as if nothing in the universe were out of order. That she could lie down and fade into one with the ether of existence. As if the fate of all things had been determined long before the birth of the universe. It made her wonder at the futility of all endeavors—including the mission to Jema.

No. That simply would not do.

Kameclara sobered up. "I fear his death more than my own demise. That I'd lose any chance at peace. I don't want to feel this way."

Sadness filled the air. "I don't have response. I just believe if you love someone, they never really leave you. Even in death."

They fell silent.

Syralise eventually snickered. "Leera was right. Emotions are sloppy. Forget what I said. I'm being hypocritical. Things were getting messy with Nolram and we had to end it."

"When did this happen? You've been seeing him for almost a decade!"

"A little while ago," she brushed it aside. "I'm kinda blue, but it's okay. We both knew it was coming." Syralise shrugged, "Maybe I'm saying all these things to you because a part of me wonders what it'd be like if Nolram were the one."

"How did you know he wasn't?"

"Don't get me wrong, we felt strongly for each other. But there's a click that was missing. I grew more apparent when I saw you with Stanten. You two have this… 'thing.'"

"Sy, I'm so confused," Kameclara droned as she buried her face in the towel. "Why am I feeling this now? The timing's so bad! We're on our way to Jema!"

Syralise huffed nonchalantly, "I guess only Ia would know. If you ever meet her, make sure to ask!" she jested.

Kameclara choked. Syralise didn't know about Isa.

"You know," Syralise changed the topic, "My dad once said you have an old soul."

Kameclara faced her partner with intrigue. "Really? What does that mean?"

Syralise shrugged, "I 'spose if you believe in ancient Teroman stuff like my dad, about reincarnation and the legend of the Goddess, it means you've lived like a thousand lives or something."

"Hmm," Kameclara grew thoughtful. She didn't want to think about Meliora, so she asked, "What about Leera?"

Syralise narrowed her eyes and tried not to laugh, "Even Stanten could tell ya, she's an asshole!"

The two stifled giggles. After the clowning died, they sat silently for a moment on the cool floor. Eventually, Syralise let out a breath, "Come on girlie, let's get back to bed. We've a long day tomorrow. You can figure stuff out about Stanten later."

"Thanks. I mean it."

Syralise gave Kameclara a tight hug before pulling her to her feet. They hung up the towel and flicked off the lights.

Kameclara hopped onto her bunk. In a playful gesture, Syralise tucked her in. They shared a low chuckle, careful not to wake Leera. Syralise then rolled into her bunk and was soon snoring.

With a weary hand, Kameclara pulled the blanket over her shoulder. Syralise's words echoed in her mind and thoughts of Stanten lingered. It instigated more of her dream to return. She tried to push it away, but it refused to be suppressed.

The back of Stanten's fingers brushed lovingly against her cheek. It awoke something in her. She turned and dragged her lips against his thumb, feeling it touch briefly against her tongue. It found its way to the nape of her neck, leaving a wet trail. Teeth chattering, a moan escaped her lips.

When Kameclara gazed down, his eyes penetrated her soul. It seemed if he'd stared into her a thousand times before. She sat naked and formless as if there was no place to hide, not even in her skin. It felt as liberating as it was terrifying. Stanten knew every ounce of her inside and out, even secrets she wasn't familiar with herself.

Kameclara replayed how she'd cradled his head. Stanten angled his face up, eyes drunk by the sight of her. She'd leaned forward to taste his kiss.

As their lips touched, his breath washed into her. Kameclara felt herself drowning, lost in the eternity of his essence.

She didn't need to tell him that she loved him.

He already knew.

Epilogue

In a field of blinking lights, Stanten floated tenderly beside Kameclara as a bodiless soul. It didn't matter they no longer held physical form. He felt ecstatic to be near her once more.

Stanten retained memories from multiple lives, but Kameclara had suffered tragic deaths in succession. She had trouble recalling.

Stanten didn't mind. He'd wait by her side, even if it took an eternity. "Do you recollect the beauty of Ima, and our time on Jema?"

"I do," she responded in a warm pulse. "You were there!"

"At least you remember me from our last life," he twinkled a sigh.

"Have we been together for more than one?" The notion teased nebulously.

"Yes. We've been together countless times and we've also spent many lives chasing after one another. This is the closest we've come in trillions of years."

"Trillions?" she blinked in exasperation.

"Nothing's impossible," Stanten winked with passion. "The fact we're together proves it. In each life we've shared, we've loved each other in different forms. I was your mother in one, twin brothers in another, and so many more… Something in our soul connects strongly.

That's the one thing I know definitively."

Kameclara shined in marvel, "You're saying it's a rare occurrence that we're together in this moment?"

"Yes, Kameclara," he pulsed affectionately, "and there's something I wanted to tell you in our last life, but could not."

"What is it?" she asked sweetly. Before Stanten could speak, Kameclara interrupted with urgency, "Something important is surfacing in my memories!"

Stanten waited patiently as she concentrated. He understood how challenging the process could be.

"My name," she palpitated, "... it's En!"

No sooner did the realization come, a commotion stirred in the distance. Stanten glanced in the direction of panic. A dark cloud approached at great speeds. He fretted, recognizing the soul eater.

Kameclara hovered in a daze after speaking her other name. There was no doubt she had come upon a profound realization. Maybe it was something Stanten could grasp too, but he didn't have the luxury to wait. She was in danger.

Using all his might, he tumbled into her. She lurched away in a wavering pattern. To his relief, a white beam of light washed over Kameclara.

"I wanted to say I love you!" Stanten called as she disappeared. "At least she's safe," he added to himself. That was his last thought as the soul eater devoured him.

... To be continued...

Book Three

Cycles of the Lights:
Stillness in the Storm

Coming in 2022

Pronunciation Guide

Carpecillero	KAR-puh-SIL-er-oh
Cromnus	CROM-nus
Deron	DARE-un
Erilph	AIR-elf
Fervir	FER-ver
Ginevra	jih-NEV-ruh
Habbada	HAB-id-uh
Heliope	HEE-lee-ope
Hurwon	HER-won
Ia	EE-uh
Ima	EE-muh
Isa	EE-suh
Jebbun	JEB-un
Jedrek	JED-rick
Jema	JEE-muh
Kame	KAH-may
Kameclara	KAH-muh-CLARE-uh
Leera	LEE-ruh
Maliote	MAIL-ee-ote
Mantipas	MAN-tih-pahs
Meliora	mee-lee-OR-uh

Pronunciation Guide

Molta	MOLE-tuh
Nanti	NAN-tee
Orareca	OR-uh-REH-kuh
Pinghe	PING-ee
Priletoria	PREE-luh-TOR-ee-uh
Procias	PRO-see-iss
Pudyo	PUD-yo
Sessa	SEH-suh
Seu	SAY-yoo
Syralise	SIGH-ruh-lees
Teppa Nevo	TEH-puh NEH-voe
Teroma	ter-OH-muh
Theol	THEE-ole
Tivan	TIH-vin
Unadine	OO-nah-deen
Wyzenkor	WIZE-en-core

The Seed of Life Timeline

Event	ans	Iman Year	Jeman Year
Priletoria Attacks	14.211 ans	2188 Iman Year	9745 Jeman Year
Vesper Controls Ima	14.213 ans	2190 Iman Year	9747 Jeman Year
Hayes Meets Isa	14.234 ans	2211 Iman Year	9768 Jeman Year
Teroman Fleet Launch	14.236 ans	2213 Iman Year	9770 Jeman Year
Teromans Arrive to Ima	14.244 ans	2221 Iman Year	9778 Jeman Year

About Ava Reiss

Ava Reiss started journaling at age eight. As years passed, volumes became littered with short stories. Ava loves legends, myths, and the fantastical. Many of those themes carry into her writing nowadays.

During her grade school years, she constantly bugged her artist uncle. She whined and begged him to illustrate for her little homemade books. Graciously, he conceded a few times—to which she was grateful. Eventually, Ava picked up a pencil and learned to draw herself.

"Only I truly know how my characters should look. If I can't draw them to look as they should, I've got no one to blame but myself," says Ava. Her novels include her illustrations.

She currently resides in Cleveland, OH with her husband and two tabbies Penny, and Piddy. Penny and Piddy star in her children's book: Space Tigers.

Follow Ava on Instagram @avareissbooks
And Space Tigers Publishing @spacetigers.publishing

Enjoy <u>The Seed of Life</u>*? Read the prequel:*

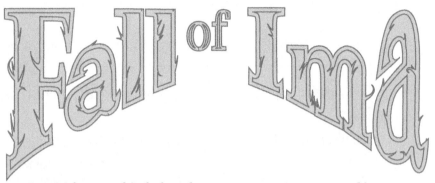

Join Meliora and Jedrek in their previous incarnation and learn how Vesper came to power.

Available now on Amazon!

Please follow Space Tigers Publishing on Facebook and Instagram for news and updates.

facebook.com/spacetigersplace
Instagram: @spacetigers.publishing

... And please leave a review on GoodReads.com!
Thank you!

Book One
C y c l e s   o f   t h e   L i g h t s :
Fall of Ima

Chapter One

Priletoria- 2184 Iman Year

Meliora ran a final brush through her hair. Its chestnut color came from her mother, but the bounce was from the late King Makarios' golden waves. As the locks recoiled from the teeth, she thought longing of her father. The brush was a gift from him. The silver handle gleamed softly, reminding of tears to soon follow.

Standing, the girl set down her brush and smoothed her gown. Pulling a dark veil over her face, she prepared to attend her father's funeral. Meliora's maid, Petra waited outside her door. The Princess spoke softly, "I thought I gave you the week off."

Petra's eyes peered to her friend and master, moistening. Like many in the nation, she loved their late King. "Your mother asked me to keep watch over you."

Meliora mustered a grin. "I'm off to see her now. Please, take time for yourself. I'd like to be alone."

Petra gave a curtsy. After checking over her shoulder to make sure no others were around, she wrapped arms around Meliora in a sympathetic gesture. After a squeeze, Petra darted to her private quarters.

Meliora watched her go. Petra had been a great friend; the two shared secrets when the council wasn't around to scold. They felt it unsuitable for the Princess to confide in a commoner. Meliora's parents felt differently and encouraged the friendship. In recent years, the two had drifted slowly. Petra was a few years older and finding interest in boys. Meliora barely began to understand the appeal.

The Princess swallowed hard to suppress rising emotions. "You promised you wouldn't cry until after the royal address," she reminded herself. Yet memories of her fourteenth birthday mere months ago brought a drop to her cheek. She'd always celebrated with her dearest of friends, Jedrek. He was born the same day, merely one year after. The jolliness had eclipsed Meliora's notice of her father's paling skin and quieter demeanor. The afterglow continued past Jedrek's return to his kingdom, Carpecillero, to which he was the youngest Prince.

Three days after celebrations, Meliora awoke to a strange noise. Alarms sounded through the halls. Wiping groggily at her eyes, she realized it was coming from the royal bedchamber. The hair on her neck rose as she recognized the high-pitched wail to be from her mother. Meliora didn't pause to slip on shoes. She dashed to the royal bedchamber, freezing a few steps from the open door. Cold stones stung her feet, but fear struck her numb.

From the room came sounds of a beast in agony. Steeling herself, Meliora forced one foot in front of the other. Peering in, she saw her father bent. His shoulders quaked with each cough, filling the room with ominous sound. Her mother had ceased wailing. Senses returned, Queen Vesper checked his vitals. Before marriage, she had been a long-time student at the kingdom's renowned temple of healing. She took charge and called out a list of herbs. When finished, attendants and nurses hurried from the room.

Servants rushed about, avoiding collisions. Some lowered curtains to keep sunlight from the King's eyes, which recently developed sensitivity. Others offered his usual medicines, but Meliora's father waved them away as his form dropped heavily onto pillows. A plume of feathers released. His features, once bold, now appeared sallow and listless. The golden bounce of his curly locks once brought Meliora joy. He loved to fling them about imitating his wife. The sight of them clinging like damp weeds made Meliora's heart twist.

Meliora slipped into the room as her father's eyes stared half-open at the ceiling. She identified a look of peace. He knew it was his time. King Makarios extended a hand to his daughter. Meliora stumbled forward, body heavy. She clasped his hand tightly. "My child," he'd wheezed. "You're a wonder." His shallow breath made continuing difficult.

"Father, please rest." She swept sweat-drenched hair from his eyes.

The King shook his head. "In my dreams... So clear, I saw you... real you..." The words drove him to another coughing fit. He cringed with frustration, neck purpling as he fought to breathe. His fingers had lost sensation in past months and could no longer write. "You're... tr- transcend-ent..." He strained a last syllable, desperate to share a message, "En!" It sounded as a groan to Meliora.

"I understand. And I love you too," Meliora spoke in her most assured tone. He appeared pleased. In truth Meliora couldn't be certain of her father's gibberish. All she hoped was to give him peace.

Angst folded in the lines of the Queen's ovular face, growing long as she squeezed the bridge of her nose. "I'm unable to accept your father will be stolen so soon." She massaged his back to ease discomfort. The King grunted in limited relief.

The Princess detected warping of her mother's emotions. "But what can we do?" Her tone bore surrender, hoping to guide the Queen along.

Vesper gave an untamed look. "There're ancient texts in the temple of healing. In a particularly old volume is mention of a Seed of Life. It's a powerful object, believed to have brought flora and fauna to the planets." A bizarre vigor elevated her pitch, "I will find this seed and learn of its powers. It must be able to save your father."

Meliora blinked, speechless. In the deepest reaches of her unfettered heart she wished her mother would find the mystical object and save her father. Yet rationale reeled her in. "If such an object exists, why has it not been used and its existence hidden from common knowledge?"

"The Seed of Life is holy. It must be protected." Vesper recited, her eyes shined with fixation, "The essence of our breath, source of our life. The Seed of Life imprints upon the watery wells and gifts to all."

Meliora gulped, having never seen her mother so stirred. Unsure what to do, she reached for her hand. Vesper responded with a determined squeeze, eyes staring unwavering at the ashen face of her dying husband.

Nurses reappeared with the herbs Vesper requested. She quickly brewed a paste and administered it to King Makarios. Meliora held her breath against the odor. She'd learned a bit from her mother. By the strong scent, the Princess knew the concoction was powerful. It firmed knowledge that her father didn't have much longer. She glanced worrying to Queen Vesper. The King had been sick before. Each time, he'd spent long hours with Meliora talking of life and death. She knew now he prepared her for the inevitable. One day he'd said, "Your mother can live in denial. If anything should happen, you'll need to help her."

"I'll always help, Papa," Meliora recalled her response. It wasn't until seeing her mother in the moment did she realize the extent of what he'd meant.

The elderly Master from the church of healing arrived late that day. He examined the King and confirmed, "He doesn't have much longer. A few months at most."

Vesper shook her head wildly. "This can't be true. What's his ailment? I can cure it!"

The Master took Vesper aside, "You're my most talented pupil with a heart that'll take you to the furthest reaches for the ones you love. But what has your spouse was passed to him from his father and his parent before him." The Master shook his head. "Such things have no cure, only a time. His is fast approaching."

"No!" Vesper leapt to her feet. She turned to leave, then remembered something. "Master, did you bring the tome I've requested?"

He called for his satchel, delivered swiftly by an apprentice. From it he retrieved an old book wrapped in heavy cloth. "It won't help," he warned with sympathy.

"I beg to differ." The Queen marched away.

In weeks to follow, numerous books arrived to her on loan from other nations. She scoured every last volume for mentions of the Seed of Life. She didn't sleep for days at a time. Despite her efforts, they were fruitless. Weeks later, King Makarios passed peacefully in his sleep.

Though saddened, Meliora rejoiced knowing her father no longer suffered. She hoped her mother would give up her fanatical search. Instead the Queen secluded herself. She shirked responsibilities, refusing to see anyone except Meliora. Planning of the funeral was left to the royal council.

Meliora shook herself from the reverie. Time had passed quickly and it was time for the funeral. She peered into the royal bedchamber. It sat empty, as it had been since her father passed. But she knew where to find her mother.

Meliora headed to the ancient wing of the palace. Once a stronghold during times of war, it was built with heavy stones. Vesper had moved her workshop there years ago, favoring its large, open rooms. She demanded her work be uninterrupted. Few dared disturb her. If the council had inquiries, they sent Meliora as a liaison.

Without natural light, torches illuminated Meliora's path. She squeezed between rough-cut walls of stone. She didn't usually mind its dinginess, but that day she shuddered.

The Princess stopped at the heavy wooden door. Knocking soundly, Meliora heard a cross voice snap. The girl disregarded the command and pushed with her shoulder. The thick door swung open. A few dozen candles lit the workspace. Aggravated eyes flashed in her direction. Upon seeing the Princess, Vesper's shoulders rolled back.

"My darling," honey words flowed. In contrast in the harsh light, a lackluster appearance startled Meliora. The Princess gave the sweetest of grins, hiding concern. She stepped forward, noticing untouched food from that morning.

"Not again," she sighed, heart fluttering. Meliora turned to her mother and cupped the woman's thin fingers. She pleaded, "You must eat. For my sake, I don't wish to lose you too." Her eyes swept down. Neither was the Queen dressed for the funeral.

Vesper withdrew one hand as the other squeezed back. She pulled a stray hair from her daughter's eyes and tucked it endearingly behind an ear. Long lashes batted sluggishly as if they were too heavy. "One day, we needn't worry about death," a creaking voice answered.

A chill tightened Meliora's knuckles. "What do you mean? We're taught death's a part of life. It's the nature of the universe."

Vesper nodded. "It is said that we don't die. We merely pass into another realm where we continue existence." A chuckle rattled her thin frame. "I'm searching for a way to bring your father back from that realm." She gestured across the disorderly room. "You see these scrolls, they've documented tales of sorcerers who've conversed with those crossed over." Queen Vesper paused as if tasting something in the air. "This means the realm of the dead isn't entirely separate from us."

The woman shambled to a table and thumbed pages. "My bane is that the last record of these tales came centuries ago. For all we know, they're merely myth." Her brow furrowed, turning to her daughter, "I've tried sacred amulets to drinking potions and deep meditation. I've fears, Mellie. Either we've lost the knowledge to see beyond our tangible world, or we were never able to do so and these tales are farce."

"Oh, Mother!" Meliora rushed to her side. The Princess wrapped arms around the Queen's neck, secretly wondering if grief had driven her mad. "Let's take this one moment at a time. I know you miss Father. I do too! You've been pushing yourself too far. Let's pause and remember the good times."

"But do you believe we can see beyond our world?" her mother begged, unwilling to deter.

Meliora sensed her need for affirmation. She searched her mind for something to say. A fond memory surfaced with a spot of warmth. "Sometimes when I'm chatting with Jedrek in the small hours of the night, we see images as if waking dreams. After sharing them through words, we discover they're near identical, only obscured like old memories. Perhaps," Meliora gulped, unsure if she'd be feeding delusion, "those images are messages from those who've passed."

Adoration glowed, the Queen's mood improved visibly. "That gives me hope," she murmured. Vesper turned back to her table.

"Mother, the funeral," Meliora reminded.

"I just need to find a substantial clue. The Seed of Life…" fragmented thoughts trailed.

Meliora took a volume from the woman's hands. She locked her gaze. "Father's gone. So is his body. What do you hope to accomplish with the Seed of Life?"

"Meliora, it *gives* life. It must be able to return your father's. If only I could study its properties. My frustration spawns from the uselessness of these books!" she smacked a manual onto a table. "They hold no clue as to where the seed could be found! Even worse, there's no description of its form!" She picked up another and flipped madly, tearing pages. "Only passive mention of its potential!"

"Mother," Meliora soothed, taking the book carefully from her and setting it aside. "Please, let us do what we can and pray for father's soul." She turned and untangled her mother's fingers from her hair.

"My child, I'm sorry," the newly crowned Queen wheezed. "I'm not as strong as you, and it's now you who cares for me." The words engorged Meliora with fresh sadness.

After much effort, the Princess convinced her mother to return to the royal bedchamber. There, Vesper dressed. They took their places as the funerary procession began.

Meliora couldn't help but notice her mother's mental distance. She wanted to be in her workshop, searching for a myth.

"How do I help her, father?" Meliora whispered under her breath. She felt emptiness expound in her soul, as he wasn't there to answer.

Made in the USA
Monee, IL
24 August 2021

75740938R00249